PRAISE FOR JENNIFER CLOSE'S

The Smart One

"*The Smart One* is emotionally engaging and thoughtful; like Anne Tyler, Close goes straight into the heart of a group of people to show all its flawed, complicated members clearly and deftly and totally without judgment. There is not one dull moment—Close is a subtle and incisive writer who gets better with each new book."

—Kate Christensen, author of *The Astral*

"The novel sings in the small moments when its women express uncomfortable truths, undercurrents of sibling resentment and parental disappointment, which usually remain unspoken. . . . Perfect for the beach or a long plane trip." —*Kirkus Reviews*

"*The Smart One* has such authentic, multifaceted characters." —Book Riot

"A well-written family drama in which all the characters keep moving forward, but not all the loose ends are completely and neatly tied. . . . Sure to please." —*Library Journal*

"Close's gift as a writer is her spare but delicious prose and unflinching way of describing her characters."

—*The Globe and Mail* (London)

"*The Smart One* focuses on the intersections of self-discovery, independence, and reliance in the modern family, all enlivened by Close's signature wit and warmth. . . . A touchingly tender, emotionally honest novel about shifting priorities and the nontraditional career paths so many find themselves on."

—*Booklist*

JENNIFER CLOSE

The Smart One

Jennifer Close is the bestselling author of *Girls in White Dresses*. Born and raised on the North Shore of Chicago, she is a graduate of Boston College and received her MFA in fiction writing from the New School in 2005. She worked in New York in magazines for many years. She now lives in Washington, D.C., and teaches creative writing at George Washington University.

ALSO BY JENNIFER CLOSE

Girls in White Dresses

THE SMART ONE

THE Smart
One A NOVEL

JENNIFER CLOSE

Vintage Contemporaries
Vintage Books
A Division of Random House, Inc. | New York

FIRST VINTAGE CONTEMPORARIES EDITION, JULY 2013

The Library of Congress has cataloged the Knopf edition as follows:
Close, Jennifer.
The smart one : a novel / Jennifer Close.—1st ed.
p. cm.
1. Single women—New York—Fiction. 2. Life change events—Fiction.
3. Adult children living with parents—Fiction.
4. Brothers and sisters—Fiction. 5. Domestic fiction. I. Title.
PS3603.L68S63 2013
813'.6—dc22 2012018662

Vintage ISBN: 978-0-307-74370-1

Book design by Pei Loi Koay

www.vintagebooks.com

Printed in the United States of America
10 9 8 7 6 5 4

For Tim,

My favorite one

PART One

From inside her apartment, Claire could hear the neighbor kids in the hall. They were running from one end to the other, the way they sometimes did, kicking a ball or playing tag, or just running for running's sake. They had their dog with them too, a big, sad golden retriever named Ditka, who always looked confused, like he couldn't understand why or how he'd ended up living in an apartment in New York.

Claire muted the TV and listened to see if the kids were going to stay out there for a while, or if they were just waiting for their parents to take them somewhere. She hoped it was the second option. It was Saturday morning, which meant they had hours ahead of them. Having them out there made her feel trapped in her own apartment. Just because she was sitting on the couch in sweatpants and had no plans to leave didn't make the feeling go away. She could sense their presence on the other side of the wall, so close to her. She could see the shadow of Ditka's nose as he sniffed at the bottom of the door. They were invading her space, what little of it she had. And it was interfering with her plan to be a hermit for the whole three-day weekend, something she was getting better and better at.

Last week, she was crossing Broadway and a man crossing the other way looked her in the eyes, pointed to her face, and said, "I want to fuck you." On the street, she'd blushed and walked away quickly. But when she got home she realized two things: The first was that the comment had pleased her. Claire was pretty, but it hadn't always been that way. She was the kind of girl who grew into her looks, who suffered through an awkward stage of braces, unfortunate haircuts, and overalls in her teen years. Now, when men called out to her, "Hey, Princess. Looking good, beautiful," she was grateful. She would duck her head and pretend to be embarrassed or insulted, but if they called out, "Smile, pretty girl," she always obliged.

The second thing she realized was that the man on the street was the first person to talk directly to her in almost three days. She didn't know whether to be impressed with herself or very disturbed. She chose a mix of the two.

THE KIDS IN THE HALLWAY were getting louder, and Claire turned up the volume on the TV, hoping that their parents would come out soon and tell them to come inside or at least quiet down. The kids' names were Maddie and Jack, and they were somewhere in the nine-to-eleven age range. Jack was older, and starting to get that shoulder hunch that preteen boys get, like the whole world was so embarrassing, he couldn't even stand up straight. Maddie was the kind of kid who believed adults found her adorable, shouting out things like "Purple is a mix of red and blue" in the elevator for Claire's benefit and then smiling and looking down at her shoes, as if she were shy. They both had dirty-blond hair and buckteeth, and Maddie would find out soon enough that she wasn't adorable or charming, so Claire always smiled at her.

She and Doug used to call them the Hamburger Helpers, because every night the smell of ground beef and onions came wafting out of their apartment. Sometimes Claire wanted to call the kids into her place to give them something to eat, anything that wasn't meat and onions in a pan. It used to be a running joke—whenever they'd smell the ground beef cooking, Doug would say, "Is it tacos for dinner?" and Claire would answer, "Nope, just some good old-fashioned Beefy Mac."

Together, she and Doug talked endlessly about the family. They wondered what possessed the Hamburger Helpers to raise a family in an average New York City apartment. Every Sunday they watched as the dad took the subway with Maddie and Jack to Fairway, watched the three of them return carrying loads of groceries, struggle onto the elevator, and go up to their apartment. Wouldn't they have been better off in the suburbs? Wouldn't things have been easier?

Claire and Doug laughed when Jack failed his spelling test and they heard the fight through the wall, heard Jack say, "Fuck spelling," to his parents. They agreed that it was only going to get worse over at the Hamburger Helpers' as Maddie and Jack hit puberty and hormones crawled all over their tiny apartment. They pitied the family and what was in store for them.

Now Claire realized the family was probably pitying her—that is, if they'd even noticed that Doug had moved out. Either way, they seemed to be getting a lot more annoying.

WHEN DOUG AND CLAIRE CALLED OFF their engagement, her friend Katherine had said, "In some ways, it's worse than a divorce." It was Claire's first night out since the whole thing happened, and she and Katherine were at a wine bar near her apartment. "I guess it's because it ended before it even started, so it's like someone dying young."

"Great," Claire said.

Katherine wasn't listening. "Or maybe it's because by the time people get divorced, they're usually like really sick of each other, and have done bad things and are ready to move on. With you guys, no one saw this coming."

Claire figured this had to be the strangest response she would get. Katherine, a friend from high school, was so perpetually messed up that you got used to it after a while. Her first week in New York, she'd watched a thirty-two-year-old woman leap off the subway platform at Twenty-third and Park, killing herself as she got hit by the number 6 train. Katherine had skipped work for two weeks, leaving her apartment only to purchase a small white Maltese for eight hundred dollars from the pet store on the corner with her parents' credit card. Things since then had been touch and go. Claire could forgive her strange reply. Surely everyone else would know how to be more appropriate.

But Claire was wrong. Apparently no one knew how to react to her news. Her two friends at work, Becca and Molly, decided that their mission would be to cheer Claire up by telling her all of the bizarre love stories they knew. Sometimes the point was clear ("My mom was engaged before she met my dad, you know!") and sometimes it wasn't, like the time Molly told her about her sister who worked as a nanny and ended up running off and marrying the father of her babysitting charges, leaving his first wife in their dust. "Isn't that romantic?" Molly asked. *No*, Claire wanted to say, *that's not romantic, it's adultery*. But she stayed silent and smiled.

Becca and Molly had been nice coworkers to have. They were all around the same age, all enjoyed getting an occasional drink after work to complain about the office, and were happy to have lunch together. She had always liked them.

Until now. One afternoon in her office, as Molly told her about all of the friends she had who were getting divorced, Claire said, "Well, at least I won't have to be Claire Winkle-pleck. Now there's a silver lining."

Molly stared at her for a moment, and then said quietly, like she didn't want to upset Claire, "So many women don't take their husband's name anymore. You wouldn't have had to do that if it made you uncomfortable."

"Right," Claire answered. "Right."

She'd decided that day that Becca and Molly had to go. It was really for the best. She began to avoid them. Whenever she saw them coming toward her office around lunchtime, she'd pick up the phone and call her voice mail, so that when they popped their heads in, she could roll her eyes and point to the phone, then wave them along, as if to say, "Don't wait for me, this could take forever, just go, go on!"

MADDIE AND JACK WERE NOW screeching and laughing in the hallway, the kind of laughing that often turned into hysterical crying, when one kid hit another and the game quickly went south. She waited for that to happen, but they quieted a little bit and resumed their game, some sort of crummy hallway soccer, she assumed. She hoped that they'd be out of there by the time she wanted to order dinner, because she didn't want to have to wave to them and say hello, have to pet the dog and smile as she accepted her food.

She probably shouldn't even be ordering out, considering her money situation, but what difference did twenty more dollars on her credit card really make at this point? The credit card balance was so high, so unbelievable, that she was able to ignore it most of the time, to pretend that there was no way she'd spent that much in the past six months. It just wasn't possible.

Her phone rang again, but she didn't bother to look at it. Her mom had been calling every day (a few times a day, actually) trying to persuade Claire to come to the shore with the family. "It's important to me," her mom said, over and over. If Claire had been anyone else, she could have told her mom the truth, that she didn't want to go and sit with her family for a week at the beach, that it would make her already pathetic life seem worse. But she wouldn't do that, because no matter how old she got, she still hated hurting Weezy's feelings, and the times that she did left her feeling so guilty she couldn't sleep. But for now, she let the phone ring. She had stuff to do, like looking at her bank accounts online hoping something had changed, and watching TV.

Claire sighed and switched the channel. She could always make something for dinner. There was a box of macaroni and cheese in the cupboard and that would be fine, she realized. Yes, if Maddie and Jack were still out there when she wanted to eat, she'd just make that. Calmed by the fact that she wouldn't have to talk to anyone today, she pulled a blanket over her and settled down on the couch to watch an old eighties movie. She figured watching people go to the prom would be soothing.

CLAIRE FIRST MET DOUG AT a Super Bowl party of a friend of a friend on the Upper West Side. They'd sat next to each other on the couch and watched the game, eating guacamole and laughing at the commercials. Anytime Claire needed a beer, Doug stood up, took her empty bottle, and returned with a full one. At the end of the night, she was happy to give him her number when he asked.

"Doug Winklepleck?" her best friend, Lainie, had said. "That's an unfortunate name." Claire agreed, but continued to date him.

After they'd dated each other for a few weeks, Doug said, "I would like to be exclusive with you, if that's what you want as well." It sounded like a business proposal, but Claire was happy to agree. Doug was straightforward, and Claire appreciated that. He had a thin face, and a nose that was almost too big, but not quite. He was handsome in his own way. He was a systems developer for a fund of funds, a job title that meant nothing to Claire and that she never quite fully understood. He had his ties on a rotating schedule and contributed the maximum amount to his 401(k). He was, by all accounts, admirable.

On one of their early dates, Doug took Claire to see the elephants arrive in Manhattan for the circus. They were marched through the Queens Midtown Tunnel at midnight and Doug told her it was something she had to see. "I can't believe you've lived here for five years and you've never seen them," he said. "That won't do."

They went to a bar on Third Avenue that had a jukebox, long wooden tables, and smelled like yeast and bleach. They played darts and shared a plate of buffalo wings, which was a tricky thing to eat on an early date. And when it was time, they rushed out to the street to wait for the arrival.

Claire stood there, leaning against Doug, buzzed from the beers and the strangeness of the night. She shivered and watched the big, sad elephants march into Manhattan. They were wrinkled and dusty and magnificent. She wanted to cry for them, wanted to run up and touch their rough skin with her hand, to place her palms flat against their hides. It was all she could do to stay put in her place. She drew in a deep breath and said, "Oh."

"See?" Doug whispered into her hair. "I told you. It's something to see."

And right then, Claire felt like Doug was the right choice, the person she'd been waiting for, and anytime she started to think otherwise, she'd close her eyes and whisper, "Remember the elephants," until the feeling went away.

THEY MOVED IN TOGETHER NINE MONTHS after they met, and then, about a year after that, Doug proposed. The ring was dull, silver, and thick, with a vine etched all around it. Along the vine were tiny dots of diamonds. Claire hated it. "I knew you wouldn't want a big, showy ring," Doug said. She'd just nodded and looked down at her hand. Of course she wanted a big ring. She'd always wanted a big diamond, even if she knew she was supposed to say it didn't matter.

And the thing that bugged her, the thing that really drove her crazy, was that Doug had never asked her. If he had, he would have known. She suspected that he surprised her with this one so he wouldn't have to spend a lot of money, which was even more annoying, because he made a good amount of money—a lot of money by anyone's standards. It wasn't like she could look at the ring and think, *Well, this is all he could afford, but I know he loves me.* It wasn't. He could have bought her something spectacular, but he decided to be practical. And who wanted practical for an engagement ring?

They were engaged for four months. Claire tried to remember where the shift happened, when things started to fall apart, but she could never quite figure it out. There were no screaming fights, no cheating, no admission of an Internet porn addiction or a hidden drug problem. They just simply began to crack.

Almost every conversation they had led them to a disagreement. Had it always been this way? Claire didn't think so, but maybe it had and they'd just never noticed. Maybe now that they were facing the rest of their lives together, everything seemed bigger and more important.

"You only want two kids?" Claire said one day. Doug nodded. He'd said this before, but she'd always thought he was flexible.

"Two is a good number," he said. "Two is affordable."

"What if one of them dies?" Claire asked. "Then you only have one left."

"Why would you say something like that?" He looked away. "What's wrong with you?"

When Claire wanted to go out to dinner three nights in a row, Doug said they shouldn't, to save money. When Doug talked about moving to Long Island, Claire told him he was out of his mind. When Claire watched reality TV, especially the singing competition show that Doug hated, he told her she was contributing to the downfall of American culture. When Doug wore his BlackBerry strapped to his hip in a holster, Claire told him he was a nerd. It went on like this, until most nights were spent in separate rooms of the apartment, watching different TV shows.

"You're always so mad at me," Doug said, more than once. "It's like whatever I do disappoints you."

"That's not true," Claire said. But she wasn't sure.

Then one night, after an argument about whether they should order Thai food or sushi that ended with Doug calling Claire overdramatic and Claire calling Doug controlling, he had sighed. "What's going on with us?"

"It's just Thai food," Claire said. But it was too late.

"Something's wrong. This isn't right."

"You can get the crab wontons," she said. Doug shook his head.

Claire stayed in the apartment and Doug moved out, saying that he would pay his part of the rent for two more months while she looked for a new place. It all happened quickly. There were two nights of talking and fighting, of Claire crying on the couch, and Doug crying a little bit too, and then it was settled and he was moving out and Claire still hadn't told anyone what had happened.

The Monday after Doug left, Claire got dressed, took the subway to work, and was standing in her boss's office talking about a grant proposal when she started crying. Crying! Like she was seven years old. It had been mortifying to stand there and try to hold back her tears, and even more so to have her boss jump up and close the door to her office, then guide Claire to a chair to ask her what was wrong.

Claire had told her everything—the engagement, Doug's moving out, the apartment, how she still needed to tell her family and cancel the plans that had been made for the wedding—and Amy had listened, nodding and handing her tissues, making sympathetic noises at certain places.

"It's such a mess," Claire said. "I'm sorry. It's a mess, I'm a mess."

Amy had sent her home then, instructing her to take the week off. "You have so much comp time. Take it. We're covered here. There's nothing that can't be done next week. Just get things sorted and settled." Claire thought how strange this was, since the extent of her personal conversations with Amy up to this point had been about the salad place across the street that they both liked. When they ran into each other there, they'd laugh and say, "Funny seeing you here," and then they'd discuss whether it was better to get walnuts or pecans on your salad, or to leave them off altogether since nuts were so packed with calories.

"I don't need a whole week," Claire said, but Amy held up her hand.

"Take it. This is your life and this is important. There's a lot for you to figure out. It wouldn't hurt to rest and be kind to yourself for a few days."

Claire was forever grateful for this. She hoped that one day she could show the same kindness to someone who worked for her. But she was also deeply embarrassed and when she finally did return to work, she couldn't look Amy in the eye. It was like she'd taken all her clothes off in front of this woman and then expected it not to be awkward. It was awful, really.

Claire had spent the whole week in her apartment. She didn't leave once. She called her mom to let her know about the engagement and refused the suggestions to come home to Philly, and screamed, "No!" at the idea of her mom coming to New York.

"I'm fine," she said. "Really. I just need to sort things out."

"Oh, Claire," her mom had said. And Claire had to get off the phone before she started crying, because those two words coming out of her mom's mouth were the worst. She'd heard them so many times before—when she got a D in calculus, when she crashed the car in the high school parking lot, when she got arrested at the shore for underage drinking.

Claire e-mailed her friends, but didn't take any phone calls. She made it seem like she wasn't in New York. *I'm sorting things out*, she typed. *I'm doing fine.*

That whole week, Claire took baths at night. She soaked in the tub, filling it with water as hot as she could stand. When the water started to cool, she would let some of it drain out and then turn on the faucet to let new, steaming water pour in. She emerged from these baths pink-faced and dizzy. She would wrap a towel around her head and another around her body and stare at herself in the mirror. She looked like a newborn hamster before it got its fur—a doughy pink blob of see-through skin, unrecognizable and delicate.

Claire hoped for some revelation during these baths. She thought that soaking in the soapy water would clear her head. But it didn't. Mostly she just tried to figure out where she'd gone wrong. Sometimes she wondered what would happen if Doug were still there. Almost always she replayed the moment in her head when the actual breakup happened, when Doug said he was going to move out, and Claire said, "What am I going to do now?" She hadn't meant to say it, didn't even realize it was coming out of her mouth until she heard it, and immediately she was ashamed. She didn't want to be that person, didn't want to hear her teary, pathetic voice in her head, admitting that she was lost, saying, "What am I supposed to do now?" like she couldn't figure anything out for herself. And so she soaked in the water and hoped that somehow the words would steam out of her.

During the days, she watched talk shows. On Tuesday, the guest was a kidnapping specialist, who talked the audience through gory details of women being dismembered and raped. Claire forced herself to watch as a reminder that things could be much worse. More than once, the man looked at the audience with serious eyes as he repeated his most important advice: "Never let them take you to a second location," he said. He pointed at a different person with each word.

Apparently, the odds of being killed went up enormously when you let an abductor take you somewhere else. Claire let this thought run itself over in her head. She ordered takeout every night, and figured she was safest in her apartment.

Claire returned to work without one thing figured out. She had considered moving, but the thought of finding a new place that she could afford seemed impossible. And so she stayed put and dipped into her savings to pay rent after Doug stopped sending her checks. She told herself that it was actually less expensive this way, because to move she'd need money for a deposit and a broker fee and a moving company. It was the right thing to do, she thought, to stay where she was for the moment. *Never let them take you to a second location,* she'd remind herself.

Of course, six months later, all of Claire's savings were gone and she'd started charging anything she could on her credit cards—groceries, subway cards, taxi rides, the electric bill. It was easy to live in New York on credit.

At least ten times a day, she signed on to her bank accounts to look at the numbers, trying to make sense of them, trying to make them add up differently. She studied the numbers, like if she looked at them long enough, more money would appear in her bank account. But that never happened. After staring at it for about an hour, she'd begin to get a panicky feeling, and she'd have to sign out quickly, clicking the button at the top, like closing the screen was going to make the problem go away.

Sometimes at night, Claire dreamt about that crazy blond lady on TV, the one who tried to fix the financially irresponsible, adding up their bills, telling them, firmly, that they needed to change their habits. In her dreams, Claire saw this woman walking up to her in a no-nonsense suit, accentuating every word as she said, *You cannot live like this. You have got to take responsibility. You have got to live within your means or you are going to end up—Broke. Without. A. Penny. To. Your. Name. Or. A. Place. To. Live.*

In the dreams, Claire would try to run away from her. When she woke up, she'd always think, *Even my dreams have money problems.* Then she'd try to tell herself it wasn't that bad.

This past month, she'd realized that she was totally screwed, that she probably wouldn't even be able to pay her full rent next month. She wondered about this in a sort of abstract way, as if the apartment were so absolutely hers that the landlord wouldn't be able to kick her out. But she knew that wasn't the truth. She knew her borrowed time was almost up.

EVERY ONCE IN A WHILE, Claire went to craigslist to look at apartment listings. She scrolled through them, clicking on the pictures of the tiny studios, usually in Brooklyn, or else so far up and so far east on the island, she wasn't even sure it could be considered Manhattan anymore. She looked at the pictures of the empty rooms, clicking through the bathroom photo that showed a bare toilet, naked and exposed in the empty white space. She'd click, click, click along, each one uglier than the one before, until she felt like she was going to throw up.

Even scarier were the apartment shares. She'd gone as far as e-mailing with one guy who was renting out a bedroom in a three-bedroom walk-up at York and Seventy-sixth. Claire set up a time to meet with him, got to the building, and then kept walking. She just couldn't face it. She knew what she'd find: a tiny place with thin walls, where she'd be able to hear everything her roommates did and said, would have to run into them in the kitchen while eating cereal, and wait her turn for the shower in the morning.

No. Sharing a place with randoms was out of the question. She was too old for that. Maybe a few years ago, it wouldn't have seemed so bad. But she was twenty-nine and she didn't want to have to negotiate refrigerator space with strangers.

What she wanted was to stay where she was. It wasn't fair that she had to leave. She hadn't done anything wrong. She'd always had a job, had worked hard, had been responsible. Why was she the only one being punished? None of her other friends had to deal with this. Even the dumb girls she'd known in high school seemed to be capable of living as adults. How had they all ended up fine and she'd ended up like this?

Claire loved the apartment that she and Doug had shared. It was a teeny bit run-down, but it was clean and in a beautiful old building. It wasn't big, but it was certainly the biggest place she'd ever lived in New York—a proper one-bedroom, with a kitchen that opened up into the living room with a counter and stools. What more could you want? Sure, she couldn't afford it, but maybe something would happen, maybe her circumstances would change.

CLAIRE'S PHONE HAD BEEN RINGING all weekend, which was really annoying. It was one thing to have to talk to people at work, but on Saturday and Sunday, she wanted peace. The first call was from her sister, Martha, reporting that a meth lab had been busted on the Upper West Side. Martha assumed that the meth lab was right next to Claire's apartment, possibly in the very same building. Martha left messages like this a few times a week. It was almost as if she searched for bad news to share, almost as if she liked it.

Her mom had called twice more, asking about the shore. Claire didn't even have to listen to the messages to know what they were about. Weezy wasn't going to stop until she got the answer that she wanted.

Her friend Lainie had also called three times, but hadn't left any messages. Lainie never left messages; she got too impatient waiting for the beep to come. Claire wasn't that concerned, because if it was a real emergency, Lainie would text her. But when her number came up a fourth time, Claire answered.

"You sound miserable," Lainie said. She didn't even say hello. She was never one to sugarcoat things. Once in high school, when Claire was obsessing over a giant pimple on her forehead, searching for some sort of reassurance that it wasn't as bad as she thought, Lainie had said, "Yeah, it's huge, but what are you going to do? Stay in your house until it's gone? Everyone knows you don't normally look like that."

"Well, hello to you too," Claire said now.

"Hi," Lainie said. She spoke quickly. "So what's going on? You sound awful."

"I'm fine."

"You're not fine. You sound like someone died. Katherine thinks you're depressed."

"Katherine thinks everyone's depressed."

"Fair enough." Lainie knew this was true. Katherine loved therapy, thought everyone should be in it, and had encouraged Lainie to see someone after she gave birth to each of her children, just in case she developed postpartum depression.

"I'm fine," Claire said again. She felt awkward on the phone with Lainie, like they were dancing on the offbeat of a song. They hadn't talked much since Doug moved out. Lainie had her third baby the month after, and was available only for quick calls, in which she often mentioned that her life was full of poop and that she sometimes forgot to brush her teeth. Claire was used to this, the way Lainie disappeared for a little while when each of her boys was born. She wasn't surprised by it anymore, or even hurt. It was just the way things happened, and Lainie always resurfaced after a few months. Just because this last baby had come at an inconvenient time for Claire, a time when she could have used her best friend, there wasn't anything she could do about it, except wait.

"Are you sure?" Lainie was saying.

"Yeah, I'm just . . . You know, trying to adjust, I guess."

"It's been six months." Lainie didn't say this unkindly, but it still made Claire's throat tighten up.

"I know. It's just weird, okay? It just sucks." Claire heard a baby crying, and Lainie sighed. Claire could tell that Lainie was picking Matthew up and bouncing him around, trying to get him to quiet down.

"I know, I know," Lainie said. But she didn't.

"I just have to figure a bunch of stuff out. I just never feel like doing anything. I have to move, I have to do tons of things, and I just feel like I can't."

Lainie was silent for a moment. "Maybe I'll come up to see you this weekend."

"Really?"

"Yeah, really. That's what we'll do. I could come tomorrow and stay the night. It's a three-day weekend and Brian can watch the boys. We'll figure it all out. We'll find an apartment, get you signed up for online dating."

"Funny," Claire said. But then she did let out a little laugh.

"I'm serious. We'll get it all figured out." Claire knew that Lainie was only half kidding. Lainie liked to solve problems and she probably thought she could come up for one weekend and easily sort out Claire's mess. Which was just a little obnoxious, but Claire didn't mind.

• • •

"IT'S AMAZING, REALLY," LAINIE SAID, "that this place hasn't driven you crazy yet." She dropped her bag on the floor and looked around at the apartment. Claire had to admit it didn't look good. When Doug had packed up all of his stuff, it became clear that almost everything in the apartment was his. They'd both known this, of course, but somehow it was still a surprise to see him take it all with him.

He'd taken all of the framed pictures from the walls, the big TV, the dresser, the desk, the big couch, and most of the stuff in the kitchen. He'd left her the bed to be nice, and so Claire had insisted he take the duvet and pillows, which he had (except for one pillow), and now the bed looked like it belonged in an insane asylum, stripped down except for white sheets and an old knitted afghan that Claire had stolen from home years ago.

The only things left in the main room of the apartment were an old loveseat, a side table, a small TV, and a lawn chair that she'd found in the closet after Doug left. There were a few things in the kitchen, enough to get by, anyway—a couple of plates, a bowl, some silverware, a pot, and a skillet. She knew Doug had felt bad for leaving her with so few things, and he kept offering to leave more, but she insisted he take his stuff. "It's yours," she kept saying. "You should take it, it's all yours."

Doug probably assumed that Claire had waited a few days and then gone out to replace what was missing, that she'd moved things around, hung new pictures, or at least covered the holes that were left. But she hadn't done a thing. And now the whole place was practically empty, like she was in the middle of moving in or out, like the whole situation was just temporary.

That night, she and Lainie decided to just stay in and order food and when the deliveryman came, Claire realized that she wouldn't be able to charge it to her card. She hadn't paid the bill and there wasn't enough credit left.

"Oh shit," she said. "I forgot, there was some security thing with my bank and they canceled all my cards. I was supposed to get new ones, but they haven't come yet."

"That's okay," Lainie said. "I got it."

"Thanks," Claire said. Her heart was pounding with the lie, but Lainie didn't seem to notice anything.

AFTER THEY ATE AND DRANK WINE and went to bed, Claire lay on her back for a long time and stared at the ceiling. Her room never got all that dark, since the light of the city came in through the blinds and she'd never taken the time to get curtains or a shade to block it out. This never bothered Claire, because when she woke up, she could always see everything in the room and never had to turn on a light to go to the bathroom, never tripped over a pair of shoes or walked into a wall.

"I have no money left," she said. She wasn't sure if Lainie was awake or asleep, and she figured that was her gamble, that she could just say it out loud and if Lainie heard, then she'd have to deal with it.

But then she saw the pillow move, and then Lainie was squinting at her. "What?"

Claire considered lying for a minute, or telling her that she was just exaggerating. But then it seemed too hard, and Lainie always knew when she was lying anyway. "I have no money left," Claire said again. "I'm broke. And I don't mean, I'm broke, like I normally mean it. I mean that I've spent all of my savings and have been living on my credit cards

for months and now there's no more room left on them, and
I don't think I can pay rent this month. Not after I pay the
minimum on the cards, and I seriously don't know what I'm
going to do."

"Oh shit." Lainie was sitting up now.

"Yeah."

"Can you borrow some money from your parents?"

"Yeah, I guess. I mean, I'm going to have to. But I don't
know what good that'll do. Even if I get through this month,
I'm going to have the same problem again next month."

"Well, you need to move." Lainie sounded firm, like moving would solve everything.

"I know, I know. I know I need to. I just put it off for so
long because I didn't want to live somewhere shitty, and it
costs so much to move—to pay the movers and put down the
deposit and all of that. At this point, I'd have to borrow ten
thousand dollars from my parents to move and that probably
wouldn't even be enough. And I'd end up in some dungeon
in Brooklyn."

Claire felt her nose start to run and knew she'd be crying soon. Lainie patted her knee, got up, turned on the bedroom light, and went into the kitchen. She came back with
Kleenex and two beers. She handed one to Claire and sat
cross-legged in front of her.

"I'm so screwed," Claire said.

Lainie nodded. "We'll figure it out," she said. "It seems
impossible, I know, but it's not. We'll figure it out."

There were times in college when the size of a paper she
had to write would overwhelm Claire. She'd sit there in front
of the computer and try to get herself to start typing, but all
she could think about was how much she had to do, the enor-
mousness of the project. It would paralyze her. People some-

times said that fear was a motivator, but she never found that. Instead, she'd sit, all night, staring at the screen and not typing a word.

And it was happening again. The amount of her debt was too big, the size of her fuckup was too large. To act on it would be to acknowledge it, to start trying to fix it, and it just didn't seem like there was any way to do that. And so she sat, paralyzed, and waited.

The next day, Lainie left and Claire sat on her couch. She was exhausted. She and Lainie had stayed up almost the whole night talking, and right around five in the morning, Lainie had said, "Look, don't freak out, okay? But maybe you should think about moving home."

"Lainie. I'm not moving home. That's ridiculous."

"Okay, that's what I thought you'd say. But listen, people do it all the time to pay off debt. You don't even like your job, and it would be an excuse to leave it. You could live rent free, get a random job, pay off all your credit cards, and then move back when you're more settled. You could take your time looking for a job and find one that you really want."

Claire was annoyed at how rational Lainie sounded. She wanted to offer up another plan, another idea for how she could get herself out of her situation, but she didn't have one. From her calculations, after next month, she was done.

"You could even temp," Lainie continued. "So it wouldn't even be like you were staying there. Temping is just that. Temping. Temporary. Beth used an agency that loved her, that's always e-mailing her for referrals. They'd die to get you. I think most of the people that go there are sort of weird or something, but whatever. It would be easy. It would be like a break, and you deserve a break after this year, you really do."

When she'd left today, Lainie had said, "Think about what we talked about. I think it's the best plan."

Claire had hugged her and closed the door, thinking there was no way in hell that was going to happen. But now here she was, alone in her apartment, and she felt trapped again, but this time it wasn't because the Hamburger Helpers were outside—it was because she had no money. None. This was it. Lainie was right. She couldn't stay, and her only option was to move home.

Last night Lainie had said, "Look at it this way—at least you have this option. At least going home is a possibility." Claire knew she should feel grateful for that, even if she didn't right now. She'd tell her parents at the shore, she decided. How bad could it be? It couldn't be worse than telling them her engagement was called off, could it?

And so, knowing that she couldn't get out of it, knowing that she had no better alternative anyway, Claire pulled her bag out of the closet and began putting together her clothes for a week at the shore with her family.

The woman that Katherine saw jump in front of the subway was named Joanne Jansen. It was a cute name—catchy and poetic, sort of like Claire Coffey. There were a few people on the subway platform that day that insisted Joanne Jansen had just fallen, that the whole thing was a horrible accident. But Katherine told Claire that wasn't true. "She jumped with her arms in front of her," Katherine said. "She jumped like a superhero, like she wanted to make sure she got to where she was going." Claire thought of that now as she packed, how Joanne Jansen had put her arms straight in front of her, determined and sure of her decision. She wished she didn't know that detail. It made it worse somehow.

CHAPTER 2

To be a manager at J.Crew, you had to be organized. That was what Martha always told people. She had, after all, risen to the position of manager faster than any other person at this particular branch. (Well, she was pretty sure of that. Someone had told her that once, and it seemed true.)

"You have to be willing to fold clothes all day if that's what needs to be done," she always said. "People don't want to scrounge around through a messy pile of pants to find the right size."

Martha was being a little modest when she told people this. You did have to be organized, that was true. But you also had to have the right work ethic, and Martha knew she had it. Some of these people treated this job like it was nothing, like the store was lucky to have them. Well, Martha was a registered nurse who had graduated at the top of her class, and she still worked harder than everyone else. She wasn't too good to take the extra time to help a pear-shaped girl find the right kind of pants. If her job was to steer that pear of a girl away from skinny cords and point her in the direction of some wide-leg chinos, then that was what she was going to do.

The store was just a ten-minute drive from her parents' house, which was why Martha decided to apply there in the first place. She'd never worked in retail before, but she figured it couldn't be that hard, and so she dropped off applications at Banana Republic, Ann Taylor, and Anthropologie. She was turned down almost everywhere.

"But I went to college," Martha would say, when the managers asked her about previous retail jobs.

Then they would shake their heads no and apologize. "I'm sorry," they'd say. "We really need someone that has prior experience."

It was a godsend, really, that the manager at J.Crew was someone that Martha had gone to high school with. They weren't exactly friends, but Margaret Crawford had sat next to Martha for years in school, and they'd had a sort of friendly alliance, since alphabetically they were always stuck together.

Margaret, it turned out, was pregnant. She told Martha that she was going to be cutting back on her hours and between that and all the college kids leaving to go back to school, they really needed help.

"You're pregnant?" Martha asked. She tried not to sound shocked, but she was. Margaret looked just a little tubby all around, but not pregnant. Martha noticed a tiny diamond ring on her left hand.

"Yep," Margaret said. She smiled and rubbed her bloated tummy. "Thirteen weeks. Can't you tell?"

"Oh, yeah," Martha said. "Now that you mention it, I can."

"So why do you want to work here anyway?" Margaret said as she read Martha's résumé. "I thought you were nursing. Career change?"

"No, not really. I was just in a job that wasn't a good fit and I thought I'd take a break from it for a while. From nursing, I mean. You know." Martha prayed that Margaret wouldn't ask her what she'd been doing in the past year since she stopped nursing.

Margaret wasn't a very pretty girl. She was average height and a little hefty, with unremarkable brown hair and a splotchy complexion. She was the sort of person who was just average at everything. She'd been in all mid-level classes in high school, had played volleyball for one year on the B team, and had some friends, but not many.

But she was nice, Martha thought. A little dim, but not completely unaware. Martha wondered for a second why they never became better friends. They could have banded together in high school, enjoyed each other's company. It could have been a little less lonely.

Martha was mulling this over, thinking that maybe now was the time when she and Margaret would connect and they would become great friends, the kind of friend that Martha had never really had before. Maybe Martha would be this baby's godmother, and they would laugh about it in years to come, about how they sat next to each other for so many years in school, but never really became friends until that one day when Martha just randomly walked into J.Crew.

"So where are you living these days?" Margaret asked.

"At home, for now."

"You're living with your parents?" Margaret asked. "Oh, no. That's awful."

And just like that, Martha remembered Margaret. She remembered the first day of sophomore year, when Margaret told her that bangs were not in style anymore and that Martha should think about growing hers out. Not meanly, really. Just with a sort of honesty that comes with being clueless.

Martha looked at Margaret's chubby tummy and shrugged. She would not be the godmother of this baby. And she would get over it just fine.

That was almost six years ago, and Margaret had long since stopped working at the store. Sometimes she came in with her daughter, Addie, who always had a runny nose and the same blotchy complexion as her mother.

"Isn't she beautiful?" Margaret always asked Martha. Martha would just smile in response. She didn't believe in lying to make people feel good. The child wasn't the least bit attractive, and she didn't think it was right to say so. Besides which, what kind of person stated that their child was beautiful and then asked for confirmation?

Margaret's husband looked like Eddie Munster, with bushy eyebrows and pointy teeth. It was no wonder that their child turned out like she did. Martha could tell that Margaret believed her husband to be very handsome. Sometimes he'd accompany her when she came to visit the store, and Margaret would hold his hand with a tight smile on her face, like she thought Martha was jealous of them. Martha would look at this unattractive family, and Margaret's stupid smile, and feel nothing but sorry for the whole group of them, most of all for that eyesore, Addie.

Martha had seen people come and go from J.Crew. She trained the college kids in the summers and welcomed the good ones back over holiday vacations. She was a tough manager, that was for sure, but she was fair. And what more could you ask for?

Folding clothes in the store gave Martha a certain sense of accomplishment that was hard to explain to other people. She wasn't OCD or anything, but she loved the way it felt to stack the clothes on top of each other, all of them the same, crisp and ready for the customers. It was her favorite part of the job.

She especially liked folding the clothes in the morning or at the end of the day when the store was closed, as she did now. It was nice to be surrounded by quiet, to know that at least for a little while, the neat stack of shirts that you made would stay just that way, and no customer would go grabbing in the middle of the pile, looking for his size and knocking the whole thing to the side.

Martha folded a stack of navy pants, pulling the crotch of each pair tightly, so that it was taut, and then folding the legs just right to get a perfect crease. She put the sizes in order, big ones on the bottom and the small ones on the top, like the big guys were holding up the little ones. *2, 4, 6, 8, 10, 12,* she said silently to herself, making sure that each size was represented.

Martha took a size 12 out of the pile of pants and put them back behind the register. She'd try them on later. She was a little surprised at how tight her size 10 pants were lately. She'd ignored it for a few weeks, but that morning she wasn't able to button her favorite pair of khakis, and so she decided it was time for new ones.

It was a little hard to admit that she might have gone up a size. Again. She'd been a size 10 for so long now. Before she went on the medicine, she was a very respectable size 8, and once, a long time ago in high school, she was a size 6. She'd never been as thin as Claire, but she'd never been big. Even in college, when her diet of pasta and pretzels had bulked her up, she still wasn't fat. And then she'd learned to deal with being a 10, a little fleshier than she was meant to be, but nothing horrendous. But now there was this. She was a size 12 and it felt like she was sliding toward obesity.

Lately when Martha got undressed at night, she noticed that the waistband of her pants left a circle of angry pink teeth marks around her stomach. She was starting to feel like a sausage stuffed into a too-small skin.

Martha closed down the registers and began gathering the receipts to bundle them. She couldn't wait for this day to be over. One of their best employees, Candace, had quit unexpectedly. "I hate it here," she'd said to Martha. "You're like a Nazi."

It was completely inappropriate to invoke the Nazis to describe anyone, and Martha told Candace just that. She asked Candace if she even knew the horror that the Nazis had caused. "Because if you did," she said, "you might think twice about calling me a Nazi and disrespecting all of the people that were murdered by them."

Candace made a strange sort of strangled sound, and threw up her hands. "You're a freak!" she said. And she gathered her things and walked out. Martha tried not to let it show that Candace had embarrassed her, but she knew that her face was red. The other employee working that day, skinny little Trevor, gave Martha a small smile and she knew that he was pitying her.

"Good riddance," Martha had said to him. Then she went back to the employee bathroom and put a wet paper towel on her cheeks until they cooled down.

Martha was stacking the register drawers to take them to the back when a teenage girl came to the door and, finding it locked, banged on the glass with her palm. Martha smiled and shrugged, then pointed to her watch to indicate that the store was closed. The girl outside gave her the finger and walked away.

Martha didn't deserve that. People felt like they could

treat her however they wanted, just because she worked in the store. Customers were sometimes rude beyond belief, acting like she was their servant as they sent her to fetch them striped shirts and printed skirts. Martha muttered to herself as she finished up her closing duties. Maybe she would just leave J.Crew altogether. She was, after all, a registered nurse. Well, she wasn't exactly registered anymore, since she hadn't worked in so long, but she could be if she wanted to.

MARTHA HAD KNOWN THAT SHE wanted to be a nurse from the time she broke her wrist when she was twelve. It was the nurses who comforted her, with their matter-of-fact answers and soothing voices. She loved the uniforms they wore, how they all had matching scrubs, like they were part of some club. They looked so important, filling out charts and taking temperatures, and she knew that was what she wanted to be. Plus, she'd always had a mind for medicine, had always done the best in her science classes.

Nursing was not a major to be taken lightly. It wasn't like the other majors at her liberal arts college—English or sociology or philosophy. Nursing was different. There were high expectations for the nursing students. You had to keep your GPA up, or you were out of the program. You did clinical work in addition to your classes. People's lives depended on you, so you had to know your stuff. That was how Martha thought about it anyway.

The other girls in the program were different from Martha. They were sillier, flightier, than she was. But they all spent so much time together, studying for tests and carpooling to their clinicals, that Martha developed a fondness for them and even began to enjoy their company.

They used to drag her out with them sometimes, to

bars or to a party to stand in a random kitchen in some off-campus apartment and drink out of red plastic cups. "Come on, Martha!" they used to say. "Blow off some steam." They used to call her Serious Martha, like that was her full name. They used to think it was their duty to try to get her to have some fun.

Martha would let them pick out her clothes for going out, even sip some rum and Cokes with them while they were getting ready. They'd do her makeup and ignore her pleas not to put on too much. "Mar-tha," they'd say, and roll their eyes. It was the same way Claire used to say her name when they were younger, when she would get so exasperated by Martha's very being, saying her name like it hurt to get it out, dragging out each syllable—"Mar-tha."

She'd go to these parties and stand there for a while. She had a feeling that she was supposed to be enjoying them. At the beginning of the night, the girls would stand next to her and include her in the conversations. But as the night went on, each of them would wander away, distracted by some boy. They were all desperate for boys. The one male nurse in their year had seven piercings on his face, including a big plug in his ear. He was nice, but no one they would be interested in. They used to call him Leo the Male Nurse, right to his face.

Even if Martha found her way into a conversation at these parties, she never really had fun. There were some pleasant moments, but those were short-lived, and all that was left was a group of horny college kids waiting to get drunk enough that they could start making out with each other. It was like one big mono pool. She would wait until all the other girls were occupied, then she'd find one of them and tell her that she was leaving. She tried to find someone who was really immersed in a conversation with a boy, so that there would be no protests, so that no one would try to convince her to stay.

On the street, Martha would breathe with relief. She always walked home, even if it was the middle of winter. She didn't mind. She liked the way the air rushed into her nose and froze her nostrils. It made her look forward to getting back to her single room and making hot chocolate in the microwave. She liked the feeling of thawing out in her cozy room, finding an old eighties movie to watch while snuggled under her covers, knowing that tomorrow she'd wake up fresh and ready to do her work, while the rest of the girls would be groggy and hungover.

Those were great mornings, when her nursing friends groaned with their heads in their hands. "Why did we do this?" they'd say. Martha would *tsk* at them, not meanly, just in a good-natured way. She'd smile sympathetically and indulge their requests for Gatorade and water. Martha was happy during those study sessions, pleased that she was learning more than the other girls, because her body wasn't wrecked from the night before. She always felt like she was a few steps ahead, so she was gracious enough to be nice to these girls, to agree to take a break so they could eat greasy food, shoveling french fries into their mouths as they said, "Why didn't we leave when you did, Martha? Why did you let us stay?"

They didn't really mean it, Martha knew. Maybe at that moment they regretted their decision, but the thing that Martha always knew was that these girls wanted to go to parties and meet boys just as much as they wanted to be nurses. And that was the difference. Martha was in school *only* to be a nurse. For these girls, it was just part of the whole package. For Martha, it was everything.

IT WAS ONLY AFTER SHE'D left college that Martha realized how much she'd loved it there—she loved the structure of it, the study schedule, and the forced socializing. She loved her single room, where she could be alone but keep the door cracked open so she could hear people chattering in the halls, the excited way people greeted one another, their shrieks of laughter. Of course, at the time, if anyone had asked her, she would have said that she couldn't wait for graduation, that her dorm was noisy and filled with immature girls who made it nearly impossible to get any work done.

But when it was all gone, she mourned it. She would never be back there again. Ever. Her life was a big silent white space. There were no tests to study for, no groups to meet. When she wasn't working, she could do anything she wanted to, but she found that she didn't like the openness of her time. It was startling, all that free space, and she ended up watching a lot of TV.

Martha got a job at a large hospital in South Philadelphia. She was hired as a floater, which meant that she rotated among departments, filling in wherever she was needed. One night she'd be in the pediatric ward and the next she'd be in the emergency room. She was always on the night shift, because she was new, and they told her she'd have to earn her way to the more desirable hours.

The hospital was large and understaffed. Martha would arrive at seven p.m. and be thrown into a pit of need. That was what it felt like. There was always so much to do, and so many people who needed things from her. The older nurses weren't particularly nice or friendly. She'd imagined that they would take her under their wing and show her the ropes. But that's not how it was. They were frustrated with her, impatient and bossy. And since she moved around all the time, she never really got to know any of them well.

Martha couldn't adjust to her new schedule. Getting to work in the evening gave her a bad feeling in the pit of her stomach, the kind that she used to get on Sunday nights in high school. She worked until seven thirty a.m. and then she'd take the train home, rumpled and exhausted, while everyone else was just starting their day. It made her feel anxious, to see them freshly showered and dressed, holding coffee and reading the paper, while she was on her way home to sleep. *I'm living life backward*, she used to think. And the thought of being a backward person made her heart pound loudly, strangely, so that sometimes it even felt like it was beating the wrong way, like it was going backward along with her.

When she got home in the mornings, she couldn't sleep. She could never quite get used to climbing into bed as the sun was shining. She would lie awake for hours, wondering if she'd done everything she was supposed to. Had she given all of her patients their medications? Had she measured right? Had she filled out the charts? She was sure she was killing her patients, and that kept her awake, always. She was so tired that her whole body ached, but her mind was always moving, always thinking, and no matter how hard she tried, she just couldn't fall asleep.

With each day, it felt worse. Martha was antsy, but never wanted to leave her apartment when she didn't have to. She didn't want to wash her dishes or do her laundry. She ate in her bedroom and let plates pile up on her desk, let glasses full of iced tea sit on her nightstand until they started to mold and little black ants crawled in them. Her laundry lay in piles, and when you first opened the door to her bedroom, it smelled like the home of a dirty person—sour and stale.

This wasn't the way Martha kept things. She'd always been clean, always been disgusted by people who sat around in their own filth. But it didn't seem to matter anymore, and leaving things to rot where they were was easier than trying to clean it all up.

Her roommate, a girl she knew from nursing school, told her that she couldn't live like this and that she was moving out when their lease was up. Martha started skipping work, napping during the days and watching TV at night. Her parents came over to see her, and her father stood in the doorway to her bedroom, looking all around, while her mother said, "Oh, Martha," and began to pick things up, gathering dirty laundry in her arms, as if the mess were the problem.

Martha quit her job and moved home. Her parents packed up the apartment for her, boxing up all of her books and clothes. "It's just my job," she told them. "It was too much. I'm burned out. I just need to rest."

But she was still so tired all the time. She slept almost all day, glad to be in a bed with clean sheets, back at home. Her parents would come upstairs to see her, insist that she get out of bed for meals. Her mom would take her on errands. "You can sit in the car if you want," she'd say. "But you have to get out of the house." And so Martha would put on clothes, and sit in the passenger seat of the car while her mother went to the dry cleaners and the bank.

Sometimes her dad would come upstairs and sit next to her bed, to talk or just read. "It will get better," he'd say to her. And for some reason, this made her cry, tears running down her face to her pillow.

Finally, her parents made her go see someone. "You need someone to talk to," they told her. "It will make you feel better." She could hear them whispering about her when she walked out of a room. But she didn't care. She knew they were worried about her. If she'd had more energy, she would have been worried about herself.

She'd gone to see a therapist and a psychiatrist. The psychiatrist she didn't much care for. He didn't seem interested in her, and she'd sat there and answered his questions, and at the end of the session he'd written her prescriptions. Just like that. When she started to take the medicine, she felt loopy and in her own world, and she wanted to tell everyone that this wasn't going to work.

Dr. Baer was her therapist, and at first Martha thought she wasn't going to be of any help either. But she kept going, and little by little, Dr. Baer began to grow on her. It was strange, like she didn't even notice anything was changing, but slowly she seemed to feel the tiniest bit better, then a bit more. The medicine seemed to balance out, or at least she didn't feel so out of it anymore. Things weren't perfect, but she slept less and got dressed more often. And one day she realized that her father had been right. Things had gotten better somehow.

A few months after that, she'd felt good enough to apply to J.Crew, and she'd gotten the job and worked hard and done well. It had really all been going well—until today. Today, Martha couldn't stand all the people yelling at her about sizes and sales. She couldn't stand the Candaces of the world thinking they could act however they wanted to, like they were special somehow. Today, for the first time in years, Martha almost wished she was a nurse again.

MARTHA LEFT DR. BAER'S OFFICE, but stood right outside the door and leaned against the brick wall. She needed a minute. Even though it was August, she was chilled and she pulled a cardigan out of her bag and put it on. The air-conditioning in Dr. Baer's office was insane. Dr. Baer was always warm (hot flashes, Martha assumed), and now, because Martha had been forced to sit in the freezing room, she probably had a cold.

Early on, when Martha first started seeing Dr. Baer, she used to go home after each session and write down what her therapist had said, so that she could remember everything. Martha wanted to remember all the advice that Dr. Baer gave. She was always so calm, so practical. Martha used to carry that notebook around with her, so she could read Dr. Baer's words whenever she wanted. It made her feel in control.

Now, after so many years of therapy, she was able to hear Dr. Baer's voice in her head wherever she went. When she was at the store, about to buy ice cream, she heard her say, "Sometimes we comfort ourselves in physical ways instead of emotional ways." When Martha turned down an invitation to anything, she heard Dr. Baer say, "It's scary to put yourself out there. But sometimes you need to be uncomfortable to live in the world."

But this visit was different. Martha got the feeling that Dr. Baer was less interested in her problems. She seemed to sigh a lot, to tap her pen before she addressed Martha. And at the end she said, "You know, Martha, it feels to me that you've had time to recover and now you may just be hiding. Maybe it's time to push yourself. Find a job that challenges you more. Maybe go back to nursing. Move out, take a trip, do something that will get you going."

This seemed to be inappropriate shrink talk. All Martha had been saying this session was that she was having some problems with her family. She was complaining about how it seemed to be her curse that whenever she tried to help people (like her sister) they acted like she was butting in. Dr. Baer had sighed and said something about small problems seeming large under a microscope. What was that supposed to mean?

At first, Martha hadn't wanted to see a shrink, but her parents hadn't really given her a choice. For the first few visits, all Martha did was cry. Dr. Baer just sat with her, handing her tissues and waiting. Dr. Baer was a petite woman with short brown hair and thick-framed glasses. She was compact, and looked like she worked out for many hours a day. She handed Martha tissues with purpose, pulling them straight up and out of the box, in one quick motion.

Martha took them, always taking notice of how muscular Dr. Baer's arms were. She didn't even know why she was crying, exactly. She just knew that she didn't want to be there.

As the sessions went on, Martha began to appreciate Dr. Baer's firm voice. She looked forward to the weekly appointment, picking out her outfit to go to the office downtown, walking down Walnut Street, looking in the windows of the clothing shops. Martha always felt important when she walked down the street to the office, like she had somewhere special to be. Dr. Baer's office was on the second floor of a building that was squished in between a Rite Aid and a Lacoste store. Sometimes when she entered the door from the street, she felt like she was entering a secret passageway. There were no markings on the door, just a small mailbox card that said MD BAER. If you didn't know what you were looking for, you'd walk right by.

Martha wasn't embarrassed about seeing a shrink (although Dr. Baer hated that word. "I'm a therapist, Martha," she would say whenever Martha called her that). She was very honest about her appointments with everyone at J.Crew. "I can't work Tuesday afternoons," she would say. "That's my shrink appointment."

When Dr. Baer took her vacation in July, Martha felt a hole in her life. The hour appointment was easily the best part of her week. Martha began to think of Dr. Baer more as a friend than as a doctor; a confidante she could talk to. That is, until today.

Outside the office, Martha watched as Duncan walked inside to see Dr. Baer. Duncan had had the appointment right after Martha's for almost two years now, and they often ran into each other in the waiting room or right outside on the street. They always gave each other knowing nods as they passed. Today, Martha wanted to grab Duncan's arm and warn him. *Watch out,* she would say. *Dr. Baer is in a mood.* They would look knowingly at each other, Duncan understanding just what Martha meant. But Duncan walked quickly past her before she could say anything.

Martha pulled a dusty Kleenex out of her pocket and blew her nose. Then she decided to walk to the coffee shop a couple of blocks away to get something to drink. She needed to sit and make sense of her last hour.

She hadn't even gotten a chance to tell Dr. Baer about the dream that she'd had last night, where she'd seen a giant orange ant and grabbed a shoe to kill it. When she smacked it with her shoe, the ant turned to look at her with big eyes. Then the back half of the ant kept moving and Martha had to chase it around and hit it again. She'd been excited to talk about the dream, since she never had dreams that vivid. It must have meant something—she was sure of it. She'd told her mom about it that morning, but her mom had just sort of stared at her in a fuzzy way over her coffee. Dr. Baer would have had to listen as she described the body of the ant, how strange it made her feel. But she hadn't gotten to talk about it. And now she would never know what the ant was supposed to be.

The coffee shop was more crowded than Martha expected. There were several people banging away on laptops with a sense of purpose, a couple of people reading the paper, and one pair of girls with their heads bent close together, whispering seriously. Martha found a small table in the middle back of the shop, and edged her way through the other customers to get there. A few of them looked up as she passed and she wondered if she looked distressed to them. She tried to catch the eye of one scraggly-looking guy who had his hands resting on his laptop and was staring off into space, but he looked back at the screen as soon as he saw her looking at him.

Martha sighed and flopped her bag onto the table. It made a satisfying thump, and a couple of people jumped. Then she sighed again and sat down, pushing her chair back so that it screeched on the floor. No one looked up. She wanted just one of these people to acknowledge her and give her a sad smile. *I just had a fight with my shrink,* she would say. Although that wasn't really true. Maybe she'd say, *My shrink just told me I'm worthless.* That would get their attention. But that wasn't true either. Martha sighed again and leaned back in her chair.

A waitress with hair that hung down her back all the way to her waist came to take Martha's order. She looked like someone who wanted to be a singer or a songwriter. She probably had a guitar at home. Maybe she even played at small clubs around the city, or at this very coffee shop.

"Do you know what you want?" the waitress asked. She had a harsh voice, kind of rough, really, and Martha hoped she hadn't pinned too much on the idea of becoming a singer.

"I'll have a mocha," she said. "But with skim milk." She was trying to cut back on her calories this week.

The waitress nodded without writing anything down, then turned to head back to the counter. "Wait," Martha called. "Can I also have a muffin? Or coffee cake? Whatever's back there." She shrugged like she didn't really care what she got, like she was just realizing that she hadn't eaten breakfast and should order something. Of course, she *had* eaten breakfast. She'd had a bagel and then a big bowl of cereal, but that was hours ago. No sense in starving herself to lose weight. That's not how it was done.

"Is cranberry okay?" the waitress asked. Martha nodded. She'd really wanted chocolate chip, or cinnamon, but cranberry would do. Yes, cranberry would do just fine.

Martha rooted around in her bag, hoping that for some reason she had the Dr. Baer notebook in there, even though she knew it was in her nightstand. She hadn't used it in so long. She did manage to find an old to-do list and a pen. She uncapped the pen and smoothed out the paper, which had been folded up into a tiny square. Now she was ready. Ready to write down all of the horrible things that Dr. Baer had said to her and to deconstruct them.

But when she wrote down, *You need to push yourself,* it didn't have the same effect. The problem was that when you wrote something down, you couldn't hear the tone of voice. And really, it was Dr. Baer's tone of voice that was the biggest problem.

At the top of the page, she wrote, *Tone of voice was disapproving and harsh.* There. That explained it better. Then she continued. *Go back to nursing,* she wrote. *Challenge yourself. Stop hiding.*

The waitress came to deliver the coffee and muffin, and

Martha made a show of moving her paper over and giving the waitress a look like, *Do you believe this? Look what I'm dealing with.* But the waitress just set the oversized coffee cup and the plate down, and placed the bill on the table next to her.

"Anything else?" she asked, but she was already walking away before Martha could answer.

Martha read over her list. She really couldn't believe the nerve of Dr. Baer, suggesting that she go back to nursing. After that nightmare of a job pushed her over the edge? All of those patients that didn't have enough care? It was too much. Way too much. She had a job now, and it was a good job, even if Dr. Baer didn't see it that way. Sure, it had gotten a little boring, but that was to be expected. And yes, Dr. Baer was right when she said that Martha was in a more stable place now. And maybe she was even right when she said it might be a time for Martha to challenge herself. Maybe.

"I hate my job," Martha had said, as soon as she walked into Dr. Baer's office that day. "Retail is killing me." She threw her bag on the floor and waited for Dr. Baer to say something comforting, something about how hard it was to wait on people, but that it taught you patience and taught you how to treat others. But Dr. Baer had just sighed, leaned back, and said, "Tell me why you hate it."

And so Martha had. She'd talked about how rude the new workers were, how she couldn't stand the way the customers talked to her. "I'm a college graduate," she said. "I could be a nurse if I wanted to."

"So, why don't you?" Dr. Baer asked her.

"I'm . . . well, you know why."

"I know why you stopped nursing six years ago. I don't know why you don't do it now."

"I have a job," Martha said. "It's not easy. And some days I complain about it."

"You don't just complain about it some days. It seems you complain about it most days. Almost every day, in fact, in recent months."

"Because I hate it," Martha told her. "But I need a job. I don't have a choice."

"It sounds to me like you do have a choice. You're making the choice to be there. So, if you're complaining about something, then make another choice."

"It's not that easy."

Dr. Baer kept pushing. She kept asking her questions about the job, asking her why she hated it, telling her that it sounded like she was avoiding things. It was really rude, when you got right down to it. That was the only way to describe it.

At the end of the session, Martha had cried a little bit. She was tired of defending her job and then trying at the same time to explain why it was so awful. Because she did hate it, she did. But she couldn't hate it completely, and she knew that too. J.Crew had saved her, and maybe that was pathetic but it was true. When it had felt like she was never going to be able to be productive again, when the world seemed really awful, she was able to go there and fold clothes.

It hadn't always been easy, but she'd been able to get up and go, at first just for a few hours at a time, and when she got home, she'd go right back to bed. But at least she felt like she'd done something. And as time went on, it got easier, and then she didn't have to convince herself to get up and go to the store. She just did it, and now it was almost effortless. But always, in the back of her mind, was the thought that she might slip back to that place, to that time when getting out of bed seemed almost impossible.

Was she fixed now? Was that what Dr. Baer was trying to tell her? It couldn't be. No one in her life would ever consider her "cured." At least once a day someone told her to lighten up. Every time she talked to her sister, Claire said, "Calm down. Stop worrying."

But she couldn't. That was the thing. Martha would have loved to stop worrying, but she didn't know how. Maybe Claire thought it was crazy, the way Martha always thought there was a murderer around every corner, or that she had stomach cancer, or that she was going to die in a car crash. But the thing was, those things happened. They happened every day to lots of people. And so she couldn't understand how other people just walked through life, unconcerned, not even considering the possibility that tragedy could strike at any moment.

How did these people just assume that they were going to live a full and safe life, when all evidence pointed the other way? When there were so many ways for people to die, so many different ways that people could get hurt—just walking down the street, or even sitting at their desks at work—wasn't it a miracle that anyone made it through the day at all?

As the session was ending, Martha had stood up and looked straight at Dr. Baer, to make one more attempt to try to get her to understand. And now, the last thing she'd said was playing over and over again in her head: "I can't fold another pair of pants with whales on them," she'd said. "I'll die if I do."

CHAPTER 3

In the Coffey house, there was always a list taped to the refrigerator. At the top, it was titled: THINGS WE NEED. When the list got too full, or most of the items had been crossed off, someone would tear it down and start a new list with the same heading. The title was always capped and underlined, as if to stress that yes, this is important, these aren't just things we want, these are things we need.

Weezy couldn't even remember when the list had started. She supposed it was when she and Will first moved into the house, over thirty years ago. They were so young then, barely out of college, and at that time they needed everything. But times were different, and they didn't ask their parents for help or just charge everything, like kids would today. Neither of them even had a credit card yet, and they had a whole house to fill. So they made a list to prioritize what they were going to buy first. Weezy remembered their deciding to buy a bed and a couch, but waiting almost two years to buy a dining room table. Most of the house sat empty for those first few years, but the list always made them feel like it was only temporary.

It was on that list that Weezy told Will she was first pregnant. She'd gotten home from the doctor, so excited, and she'd added *A Crib* to the list. *So clever*, she thought. She stood back and looked at it and laughed and even jumped up and down a little bit. She was giddy the whole day, waiting for Will to come home and find out that they were going to start their family. It was almost perfect, the way she asked him to check the list to see if she'd added milk, and how he scanned it quickly, taking a moment to let it sink in, to believe what he'd read. He turned around to face her with a look of disbelief on his face. Neither of them could believe it, really, that they were capable of something so amazing, so fantastic. They were so proud of themselves, as if no one before them had ever accomplished such a thing.

Of course, when Martha was two months old, and Weezy found out that she was pregnant again, there was no such moment. Instead, she'd sat on the kitchen floor and cried up a storm. She never told Claire this story. They were delighted when the baby came, of course, but on that day, newly pregnant with a fussy infant, she had cried. Holy moly, had she cried.

Once the list had been up there for so long, it just seemed necessary. Each family member wrote down whatever it was they needed, and it was all in one place. Today, the list contained the following items: *Grape-Nuts, lightbulbs, car inspection (Volvo), AA batteries.*

When Max was home, the list was filled with food: *Cheetos, Oreos, turkey, Honey Nut Cheerios.* Max still ate like a teenager, ravenous, shoveling food in his mouth like he hadn't eaten in days. He was twenty-one now, going to be a senior in college, but he seemed younger to Weezy. His limbs still looked too long for his body, his smile a little sheepish, like he knew that he had grown up to be handsome, but he had no idea how or when it had happened.

Once, when Claire was in high school and in a particularly foul adolescent mood, she added *A Life* to the list. It was after they'd forbidden her to go on a weekend trip with a group of friends to someone's unsupervised shore house. Claire had screamed in the way that only a fifteen-year-old girl can. She'd narrowed her eyes and accused them of abuse, and denying her the right to any fun at all. "Just because you have no lives," she'd said, "and just because you are socially void, doesn't mean that I have to be."

Will had found the list in the morning while making coffee, and he'd brought it upstairs to Weezy, who was still in bed, and the two of them had laughed and laughed. "What a little shit," Weezy had said, and Will snorted. They saved the list, thinking that someday they'd show it to Claire, maybe when she had a teenager of her own. "To show her what a horror she was," Will said.

Martha had once added *Peace* to the list, during the first Iraq War, and Weezy was touched that she had such a sensitive daughter. (She was also a little concerned about Martha's obsession with war, natural disasters, and just horrible news in general, but she tried to focus on the sensitive part.) Claire had ripped down that list, saying that she didn't want any of her friends to see it, because it was "beyond embarrassing."

"Why do we even have this list?" Claire had asked that day. "Things we *need*? It makes us seem so desperate. God, we aren't poor."

Weezy loved lists. They made her feel powerful. Today she sat down with her coffee to make a list for the day. *Shore*, she put at the top. Then underneath that she wrote, *grocery store*. She put her pen down and took a sip of coffee. She'd been trying to get commitments from all of her children to go to the shore house for a week in August. She and Will would stay on for another week after, but she wanted all of her children there together. Was that too much to ask?

They'd all been responding in a casual way, "Sure, Mom, probably." And now here it was, August 1, and she still didn't have a real answer from any of them. Not even Martha, who was living with them. It was like none of them knew that things took planning, like they all expected her to just wait for them to make up their minds, and then rush around to get ready for it.

Weezy called Claire for the third time that week. As soon as she said, "Hello," she could hear Claire sigh. "Mom, I told you I'd try. I'm not sure if I can take the time from work."

"It's less than a month away," Weezy pointed out. She tried to stay calm. "Have you even talked to them about it? Have you asked? I'm trying to finalize everything."

"I'll ask today, Mom. I promise. But they might say no."

"Well, see what you can do. Your sister would love to spend some time with you. And Max, too. He's bringing Cleo. And your Aunt Maureen will be there for sure, although it's looking like Ruth and Cathy can't make it. Neither can Drew, which is too bad."

"Max is bringing Cleo?" Claire asked.

"Yes. He asked if he could, and I said it was okay, of course."

Claire stayed quiet for a few moments and Weezy wondered what she was thinking. They'd all met Cleo last year, when Max had brought her for a visit. Right after they'd all been introduced, Weezy and Claire went to the kitchen to get drinks for everyone, and Weezy whispered, "She's a bombshell." It was the only word she could think of to describe Cleo.

"Mom." Claire laughed. She'd started to say something, but then stopped and nodded. "She really is, isn't she?" And the two of them had bent their heads together and giggled like girlfriends at the pretty little bombshell that Max had brought home.

Weezy had warned her sister before she came over for Thanksgiving. "Just so you know, Max's girlfriend is quite a showstopper." Maureen had laughed and said something about Weezy's being a protective mother. "No, it's not that," Weezy said. "She's just . . . she seems older. She seems, well, very sexual."

Maureen had laughed again, but when she got to the house and met Cleo, she was visibly taken aback. She recovered, walked over to Cleo to introduce herself, and tripped just as she got near her. Maureen put her hands straight out, ended up pushing Cleo down on the couch to break her fall, and the two of them landed tangled together. They pulled themselves up and off of each other, and then sat side by side on the edge of the couch.

"I'm Max's clumsy aunt," Maureen had said. Claire, Martha, Cathy, and Ruth had watched the whole thing with their mouths hanging open. Cleo brushed off her arms and insisted she was okay, that there was no problem. She'd even laughed.

Later in the kitchen, as Weezy poured Maureen a glass of wine, she said, "I told you."

"You weren't kidding," Maureen said. "Good lord."

It wasn't that she didn't expect Max to bring home a lovely, pretty girl. She did. But Cleo was something else altogether. She seemed out of place in their house, like a runway model that had been dropped out of the sky and into their Thanksgiving. She was nearly as tall as Max, and she wore strange, funky outfits that looked amazing on her, like the fake fur vest that kept shedding, so that little tufts flew behind her when she walked, making Will sneeze.

Weezy was immediately worried that she was too much

for Max. She wanted Max to date someone just a little less stunning, someone who didn't seem like she would break his heart so easily. And so, although Cleo seemed perfectly polite and nice, Weezy prayed every day that they would break up.

Claire had defended Cleo. "Just because she's so pretty doesn't mean she's not a good person," she'd said. Claire was always protective of Max, and she'd gone out of her way to be nice to Cleo.

But Weezy could hear something in Claire's voice now, like she didn't want Cleo to go to the shore for some reason. Maybe Claire finally sensed that Cleo wasn't the right match for Max? Weezy started to ask Claire about it, but Claire interrupted her.

"Okay, Mom. I'll ask at work and let you know, okay? I'll call you later."

Weezy hung up and started to cross the item off her list, but then realized she couldn't because it wasn't taken care of yet. She did add *Empty dishwasher* to the list, and then crossed it off, because she'd already done that and it made her feel like she had accomplished something.

She sipped her coffee, which was starting to get cold, and tried to plan out her day. There was so much to do, and already she was exhausted. How was it that even as her children got older, it seemed harder to get things done? It was supposed to be the other way around, she was pretty sure of that. But it seemed like the more she tried to get things in order, the more she tried to corral them, the more they squeezed out of her grasp like a group of little greased pigs, determined to do the opposite of whatever she wanted.

WEEZY COFFEY HAD ONCE BEEN Louise Keller. No one called her Weezy until she met Will, when they were freshmen at Lehigh University and were seated next to each other in World Civ class. She'd introduced herself as Louise, but the next day Will called out to her from across the quad, "Hey, Weezy!" It made her laugh, made her heart beat faster to hear him call her that. (Of course, if she'd known it was going to stick, she would have put a stop to it right away.)

They were in college, and everyone was new to everyone else, and this crazy nickname took the place of her real name. Half of her friends from college never even knew her as Louise. With time, even her parents and sisters adopted the name, and eventually she just stopped fighting it. She almost forgot that she'd ever been Louise in the first place.

Even her own children sometimes referred to her as Weezy when talking to each other or to their friends. And a couple of times in high school, when Claire was annoyed, she'd say, "Chill, Weeze," which made her sound like a frozen treat.

Weezy had graduated from Lehigh with a degree in education, even though she had never really wanted to be a teacher. Her mother had pushed her toward it, telling her that it was a doable profession for women. Weezy took a job in a sixth-grade classroom for one year, and then she'd gotten pregnant with Martha and then Claire, and she never went back.

She hadn't missed it. After her first week of teaching, she knew she wasn't going to like it, but she had committed to it, so she gave it a try. The kids she taught were right on the brink of adolescence, that time when they don't quite fit in their bodies, when they can turn nasty in a second and gang up on each other, on teachers, on anyone, really.

It didn't make sense for Weezy to work those first few years, not with two babies at home. When both of the girls were in school, she'd started looking into other jobs. "But not teaching," she told Will. She wasn't even sure that she wanted to go back to work, but she felt like she should. Not for money reasons—they'd actually been quite fortunate, inheriting enough from Will's father to buy the house, and it wasn't like they lived an extravagant life. No, it was more that Weezy had always talked about how women had the right to work, how they were equal, and now she felt that she should act on it.

She'd worked on and off for years—at the front desk of a medical office, as the office manager of a small law firm, and most recently at an accounting firm running the day-to-day operations of the office. She'd been there for almost six years, and she couldn't say she was sorry when they started suggesting they were going to eliminate the position.

The secret she never told anyone—not Will, not Maureen, and certainly not her mother—was that she much preferred the times when she was at home, when she wasn't working. During those years she was able to make her life more orderly, was able to spend more time with the kids and Will. And even though it had felt chaotic a lot of the time with three kids and a dog, she still loved it.

Her favorite times were Sunday nights, when the house was clean and picked up, the laundry was done, the lunches for school were made and sitting in brown bags in the refrigerator, homework was done, and everyone was asleep. It was those nights when Weezy felt she'd accomplished the most, when the quiet of the house buzzed through her, made her feel like she'd won a prize.

Maybe it would have been different if she'd majored in something besides education, something that she was interested in. But then again, maybe not. Her parents had always told her she was the smart one, right in front of Maureen, like Maureen wasn't even there. In their eyes, Maureen was the pretty one. "Maureen will marry well," her mom said once, but that wasn't true. Maureen had married an awful man, and they'd stayed together long enough to have two kids and then he'd left, moved clear across the country and barely saw his children.

No, it had been Weezy that had married well, married a kind man who was a caring father and a good provider. It had been Maureen who had found a career she loved and raised Cathy and Drew practically on her own. Sometimes Weezy wondered if they'd almost done it on purpose, fulfilled the part of their lives that their parents doubted they would, just to show them they could.

Weezy found herself overcompensating when she talked about women in the workplace, as if her children were going to pick up on her desire to stay at home and get some sort of subliminal message that told them women couldn't make it. No, she didn't want that. She couldn't raise two daughters and let them think there was anything they couldn't do.

Her rants became almost background noise to her children. They were so used to hearing her go off on the way the world viewed women, in a commercial, or a TV show, or a billboard. She wanted to make sure that they knew it wasn't right, but sometimes she wasn't even sure if they were listening.

She remembered once overhearing a friend of Claire's say that she "wasn't a feminist or anything," and Weezy had scolded her. "Do you know what a feminist is?" she'd asked. "Do you even know what you're saying by denying that? Do you think you're worth less simply because you're a woman?"

The girls had all giggled at being called women. They

were twelve and uncomfortable at the thought. Claire had sat there, her face red and hot, trying to get Weezy to stop talking, rolling her eyes to the top of their sockets, saying, "God, Mom, come on, stop!" But Weezy didn't care. So her child was humiliated by her—so what? Wasn't that the job of a parent? And when Claire was embarrassed enough to answer back, embarrassed enough to react, well, then at least Weezy knew that she'd been heard.

WEEZY COULD HEAR WILL WALKING around in his office upstairs on the third floor. Sometimes it sounded like he paced back and forth across the room all day long. Will was the head of the sociology department at Arcadia University, a small liberal arts school near their house. He'd started working there in the eighties, when it was still called Beaver College. It had existed as Beaver College for over a hundred years, but as the Internet grew, parents who went searching for "Beaver College" didn't find the school's homepage— instead they found themselves on some pretty disturbing pornography sites. And so the school decided to reinvent itself.

Will was a popular professor at the school, teaching classes in sociology and in cultural anthropology. His most popular class was Society and the Cyberworld, which looked at the way culture changed because of technology. He used the name change of the college as his first example, pretending to be a prospective student as he searched the Internet, then faking his surprise at what he found. He always made the kids laugh, as he covered his eyes and shook his head at the results. His students loved him, found him entertaining and engaging. They begged to get into his classes, even after they were already full. He was almost a campus celebrity.

Will had written a book in the late eighties called *Video Kids,* which had become something of a phenomenon. It was a look at the effect that television and video games had on children. He hit something in the culture at that moment, and his book had become a best seller. He'd appeared on talk shows, and was still invited to sit on panels and give speeches.

It had been somewhat of an amazing time when the book came out. They'd been plugging along just fine, and then all of a sudden Will was a celebrity. He'd gotten a two-book deal with the publisher, and the movie rights to the book were snatched up. The good news just kept coming, and Will's job as a professor turned into something much more profitable.

Of course, the next two books that he'd written, *Video Adults* and *The Anger We Teach,* hadn't done nearly as well. The movie rights were still being optioned by the production company, but at this point there was almost no hope of those books' ever being made into anything. Will was at work on his fourth book, which he was reluctant to talk about at all. Weezy understood that. She knew he'd been shaken after the mild reception of his two follow-up books. She reminded him that since he started out so high, anything would seem like a letdown. And *Video Kids* was still used as a textbook for college classes all over the country, which made for some nice royalties. But Will had seen his requests for speaking engagements and panels diminish in the past few years, and Weezy knew that he was anxious for another success.

Will had even cut back on his classes this year, and now was home three full days during the week, which took some getting used to. He was teaching three different sections of Society and the Cyberworld, but he could do the class in his sleep and he had teaching assistants, so it wasn't a big time commitment.

It was amazing to Weezy that Will could spend days locked away, studying how other people lived their lives and what it meant for them, and how the culture influenced choices, and vice versa, but she could barely get him to talk about his children for more than five minutes. His attitude was that they were grown, that he and Weezy had done their job and now it was up to the children to choose their own paths. It drove Weezy up the wall.

"What do you want me to say?" Will would ask sometimes, when she went on about Claire's calling off the engagement.

"I want you to have an opinion," Weezy said. "I want to know what you think."

"I think Claire's a smart girl. I think if she thinks it was the right decision, then it was." And that was all he offered. *Claire's a smart girl.* Like she was just a distant relative he didn't know that well, instead of their own daughter. They'd always assumed Claire would be fine. She was the most independent one, the one who was ready to live on her own by age five. But then, last year, Claire's plans had all fallen apart, and Weezy felt like they'd failed her, like they hadn't been paying enough attention. Will still believed she'd work it out.

Weezy wanted to shake him until he got some sense. "These are our children," she wanted to say. "Our flesh and blood, the people we made, and you really don't care what they do with their lives?"

WHY DID EVERYONE ACT LIKE it was so wrong of her to want her children to be happy and healthy and successful and settled? Wasn't that what everyone wanted for their children? Was she really supposed to stop caring, stop getting involved, now that they could vote and drive?

Will always pointed out that he and Weezy hadn't had the

same support that they gave their kids. "Once I was eighteen, I was on my own," Will said. And Weezy knew that he was right, but why did they have to raise their children the same way they'd been raised? That didn't seem right. Wasn't there some sort of cultural evolution that took place? Will of all people should be interested in that.

Her children were her greatest accomplishment. Wasn't that what every mother said? Well, it was true. And Weezy didn't know how she was supposed to stop being a mother now. She'd grown them, raised them, and now she was still raising them and she probably would be until she died. What was wrong with that?

Weezy had loved being pregnant. It had agreed with her—everyone said so. She didn't have any of the vomiting or swollen ankles that Maureen and her friends had. Her cheeks got rosy when she was pregnant, and she loved the feeling of her babies swimming inside, loved watching her stomach move with the fists and the feet of the baby. Toward the end of each pregnancy, she mourned just a little. She was excited for the baby to come, but she knew the things that went with it: bottles, diapers, spit-up. She loved how neat and tidy being pregnant was, carrying everything with you, giving the baby everything it needed without having to think about it.

It was harder once they came out, harder with each year that went by. Weezy wanted her children to have everything they needed and more. But it was hard to figure out just what that was. Sometimes she got fixated on things that she wanted the kids to have. She was determined to get bunk beds for Claire and Martha, something she'd always wanted so badly when she was younger. She used to picture herself and Maureen building forts, and talking to each other in their bunks, late into the night. What little kids wouldn't want that?

Her girls hadn't seemed as interested, but Weezy pushed for it. "You'll love them," she kept saying. It turned out that they were both too frightened to sleep on the top bunk. Martha cried the whole first week she was up there, so Claire agreed to switch, but ended up falling out of it a few days later and spraining her wrist. Weezy tried to remain hopeful that they'd end up falling in love with the bunk beds, but after waking up to find them both squished into the bottom bunk for almost a month straight, she gave in and had Will take the bunk beds down.

So maybe Weezy hadn't always been right about what would make the children happy. But that didn't mean she was going to stop trying or step back and let them search all by themselves. They didn't know what they wanted. She was their mother, and she couldn't help it. She was involved.

That was why she was hell-bent on getting them all to the shore. They didn't know how important this time would be to them later. Maureen seemed to have given up on her kids' coming to the shore. "They're busy," she said. Maureen's daughter, Cathy, was living in Ohio with her partner, Ruth, and her son, Drew, was all the way in California, and somehow this didn't seem to bother her. It seemed absurd to Weezy—they'd all gone to the shore together when the kids were little; it had been a tradition. Maureen should have encouraged her kids to keep coming. Didn't she want them to be able to look back on the family vacations and appreciate all the time they'd had together?

"They're adults now," Will said, when she complained about getting the kids to clear their schedules for the shore. But they didn't really seem like adults to Weezy—Claire didn't even do her own laundry. She had it sent out to the cleaners around the block. Martha was still living at home. And Max was practically a child, still in college, likely to eat cereal for dinner if no one was there to cook for him. They weren't adult enough to know what was good for them, that was for sure. So she was going to get them to the shore, come hell or high water.

Weezy and her family had been going to Ventnor City since she was a little girl. Her father's family had acquired the house, and every summer her father and his brothers used to pack up their families for the summer and head out there. The husbands went back to the city during the week and returned each weekend to the shore, where the children greeted them like long-lost explorers, running out to meet them at the car, jumping on them like monkeys, wrapping their sunburned arms around their necks and saying, "Daddy, we're so glad you're back."

There were four bedrooms in the house where the adults stayed. Weezy and Maureen and their cousins were crowded on cots on the sleeping porch, lined up like little soldiers, waiting for a breeze to cool them down. From there, they would listen to the sounds of their parents outside on the front porch, getting drunk with the other neighbors, laughing and singing, smoking cigars, and saying, "This is the life."

Those were the best summers of Weezy's life. She firmly believed that. She was shocked when her own mother, Bets, had told Weezy that she'd always hated going to the shore. "It was so crowded, and no one had any privacy. Your aunts weren't the best company, and anyway we had to cook and clean and what kind of a vacation is that?" After Weezy's father died, Bets never went back to the shore house.

But Weezy didn't care what Bets thought. She wanted her kids to have the same summers that she did, full of hot dogs, taffy, and sea salt. Of course, it was different now. The house was split between Weezy, Maureen, and nine other cousins, and no one (including Weezy) wanted to double or triple up on families and be squished the way they once were. She and Maureen always went together with their families, which was plenty. And for the past few years, Maureen's kids hadn't come, so it was just one extra person.

Weezy had claimed the last two weeks in August early on, and thankfully no one had challenged her on it. She and Maureen had brought their families there every summer for the past thirty years. Weezy was afraid to miss even one year, worried that if she did, one of the other cousins would take her time slot. Even the year that Will's mother died in August, they packed up the week after the funeral and went. It was good therapy to be by the ocean, Weezy thought, and what good would it do to sit at home?

The end of August was Weezy's favorite time, right before the end of summer, when fall and responsibility and schedules were so close that you could smell them in the changing air, and everyone rushed around to get as much sun and ocean as they could before they had to return home. That was all she wanted for her children, who were no longer children—to smell like sunscreen and play mini-golf and shuffleboard, and jump in the waves. If she could give them this one thing to carry with them, then maybe it would make everything else okay. And so she forced this gift on them, summer after summer, whether they wanted it or not.

WEEZY WAS IN THE TV ROOM sorting through the beach towels and her summer clothes. She had them all spread out on the couch, trying to decide which things to give away and which things she could keep. She needed to make a list of things to get for the shore and start shopping, because really she was already behind.

She held a black one-piece bathing suit in her hand, debating whether or not to just pitch it. She hadn't bought a new bathing suit in years, and she knew it was time, but the thought of standing in a dressing room to find a new suit that would (to be honest) just stay hidden underneath her cover-up seemed like a waste of time. Not to mention an unpleasant errand, to say the least.

She was still holding the suit when the door slammed, making her jump. Then she heard Martha clomp to the kitchen and open the refrigerator.

"Martha? Is that you?"

Martha came around the corner with a glass of Diet Coke in her hand. "Mom," she said, "that bathing suit is like a million years old."

"I know, I'm tossing it." Weezy put it down on the couch. "How was your afternoon?"

"Fine," Martha said. She sounded down and Weezy felt her heart drop. She was used to Martha's moods, but she'd hoped for a good one today. Now dinner would be strained and silent. Maybe they would eat in front of the TV.

"Is everything okay?" Weezy asked. She tried to make it sound like a light question, so Martha wouldn't think she was prying.

Martha sipped the fizz off the top of the glass and sighed. "It's fine. Just a bad day at work."

"I'm sorry to hear that."

"Yeah." Martha sighed again. "I'm just kind of over it.

J.Crew, I mean. I'm thinking about looking for some other jobs. Maybe even think about going back to nursing."

Weezy stayed silent, not wanting to say anything that would make Martha change her mind. She had wanted Martha to do something else for so long, but she hadn't wanted to push it. It had driven her crazy to watch Martha rot away at that store. It was a waste of talent. But she hadn't been able to say so. She'd remained quiet and patient, at least in front of Martha. At night to Will, she would whisper, "What is she going to do? Work there for the rest of her life?"

"Really?" Weezy finally said. "That's interesting."

"Whatever. It's just something that I'm thinking about. I don't even know if I'll go through with it." Martha took her Diet Coke upstairs, leaving Weezy to worry in the TV room.

Will teased her that she spent twenty-three hours a day worrying about the kids. But what did he expect? Of course she worried about them. That was what mothers did, wasn't it? Will had the luxury of knowing that she was taking care of the worrying and so he didn't have to. He could rest his head on the pillow at night and sleep well.

When the kids were little, she'd worried about their getting hit by a car. She was a firm believer in hand-holding. Max and Martha had been like obedient little suction cups when they reached the street, holding their hands up to her, clinging to her with trust. Claire was the first one to pull away, to hold her arm stiffly by her side, glaring up at Weezy, wanting her independence.

When they were in high school, Weezy worried that they'd get in a car with someone who'd been drinking. When they were in college, she worried that the girls would be raped, that Max would be mugged, that they'd fall down the stairs at a wild party and break their necks, that they'd try drugs, drink too much, or vanish. The list went on and on. She kept most of her worries to herself, knowing that if she shared them with Will, he'd just think she was overreacting.

And then she worried that all of her worrying had made Martha the way she was. Maybe as a child Martha sensed Weezy's fear of the world, absorbed it as a little person, and let it overtake her. Or maybe it had been passed down in her genes, a worrying gene that mutated and grew in Martha.

She wondered if having the girls so close together hadn't given her enough time with either of them. They were less than a year apart and so different in every way. Had she made them the way they were? She would never know.

And so she continued to go through her clothes and worry. She worried that Claire was unhappy, that Max would get hurt by Cleo, that Martha wasn't going to be able to get back to nursing. There was always something. That's what Will never got. You could worry from morning until night, and even then, there'd be something more, something else that you needed to add to the list.

CHAPTER 4

Right from the start, Cleo knew she wanted to go to a college with a campus. She wanted green lawns and trees. She wanted a quad with brick buildings and college kids reading books on the grass. Basically, she wanted to go to college in a picture.

"Why?" her mom kept asking. "Why narrow it down before you even start looking?"

"Because," Cleo said. She left it at that. Cleo had grown up in New York, lived on the Upper West Side her entire life surrounded by buildings and people, and she was ready for something different. There was no explaining to Elizabeth why she wanted—no, *needed*—a campus. She couldn't say that she was craving greenery, that she imagined herself walking across grass, wearing a backpack, while leaves fell in front of her. She couldn't say that she wanted to go to a school that had a campus because that was how she'd dreamt it would be. Elizabeth was not a dreaming woman, and would never understand.

Cleo also couldn't say that she wanted to go somewhere different, somewhere no one else from her high school had even considered going. She'd listened as the guidance counselor had listed all the usual colleges, and she'd pressed the woman for more options until she'd come up with some.

When she stepped onto Bucknell's campus, she knew it

was the place for her. Their tour guide was a cute girl named Marnie, with a brown ponytail and a raspy voice. She was the kind of girl that looked like she always had a party to go to. Marnie laughed as she pointed to all the brick buildings, told them that she was a philosophy major (which made Elizabeth snort), that she was from Quakertown, Pennsylvania, and that her boyfriend was on the baseball team. "He's the pitcher," she said proudly, like they should all be jealous. Cleo found that she was.

After the tour, she and Elizabeth went to have lunch in Lewisburg, at a little place called Maya's Café. Cleo tried to contain herself as they walked down Market Street, even though she wanted to point at the old-fashioned movie theater and squeal. Elizabeth didn't like squealing and wouldn't be amused.

They each ordered a BLT and as they waited, Elizabeth pointed to the glossy brochure and then ran her finger down it, like she was trying to read it a different way. "I've never even heard of this school," she finally said. "You should keep exploring other options."

"Okay," Cleo said. She took a sip of her Diet Coke and slid the brochure back across the table toward her. She didn't want Elizabeth touching it.

"I mean, my God, it's small. What did they say? Nine hundred people in the freshman class." Elizabeth shuddered, like this was unthinkable.

There was no point in arguing. Cleo knew she'd end up at Bucknell, but she also knew it wouldn't happen by pitching a fit. She was only a junior. She would go on other college visits, she'd pretend to consider them. And when it came time, she'd make her choice and Elizabeth would let her go.

CLEO'S DAD WAS "NEVER IN THE PICTURE," which was a phrase she heard her mom use once, so she stole it and used it whenever anyone asked questions. She found that it shut them up right away. There was something final and not quite nice about it. He was "never in the picture," as if to say, don't ask anything more.

Even if people had asked questions, Cleo wouldn't have been able to answer them. Her mother told her that her father had been someone she worked with in Chicago at the Board of Trade, when she was "right out of college and dumb." Once, when Cleo pressed for more information, her mom said, "He had a wife and a family and he wasn't interested in a new one." Cleo never shared that information. Even if her own mother wasn't ashamed that she'd had an affair, Cleo found the whole thing humiliating. She was constantly afraid that her classmates would find out, that she would let it slip one day that her mom was a homewrecker.

After Elizabeth got pregnant, she moved to New York and got a job at a consulting firm, where she worked long hours and loved every minute of it. When Cleo was younger, she'd hated to listen to Elizabeth on work calls—she was always pushing people to do what she wanted, always sounded so angry and annoyed. Cleo knew why everyone caved around her, why Elizabeth just kept rising at the company. A coworker of Elizabeth's once told Cleo, "Your mother is a force to be reckoned with," as if Cleo didn't know that already, as if that wasn't the most obvious thing in the whole world.

Elizabeth was different from other mothers—Cleo knew that from the time she was about four. Some of the other mothers who worked hugged their children tightly when they dropped them off at school, declared how much they'd miss them, and surprised them by showing up early and taking them out of school for the day.

When Elizabeth dropped Cleo off, she'd walk her to the door, give her a light pat (usually on the head or back, sometimes on the arm), and walk away quickly. The few times that Cleo whined or clung to her, Elizabeth had been annoyed. "I have to go," she would say. "That's how it works. You stay here, and I have to go."

It wasn't that Elizabeth was a bad mom—she was just different. Cleo never felt bad for herself or imagined that she was missing out on anything. Mostly, she just wondered how they were even related.

"If I'm adopted," Cleo said once when she was twelve, "just tell me now. I can handle it."

Her mom had looked up from the computer, serious, and for a moment Cleo thought this would be the big reveal, when her mom admitted everything. Then Elizabeth had thrown her head back and laughed. Cleo had been insulted. "It's not funny," she said over and over, until Elizabeth was able to talk.

"I promise you, you're mine. You're not adopted. I grew you, I gave birth to you. Sorry, kid. This is it."

Elizabeth wasn't a liar, and she certainly wasn't one to lie to protect feelings, and so Cleo didn't argue. (Though she was deeply disturbed by the idea that she'd been "grown" by Elizabeth, like a plant or a sea monkey.) As she got older, Cleo could see that she looked just like Elizabeth, almost identical, really, and so she tried to ignore the thought that her real mother was living somewhere else.

How else could she explain the differences? Elizabeth was entirely unsentimental. She barely kept photographs, let alone souvenirs or letters or any sort of memorabilia. Cleo kept it all. She kept every birthday card she'd ever gotten, even the ones from people she didn't like. When she tried to throw them out, she found that she couldn't—they looked so sad in the trash, the balloons and smiling animals staring up at her, and so she ended up pulling them back out and putting them safely in a box.

Cleo saved tests and old notebooks, papers that she was especially proud of, notes from her classmates. She saved the cap from the first beer she ever drank (a Miller Lite). She hated to give away clothes, even if she never wore them or they didn't fit anymore. It seemed so mean to just discard them, like they had feelings and would be hurt when boxed and sent to Goodwill.

It was problematic to be a "low-level hoarder" (as Elizabeth called her) while living in New York. Their apartment at Seventy-ninth and Riverside was nice—spacious even, by most standards—but it was still an apartment in New York. Sometimes Elizabeth would reach her breaking point, and lay down the law, sounding more like a mother than she usually did. "You need to get rid of this stuff," she'd say, looking in Cleo's closet. "What is all this junk?" She'd hold up a stuffed elephant by its ear, and toss it on the floor, like it was going to be the first thing they threw out.

"No," Cleo would say. She'd rescue the elephant. "I'll clean it out, just don't touch anything, please don't touch a thing."

It was the same thing she'd made her mom promise when she went off to college. "My room is off limits," she said. "You aren't allowed to throw out one thing—not one thing—while I'm gone." She made Elizabeth swear up and down a million times before she was satisfied. And still she sometimes worried that Elizabeth would get the urge to clean and would throw out all of her memories—her stuffed animals and dolls, her favorite books, her journals—would bag them up in big black garbage bags, until there was nothing left of her.

ELIZABETH WAS IMPATIENT WHEN CLEO moved into the dorm. Most of the other mothers were making the beds, dusting, or folding clothes. Elizabeth sat on the desk chair and watched Cleo do all of these things, looking at her BlackBerry or her watch every few minutes. Elizabeth hadn't offered to help, but even if she had, Cleo would have declined. Cleo wanted to put everything together herself. She knew that if her mom helped, she'd rush through it, and she didn't want her underwear thrown in a messy pile in a drawer. She and Elizabeth didn't have the kind of relationship where she trusted Elizabeth to fold her underwear.

Every so often, parents or other kids moving into their rooms on the hall popped their heads in to say hi. Elizabeth, who was wearing jeans that looked crisp and pressed, flats, and a button-down, barely smiled at these people. "Hello," she'd say quickly, nodding her head at their response as if agreeing with them, *Yes, it is a pleasure to meet me, isn't it?*

Cleo was used to the way her mom didn't quite fit into social situations. It wasn't that she didn't know what to do or say to come across as normal and friendly—she just didn't care. "Be your own person," she always said to Cleo. As if there were a choice to be someone else.

Once in sixth grade, when Cleo was crying because Susan Cantor cut her out of the lunch table, told her she couldn't sit there anymore, Elizabeth had said, "Why do you care about those girls? If they don't want to be your friend, why do you want to be theirs?"

Whenever Cleo went out of her way to be nice to people, writing letters to her grandmother, being polite to her friends' parents or to her teachers, Elizabeth would sometimes comment later, "Good God, Cleo, you can't get everyone in the world to like you. Why try?" Elizabeth was used to being disliked—Cleo suspected she even enjoyed it—and she couldn't imagine why her daughter wasn't the same. "You're such a people pleaser," she'd said on more than one occasion, in the same way people said, "You're such a liar," or "You're such a cokehead."

Cleo's roommate, a small Asian girl named Grace, had already moved her things in and gone off to try to meet up with the dance troupe she wanted to join. "I'm passionate about dancing," she'd said when they met. Cleo had nodded and tried to think of a fact she could share. "I was on the school paper," she'd finally said. Grace had nodded like this was satisfactory.

"I'm almost done, Mom," Cleo told Elizabeth. She was done with her bed and was on to unpacking her clothes into the drawers. Just then she turned and saw a man at the door to the room, "Knock, knock," he said. Cleo screamed, and he smiled apologetically.

"Sorry," he said. "I didn't mean to sneak up on you! I just came to offer my services." He held up a hammer and a box of tools. "My wife and daughter suggested I see if anyone on the hall needed help hanging things up. I suspect they just wanted me out of the room." He winked at Elizabeth, and she gave him a small smile. Cleo laughed loudly to make up for her mom.

"That would be amazing," she said. "I wanted to put this shelf up, but I'm actually not sure how to do it."

"That should be no sweat. I'm Jack Collaruso, by the way. My daughter, Monica, is moving in down the hall." He stopped to shake Elizabeth's hand and then Cleo's, and then he turned to the wall and began making marks with a pencil. "Monica's our oldest, so my wife's not handling this so well."

Elizabeth made a sound then, a sort of agreement grunt that made it clear she wasn't very interested in Monica or her mother's emotional turmoil. For twenty minutes, the conversation continued like this. Jack would say something, trying to include Elizabeth in the Club of Parents Dropping Their Children Off at College, and Elizabeth would give a borderline rude reaction, while Cleo went out of her way trying to be charming and polite to make up for it. By the time the shelf was hung, Cleo was sweating.

As Jack was finishing putting up the shelf, a dark-haired mother and daughter poked their heads in. "There you are," the woman said. "We thought we'd lost you."

"You told me to go be helpful," Jack said. The two smiled at each other and Cleo got the feeling of watching a play or a sitcom about a couple taking their daughter to college.

"This is my wife, Mary Ann, and my daughter, Monica," Jack said. He put his arm around Monica's shoulders and smiled. Monica looked at the floor, and Cleo wanted to tell her that she had no reason to be embarrassed for her parents when Elizabeth, who was clearly the most embarrassing parent, was sitting right there.

"I was going to run down and get a cup of coffee somewhere. All this unpacking and crying has made me tired," Mary Ann said.

"Mom." Monica rolled her eyes, but smiled.

"Why don't you come with us?" Mary Ann was smiling and looking at Elizabeth, who looked at Cleo and then stood up.

"Coffee sounds good," Elizabeth said. Cleo let out a breath and Elizabeth gave her a look that said, *You need to relax.*

"That's great. It will give these two a chance to get to know each other." Mary Ann squeezed Monica's arm and smiled.

After their parents left, Cleo and Monica looked at each other for a few seconds. Cleo wondered if they were just going to stay like that forever, just silently staring until their parents got back, and then Monica said, "So, where are you from?"

"New York. What about you?"

"Boston. Well, just outside. Lynnfield."

Cleo nodded. "I've heard of it," she said, although she hadn't.

"Hey," Monica said. She was staring at Cleo's bed, where the gray ears of a formerly pink bunny were sticking out from behind a pillow. It was Cleo's baby blanket—a bunny head attached to a blanket, which used to be pink but was now faded. Monica walked over to the bed, and Cleo tried to think of something to say. Should she deny it was hers? Say that Elizabeth brought it? Or would that make it worse? Cleo had had the blanket for as long as she could remember. It was a thing that you gave babies—they were called snugglies or something like that. Cleo always called hers Bunny Nubby, and when she was younger, she had liked to hold it in her right hand and press it against her face while she sucked her thumb. She'd thought about leaving Bunny Nubby behind, but when she imagined sleeping in a strange room, she knew she wanted him there. When Elizabeth had seen her pull it out earlier that day, she'd made a face and said, "Oh Cleo, really?" And so Cleo had hidden it behind the pillow so no one else could see it and so Elizabeth wouldn't make any more comments.

And now Monica was walking right over to it, leaning over and plucking Bunny Nubby out from behind the pillow, dropping it on the bed and then running out of the room. Cleo stood there. She felt dizzy. What was Monica going to do? Announce to the hall that she had a baby blanket with her? Wasn't this sort of behavior supposed to be done with? Wasn't this the kind of thing that girls in junior high did to each other? Bunny Nubby was lying crumpled on the bed, and Cleo was just about to go and rescue him, put him in her drawer or somewhere safe, when Monica came running back in the room, breathing hard and holding her own matching bunny blanket.

"Look," she said. She sounded delighted and held her blanket next to Bunny Nubby. "Twins!"

FROM THAT POINT ON, Cleo and Monica were always together. Most people they met assumed the two had known each other before they'd gotten to Bucknell, that they'd gone to high school together or had been friends for a long time. Their names were almost always said together, Monica and Cleo, like they were some sort of celebrity couple. Cleo loved this. She'd had friends before, but never a best friend. She was always the girl that was the addition to the group, the peripheral friend that was nice to have there but wasn't missed if she wasn't; and while she was fond of her high school friends, she didn't miss them all that much.

Monica's roommate, a girl named Sumi Minderschmidt, had never shown up. A week into the semester, Monica found out that Sumi had decided to go to Villanova instead. "Poor Sumes," Monica said. "Confused until the very end."

They loved Sumi's name, and would often say things to each other like, "You know who loves Lucky Charms? Sumi Minderschmidt," or "Who do you think you are? A Minderschmidt?"

Cleo was in heaven. She and Monica had inside jokes that

could make them double over with laughter, make everyone else look at them with jealousy. They were a pair, a team. And so, a few days after they found out that Sumi wouldn't be joining them, Monica blurted out, "You should just move in here." She said it quickly, like she was professing her love for Cleo and was afraid she was going to be rebuffed.

"Okay!" Cleo said. She was delighted. She'd been thinking the same thing, but hadn't wanted to be the one to bring it up. It was Monica's room, and she thought maybe she would want it all to herself, but Cleo was so sick of Grace and her spandex dance outfits, and the way she slept with an eye mask and a noise machine set to "Babbling Brook" that made Cleo have to pee. If Cleo ever left the room while Grace was sleeping, she'd hear about it the next day. "You woke me up," Grace would say. "We can't have that happen. I just really need my rest for dancing."

And so the girls got permission from the RA, a senior named Colleen, who was never there much anyway, and moved all of Cleo's things into Monica's room. They were perfect together as roommates. They ate pretzels dipped in peanut butter and talked seriously about which famous person they would choose to be their boyfriend. "It can't just be about looks," Monica would always say. "It has to be about their personality, too."

Monica's Boston accent was surprising and harsh, and at first Cleo found herself reaching out her hand and placing it on Monica's arm, as if that could somehow soften the edge of her words. But soon she got used to it, the way that she could hear Monica talking loudly down the hall, the way her voice was sort of like a chicken squawk. Cleo found that she started to like the way it sounded, and she sometimes used the word *wicked* herself, when the situation called for it.

They made up dance routines in their room, after drinking vodka mixed with orange guava juice that they carried back from the dining hall in huge cups. They accompanied each other to parties of upperclassmen, where they were always welcome. Cleo found that their prettiness was somehow multiplied when they were together, that people seemed to notice them more and gave them more attention. She thought maybe it was because when they stood next to each other, Monica's hair looked darker and hers looked blonder and the difference was striking. But that was just a theory.

They shared each other's clothes and Cleo always put eye makeup on Monica, after suggesting nicely that sometimes she was just a tad too heavy on the shadow. It was everything Cleo could have hoped for college, and so midway through freshman year, when Monica suggested they move off campus, Cleo was all for it.

"My cousin is a senior and living in one of the best off-campus houses. If we don't take it now, some junior will get it and keep it for two years. We have to do it. It would be a crime not to."

"But are we even allowed?" Cleo asked. She hadn't heard any other freshman talking about moving off campus.

"Well, legally it's allowed," Monica said. She bit her bottom lip. "I mean, they don't really like sophomores to move off, but they make special exceptions sometimes, and my dad thinks he can help."

Monica never said specifically, but Cleo got the feeling that her dad, who was a Bucknell alum, donated a lot of money to the school—money that had helped Monica get accepted, and also get into the best freshman dorm, and into any classes that were filled.

They decided to ask two girls from their hall, Laura and

Mary, to move in with them. The four of them sometimes went to eat dinner together, or pre-gamed in one of their rooms, and it seemed like the logical choice. All four girls got permission from their parents and then from the housing board to move off campus. For the rest of freshman year, the four of them talked endlessly about how amazing their house was going to be and the parties they could have. Sometimes, in the dining hall, Cleo would say to Monica, "I can't wait to have our own kitchen next year," just to remind whomever was around them that they were special, that they were moving off campus.

In New York that summer, Cleo felt like she was just counting the days until she could get back to Lewisburg. It seemed now that Bucknell was her real life, and New York and Elizabeth were just a holding place to wait until she could get back there. Cleo went to visit Monica in June, and stayed in her big sprawling house in Lynnfield, slept in the spare twin bed in her room, and went with her to a party at a high school friend's parentless house.

While they sat outside that night, drinking Keystone Lights by the pool, the two girls talked about their sophomore year, told all the other kids there about their new house and the parties they were going to have. She and Monica sat at the edge of the pool, their feet in the water, and they laughed at everything.

"I've missed you so much," Monica said. "You're just so much more important to me than my high school friends."

Cleo loved everything about Monica. She loved where she grew up, how she was meticulous about putting her clothes away as soon as she changed, the way she drew little animals on the corners of her notebooks. She had a best friend and everything just fit. Cleo was filled with happy; everything was right in the world.

• • •

SOPHOMORE YEAR STARTED PERFECTLY. The girls moved in at the end of August, tripping over each other as they unpacked and ran from room to room. They hung up posters and bulletin boards, bought throw pillows and pots from Target, stocked up on macaroni and cheese and big plastic bins of pretzels. They were as happy as four little clams.

For the first few months, things went amazingly well—swimmingly, as her mom would say. Then two things happened, although Cleo couldn't say which had happened first, or if one thing caused the other, or if they just happened at the exact same time. The first thing was that Monica became severely anorexic. She started running for hours each morning, first at the gym on campus and then, when spring came, outside. After her run, she'd do sit-ups in the common room. As they all stumbled out of their bedrooms to make it to class in the morning, they'd find Monica flying up and down as she worked her abs, her arms crossed in front of her chest in an X, counting her progress in an angry, loud voice. "One, two, three, four," she would huff. When she got to "twenty-five," she'd stop for a few seconds, lying on the floor and staring at the ceiling, and then she'd start all over again.

"She's like a soldier," Laura whispered one morning. It was an accurate description and it made Cleo nervous.

This seemed to come out of nowhere. Monica was anything but fat, and while both of the girls drank Diet Coke and frequently looked in the mirror and said, "I'm a cow," or "Look at my giant ass," it didn't mean anything. It was just what girls did. Cleo hadn't seen any behavior that would have led her to believe that Monica was going to be one of them: an Eating Disorder Girl. At Cleo's high school, there was one in every group of friends—a thin, chilled girl with bags under her eyes who was eventually taken out of school to go to a rehab clinic and returned eating measured foods and seeing the school counselor once a week. She couldn't understand how she'd missed this in her best friend.

Monica kept a notebook to write down every piece of food that she ate. Once, Cleo looked over her shoulder as she wrote down, "Baby carrots, lettuce (NO dressing!), gum, water."

"It doesn't seem like you're eating enough," Cleo offered.

Monica slammed the notebook shut. "I'm being healthy," she said. "Not like the rest of you, eating candy and french fries all day."

She stomped off to her room, where she spent most of her time with the door closed listening to music. She was always tired and cold, sometimes coming out to nap on the couch in the common room, because the sun came through the windows, and she could curl up there like a cat trying to warm itself.

When the rest of them ate, Monica watched them closely. "Is that a waffle?" she'd ask, sniffing the air. She'd sit and stare as Cleo put syrup on her Eggo, suggesting that she add butter, or maybe more syrup. Then she'd fill a glass of water and drink it while she watched Cleo eat, with an almost erotic look on her face. It was really freaky.

Cleo noticed one day that Monica's arms were covered with peach fuzz, and she knew she had to call her parents. They came right away and took Monica out of school for the last month of sophomore year, keeping her home all summer and the first semester of junior year. They left everything in her room, paid her rent, and told the girls she could return when she was better. Sometimes Cleo would open the door and look in Monica's room, which was just as she'd left it— the bed was made, there were books stacked on the desk, a box of Kleenex on her nightstand—except there was a fine layer of dust over everything, so that it made Cleo feel like time had stopped. She would stand there and stare at it, until it made her feel too lonely, and then she'd shut the door and go to her own room.

Once Monica was gone, Cleo wished she wasn't staying in Lewisburg for the summer. The house felt empty, and even though Monica had been in her own calorie-counting world for most of the year, Cleo missed her greatly. But the arrangements were made, and it was too late to back out of the summer job working in the Visitors Center. And so she stayed.

The second thing that happened that year was that Laura and Mary turned into complete and total bitches. The house had always been a little divided, like they were on two teams—Monica and Cleo on one and Laura and Mary on the other—but they still all got along pretty well. And then once Monica got sick and left, the other girls seemed to blame Cleo in some way. They were annoyed at her all the time, made passive-aggressive comments about her jacket's being left on the couch, or the amount of noise that she made. Post-it notes were left on milk cartons and said things like, *This is Mary's Milk. Unless you're Mary, then hands OFF.*

Cleo had used Mary's milk on her cereal exactly once, and then she found the note there the next day. She honestly couldn't figure out how Mary could have known, until she looked at the side of the plastic carton and saw little black lines to mark the level of the milk. She placed the carton back in the refrigerator carefully, and closed the door softly, as if someone was going to jump out and catch her.

It became clear that it had been a mistake to move in with these girls so soon. Everyone else in their class had waited an extra year to make their permanent living choices, giving them time to weed out the crazies, to form real friendships, and now they all had their own living pods that were full and had no room for Cleo.

IN JUNE, RIGHT AFTER SOPHOMORE YEAR ENDED, Cleo went to a party with a girl she knew from her Foundations of Accounting class. It was at that party, standing by the keg in a dirty kitchen with a sticky floor, that she met Max. They were both holding red plastic cups, and waiting in line to get them filled. This was a story that pleased Cleo. It seemed like such a perfect way to meet a boy in college, the way he'd started talking to her in line, then pumped the keg and taken her cup to fill it first, tilting it perfectly to make sure there was no foam on top.

She liked him immediately, mostly because he was taller than she was. Cleo was five nine, and it was surprising how many boys she towered over, especially when she wore heels. But Max was well over six feet tall, and her head just cleared his shoulder. The two of them hung out the whole night at the party, and once when she went to the bathroom and they were separated for more than ten minutes, he came up behind her and put his arm around her shoulders. "There you are," he said. "I was afraid I lost you."

At the end of the night, Max said, "I really liked talking to you." He said this like it was something that boys in college said all the time, when Cleo knew from experience that it certainly was not.

Max was so easy—and not in a bad way. He was so sure of himself, so honest, so happy. After that first night, he was always around and Cleo was thrilled to have someone to hang out with, someone to distract her from her haunted house of eating disorders and milk Post-its. He always wanted to actually do things. Unlike most of the boys at Bucknell, who sat around in sweatpants and played video games, Max suggested real activities, like playing tennis or going to see a movie.

By August, they were a serious couple, by the college definition. When Max's parents came up to visit one weekend, he asked Cleo to come to dinner with them, and so she put on a sundress and waited for them outside of her house, feeling more nervous than she ever had before.

They ate dinner at a steakhouse, and Max's mom encouraged Max to get the biggest steak, made sure that all the leftovers were wrapped up for him, and asked about ten times what he was making himself for dinner these days.

Max's mom fascinated Cleo. Weezy was doting. Cleo had never used that word much before, but it was the only word to explain Weezy's relationship with Max. When she walked into his apartment, she almost immediately began to clean it, stocking the kitchen with groceries she'd bought, dusting shelves and changing sheets.

During her first visit to the Coffey house, she and Max were sitting on the couch when Max mentioned in an offhand way that he was hungry. "Do you want a snack?" Weezy asked. She got up and went to the kitchen, began returning with options, holding up bags of chips and cold cuts, like she was one of those ladies on a game show, presenting the contestants with their prizes.

It was no wonder Max was such a happy person. Sitting there, watching Weezy fall all over him, she got it. His whole life, people had been doing things for him, telling him how cute and funny he was—and he was all of those things, but still. Cleo couldn't remember the last time her mom had made her a snack. She might have been around five years old, and the only reason her mom got involved was because the granola bars were on a shelf that was too high for her to reach. After that, the granola bars were put on a lower shelf so that Cleo could help herself to one whenever she wanted.

The first time that Cleo met the whole Coffey family, she was overwhelmed, to say the least. They were loud and could be crass. They hugged often, sometimes for no reason at all. With no warning, they'd just reach over and pull the person standing next to them into an embrace. They touched each other's hair and squeezed shoulders when they passed by. More than once, Cleo jumped when a hand surprised her.

"You have a family of touchers," she told Max. Then she tried to take it back and explain what she meant, because it sounded like she was accusing them of something. But Max just laughed. It was nearly impossible to upset him.

WHEN MONICA RETURNED, HALFWAY THROUGH junior year, Cleo was ecstatic. She couldn't wait to introduce her to Max, to talk to her every night, to have a friend in the house again. But Monica wasn't interested in any of it. She spent most of her time shut away in her room. She seemed mad at everyone, like they'd all betrayed her. Cleo apologized for calling her parents, but it didn't make a difference. Monica just shrugged like she couldn't care less. When Cleo talked to her—about school or Max or parties—she'd just look back at her, visibly bored. It was as if they'd never known each other before.

Cleo didn't know how to make it better. For a few days, she'd give Monica space, and then she'd decide that it would be better to spend more time together, so she'd force her way into Monica's room, sit with her and do homework. But nothing seemed to work. Monica was different and no matter what Cleo did, it wasn't getting better. It was lonelier than when she'd been gone.

Max lived on the top floor of a house in Lewisburg that was converted to a two-bedroom apartment. At the end of junior year, his roommate, Charlie, was asked by the college not to return the following year (a polite way to kick someone out), and Max asked Cleo to move in with him.

"Come on," he said. "It's perfect. I don't want to get some random to move in, and you're here all the time anyway."

That was true, but Cleo wasn't sure. "I'm not sure my mom would like that."

"My mom wouldn't like it either," Max said. "We just won't tell them."

Cleo was, first of all, just a little offended at the thought that Max's mother wouldn't like their living together, even though she'd just said the same thing about her own mom. Still. It was different.

"Just think about it," Max said.

And so she did. She thought about what it would be like to give up her house and move in with Max. How she could use his milk whenever she wanted, how he would never yell at her if it was her turn to buy the toilet paper. It was tempting. Very tempting.

But it was a crazy idea. Couples in college didn't live together. They'd barely been dating a year, and what were they going to do? Live together for the rest of their lives?

"You're overthinking it," Max told her.

But Cleo didn't think she was. She tried to picture herself living there, tried to imagine what it would feel like to wake up with Max every morning, to have all of her clothes there in a real dresser instead of the Tupperware box that she kept them in now. But then she thought about what would happen if they broke up, how she'd probably end up sleeping in the other bedroom since it would be impossible to move midyear.

That was enough to make Cleo decide to stay in her own house. Also, she felt disloyal leaving Monica, even if she barely spoke to her anymore. It was just one more year, and really she could do anything for a year. Maybe things would change and senior year at the house would end up being fun. Maybe Monica would go back to her old self. Anything could happen.

A few days later, Laura came out of her bedroom holding a cardboard wheel and looking full of purpose. Laura, a sturdy girl from Iowa, had gained all the weight that Monica had lost over the years, and was now bordering on being truly fat. People always used to say that Laura "had a really pretty face," but Cleo didn't think they even said that anymore.

"What is that?" Cleo asked. She was sitting cross-legged on the couch, eating a bowl of Life cereal and flipping through a gossip magazine.

"It's a chore wheel," Laura said. "Well, more than a chore wheel, really. See, there's a part here that also reminds us whose turn it is to buy toilet paper and toothpaste and dishwasher soap. So it's fair."

Fairness was something that Laura talked about often. When Cleo first started dating Max, Laura mentioned that she thought they should have a rule for how many times a boyfriend could sleep over in one week. "It's not fair to the rest of us if there's a stranger here all the time."

"He's not a stranger," Cleo said. "He's my boyfriend."

"Still," Laura said. "We have to be fair."

And that was why Cleo ended up spending all of her time at Max's, keeping clean underwear and pajamas in the Tupperware box that he had in his closet.

Now Laura stood in front of Cleo, clutching her cardboard wheel, and called Mary and Monica out of their rooms to show them her creation.

"See?" She pointed to the wheel. "For one week, it will be someone's responsibility to clean the bathroom, and someone else will be responsible for the kitchen and so on. Then we'll switch."

"Fine," Monica said. "Fine with me." She sat on one of the futons in the room, hugging her knees to her chest and looking bored. She was pretty agreeable these days. "The bathroom's disgusting anyway."

Cleo tried to catch her eye, to look at her so that she could see that Monica really thought this was stupid too. She wanted them to roll their eyes at each other and then go into one of their rooms and laugh about how crazy and annoying Laura was being. But Monica kept her eyes down, picking imaginary fuzz and stray hairs off of her leggings.

"Wait," Mary said. "What if, like, let's just say it's my week to clean the kitchen and then Cleo leaves her cereal bowl in the sink. Do I have to clean that?"

"I don't leave my bowl in the sink," Cleo said.

"Okay, sure," Mary said. She snorted and shook her head.

"I don't. I don't leave my dishes in the sink."

"Okay, guys," Laura said. "I mean, the fair thing is for the kitchen person to just be there for the big stuff, like emptying the dishwasher and just making sure it's clean. We're all still responsible for our own mess."

"Are we?" Mary asked. She looked at Cleo.

Cleo was still staring at Monica, willing her to look up and defend Cleo, or at least acknowledge that the girls were ganging up on her. But Monica only looked up to say, "So are we done?"

Cleo stood up and put her cereal bowl on the coffee table. Her hands were shaking and she knew she was about to cry. "Actually, I think a chore wheel sounds like a great idea," she said. "Fantastic, actually."

"Really?" Mary said.

"Yes, really. I'd also like to say that I won't be living here next year. I'm moving out."

"What?" Laura asked. "You're just telling us now? What if we can't find a new person? This is so unfair."

"Everything's unfair," Cleo said. She knew she wasn't making sense and she didn't care.

When she told Max, he screamed, "Yes!" He hugged her around the waist and her feet came up off the ground. "This is going to be great," he said. "You'll see."

THEY MOVED ALL OF CLEO'S STUFF into the apartment right away, and spent the summer working and going to barbecues. Cleo had gotten a marketing internship, working for the Little League World Series in Williamsport. Elizabeth had advised her to take an internship in New York, but Cleo remained firm.

"You don't even want to go into marketing," Elizabeth said. "And you don't even like sports."

"I like sports," Cleo said. "And maybe I will want to go into marketing."

"This is a mistake, Cleo. When you're up against another candidate that did an internship at a well-known firm in New York, and then they look at you and see you wasted away your time as a ball girl in some stupid town, do you really think you'll win?"

Cleo was determined to show Elizabeth that she was wrong. Also, she didn't want to be away from Max, so an internship in New York was out of the question. She didn't give Elizabeth too much information about her job. She wasn't a ball girl, but she was mostly just typing out schedules and directions to send to the parents of the players, and getting coffee for people in the office. She was pretty sure there was no marketing involved whatsoever.

At the apartment, Cleo pretended they were married. They played house, making dinner (usually just pasta and jarred sauce) and drinking wine, like they were adults. She knew that her old roommates were wrong when they told her she was making a mistake. "This will end in disaster," Mary had said as she packed up.

Cleo had become friends with some of Max's friends, but it felt like they were on loan, like they never really made the switch to being hers. She had really started to like his friend Ally, had started to think that maybe she would be the one that Cleo clicked with, until she heard her say at a party, "Cleo's totally nice. She's supersweet. She's just, you know, sort of a loner."

A loner? Cleo had been waiting for the bathroom when she heard this, and Ally was around the corner, out of sight, talking to someone else. She wanted to ask Ally what she meant by that, but she didn't. Instead, she stood there praying that she could get into the bathroom before Ally saw her.

Later that night, she'd told Max what she'd heard. "Do you think I'm a loner?"

"No." Max laughed.

"It's not funny. Why would Ally say that? I thought she liked me."

"She does like you," Max said. "Don't let it bother you."

"I can't help it."

"Look, Ally can't be alone for five minutes without going

crazy. You know that. She can't eat alone, she can't walk to class alone, and she certainly can't study alone. She's probably just jealous of you."

"It didn't sound like she was jealous."

"Well, then she's intrigued. You do your own thing, that's all. You don't need a clan of girls around you at all times."

"I guess," Cleo said. But it wasn't that she didn't need it, she'd just never had it. She'd learned to live without.

Cleo felt like she'd failed in some very real way, to be almost a senior in college and not have one single girlfriend to show for it. It was her mom's fault, probably. Elizabeth didn't have any friends, not really. She had work people that she went out to dinner with sometimes, or to the Hamptons with, but not real friends that she relaxed and spent time with. And now Cleo was all fucked up because of it. She'd never seen an example of how to have friends and now maybe she never would. She could go on a talk show about it.

One night she and Max were watching TV, and she said, "You're my best friend, you know."

Max smiled. "Why do you sound so sad about it?"

"Don't you think it's weird? That you're my best friend? My only friend, really? That I don't have any girlfriends?"

Max thought for a minute. "No. I think you got in with a bad crowd early on."

"A bad crowd?"

"Yes, a bad crowd. Any house with a milk tracer and a chore wheel is a bad crowd. In my book, at least."

"I guess so."

Max came closer to her and pulled her head down to his chest. "You're my best friend, too," he said.

"You're such a liar."

"I'm not. I'm not lying at all."

"What about Mickey?"

Max wrinkled his nose. "He's fun, but you smell way better." He lifted up her shirt and started kissing her stomach. "Way better."

IN THE MIDDLE OF AUGUST, they packed their bags and headed to the shore for a weeklong vacation with the Coffeys. They'd agreed to keep their living arrangement a secret from their families, and Cleo was terrified that she was going to blurt it out during the trip. Max told her she was being paranoid, but she knew better.

Around the Coffeys, she became a strange version of who she was. She tried to be chatty, but her voice came out higher than it usually was. She tried to be casual, but she felt uncomfortable everywhere. It was exhausting.

Cleo was almost certain that Aunt Maureen was bordering on a drinking problem, although when she suggested this once, Max laughed. "She just likes to have a good time," he said.

On the drive to the house, Cleo asked how Claire was doing. She was nervous about seeing her after the whole engagement disaster.

"She's good," Max said.

"Well, she can't be good. She just called off her wedding."

Max had shrugged. "I mean, it sucks, but I think she's handling it fine."

"It's just so sad. I feel so bad for her," Cleo said.

"Well, don't ask her about it."

"You don't think I should say anything?"

"No," Max said. "You know Claire. She doesn't like to dwell on things."

"Yeah, but I'll feel weird not mentioning it."

"Trust me, she doesn't want to talk about it."

So now there were two things that Cleo wasn't supposed to talk about. She took a deep breath and looked out the window.

"Are you okay?" Max asked.

"I'm just nervous, I guess," she said.

Max reached over and took her hand. "It'll be fun," he said. "I promise."

Cleo felt very grown-up just then, driving with her boyfriend to join his family on vacation, discussing the things that they weren't to discuss with the rest of the family. And the two of them drove almost the whole way like that, holding hands, sometimes linking their fingers, sometimes just resting against each other. It thrilled Cleo a little bit to be doing this, traveling in a car, with her live-in boyfriend, driving through the night with their secrets between them.

CHAPTER 5

The house at the shore looked like it belonged in a fairy tale. When Claire was little, she used to call it the Gingerbread House, because it was tan and pink with sculpted posts, and rising turrets that looked like the perfect place for hiding a princess. She'd been there every year since she was a baby. Even the year she was in college, when she had her own shore house with friends in Ocean City, she still stayed at the Gingerbread House for the last two weeks of August.

She'd pretended to be annoyed that summer, pretended that her parents were making her stay with them, but really she was grateful. She'd been sharing a room with Lainie, which meant that she was also sharing a room with Brian. The room smelled like mildewy towels and had two twin beds with thin mattresses that dipped in the middle. Every night, Claire had to get upstairs before Lainie and Brian, put on her Discman, face the wall, and pray for sleep so that she could ignore whatever happened when they came in. The alternative was to sleep on the couch downstairs, which always felt wet and smelled worse than the bedroom—a mix of feet and old cheese.

There was sand all over the house, dirty dishes every-where, and every morning Claire woke up sunburned and hungover. She was filled with relief when it was time to go to the Gingerbread House. She packed up her clothes quickly, saying, "This sucks, I can't believe I'm missing the end of the summer here. Yeah, my parents are so annoying."

Claire loved the Gingerbread House, loved waking up to the sound of waves and the smell of sand. It was part of the reason she'd finally agreed to go this year. Well, that and also because she didn't have enough money in her account to pay September's rent.

She'd taken the train to Philly on Saturday, and her parents and Martha had picked her up at the station and they'd all headed right for the shore. Everyone was in a great mood. Her dad was whistling, her mom was almost bouncing up and down in her seat, and Martha wasn't discussing any recent tragedies. Claire started to feel calm for the first time in months. This was exactly what she needed. She had three new books to read, and the thought of lying on the beach and resting in the sun sounded like the most wonderful thing in the world. And then when the time was right, she'd tell her parents that she was broke. And moving home.

But that would all come later. She could wait until the end of the week to fill them in. Actually, it was preferable, since she could just leave right after. In the meantime, she'd enjoy her vacation, go for a walk on the beach or the board-walk. Eat saltwater taffy. Just relax.

When they were younger, all of the cousins stayed in the same room. Cathy, Martha, Claire, Drew, and Max were all tucked away in bunk beds and sleeping bags. One summer, Martha forgot to put sunscreen on her feet and they burned, badly. She'd insisted that the fan in the room had to stay pointing right at her feet to cool them down, instead of circu-lating the room like it normally did. They'd all disagreed, of course. But as soon as Martha thought they were all asleep, she'd pull the lever on the fan to make it stop, and one of the other kids would realize it and yell, "Martha!" But they were all laughing, not really annoyed, just thrilled with their own little game they'd created.

Had they ever slept during those summers? They must have at some point, but Claire didn't remember it. She remembered sandy beds and Cathy telling them stories about girls that were kidnapped. "I knew a girl," she said, "that was taken right out of her room, pulled right through the window."

"You did not," Claire said. But she wasn't sure. Cathy always sounded sure.

Usually, as they were drifting off to sleep, Drew or Max would fart loudly and all the girls would scream, and there'd be a big to-do over airing out the room and running into the hall. Weezy and Maureen tried their best to get them back to their beds, yelling threats and using their full names, "Claire Margaret, Martha Maureen, Catherine Mary." It rarely worked.

During the days, they'd run as a pack, going to the beach and then to the boardwalk to play skeet ball and walk around. The girls would get wrapped braids in their hair, feeling very special and exotic when school started and they still had a tiny seashell attached to their hair.

They always went to the same little candy store. It was made to look like one of those old-fashioned places, with bins of colored candy balls, swizzle sticks, and fudge. They always chose Atomic FireBalls and Super Lemons—candy that was more pain than pleasure, that tested the will of all the sun-burned kids that ate it. They'd stand in a circle outside the store, count to three, and pop the little sugar balls into their mouths. They'd groan and scream, wriggle back and forth and bend over laughing in a mix of agony and total pleasure, drooling colored sugar and waiting to see who could keep the candy in their mouth the longest. Martha always won. Usually the others would have to spit the candy out in their hands, take a break, and try again.

It was funny—her cousins hadn't come to the shore in years, but whenever she thought about it, she imagined them there. The house had been redone and the sets of bunk beds in the big room replaced with a huge king bed. But still, when Claire pictured the house, she saw all of them bunked down in the big room, scaring the bejeezus out of each other and laughing until they thought they were going to die.

THEY ARRIVED AT THE HOUSE a little after five o'clock, and when they opened the front door, they heard music playing and saw smoke coming from the back patio. They heard laughing, and even though they all knew it was Max because his car was right out front, and because he'd told them he'd arrived the night before, Weezy stepped in nervously and called, "Hello? Max?" as if an intruder had broken into the house and started grilling out back.

Max appeared at the screen door with a big smile on his face. "Hello, family," he said. He raised a spatula in the air. "Cleo and I decided to cook you a welcome meal!"

He was pretty drunk, Claire could tell, and she wondered what time he'd started drinking. Weezy just clapped her hands together. "Oh, Max," she said. "How sweet is that?"

It would, no doubt, be something she talked about for months, the way Max cooked for them out of the blue; went to the grocery store all by himself, with no one asking (as if he were an incompetent), and then made dinner, like he was performing a miracle of some sort. Once, when Max was in high school, he'd folded towels that were in the dryer and Weezy had gone on about it for weeks, until Martha said, "Claire and I fold laundry all the time," to try to shut her up. It was one of the few times that they'd been on the same side, Claire and Martha, but they were just so sick of listening to Weezy talk about Max and his amazing laundry abilities.

Max turned to Claire and gave her a hug that lifted her off the ground. "Clairey!" he said. "Clairey's here." He set her down gently and Claire laughed. This was, of course, why he was Weezy's favorite, after all. He was adorable and charming, even when a little bit tipsy—maybe especially when he was a little bit tipsy. He turned to Martha and bowed. "Welcome, miss," he said.

Cleo walked in from the patio then, carrying an empty platter and wearing nothing but a bikini. "Oh, you're here already," she said. "We thought we'd be done cooking by the time you got here."

"Well, this is such a treat," Weezy said. "Personal chefs on our first night here." Cleo smiled and looked down at the ground. Then Weezy hugged Cleo, which must have been awkward since the girl was practically naked. Claire noticed that her father stayed on the far side of the kitchen and just waved. She didn't blame him.

"We made chicken and salad," Cleo said. "We thought you'd be hungry when you got here."

"That we are," Will said. He looked around the kitchen, still averting his eyes from Cleo. "You didn't happen to pick up any brewskies, did you, son?"

Claire closed her eyes for a second and took a deep breath. Her father had never used the word *brewskies* in his whole life. He'd never called Max "son" either. She was embarrassed for him, but figured it wasn't fair to judge. After all, when you had a twenty-one-year-old near supermodel standing in all of her naked glory in the kitchen of your summerhouse, you were bound to be a little rattled.

She would change eventually, Claire figured, but it never happened. Cleo ate dinner in her bikini, she cleared the table in her bikini, and then she sat and had a glass of wine with the whole family in her bikini.

When Maureen arrived later that night, she walked in, looked right at Cleo, and let out an "Oh!" Then she tried to recover and said, "I guess you're ready for the beach." Cleo just smiled.

And that was just the first night. It seemed that Cleo intended to wear nothing but her bikini for the entire vacation. In the mornings, she was in the kitchen, sipping coffee, bikini-clad.

"I mean, she's great, but don't you think it's a little weird that she never puts anything else on?" Claire asked Martha. Martha just shrugged, which bugged Claire. Normally, this was the kind of thing that Martha would jump right in on, getting upset and whispering behind Cleo's back. But she barely seemed to notice.

"I can't believe we have to share a room," Claire went on. This surely would make Martha angry. "Just because Mom doesn't want Max and Cleo in the same room, we have to share. They each get their own space." Martha just shrugged again, and Claire grabbed a towel and left the room.

ON SUNDAY NIGHT, THE WHOLE FAMILY sat outside making s'mores after dinner and Claire drank glass after glass of white wine. Weezy kept talking about what activities everyone wanted to do, like they were at some sort of summer camp; Will read the paper and called Max "son"; Maureen kept getting up to sneak around the house and have a cigarette, like they all couldn't smell the smoke on her when she got back; Martha was lost in her own thoughts and stared at the stars; and Max and Cleo used any excuse to touch each other, which would have been inappropriate for a family vacation anyway, but since Cleo was half-naked, it was downright pornographic.

"Aren't you cold?" Claire asked.

Cleo laughed. "No, I never get cold at the beach. It's like the sun warms me all day and stays with me into the night. I could live at the beach."

Claire snorted into her glass. Then she let herself admit that if she looked like Cleo did in a bikini, she would consider wearing one as much as possible too.

The night ended with everyone playing Scrabble, which Claire thought would make her feel better since she would surely win. She ignored it when Weezy said to Cleo, "Watch out for Martha! She's a killer at this game." Claire wanted to point out that Martha almost never won Scrabble. It was Claire's game.

It turned out that in addition to having a body that was meant to live in a bikini, Cleo also had an incredible vocabulary. After she got a triple word score by turning *dish* into *dishabille*, Claire made a comment about memorizing the dictionary and Cleo actually blushed.

"My first nanny was French, and she always had trouble with English. She was always asking me, 'What's the word for this?' and I wanted to make sure that I could tell her, so I kept a dictionary with me. Then it just became a habit. I read dictionaries all the time. And thesauruses. I just love words, I guess," Cleo said. She shrugged and smiled a little bit and Claire made herself smile back. Of course Cleo read the dictionary for fun. If life was going to be unfair, it was going to go all the way.

The end of the Scrabble game was a bit blurry to Claire, but she did remember dropping her glass of wine on the floor, the glass smashing and spraying everywhere. She tried to clean it up, until Maureen came in to help and sent her out of the kitchen because she was barefoot.

CLAIRE WOKE UP ON MONDAY, groaned, and rolled over to bury her face in her pillow. She could feel a burn on the edge of her scalp where her sunscreen had, of course, worn off the day before. She could hear everyone downstairs in the kitchen, dishes clinking, her dad telling some story about peaches, or something that sounded like that. Claire pulled the covers over her head. If she waited long enough, maybe they would all go to the beach without her.

At first, Claire thought she'd tell Weezy about her situation. Then she changed her mind and thought she'd tell Will, because he'd be calmer and would keep Weezy calm too. But then she thought no, that wouldn't work. Will would just sit there and listen, not sure how he was supposed to respond. Will was never the one they would go to when they asked permission for anything. And if it ever happened that they did come across him first, and asked to go to a friend's house or anything of the sort, Will always looked surprised to see them, like he couldn't quite place who they were, and then he'd say, "Ask your mom."

So it would have to be Weezy that she told. It would be fine. She'd just wait until the end of vacation, go up to her mom, and say, "I'm out of money. I'm moving home." Simple. She was going back to New York on Sunday, which meant that she had seven more days to do it.

Claire took a shower and then threw her wet towel on Martha's bed. If Martha came up and saw it, she would lose it. She was such a neat freak. Growing up, whenever they got new sneakers, Martha made a point to keep hers as white as possible for as long as she could. She'd step over puddles, avoid any dirt, and stare at her unblemished shoes with pride. Claire's Keds were usually dirty by the end of the week, and it used to drive Claire crazy, to watch Martha step around messes, so pleased with herself and her white shoes.

"That's probably the only reason why you wanted to be a nurse," Claire told her one time. "Because you knew you'd get to wear really white shoes."

Once, when they were playing kickball outside with the neighborhood kids, Martha refused to take her turn for fear that her shoes would get filthy. Claire walked right up to her and stepped all over Martha's feet with her own dirty sneakers. Martha looked down at her shoes and let out a howl, then pushed Claire on the ground.

"Why did you do that?" her mother asked Claire. "Whatever possessed you to do such a thing?"

Claire had no reason to give and was sent to bed right after dinner that night—no TV, no Jell-O Pudding Pop. She couldn't explain to her mom why she wanted to get Martha's shoes dirty. She wasn't even sure she knew herself. All she knew was that she couldn't watch Martha protect their whiteness anymore, couldn't stand to hear the other kids laugh at her while she stood to the side and refused to participate. And so she'd put a stop to it.

MARTHA WAS STILL BEING UNUSUALLY quiet. On Tuesday, she and Claire sat on lounge chairs at the beach, and Martha wrote in her journal, sighing and turning her face to the sun with her eyes closed. Cleo and Max were frolicking in the ocean—that was the only word for it, *frolicking*—splashing each other and embracing as the waves crashed over them.

"What's going on with you?" Claire asked. It really wasn't normal for Martha not to be talking all the time.

"If you must know," she said, "I'm considering a career change."

"Going to the Gap?" Claire asked. Martha shut her journal loudly and started gathering her things. "I'm kidding, I'm kidding." She put her hand on Martha's arm. "I'm sorry, come on, I was just kidding. Tell me."

Martha sniffed, acting like she wasn't going to say any more, but Claire could tell she wanted to talk about it. Finally she said, "I'm thinking about going back to nursing."

"Really?" Claire asked. "Wow."

"What's that supposed to mean?" Martha asked.

"Nothing, just—wow. I haven't heard you talk about nursing in a long time."

"Well, I've just been thinking about it lately. I think it's time. But not in a hospital. Maybe at a doctor's office or something."

"I think that's great," Claire said. "Really, I do. You always wanted to be a nurse and you were good at it."

Martha looked over at Claire. "Thank you," she said, and then she started writing again.

Claire considered telling Martha everything. Confessing about the apartment and the credit cards and all of it. But she knew that if she did, Martha would let her mouth fall wide open, stare at her, and then go tell Weezy. She wouldn't be able to stop herself. Martha told Weezy everything, which was weird. It should have been the other way around, her loyalty to Claire, but it never had been and it wasn't going to start now. So Claire kept her mouth shut.

She wished that she could tell Doug about everything. It didn't make sense, of course, because if she and Doug were still together and he was there to talk to, she wouldn't be in this situation. It had helped a little to tell Lainie, but it wasn't the same. She missed having one person to give her undivided attention and advice, to be almost as responsible for her actions as she was.

Probably it was just loneliness that made her wish for Doug. That was normal, right? It was a shitty situation and she just wanted help, that's all. She sighed and rolled over on her stomach so she wouldn't have to watch Max and Cleo anymore. It was dumb, but it made her feel worse to watch them being happy. And she found she couldn't stop watching them, even though it made her feel horrible. It was like when you had a cut on your lip that you kept biting at—it hurt, but you couldn't leave it alone.

Now Doug and her money problems were all in a mix in her head. She shouldn't have started thinking about it. Lately, she tried to remember only the really annoying things about him. The way he read only nonfiction books on truly boring subjects. How when he slept he let his limbs fly everywhere, and how she was never really comfortable when she was in bed with him; how she remained still and rigid, right on the edge of sleep, tucked in the corner of the bed.

But then she remembered other things, like how he always unpacked her laundry when it was delivered, and stacked her mail on the desk. Or she remembered the time they were at a bar, drinking beer in the afternoon, watching a baseball game. The bar was pretty empty, just a few people watching the game, and one single guy on a stool at the end of the bar, wearing a knit hat and frowning at his beer and then at the TV. And Doug had leaned over and said, "Hipsters are so joyless," and Claire had been so surprised that she'd spit her beer on the bar.

The thing was that it didn't really matter what she thought about when she remembered Doug. Because the truth was that she would have married him if he hadn't ended it. And that was the scariest thing of all. Because it meant either that she was stupid enough to commit to someone who wasn't really right for her or that she did love him and he left her and broke her heart. And honestly, sometimes she wasn't sure which one it was.

ON THURSDAY, CLEO ASKED CLAIRE if she wanted to go shopping on the boardwalk with her. The shops down there were full of animals made out of seashells and T-shirts that said things like AA IS WHERE I GO TO MEET DRUNK SLUTS, and REHAB IS FOR QUITTERS. But Cleo looked eager and so Claire agreed. Who knew? Maybe Cleo would find a beach cover-up that she liked.

They walked in and out of the little shops, quietly browsing through the ashtrays and postcards. Every once in a while, Cleo would hold up a T-shirt for Claire to read, and they'd both laugh.

Claire turned to examine a shelf of glass pipes, as though she were really looking to buy one. She picked up a red and brown swirled pipe, looked at it closely, and then put it back down. Cleo was watching her, probably wondering if she was a secret pothead, and Claire was just about to make a joke about it, when she heard someone calling her name.

She turned to see a girl in a jeans skirt and bikini top running toward her. "Claire!" the girl called out. "Claire, hi!" It took her a second to realize that it was Heather Foley, a girl she used to babysit for, and before she had a chance to say hello, Heather had thrown her arms around Claire's neck and was squeezing tightly.

"I'm so happy to see you," she said. "I didn't even know you were here."

The Foley family owned the house next to the Coffeys' and had been going to the shore for as long as Claire could remember, before they even had any kids. For a couple of summers, Claire had been a mother's helper for the family. It was a job she liked, holding the children's hands as she walked them toward the ocean, making peanut-butter-and-jelly sandwiches for lunch, putting them down for naps in their stuffy summer rooms, promising that they could go back down to the beach as soon as they woke up.

Once when she was trying to get Bobby Foley ready for bed, begging him to put his pajamas on, he'd declared, "No pajamas. I want to sleep naked like my dad does." As soon as Bobby finished saying this, Claire looked up to see Mr. Foley standing in the doorway. He'd walked away as though he hadn't heard anything, and Claire almost died of embarrassment. To this day, when she saw him at the shore, she always thought, *I know that you sleep naked.* It seemed too much information for her to handle, too personal for her to process.

Heather finally released her grip and Claire stepped back to look at her. "Oh my God, Heather. Look at you!" She sounded like an old person, but she couldn't help it. Heather looked so grown-up. She'd just finished her freshman year at GW, she told Claire. She'd gained a little bit of weight in her hips and breasts and had that happy, pudgy look that freshman girls get. She was deeply tan, almost unnaturally so, like she'd been working on it all summer long.

"This is Cleo," Claire said. "Max's girlfriend."

"Hi," Heather said. Claire could tell she was trying not to stare.

"So what are you up to this summer?" Claire asked.

"I'm waitressing at the fishery. It's so fun. There's tons of kids working there that I know from high school and stuff."

"That's great," Claire said. She was about to ask how her first year of college was, just to make sure that she sounded completely like an old lady. But she noticed that Heather was looking at something, her face getting red. Claire turned around to see a college-age guy in a bathing suit, taking huge bites out of a cheeseburger, as though it were just a little snack.

"Oh my God," Heather said.

"Who's that?" Claire asked.

"Bradley." Heather was barely whispering and Claire had to lean in to hear her. "He works at the restaurant with me. We're sort of—I don't know."

"Ohhh," Claire said. She smiled. She remembered summers at the shore, running around with her friends and chasing boys. Every day exciting, not knowing who you were going to see or what was going to happen. Claire hadn't felt like that in a long time. She hadn't even wanted to feel like that, which was maybe more disturbing. The thought of dating again, of getting back into that whole mess, was so tiring. But watching Heather skitter around, trying to pretend like she wasn't watching Bradley, almost reminded Claire of why it was so fun. Almost.

When Heather was about three, she always wanted to brush Claire's hair, which really always ended up getting it in knots. But one time, she'd sat there patiently, letting Heather run the brush back and forth so that her hair covered her face. All of a sudden, Heather had started laughing, really laughing, like she'd seen something so funny she couldn't believe it.

"What?" Claire had asked her. She peeked out from behind her hair and saw Heather lying on her side, still laughing.

"You look like a donkey," Heather said, and she rolled back and forth on the floor.

That was how Claire always remembered her. And now, here she was all giddy and excited about a guy, a Bradley. How had that happened?

ON FRIDAY NIGHT, THEY HAD a Mexican feast. That's what Weezy kept calling it, when it was really just fajitas and refried beans. She moved around the kitchen with a great sense of purpose, repeating the phrase "Mexican feast," while Maureen sat at the counter and chopped jalapeños and Martha used the blender to make margaritas from a thick syrup, ice, and tequila.

Max and Claire set the table, and each time that Weezy said, "Mexican feast," Max held up another finger to count. They were up to eight.

"Martha, did you tell Maureen about your job?" Weezy asked. Martha shook her head.

"What's going on?" Maureen asked.

"It's nothing, really. I've just been thinking about maybe leaving J.Crew. Maybe going back to nursing."

"That's great."

"Well, it's just an idea. I actually have to look into getting recertified and all of that. I'm not exactly sure what I need to do." Martha looked overwhelmed just getting the words out.

"You'll do it. We'll figure it out. We can look it up online after dinner. I'm sure it will be no trouble." Weezy's peppy comments came out all in a row, and Max and Claire smiled at each other.

"You know . . . ," Maureen started. She held the knife in her hand and looked off in the distance, like she was trying to remember something. "I have a friend that runs a high-end caretaker business. Well, more of a friend of a friend, really. She places really smart, bright people in the homes of the elderly—the really rich elderly."

"Really?" Martha asked.

"Yeah, and I was just thinking. That might be a nice way to ease your way back into it, you know? You could look into getting recertified, sort of reacquaint yourself with some parts of the job. And it pays pretty well."

"That sounds interesting," Weezy said. She looked so hopeful that Claire wanted to smack her. Weezy couldn't hide how badly she wanted things to go well for Martha, all the time. "Don't you think that sounds interesting?"

"Maybe," Martha said. "Of course, the work I did as a nurse is totally different than a caretaker."

"Oh, of course. We know that. But just like Maureen said, it would be a good way to ease your way back in." Weezy was holding her hands together and staring at Martha.

"Okay, well, I'll think about it."

"I'll get you in touch with the woman when we get back," Maureen said. Martha nodded.

Weezy practically danced the fajitas to the table. She made a big deal of sipping her margarita and proclaiming it delicious. They all sat down and began assembling their fajitas. Max took three right away and piled on every top-ping there was, while Weezy repeated the conversation about Martha's possible new job to Will, who had been upstairs while it happened.

"It's very exciting," Weezy said. "It just sounds great."

They'd be talking about this all week. Whenever Martha did anything—got a raise, had a fight with a coworker, folded a shirt at her job—they all talked about it like it was the most interesting thing in the world, like she had done something so fantastic they couldn't believe it.

"Max, when do classes start?" Claire asked. She wanted to change the subject.

Max looked up from the huge fajita he was about to put in his mouth. "Um, next week. I have only four classes, though, so I don't have anything until Wednesday."

"How can you have only four classes?" Martha asked.

"Got 'em all done," Max said. He smiled and shoved the fajita in his mouth.

"I had full semesters all through college," Martha said. She was looking at Cleo, who was the only one polite enough to listen. "Nursing is tough, I'll tell you that much."

Max put his hand on Cleo's thigh, which was bare, since she was of course still in her bikini. Claire wondered if her dad still felt uncomfortable eating with a half-naked stranger, or if he was getting used to it.

"What's your major, Cleo?" Martha asked.

"Economics and French," she said.

"That's an interesting combination," Weezy said. "I wouldn't have thought those two go together."

"They don't, really." Cleo laughed a little. "I wanted to study French, but my mother told me it was a waste of time and that I had to pick something in the business school. But

I figured out I could do both if I took some summer classes and a couple extra here and there. I just love my French classes."

"That's great," Weezy said.

"See?" Max said. "Cleo balances me out with her classes."

"That's just how Martha was with her nursing classes," Weezy said. "She always had a mind for medicine, always got A's in her science classes."

"So did I," Claire said. "I always got A's in science too."

Weezy turned to look at her and gave her a small nod and a little smile. Claire knew she shouldn't let it bother her, the way her parents talked about Martha's success in school, but it did. It was like they thought if they focused enough on how smart Martha was, no one—maybe not even Martha herself—would notice that she didn't have any social skills; like if they talked about it enough, they could make up for everything else. It was just that in the process, they made it sound like Claire and Max were dumber than dirt.

"Martha, do you like the fajitas?" Weezy asked. Max and Claire laughed. "What?" she asked.

"Of course she likes the fajitas," Claire said. "It's her favorite meal. Isn't that why we had them in the first place?"

"Everyone likes fajitas," Weezy said. "You all like them." She sounded defensive.

"I wish Cathy and Ruth and Drew were here," Martha said. She looked at Maureen and smiled.

"Me too," Maureen said.

"We all do," Weezy said. "Hopefully they'll be able to make it next year."

Claire wasn't all that upset about Cathy's not being there. They got along fine now that they were adults, but when they were kids, Cathy used to love teasing Claire, finding any reason to leave her out of a game or trick her into eating sand.

One summer Cathy had repeatedly called Claire a virgin, and Claire—assuming it had something to do with being Jesus's mother and sure that it didn't apply to her—had yelled back, "I am not! I am not a virgin!" They were all on the crowded beach, and Claire had yelled this over and over, until finally Weezy came over and told her to stop, then leaned down to explain in a quiet voice what that word meant. Claire only partly understood what Weezy was saying to her, but she knew enough to be mortified. She thought she was going to die right there on the beach.

That's still how she remembered Cathy, even now, all grown up. Claire thought of her as that girl who loved to make her cry, who took so much pleasure in bossing other people around.

"We should go to Atlantic City tonight," Max said. He looked at Claire. "Come on, let's do it. I'm finally legal to gamble." Cleo perked up and looked at Claire for her answer. She was probably dying to get out of the house. If family time was hard when it was your own family, it had to be twice as hard when you were the girlfriend.

Claire was tired from the sun, the talk of Martha, and the whole week. She'd been planning to go sit on the porch after dinner and read. She was trying to think of a way to let them down gently, when Martha said, "I'm in, let's go!"

Max let out a whoop and Weezy laughed. "Blackjack," he said. "We can play blackjack. I've gotten really good."

"You're gonna go?" Claire asked Martha.

"Yeah, I'll even drive. I barely touched my margarita."

Claire was trapped. She couldn't say no now that even Martha was going. "Let's do it," she said. She figured it couldn't hurt. Who knew? Maybe she'd win big, hit the jackpot, and be able to pay her rent next month and put off telling her parents and moving home for another month or so.

Cleo was laughing and clapped her hands like she was a child. "Just give me a minute to change," she said, and ran out of the room. Well, at least she wouldn't be wearing her bikini to the casino. That was a plus.

Weezy was telling them all to go. "Have fun," she said over and over. She was so happy to have all of her kids heading out together, especially happy to have Martha be a part of it, and so she took the plates out of Claire's hands as she tried to clear the table, and said, "Leave this for me. Just go have fun."

THE CASINO WAS FULL OF crazy people. Crazy, dirty people. Claire noticed that an abnormally high percentage of people were missing a limb. They'd gone to the Taj Mahal casino partly because it was one they'd heard of and partly because in the car Cleo had said she'd heard it was beautiful there.

"Beautiful?" Claire had asked. "I'm not sure any casino can be called beautiful, but sure, we can go to that one."

"I've never really gambled before," Cleo said to Claire and Martha. "Have you guys?"

"Not a lot," Claire said. "We came last year, and Max gambled, even though he wasn't legal." Claire laughed and kicked the back of the seat.

"Hey, that wasn't my idea," Max said.

"You made Max break the law?" Cleo said. She was smiling as she looked at Claire.

"No," Claire said. "It was my—it was Doug. He was here last year, and he wanted Max to do it."

"He's like the worst gambler ever, too," Max said quickly.

"He talked about statistics the whole time and made it so boring."

"Gambling makes me nervous," Cleo said. "The possibility that you can gain or lose so much in a second is scary." No one answered her, and they drove the rest of the way in silence.

Once they walked into the casino, Martha headed straight to the slots and began feeding twenty-dollar bills into a machine called Wild Cherry. "I'm not going to waste my money gambling on blackjack," she said.

"Right," Max said. "Because slots are really the smart way to go."

Martha pursed her lips at him and kept playing. They left her at the slot machines and went to the bar to get a drink because Cleo had wrinkled her nose at the free drinks they were passing out. Then they walked around looking at the different minimums for the tables and trying to find one they liked. When they passed Martha again, about forty-five minutes later, her eyes were glazed, and her lips were parted, with a little string of spit between them, as she pushed the button to make the slots go, and listened for the *bing, ring,* and *ding* of the cherries and sevens and big-money signs.

"I think we've created a monster," Claire said.

"Martha," Max said. She didn't look up right away. "Martha," they all called together, and she looked up, spacey and surprised.

"Have you won?" Cleo asked.

Martha shook her head. "Not yet, but I have a good feeling about this machine."

"Are you sure you don't want to come with us?" Claire asked.

Martha shook her head.

"No, no. I'm good here," she said, turning back to the machine.

"Okay, well, if you need us, we'll be over there, okay?" Claire pointed in the direction of the tables. Martha nodded distractedly.

"Good God," Max said. "We're gonna have to call Mom and Dad to drag her out of here."

"The scary thing is, she kind of fits in," Claire whispered to Max. It was true. Martha was wearing a large tented flowered dress, and her hair was pulled back in a messy ponytail. She looked older than thirty, and she clutched her purse on her lap while she touched the machine like she was communicating with it. On either side of her were older women, just as sloppily dressed, petting their own machines. Claire got the chills watching her.

"Well, at least if she started coming here, it would be something social she could do," Max offered.

"Max, that's mean," Cleo said. She looked shocked and Max muttered an apology.

"Come on," he said, putting his arm around her. "Let's go gamble."

At the blackjack table, there were only two seats open, so Claire and Max sat down in the middle and Cleo stood behind them. "I just want to watch first," Cleo said.

The man to Max's left looked a little off and anytime someone else at the table got a good card, he pounded both hands in front of him and said, "Sonofabitch," all as one word. Max leaned over and squeezed Claire's shoulder and the two of them bent their heads down, trying not to laugh.

Claire watched Cleo place her hand on Max's back, just lightly, like she wasn't even thinking about it. It was almost like they were the same person, and Claire felt a sharp pain.

She was jealous of her younger brother and his girlfriend. Max had a life, a love life, and she didn't. Even Heather Foley had a love life. It was like somewhere along the way, Claire had stopped being a real person.

When Cleo finally sat down, she got blackjack on her first hand. She squealed and clapped her hands again. She was very careful to place her winnings to one side, and when she was up about forty dollars, she decided to stop. "I should quit while I'm ahead, right?" she said.

"That's very mature of you," Claire said. She had lost eighty dollars and was trying to stop herself from going back.

"You can't win if you don't keep playing, though," Max said. Cleo just smiled and shook her head.

They went to retrieve Martha from the slot machines, and she printed out her slot ticket and went to get the rest of her money. "I lost forty dollars," she said on the way home. "But I know if I could've kept playing, I would have won big."

That night, as Claire tried to fall asleep, she heard the sounds of the casino in her head—cards being flipped, people cheering or groaning, and the *bing* of the slots as they rolled around and around.

SATURDAY AT THE SHORE WAS cloudy and cool, but Claire and Martha went down to the beach anyway, bundled up in sweatshirts and pants. They were leaving the next day, so they figured they would try to get as much out of the end of their trip as they could. They sat on beach chairs and watched the wind chop up the water. A storm was coming in, and the dark clouds were getting closer.

Both of the girls held books in their laps, but neither of them made a move to open them. Martha took in a deep breath and let out an audible sigh, which Claire knew was a sign that she wanted to say something.

"What?" Claire asked her.

Martha shook her head and sighed again. "It's just watching the ocean like this, right before a storm, it makes me think of the tsunami in Thailand, and how all of those people were just minding their own business, living their lives, and the ocean just swallowed them."

"That's what you're thinking about right now?" Claire asked. She shouldn't have been surprised, but she still was. Claire had been thinking about how she still had to tell Weezy everything, and how maybe it was a good idea to go back to New York first and do it over the phone, because then she could just hang up right after and be done with it. Yes, that made more sense. And so she was wondering what she was thinking before, planning to tell Weezy in person, and Martha was thinking about a natural disaster that had happened six years earlier. She wasn't sure whether she should be annoyed at Martha or ashamed of herself for thinking only about her problems.

"I think our brains work differently," Claire finally said.

"Yeah," Martha said. "I think they do."

The two of them sat there for another hour, books on their laps, watching the storm crawl closer and closer, witnessing the waves getting bigger and angrier, until they felt drops hit their faces and heads, and were forced to pick up their chairs and walk back to the house in the rain.

WHEN CLAIRE OPENED THE DOOR to her apartment, she was hit with a wall of hot air. This was always how it was when she got back from a trip; the air seemed unbreathable, like no one would ever be able to survive living here. She saw the rent envelope slipped under her door and her stomach twisted. She moved it aside with her foot, dragged her suitcase inside, and went to sit on the couch.

All the years that she'd lived in New York, Claire always felt giddy when she returned after a trip. It was nice to get away, to get out of the crowded city, but she always had the sense that when she got back, she was where she belonged. But now, looking around at the dusty old apartment that she couldn't afford, she didn't feel that. She just felt dread. She didn't belong here anymore, in this apartment. And it didn't even matter if she did, because she was going to be kicked out soon anyway.

And so, she took out her cell phone and called Weezy, who was still at the shore. There was no time like the present, especially if you were totally out of options.

PART Two

When you live in a house your whole life, you know all of its noises. You know that two short buzzes is the end of the dryer cycle, that one short buzz is the back doorbell. You know that when the furnace kicks up, it starts with a clank, waits about thirty seconds, and then you hear the air coming out of the vents. You know every corner and twist in the house, that it takes sixteen steps to get up the stairs, three large leaps to get down the hall. You could find your way around the whole place blindfolded if you had to.

Claire loved this about going home—loved that she knew every corner, that everything was familiar, that the house would creak and groan her to sleep. But this time, the noises were not comforting. Each squeak of the floor made her want to cover her ears. She could hear her father breathing heavily as he walked down the hallway (was he that out of shape?), could hear her mom humming as she made coffee, could hear Martha in her room, thumping her feet against the headboard as she always did when she read, so that it bumped against the wall, over and over, until Claire was sure she was going to scream.

This reaction shouldn't have surprised her, but somehow it still did. Moving home wasn't exactly what she wanted; it was just the only possible way out of her mess. When she'd finally gotten the courage to call Weezy, she didn't waste any time. As soon as Weezy answered, she said, "I'm having money issues."

She had sounded like a polite older woman who didn't want to give the specifics of her financials, who thought that talking about money was rude. But at least it was out there. It had taken almost an hour for Claire to fully explain the situation, to really make it clear that she was in trouble. And still, when she'd said, "I think I have to move home for a while," Weezy was surprised.

Once things got moving, they happened quickly. Claire gave her landlord notice and said she'd be using her security deposit as her last month's rent. It was unclear if this was legal or not—everyone had a different opinion—but it didn't matter. If they were going to come after her, let them. She just needed to get out of this city. She figured she wasn't even staying the whole month of September, so maybe they'd look the other way.

At work, they weren't all that surprised. Amy had nodded like she'd seen it coming. "Sometimes you just need a change of scenery," she'd said. Claire had agreed and quickly left the office. Becca and Molly were surprised, but not sorry. They wished her luck and said they'd miss her, but didn't sound very convincing.

On her last day, they all stood around and ate cupcakes, as was the tradition, and they all said things like, "Enjoy those cheese steaks" and "Bet you won't miss the crowded subways in the morning!" At the end of the day, Claire wasn't the least bit sorry to leave the office and never go back.

Her apartment was packed up easily, partly because it was still almost empty from when Doug left, and partly because she sold what little was left of the furniture on craigslist. She didn't want to pay for storage and didn't want a bed—or anything else—that she and Doug had shared. She was happy to open her door to strangers, let them come in and give her cash, and watch them leave carrying her possessions.

Martha had warned her to have someone else in the apartment with her and to leave the door open while the buyers entered. "You should also alert your doorman to the situation. Make sure he knows why they're coming to see you."

"Why?" Claire asked.

"Claire. Come on. People looking to murder innocent people use craigslist all the time."

"Right," Claire said. "I'll be careful."

There was no good-bye party, no send-off with her friends like they'd done for everyone else. "I'm not really leaving," she kept telling everyone. "I'm just figuring stuff out." Her friends nodded like they didn't quite believe her and hugged her like she was never coming back.

It shocked her, really, how quickly it had all been done, how fast she'd ended up back home and sleeping in her bed. For the first few days, she felt relief. Her debt was still with her, but at least she could stop worrying that she was about to get evicted. The worst was over, and she started to make a plan, set up an interview with a temp agency, and unpacked her bags. Then on the fourth day, she'd woken up and listened to all the noise around her. And that was when the panic had started to set in.

Her bedroom still had faded stuffed animals on the shelves, collages of old high school friends that she hadn't seen in years, plastic glow-in-the-dark stars on the ceiling (why had she thought that was so cool?), and a poster of Dave Matthews on the back of the door. It was like moving right back to high school. Nothing had changed.

There was a point each morning (and this had been happening since the breakup) when Claire first woke up and didn't remember what had happened. It was about a thirty-second window, give or take, when her mind was free of everything, when she didn't think about the wedding's being called off, about Doug's moving out, about her mounting credit card debt, about moving home. It wasn't that she forgot exactly—it was just that her mind didn't remember right away, and for those seconds she felt normal. And then it all came rushing back in, her head filled up with the events of the past year, and she was embarrassed and horrified all over again, like it had all just occurred. She'd lie there as it happened, roll over so that her face was in her pillow, and start thinking about how she was going to undo everything, how she was going to go about fixing the mess that was her life.

At night, she would look at the stupid plastic stars and think, *What the hell was I thinking?* She let the thought run through her head over and over. She let herself repeat it, stressing different words each time—What *the hell was I thinking? What the* hell *was I thinking? What the hell was I* thinking?

Even the dog seemed confused by the situation. Ruby walked around at night, poking her head into each room to make sure all of the family members were there. She'd go to look in Max's room, staring at the bed as if she just wanted to make sure that he *wasn't* there. When she came to Claire's door, she'd perk up, her ears springing alive, and she'd wag her tail and come to greet her. But Ruby seemed overwhelmed by this change, and she'd sometimes tilt her head at Claire before leaving the room, sighing as she walked away to continue her inspection.

Claire's first night home, Weezy made a special dinner and they all toasted, "Welcome back," like Claire's return was something to be celebrated, like it wasn't a total failing of her attempt to live as a successful adult.

. . .

AT THE TEMP OFFICE, CLAIRE TOOK a typing test and a computer proficiency test. The woman kept looking up at Claire and then back down at the résumé like it was going to answer the question of why Claire was here in the first place.

"Now, why did you leave your last job again?" she asked.

"I'm looking for a change and I thought it would be easier to figure out what I wanted to do if I took some time off and moved back home for a little while." Claire had said this exact sentence to her about four times now. She was pretty sure the woman thought she was lying.

"Well, we shouldn't have any trouble placing you. There's a spot I'm thinking about that's just a three-month placement."

"That would be great. I'm not looking for a permanent job."

"Right." The woman nodded. She looked again like she didn't believe Claire. "Well, I think it would be a great fit. It starts in a week or two, and I can get you in there to meet them tomorrow if that works?"

Claire nodded. They set up the appointment and shook hands. Then Claire went back home, took off her skirt and jacket, put on pajama pants, and got back into bed.

WEEZY WAS TRYING TO BE HELPFUL, but it was getting on Claire's nerves. Which of course made her feel awful, since Weezy had been so nice about everything, had accepted Claire back home like it was no big deal. But still, every time Weezy asked about her plans or asked her how she was feeling, Claire thought she was going to lose it.

The morning that Claire was scheduled to meet with the office, she and Weezy sat at the kitchen table drinking coffee together in their pajamas.

"Are you nervous?" Weezy asked.

"No."

"Not even a little?"

"No. It's not a real job. It's just a temp job."

"Still," Weezy said. "It can be scary to interview."

"I guess."

"You know," Weezy said, "there are so many kids your age that have moved back home. Remember Mark Crowley? You went to first grade with him, but then he transferred to the public schools because he had all those learning problems? Well, anyway, I saw his mother in the grocery store last week and she told me that he'd lost his job in New York and moved home. Just like you."

"I didn't lose my job," Claire said.

"Well, you don't have one. You know what I mean," Weezy said. Claire was sitting in her pajamas at ten thirty on a Tuesday morning, drinking coffee with her mom. Yes, it was pretty clear that she didn't have a job.

"I'm just saying," Weezy continued, "that it's an epidemic, a trend. It's the economy, of course, but still it's interesting, isn't it? All these adult children returning home again? Moving back in with their parents? It says something about this generation, I think. And our generation for welcoming you back." Weezy looked off into the distance, thoughtful with this new revelation.

"You sound like Dad," Claire said.

Weezy leaned forward in her chair and looked out the window at the house across the street. "For a while, I thought the younger Connors girl was living at home, but now I think she just stays there sometimes. I think she brings things to her parents, their groceries and all of that."

"Hilary?" Claire asked. "Hilary still lives around here?"

Hilary and Sarah Connors had grown up across the street.

They'd never been friends, but they knew each other and played with each other sometimes out of convenience. When Sarah went to college, she started dating this boy and eventually dropped out. There were rumors that he was a drug dealer, but no one really knew what was happening. Then Sarah and her boyfriend went on a crime spree through a neighboring suburb, shooting a gas station clerk and robbing seven different people, before the two of them holed up in an old hardware store that had closed down. The police surrounded them, until they heard a gunshot and then they stormed in to find that Sarah had shot her boyfriend in the head. It made national news, and reporters and police cars were outside of the Connors' house for months.

"I can't believe they still live there," Claire said. She looked out at the house, a normal two-story brick house with yellow awnings. It looked dark and quiet.

"It's their home," Weezy said. "They shouldn't feel like they have to run away."

"I would. I would leave the town, leave the whole state, probably go all the way across the country. I'd go somewhere where people didn't recognize my name and my face. Wouldn't you?"

"Maybe."

"It has to be so miserable there. To stay in that house with all of those memories."

"Maybe they remember the good things that happened there."

"Would that really be what you remember?"

"Some people don't have the tools to start over when something like that happens," Weezy said. "Some people could, but other people—they just stop, and stay where they are and that's that."

"Sarah was always weird," Claire said. It was the first thing that she and Martha had agreed on after the strange and tragic day happened. "She was always a little off," Martha had said. Sarah had been a year ahead of Martha in school, and Hilary was a year younger than Claire. There was one picture of the four girls playing in the backyard one summer, all in bathing suits, laughing and running through the sprinkler. Claire couldn't remember it.

"It was the drugs," Weezy said. "She got mixed up with the wrong people." They'd had this exact conversation dozens of times since the whole thing had happened, but somehow it never got old.

"I guess," Claire said. "Poor Hilary." She imagined the girl grocery shopping, lugging bags over to the house that her parents didn't leave. How creepy.

Sarah had once stolen a toy of Claire's, a little plastic Care Bear that had been a Valentine's Day present. Claire had asked Weezy if she could take it to school to show her friends, and Weezy said no, so Claire snuck it in her backpack in the morning. That night, when she realized that she'd forgotten it in her desk, she started to cry.

The next morning, Weezy walked into the classroom with her, assuring her that it would still be there, but it wasn't. That day, on the playground, Sarah Connors had a little blue bear in her hand.

"That's mine," Claire yelled. She told the teachers, but no one could prove that Sarah had walked through the classroom and stolen the bear. She told Weezy that night, but there was nothing to be done.

"I told you not to take it to school," Weezy said, as Claire cried. She was firm on this point, although when Claire woke up that Saturday, there was a new little blue bear on her nightstand.

But it wasn't the same. Claire wanted the original bear, the one that had been taken. She hated the thought of it's being at the Connors' house, which was dirty and smelled like moth-balls. "Your sister stole my bear," she said to Hilary once. Hilary just shrugged and looked embarrassed. You couldn't blame her, Claire knew. She couldn't pick who her sister was.

CLAIRE PUT ON THE SAME OUTFIT that she'd worn to the temp interview and drove to the office of Proof Perfect, where she was set to meet the woman she'd be filling in for and a few others.

Amanda Liebman met her at the elevator, looking like she was about to give birth right there in the front lobby. She had both of her hands on her back, and was red in the face. "Claire?" she asked. Claire nodded and Amanda puffed a little as she turned and motioned for Claire to follow.

Amanda sat at a desk at the front of the office. Behind her, on the wall, hung letters that spelled out PROOF PER-FECT. There was a hallway to the right and left, but all the offices that Claire saw had their doors closed. Once they were seated at her desk, Amanda seemed a little calmer. "I'm car-rying around so much extra weight at this point that even standing feels impossible."

Claire nodded again. "When are you due?"

"In two weeks, but I want to keep working up until the very end so that I can take all of my time with the baby. I've already saved up all my vacation and personal and sick days, which wasn't easy, so I don't want to waste it now just lying around and waiting."

"Right."

"So, my title is Office Manager and Senior Executive Assistant. Basically, that means that I answer the phones, and then do whatever the account managers want me to do, or don't want to do for themselves. It's a lot of Xeroxing and other random stuff. All the higher-up people have their own assistants, so you don't have to worry about them."

"Okay."

"Some of the managers are a pain in the ass, but it's not rocket science, so you'll be fine."

Amanda went on to show her the phones.

"So, will they let me know if I get the job?"

"Oh, you got it."

"Really?"

"Yeah. Everyone else that comes in here wants a permanent job. They're hoping to get placed here after this job is done. You're the only one that wants it for what it is. So, congratulations, it's yours."

"Great," Claire said. She wasn't sure that it was.

Amanda started to get up to walk her to the elevator, but Claire told her she could get there on her own. She was just walking out into the lobby when Amanda called her name.

"One more thing," she said. She stuck out her foot from behind the desk. "The dress code says no sandals, but my feet are too fat to wear any of my shoes right now, so fuck it. But if you come in wearing sandals, they'll go ape shit."

"Got it. Thanks."

CLAIRE WENT OVER TO LAINIE'S that night to drink wine. It was still pretty warm out, even at the end of September, and the two of them sat on chairs on the porch, a bottle of wine between them. Brian was inside on the couch, asleep with his mouth open and the TV on.

She couldn't get over the fact that Lainie lived with her husband and three children in a house that was down the street from where Claire grew up. How had this happened? Lainie became more adult every day, and Claire was back sleeping in her childhood bedroom.

"So you got a job already," Lainie said. "That's good news." She held up her glass and Claire clinked it, then the two of them drank.

"I guess so. The thing is I don't start until this lady has her baby. It could be tomorrow or it could be in three weeks, which sort of sucks."

"Then just relax. You've been not working for like a week. You should sleep in and enjoy yourself."

"I can't. At least not in that house. I just feel like I should be doing something, not sitting around all day with my parents and Martha. It's driving me crazy."

"Really? It sounds amazing. You can do whatever you want." Lainie had grown up in the middle of five sisters, who shared everything from underwear to makeup. She'd never had her own room, and Claire was pretty sure she'd never want to.

"It's not. It's just really boring. All I want is to not stay there all day."

Lainie looked sideways at her. "Do you want to babysit?"

"For you?"

"Yeah, for me. Our nanny's mom is sick and she's going home for a couple of weeks. I was going to ask Kristen to do it, and then get my mom and Brian's mom to fill in, but if you're really looking for something to do, that would be awesome. It's just for the mornings, mostly, and some early afternoons."

"Sure," Claire said. "Why not?" She hadn't babysat in years.

"Great," Lainie said. She smiled and sat back like she'd figured everything out. "Plus I'll give you free classes at the studio."

"You already do that."

"Yeah, but now you'll really earn it."

CLAIRE HAD FORGOTTEN HOW BORING babysitting actually was. She'd blocked out the way that when a four-year-old is building a tower out of blocks, sometimes all you can do is keep looking at the clock, sure it's standing still or maybe even going backward. Babysitting could be so quiet, so devoid of conversation, and just when she thought she'd go crazy, it became loud, a fever pitch of whines and screams and toys hitting the floor.

Claire remembered babysitting for Bobby Foley once, the summer he was obsessed with Pokemon, and they'd been sitting on the floor in his bedroom playing. He started showing her all the Pokemon cards that he had, explaining to her the difference between the characters, how some could fly and some could run fast, and she'd been nodding and then just lay down on the floor while he went on, seriously, ranking his favorites, telling her what who would win in a fight.

She'd murmured, "Mmm-hmm" every once in a while, closed her eyes for just a second, and then woke up twenty minutes later when the door downstairs slammed shut. Bobby was still next to her, babbling on, and she didn't even think he noticed that she'd been sleeping. Claire had shot straight up and wiped the drool off her face, her heart pounding as she tried to look awake before Mrs. Foley came in the room.

She'd been horrified after that, felt like the world's most irresponsible babysitter. And now she was babysitting again, spending her days with three little boys, who seemed just as bored with her as she was with them, glancing at her every once in a while to see if she was still there. Tucker screamed every time Lainie left, and then spent the rest of the time wandering his pudgy baby body around the house, picking up anything that wasn't nailed down—shoes, the remote control, cell phones, coasters—and rearranging all of it. Every once in a while he'd stop to stare at Claire, trying to figure out if she was responsible for the absence of his mother.

Jack didn't seem to be taking to the situation any better. He was a judgmental child and always had been. When he was a baby, he'd look around the room at everyone, his mouth turned down, his dark eyes taking everything in. Lainie had taken Jack everywhere with her, to bars or friends' houses, where they would put him to sleep in a bed, with jackets stuffed on either side of him so he wouldn't roll off. He'd stare at them while they drank wine, his little baby lips pursing and un-pursing as he listened to them talk. Now, when Claire arrived, he gave her the same look, as though he couldn't quite figure out what she was doing at his house. She wanted to tell him that she didn't know what she was doing there either.

Each morning when Claire arrived, the boys were half-naked—sometimes in just a diaper, sometimes wearing a shirt, or one sock, or a pair of pants. Lainie was always rushing around no matter what time it was, pausing to put an item of clothing on one of the boys, or stopping to smell their butts to see if they needed a new diaper. Claire would stand in the corner and watch as Lainie raced around and finally ran out the door. It made her tired just to watch.

The third morning she was there, Claire poured Jack some cereal and leaned against the counter to watch him eat. Jack took a bite and then looked up at her. "This milk tastes spicy," he said.

"It tastes spicy?" Claire asked and Jack nodded. Claire picked up the carton and sniffed it, and a thick, sour smell hit her nose right away. She gagged twice and ran over to the sink, sure she was going to throw up.

"What's wrong?" Jack asked.

"Nothing," Claire said. "Don't eat that, okay? The milk is bad." She took the bowl from him and poured it down the sink, holding her breath as she washed the little O-shaped pieces of cereal down the disposal. She went to the refrigerator and looked at the options. "Do you want some toast?"

"Are you having a baby?" Jack asked.

"What? No."

Jack shrugged. "That's what my mom does when she's having a baby," he said.

"Right," Claire said. "It was just that the milk made me feel sick."

"Milk is good for you," Jack said.

"You're right, it is."

"Do you have any babies?"

"Nope. No babies."

"Who is your mom?"

"My mom is Weezy. You know her, she lives down the street. And you know my dad, Will, and my sister, Martha. And you've even met my brother, Max."

"Weezy is your mom?" Jack asked. He looked like he didn't believe her for a second.

"Yep."

"Do you live with her?"

"I do now. I was living somewhere else, but I moved back."

"I'm never leaving my mom," Jack said.

"Okay," Claire said.

"I don't think Weezy is your mom," Jack said. "Because we see her when we go to the playground sometimes."

"Okay," Claire said. "Whatever you say."

"What?"

"Nothing."

Claire was exhausted by these conversations. Exhausted from sitting around and watching Jack and Tucker play. The one thing she did like about babysitting was holding Matthew. He was at a great age—small enough that he was nothing but a bundle of baby, but big enough that she wasn't afraid she was going to break him.

She liked holding him while the other two boys napped, feeling his solid little weight in her arms. He was totally relaxed, his mouth slightly open, and every once in a while his chin would quiver, and he'd sigh. Claire was jealous of him while he slept, and hoped that if she held that warm little body, some of his calmness would rub off on her.

SOMETIMES AFTER LAINIE WOULD GET HOME, Claire would just end up staying at the house for a little while. It was so much easier to be there than to be at her own house. She'd watch as Lainie and Brian came back from work and still never stopped moving, making the boys dinner and getting them ready for bed. Claire at least liked the feeling of being able to sit and watch, knowing she wasn't responsible for any of it.

It also amazed her how easily Lainie had become a mother. When she was first pregnant with Jack, Claire couldn't believe it. But then Lainie had the baby, and she walked around with Jack popped out on her hip, like he'd always been there. Then she had the next two, and she was a mother of three. There was no adjustment period, she just did it. How had it been so easy for her? Claire had barely gotten to the first step of creating that life and it had all fallen apart.

"We're going to have a party," Lainie said one night. She was walking around the room, gathering all of the toys and shoes and socks that had been thrown around during the day. She picked it all up in her arms and then dumped it in the bin in the corner of the room.

Lainie loved having parties and used any excuse to do so. Claire suspected that she loved having everyone come to her, but no one minded because Lainie always threw a good party.

"Yeah, doesn't that seem like a good idea?" Brian asked Claire. "Lainie just put a banana peel into the toy box and she wants to have a hundred people over here this weekend."

"I didn't put a—oh, wait. Yes, I did," Lainie said as she pulled a banana peel out from the toys. "Why didn't you tell me? Anyway, it's not going to be a hundred people." She turned to roll her eyes and shake her head at Brian. "Just a party for fall, one last time to barbecue before it's too cold. Plus, Claire's back, so we should celebrate that. We have to have a party."

"Sounds like fun," Claire said. It was her last day babysitting for the boys. The nanny had returned earlier in the week and was coming back to work. ("Thank God," Brian had said. "I had this feeling she was never coming back to the country.") Claire would be starting work soon anyway.

Amanda had called to tell her that if she didn't go into labor this week, they'd be inducing her on Monday.

"Do you want to come take a class tomorrow?" Lainie asked. She was always trying to get Claire to the studio, trying to convert her to the world of Pilates. But Claire was hesitant—the machines frightened her. Still, she agreed since she had nothing else to do.

AT THE PILATES STUDIO, LAINIE WAS treated like a celebrity. She introduced all the women to Claire as though they were her close friends. "This is Barbara and this is Joanie. I'm so glad you are getting a chance to meet!" She acted like these middle-aged women with fallen stomachs and wiggly arms were the same age she was, just a bunch of gal pals getting ready to work out together.

Lainie had started taking Pilates right after Jack was born, and the teacher was so impressed with her that she suggested she do the teacher training. "But you've been going to the classes for like two months," Claire remembered saying to her.

"I know, it's crazy," was Lainie's response.

And it was crazy, how Lainie stumbled onto this career. She'd never done well in school, which Claire thought was mostly because she never wanted to sit down long enough to study or do homework. She rushed through everything, scribbling down answers to tests, knowing that they were probably wrong. It was like she was just trying to get on to the next thing. She was never bothered by her grades; she'd just look at her B's and C's and nod, like *Yep, that's about what I expected.*

But at the studio, Lainie excelled. She quickly became one of the most popular teachers there. Her classes were always full, and they kept adding more to her schedule. One day, a student of hers approached her and asked if she'd ever thought about starting her own studio. "I'd back you," the woman said. "I'll be an investor. I know you'd be wildly successful."

And she had been. Lainie always called that woman her Fairy Godmother, which seemed perfect to Claire, because at least then Lainie was acknowledging that she was living in a fairy tale. Two years later, a large portion of the studio's mortgage had been paid off, Lainie had hired three other teachers, and the place was thriving.

Claire was always amazed when she went to the studio. Amazed at the way these women flocked there, not for Pilates, but for Lainie. They seemed to think that if they remained devoted, they would one day turn into her. There were loads of women in their thirties who had just had children and believed that Lainie could save them, could get them back to the body they used to have. They'd look at her and think, *Well, she's had three children, and look at her. All I need to do is some Pilates!* They were Lainie's disciples, her faithful following. They believed.

Claire wanted to pull these women aside and whisper to them, leaning in close to say, "Look, I know you think you can have a stomach like that if you take these classes, that if you do enough Pilates, your arms will look just like hers. But they won't be. She always looked like that, even before she ever started this, when she never exercised and ate fast food all the time. It's not real."

It was like when you were younger and believed that it was just a matter of time before you would become a gymnastics gold medalist, or a Broadway star. But then you got to a certain age, and you realized that the gymnasts at the

Olympics were all younger than you, and that you couldn't sing either; and just like that your visions of being a balance beam superstar or playing Annie onstage were gone.

Claire's friend Allison, who was extremely flat-chested, once confessed that she'd believed for years that her breasts would grow. "In high school, I just thought I was a late bloomer," she said. "In college, I just figured it would happen later for me. And now, I'm twenty-nine and I think it's time to admit that this is it. I'm never going to have boobs."

People couldn't help but hope for what they wanted to become—even if it meant deluding themselves. And so Claire felt bad as she watched the parade of women that marched into Lainie's Wednesday afternoon mat class, their bodies wrapped in expensive, cute spandex outfits, their hair pulled back in ponytails. Claire set herself up in the back corner, and as the class went on, as they all struggled through the exercises, she felt nothing but pity for these sweating women, who lay on their backs and sent their arms flying around, believing that they would be different soon.

THAT SATURDAY, CLAIRE WALKED OVER to Lainie's to help her get ready for the party. Jack was on the sidewalk, drawing what looked like a monster with chalk, and when he saw her he stood up and said, "My mom's not going to work today."

"I know," Claire said. "I'm here for the party."

"The party didn't start yet."

"I know. I'm here to help. Plus, remember Silvia's back. I'm not even babysitting you anymore."

Jack looked at her, like he was trying to figure out if she was lying, if she was really there to babysit him again and just trying to trick him. Finally he nodded at her and went back to his drawing, and Claire walked into the house.

Lainie had invited a random group of people to the bar-becue. There were some old friends from high school, her older sisters and their husbands and kids, her younger sisters and their boyfriends, some people that Brian worked with, some women that worked at the studio. Claire was enjoying this randomness, and was talking to a woman named Susan about New York, when the front door opened and Fran Angelo walked in wearing a Phillies T-shirt with a hole in the collar, and an old, faded Eagles hat, like he was an ad for Philly sports fans.

Fran was a friend of Brian's in high school, but she hadn't seen him in years. Probably not since she moved to New York. Was it possible that it was that long? She was trying to figure it out, thinking that he actually didn't look all that different—a little older, sure, and maybe worn down, but no, not that different—when he took his hat off, pushed his hair back and then replaced it, and Claire realized that she was staring and looked away.

He had been a handsome teenager—the kind of boy everyone was in love with. His full name was Frances John Callaghan, and it said a lot that he was never, not once, teased for having a girl's name. All through high school, Fran had dip in his mouth and a bored look on his face. He was tall, well over six feet, and had dark brown hair that was just long enough to tuck behind his ears.

Susan was still talking, but Claire had lost track of their conversation, and nodded energetically to make up for it. She was no longer staring right at Fran, but was tracking his movements from the corner of her eye, and watched him walk through the front hall and out the door to the backyard. Claire excused herself from Susan, and went upstairs to use the bathroom. She closed the door behind her and let out a breath that she'd been holding. She shook her head, telling herself that she was being really pathetic acting like this, getting all nervous just seeing a boy she used to like about a million years ago.

Claire and Fran had made out just once, during a party at their friend Brad's house. She never really knew why Fran decided to pursue her that night. Maybe he knew that she had a crush on him, maybe she was the only girl there that hadn't fooled around with him yet, or maybe he just didn't feel like trying very hard. Whatever the reason, as soon as she got to the party that night, he'd called her name and waved her over to the couch where he was sitting, then pulled her down onto his lap. He put his arm around her waist, and used his other hand to hold the can he was spitting his dip into. Claire tried to suck in her stomach, tried to make herself lighter so that she wasn't putting all of her weight on him, which just resulted in her body's being completely stiff.

"Relax, babe," he'd said.

They sat like that for a while, and Claire drank a beer, wishing to be drunk so she wouldn't have to track every movement that she made, be aware of every single breath. They didn't talk much, although she kept bringing up different topics, like where Brad's parents were, and how he'd moved all the breakable things upstairs. Fran seemed bored, she remembered, just watching everyone at the party like he was waiting for something good to happen. That was the main difference between them, really. Claire was always excited to be at a party, and if it turned out to be fun, that was just a bonus. There was always the promise of a great night, always the chance that something good could happen, and so she was often visibly enthusiastic. Fran, on the other hand, looked like he'd done this a million times before, like high school was so boring to him he couldn't even stand it, and like he had very little hope that anything truly exciting would happen.

Finally that night, Fran had squeezed her leg and said, "Come on." They stood up and he led her out of the room and up the stairs, like he knew just where to go. Claire let herself follow behind him, holding his hand, and thinking, *This is really happening right now.*

His mouth tasted like cinnamon gum and tobacco, and she kept rubbing her hands on his face and through his hair. They basically just kissed—well, and she took her shirt off, which she confessed only to Lainie—and when the whole thing was over, Claire wondered if it had really happened.

The events of that night just made her crush grow, and for the rest of high school, she liked him so much that she found it nearly impossible to talk to him or be around him without losing her breath or having her heart beat so loudly that she thought people could see it through her shirt. He also made her sweat, which was the most unfortunate part, although it didn't really matter, because he never seemed interested in her again.

Claire waited all through high school for something more to happen, or at least for someone to mention it to her. She thought maybe Brian would tease her about it, but he didn't, which seemed like a bad sign since she figured that maybe Fran had said something bad about her and Brian didn't want to get involved. Claire would have almost thought she'd made the whole thing up, until the end of senior year, when Brad told her that Fran had made a list of every girl he hooked up with in high school and had given them all grades. "You got a B-minus," he told her. And Claire felt relieved, of all things, so happy that she was above average, that she hadn't failed or done anything ridiculous that would have earned her a bad grade.

Claire washed her hands in the bathroom and talked to herself in her head. It was ridiculous, all of it. First of all, where did he get off grading girls? And second, how disgusting was it that she was happy about the grade? She dried her hands on the towel and walked back downstairs and into the kitchen, where Lainie was peeking in the oven.

"Fran Angelo is here," Claire said. She said it quietly and looked around to make sure no one could hear her.

"Oh, good," Lainie said. She leaned down and pulled out a tray of mini hot dogs wrapped in dough. "Brian thought it was dumb to make pigs in a blanket, since we have hot dogs for the grill too, but I told him he was crazy."

"You never told me he was coming," Claire said. She watched Lainie poke at the little hot dogs and start taking them off the cookie sheet with a spatula.

"So? What's the big deal?"

"Nothing. I just haven't seen him in forever."

"Oh, yeah. Well, Brian's been seeing a lot of him lately."

"Really?"

"Yeah. And anyway, I thought you'd be happy to see him. You were the one that was obsessed with him."

"Lainie, shhh. I wasn't obsessed with him. I just, you know."

"Yes, I do know. You were obsessed with him." Lainie smiled and popped a hot dog in her mouth.

"Shut up. Anyway, he was such a jerk."

"No, he wasn't."

"Yes, he was. Remember he graded me? He graded everyone?"

"Oh my God, Claire. That was like a million years ago."

"Still."

Claire found it fascinating how Lainie could distance herself so much from high school when she was married to her high school boyfriend. Did she really not care about any of that stuff? Because Claire felt each memory freshly, like it had happened just the week before, like it was still happening twelve years later.

"You know . . . ," Lainie said. Now she was the one to look around and lower her voice. "He was engaged to this girl, Liz. She broke it off a couple of months ago and now he's living back at his parents' house."

Lainie finished arranging the hot dogs on a tray and filled some little dishes with ketchup and mustard. "Are you coming?" she asked.

"I'll be right out," Claire said. She poured herself a glass of water and drank it down all at once. So she was in the same position as Fran Angelo. She'd gone to a good college, and he'd gone to some random small state school. She'd moved to New York and gotten a good job, and then what did you know? None of it mattered. She and Fran Angelo were basically living parallel lives, tied in the exact same place in their lives. Well, wasn't that just a pickle?

CLAIRE WASN'T AT ALL SURPRISED to learn that Fran Angelo still made her sweat. She walked outside and waved to him from across the lawn, and he smiled and waved back, so she walked over to him. They stood for a while, each of them holding a bottle of beer, and then they moved over to some lawn chairs that were a little bit out of the center of the party, and conveniently located next to the cooler. Claire watched as the table next to them filled up with their empty beer bottles, two at a time.

Maybe it was because she knew Fran's situation, or maybe it was because she was getting drunk in the afternoon, but Claire felt free to share. It didn't take long before she was telling Fran about Doug and the apartment and moving home. He'd nodded and then told his story. And before long, the two of them were deep in conversation, cutting each other off to tell the details of their own broken engagement.

"She kept the ring," Fran told her. When he said this, it almost felt like he was sharing too much, but Claire didn't care. She was fascinated.

"Did you ask for it back?" Claire asked.

"No," Fran said. "That would've been a dick move. But she should have given it back anyway, you know?"

"I wonder why she wanted it."

"Because she's a bitch." Fran was drunk now, and honest and angry, and Claire didn't judge him one bit for it. They sat together and drank more beer, watching the party from the sidelines as it got dark outside, their own little angry team.

AFTER EVERYONE LEFT, CLAIRE SAT on the porch with Lainie and Brian, having a glass of wine and discussing Fran and the whole situation. Brian called Fran's fiancée a bitch, and Lainie interrupted.

"You can't just call her that because she broke up with him, like that's the end of it. There's a whole other huge part to the story." Lainie's teeth and lips were a little purple and she was speaking loudly.

"What am I leaving out?" Brian asked. He leaned back in his chair and lit a cigarette.

"Well, first of all, you know I love Fran and I'm on his side, but it's not like he was the best boyfriend. He went out all the time."

"Going out isn't a reason to break up with someone."

"Brian, come on. She told me once that he sometimes didn't come home, and yeah, maybe he just got drunk somewhere and passed out, but maybe not. Who knows where he was? I'm not so sure he didn't cheat on her."

"What makes you think that?" Brian asked.

"Are you serious? Remember last Fourth of July? We were at the parade and then we went out with them after, and he was with that random girl at the bar?"

"So? Sometimes guys talk to girls in a bar. It doesn't mean they're cheating."

"He was sitting there with his hand on her thigh. I'm just saying, you don't sit there and put your hand on some other girl's thigh, do you?"

"No, Lainie. I don't. And I wouldn't. But he did, and we don't know what else happened. Maybe nothing."

"Claire, wouldn't that piss you off?" Lainie asked. "Wouldn't that be totally out of line if someone you were engaged to did that?"

"Yeah," Claire said. "I mean, I guess so."

Lainie nodded and sat back in her chair and took a sip of wine. She looked satisfied that she had finally convinced them of something.

THAT NIGHT, CLAIRE HAD TROUBLE sleeping. She was a little drunk, and had been out in the sun and eaten too many little hot dogs and received too much disturbing information. The hot dogs and stories were swimming around in her head and threatening to make her sick.

The year she was in third grade, she had developed insomnia for no apparent reason. She would just lie awake at night, wondering and worrying why she couldn't sleep. She'd read sometimes, and made her way through the Baby-Sitters Club books, one right after the other. "Don't worry about sleeping," Weezy always used to tell her. "Just lay there. Resting is just as good as sleeping." The problem went away one day, just as quickly as it had appeared, but whenever Claire couldn't sleep she always thought of Weezy's advice: "Resting is just as good as sleeping." (Which was total bullshit, by the way.)

Figuring she was less likely to get sick if she was sitting up, Claire finally got up from her bed and started looking through her dresser drawers. They were all still stuffed full of random things—a couple of the old Baby-Sitters Club books, collages made from magazines, notes from Lainie, a couple of games of MASH, and tons of those fortune-teller things, made by folding paper and filling them with predictions from the future.

It was around sixth grade when she and Lainie became obsessed with telling the future. They played games to find out what their professions would be, used a Magic 8 Ball, a Ouija board, whatever they could find. They never pulled a top off of a Coke can or the stem off an apple without believing that it would tell them the initial of their future husbands. Even now, sometimes, Claire would find herself twisting an apple stem around, silently saying the alphabet, waiting for the letter when it would fall off. It was funny to think of it now, the way they thought these things would just happen to them. You'll be a Lawyer and Live in a Mansion and marry Michael Kelly! When did they start realizing that there was more to it than that?

Farther down in the drawer, Claire found a couple of mix tapes with titles like *Claire's Driving Songs* and *Spring Fling Mix*. She wondered briefly what high school kids did these days instead of making mix tapes for each other. Did they trade playlists on their iPods? That seemed so boring and sad. They'd have nothing to show for their years in high school.

Claire sorted through all this stuff, and she thought about Fran and his ex-fiancée's ring. She'd given her own ring back to Doug when things were final, handed it over to him and said, "Here," like she was giving him a pen that he'd asked for. He didn't insist that she keep it, and at the time she wasn't sorry to see it go.

But now, she kind of wished that she'd kept it, just so she could hold the ugly thing between her fingers and know that she hadn't made the whole thing up, that it had actually happened. She had all this shit in her room, all these pieces of paper with sixth-grade fortunes written on them, all these tapes in their plastic cases that were proof that her life had happened. But for Doug? For Doug she didn't really have anything. Not even a stupid, dull ring.

CHAPTER 7

Martha resigned from J.Crew the week she got back from the shore. "I am giving my notice," she announced to the staff that day. "I want you all to know that this is a personal decision and has nothing to do with my relationships with each of you. I have loved our time together, but it's time to make a change."

One girl, who had just started the week before, kept looking around at everyone as though they could explain just what was going on. Martha thought somebody should tell her that it was rude to keep swiveling your head around during a speech.

"I'll miss you all," Martha continued. "But not as much as I'm going to miss my discount." She had practiced that line in front of the mirror the night before, and was expecting a big laugh, but there were just a few chuckles. Her speech was wasted on these people. She wrapped it up and sent them back to work.

"I really am going to miss some things," Martha said to the other manager, Wally. They were going over the schedule, moving things around so that in two weeks, when Martha was gone, they wouldn't be shorthanded. "I wasn't just saying that. I'll miss when the new shipments come in, the excitement of opening the boxes and seeing the new things. It's like Christmas, sort of."

"Sweetheart, I say go and don't look back. Live a life without these plaid skirts and ruffled tops. You'll be free!"

Once, Martha had gone out for margaritas with Wally and his boyfriend, Anthony. Anthony had called J.Crew a "preppy hell," and Martha had been beyond insulted. She'd thought that Wally would be too, but he just laughed and so she tried not to show how hurt she was, since she liked Anthony and he was generally very pleasant.

"You're right," Martha said. She deleted her name from the schedule and felt a little thrill. One second it was there and the next it was blank. "You are so right."

AUNT MAUREEN'S FRIEND LINDA, who ran the caretaker business, had been thrilled to hear from Martha. "You're perfect," she kept saying during the interview. "You're just the kind of person we look for."

Martha was flattered. Linda explained how their client base was "wealthy and sometimes high profile." She whispered this sentence, as though someone were spying on them. These people wanted a higher-level caretaker than was usually offered, and it took the right kind of person to fill that job.

At dinner that night, Martha told her family all about the company. "It sounds pretty amazing," she said. "Which is good, because it's going to be a long trek back to nursing." She sighed and put her fork down.

"One step at a time," Weezy said. "You'll get there."

MARTHA WAS SENT ON AN INTERVIEW on the Main Line in Villanova, which was almost forty minutes away. Linda explained that this was a new client, a family that needed someone to stay with their father on the weekdays. "It can be tricky to navigate a new client," she said. "Often the patient doesn't feel that he needs the extra care, and the family is uncomfortable about the whole thing. Tread lightly."

Martha kept repeating that to herself as she drove to the house. "Tread lightly," she said. She wasn't sure exactly what it meant, but it sounded important and sort of tricky. She could handle it.

Martha set out early to get to the house, afraid that she was going to get lost even though she'd printed out the directions and had a GPS in her car. She figured she could just sit in the car and drink her coffee if she was early, but when she pulled up to 24 Rock Lane, she didn't think that was such a good idea. It was the biggest house she'd ever seen, and since there were only about three giant houses on the block and each one of those houses had an enormous driveway, hers was the only car on the street. If she parked there, they'd probably report it to the police.

She drove down the windy road once, then around the block and came back to the house. She was only about twenty minutes early, which wasn't too bad. It would just show them that she was punctual, so she pulled into the semicircle driveway and parked her car.

When Martha rang the doorbell, she heard a deep and echoing chime ring through the whole house. She waited at the door for about five minutes, and just when she was about to ring it again, the door swung open. Standing there was a woman in her mid-forties, wearing dark slim jeans and a light pink button-down shirt. She had long blond hair that hung straight down her back, much longer than women her age normally wore it, but somehow it looked just right. She was very slim—almost bony—but in an attractive way, Martha thought.

"Come in, come in," she said. "I'm Ruby."

"That's my dog's name," Martha said.

"Really?" Ruby didn't smile. "My real name is Ruth, but no one ever calls me that."

"That's my cousin's girlfriend's name." Martha couldn't stop herself from saying these things. They just kept coming out. Ruby just nodded, like this was a fact she already knew.

"Would you mind taking off your shoes?" Ruby made an apologetic grimace, and Martha saw that she had a gap between her two front teeth, like that actress whose name she couldn't remember. It seemed a strange thing, to have such a glaring orthodontic disaster on that face. Surely they had money for braces in this family. How had that been over-looked? Martha slipped off her shoes and prayed that her feet wouldn't smell. She wished she'd painted her toenails, but she didn't know that she'd be baring her feet in this inter-view.

"It's just that the nurses have said that any dirt in the house could cause a problem, and we have the cleaning lady only a few times a week now. But the house is so big and it gets so dusty in here." Ruby made another face, like she was put out by how huge the house was.

"Not a problem," Martha said. She noticed that Ruby was also barefoot, and that her toes were painted a perfect deep red. Her feet looked tan, and even her toes looked thin and elegant. Martha covered her left foot with her right foot and hoped Ruby wouldn't look at her toes.

Ruby motioned for Martha to follow her, and she led her to a sitting room off the front hall. Martha sat down in a light pink flowered chair, and crossed her feet again. Ruby perched herself on a strange little piece of furniture in the corner, a green stool, that was shaped like a mushroom. Was it a muffet? Martha had never seen one, but she was pretty sure that's what it was.

"So, I brought a copy of my résumé, although I know you've already seen it." Martha handed the piece of paper over to her, and Ruby took it but didn't look down.

"I don't know how much the agency told you, but I can fill you in. My father's almost eighty and he's been having some trouble lately. He's generally been in really good health, but a couple of months ago they found some tumors on his spine. They were benign, but they had to operate, and the surgery was hard for him to recover from. We got night nurses to come in, just to make sure that he didn't need anything, and that seemed like it was enough. But then last week, he was walking to the bathroom and he fell. He was alone, because Jaz had run out, and so he was on the floor for almost an hour."

"Oh no," Martha said. She wasn't sure if Ruby wanted a response, but she felt like she should give one. Ruby nodded and looked pleased.

"He didn't break anything, thank God. But there was some bruising and he's still a little sore."

"Who—who is Jaz?"

"Oh, Jaz is sort of the keeper of the house. She was our nanny when we were little and then she just stayed on, because we couldn't have made it without her. She does the grocery shopping and just sort of makes sure things run. You know, some light cleaning, the daily dishes, garbage, that sort of stuff."

"Great," Martha said.

"We thought it would be enough, to have Jaz here during the days when my father was here, you know, to stay with him until the night nurses came. But Jaz has said that she can't do that, that she needs to be able to run errands. She's kept a pretty loose schedule for the past few years, so I guess that's hard to change." Ruby shrugged, like she didn't really believe this, but there wasn't much to do about it. She closed her eyes, arched her back, and stretched her arms up in the air.

"So, you need someone during the days," Martha said.

Ruby righted herself and opened her eyes. "Right. Sorry, I'm just exhausted. I've been filling in most days until we got this solved. Anyway, it's not such a hard job. He really doesn't need much attention, just someone here to make sure that he has what he needs, that he can get his meals, all of that."

"Great," Martha said again.

"He's not much for television, though, which can limit his entertainment. I should tell you that."

"Mmm-hmm."

The doorbell rang, and the chimes went through the house again. "Would you excuse me?" Ruby asked. "That's probably the cleaning lady. I've told her to use the key, but . . ." She turned her palms up, like, *What can you do with these people?* Ruby pronounced *cleaning lady* very clearly, like she wanted to say *maid* but knew she shouldn't.

Martha heard the door open in the other room and heard Ruby say to the lady, "I'm not going to tell you again, use your key!" She said it in a funny tone, like she was trying to make a joke, but it came out sounding kind of mean. The woman scooted through the hall and into the other room without looking at Martha.

Ruby came back into the room and shook her hair back, gathered it in her hands like she was going to pull it back in a ponytail, and then let it go again.

"So, do you have any more questions? I'm trying to think if I forgot to tell you anything. Let's see. My brother and I come by pretty often. We take turns, and try to check in at least every other day, although sometimes we can't make it. And what else? Well, we'd need you to start right away." Ruby looked at Martha as though she was waiting for an answer.

"I think that sounds perfect," Martha said. This was the easiest job interview she'd ever been on.

"Really?" Ruby asked. She clapped her hands together and smiled. "That is just great, just so great. You have no idea what a stress this has been."

"I can imagine."

"Would you like to meet him? My father?"

"Yes, that would be great."

Ruby led her down a long hallway and they turned left past the kitchen. The walls were dark wood and the floors had dark oriental runners. Martha had trouble seeing, her eyes not adjusting to the lack of light right away.

"My father's bedroom used to be upstairs, of course, but a few years back we converted his study into a sort of bedroom area. It's just easier for everyone."

Martha nodded, even though Ruby wasn't looking at her. "That sounds efficient," she said.

Ruby stopped outside of two double doors. She knocked lightly on one and then slid it open. "Hello, hello!" she sang out. Behind her, Martha saw a man in a leather chair with a blanket over his legs. His hair was neatly combed and he was wearing a deep blue sweater. He looked sort of tiny. He had the paper on his lap, and looked up slowly when they came in. On the other side of the room, a large black woman sat reading a book with a vampire on the front cover. She put it down when they walked in and stood up.

"Well, look who it is," she said. "It's Ruby." Ruby smiled and looked down.

"Hello," Mr. Cranston said. He looked back down at his paper.

"We were just having some reading time," the woman said. She looked at Martha, and then back at Ruby.

"Jaz, this is Martha," Ruby said, but her eyes stayed fixed on her father.

"Martha Coffey," Martha said, extending her arm out. Jaz laughed and shook her hand.

"Nice to meet you, Martha Coffey. Are you the person the agency sent over?"

"That's me."

"Well, come meet Mr. Cranston." Jaz led her over to the man, and Martha shook his hand, and he said hello again, but it was clear he just wanted to get back to the paper.

"Let's give Mr. Cranston some peace," Jaz said. They all walked out into the hallway and Jaz shut the door behind her.

"Well," Ruby said, "do you want to just hang out here with Jaz for a while and she can fill you in on the details of the job?" Ruby looked at Jaz hopefully.

"Oh, chicken, that's fine," Jaz said. "You can get out of here." She sort of swatted Ruby's butt, which surprised Martha, and Ruby jumped and laughed.

"Thanks, Jaz," she said, and she walked away quickly.

Martha and Jaz looked at each other in the hallway for a moment.

"So, that's it?" Martha asked. "I got the job?"

"Oh lord, yes. That girl would've given the devil himself the job if it meant she could have her days free again."

"Oh," Martha said. She looked down at her naked feet.

"Oh, now, I don't mean that you're not qualified. We're lucky to have you. Come on to the kitchen and we'll have some tea and talk."

The kitchen, unlike the rest of the house, was bright and inviting. The wallpaper was covered in colorful fruit, and the tabletop was a shiny marble. Martha took a seat on one of the wooden stools and waited as Jaz filled the red teakettle and arranged the teacups.

"I was Ruby and Billy's nanny when they were little," she said. Martha nodded and she went on. "And then when they were older, I just stayed on, to drive them places and make sure that things were in order. It's funny, you know. Not what I had planned for my life, but that's how it works sometimes."

Jaz set down the mugs and a wooden box full of all different kinds of tea. Martha picked out a mint tea bag and put it in her mug, while Jaz filled it with boiling water. She blew on her tea and waited for Jaz to start talking again. She already liked her a great deal.

"It's hard here, for Mr. Cranston alone in the house. His wife died about five years ago now, but he doesn't want to go anywhere—refuses, actually, to leave the house." Ruby lowered her voice for this part, like Mr. Cranston was eavesdropping outside.

"I can imagine it's hard," Martha said.

"It would be easier if he went somewhere with more care, but he wants to stay in his house, so what can you do? The children can't talk him out of it, and Lord knows, he has the means, so here we are."

Martha and Jaz talked for almost two hours. Jaz told her about Ruby's teenage years, how she ran away, stole some of her mother's jewelry, crashed a car. "That child caused her parents so much heartache," she said. She told Martha about Billy and Ruby, how they weren't on speaking terms anymore, how she was the only way that they got messages to each other. "Despicable," she said. "Their father is in the last part of his life, and they can't even get over themselves to come together for him."

Martha told Jaz about nursing, how she wanted to get back to it, how she had failed at it before. She told her about J.Crew and how she excelled there but wasn't happy. Jaz listened, nodding her head and saying, "Mmm-hmm" every once in a while. When Martha was done, Jaz set her cup of tea down and put her hand over Martha's.

"Child, listen. You're on a journey. You didn't like the way life was going, so you're rewriting your own story. That's what you have to do. You don't see it now, but this is the most important part of your life. If you don't like the story that's being told about your own life, you've got to change it. You've got to tell a different story."

When Martha got home that day, she took out her notebook and wrote down Jaz's words. *You've got to tell a different story.* She looked at it before she went to bed that night and smiled. Who needed Dr. Baer? She had Jaz, who seemed much smarter, was nicer, and gave her tea to boot.

CHAPTER 8

It was Weezy's secret. No one needed to know. She wasn't hurting anyone, not even a little bit. It was just something to fill her time, something to lift her spirits. But if Will found out, he'd think she was crazy. And her kids— well, they would probably call the nuthouse and make her a reservation right then and there. That's why she kept it to herself. No one needed to know.

It wasn't like she meant to do it. No, it had all been innocent enough. Weezy had been smack in the middle of planning Claire's wedding when it was called off. Just like that, it was over. She'd been talking to caterers and venues, had meetings set up, had been enjoying all the research, and then one day Claire called and it was all done.

She'd never thought she'd be the type of person to get so involved in wedding planning, but she was wrong. It was a whole different ball game since she and Will had gotten married in the Starlight Room, with a lovely, simple lunch reception. For her own wedding, she'd made her dress, worn her hair straight and down. They'd all eaten and danced and that was that.

But when she started researching for Claire's wedding— oh, the excess! There were photo booths to be rented, personalized matchbooks and napkins to be had. Caterers sent her sample menus, with wonderful descriptions of bacon-wrapped dates and Boursin-wrapped snow peas. They sent pictures of the food, names of signature cocktails, options for monogrammed cupcakes and chocolate fountains. And that was just the food! There were also blogs of local brides, detailing every step of their weddings. There were forums of angry brides, trashing photographers and caterers and florists. It was a whole new world, and Weezy was fascinated.

Claire called off her wedding on a Monday. Weezy had already arranged to meet with one of the caterers the very next day, and she was too shocked to call and cancel. How do you explain a thing like that over the phone? That morning, she found herself driving toward the offices. She didn't tell Will where she was going. No, he wouldn't have understood. He would have picked up the phone and canceled the appointment himself, just said she couldn't make it, with no explanation. But he didn't understand. She'd been dealing with Sally Lemons, the owner of Lemons and Limes, for weeks now. They had a relationship, a correspondence e-mailing menus back and forth. She couldn't just cancel over the phone. That would be extremely rude. And so she got in her Volvo and drove to the office.

She had fully intended to tell Sally in person that the wedding was off. It was the right thing to do, to end this face-to-face. But when she walked into the room, the table was already set with the ivory and taupe linens that they had discussed, and a man handed her a glass of cucumber lemonade. "This is what your guests will be greeted with," he told her. She took a sip and decided to stay. She could tell Sally later.

And so they ate. They ate pan-roasted halibut with fingerling potatoes, and beef tenderloin with goat cheese medallions. They tried bruschetta and marinated mozzarella.

They sampled wedding cakes and pecan diamonds. Weezy left Lemons and Limes, stuffed full and a little guilty. She'd drunk several glasses of wine without meaning to; every time she came close to finishing one, it was refilled right to the top. At the end, Sally had given her a warm handshake, saying how sorry she was that Claire couldn't make it, that they could do another tasting when the menu was decided, that she'd be in touch to work out the details.

Weezy had sat in her car in the parking lot for almost an hour after the tasting. When she'd stood up to go, she was dizzy and, she realized, a touch drunk. She felt almost giddy, like she'd stolen something, only she hadn't. It had all been free. Sally had talked to her like she was in charge of something big. She'd treated Weezy with respect and that was nice. The wine was just a bonus.

And that was how, months later, Weezy still hadn't told any of the vendors that the wedding was off. She'd told them it was postponed, of course. She had to. The date she had originally given them was looming, and there was no way around that. "You know kids these days," she'd said. "Their lives are so busy they can't seem to find the time to get married!" But she still sent a note to Sally every couple of weeks, just to ask about new items on the menu, or to discuss what to do for a guest with a gluten allergy.

And so what? So what if Weezy was planning an imaginary wedding? People did far worse things, and anyway, maybe she'd use this information somehow at some point. Still, if anyone had caught her, she would have been completely mortified. And so, when Will walked into the kitchen and she was on her laptop, pricing out letterpress invitations as opposed to engraved, she slammed her computer shut and sat up straight.

∙ ∙ ∙

"HI," SHE SAID. She tried to act casual.

"Hello," he said, and stretched his arms out to the side, which made his shirt pull tight against his round belly. "Just taking a break to get a drink. Don't let me interrupt."

Weezy was just the littlest bit annoyed (as she was at least once a day) that Will had a room to work in all to himself, while she was relegated to a built-in desk in the kitchen. When had she agreed to this arrangement? Her desk was often littered with things that people just dropped there, receipts or empty envelopes and sometimes even food wrappers. And there was no privacy with people parading through the kitchen. Will came down several times throughout the day. Of course he was going to interrupt. Why even say that? *Don't let me interrupt.* It was ridiculous.

"How's the writing coming?" she asked. This question was a reflex. She asked it so often, with so little real interest. It was like saying, "How are you?" to an acquaintance in the grocery store.

"Good," Will answered.

"Are you ready for your class today?" This was another pointless question. Will had been teaching the same two classes for the past five years now, and he could do them in his sleep.

"Yep. I'm all set."

"Mmm. What time are you headed over?"

"I have office hours at four."

They were silent for a few minutes and Weezy looked out the kitchen window. "The Connors are having some work done on their house," she said. "I wonder if they're getting it ready to sell. There's been people coming and going all day."

"Huh," Will said. He half looked out the window, as

though he was curious about this, which Weezy knew he wasn't. Will didn't really care or keep up on any of the neighborhood news.

It was the mothers that remembered everything anyway. That's what Weezy had learned after three decades in this house. The mothers knew what was happening in the neighborhood. They knew the history, the scandals, the stories, the transgressions. They were the ones that kept the details straight, that passed information to the new people on the block. They gave the prompts to the fathers—"You know who I'm talking about, the one that got pregnant, no, not the Brennan girl, the other one, the Sullivans' daughter."

They knew who had gotten divorced, who was getting divorced, and who would probably get divorced soon. They knew who had cheated and who got the best settlements. And the fathers would always just nod as they listened to all of this, the stories sounding vaguely familiar, or at least more familiar than unfamiliar, like it had been overheard at a picnic somewhere, discussed at a barbecue, or whispered in the kitchen while dinner was being prepared and the kids were in the next room doing their homework.

As the kids had grown up, the neighborhood gossip had slowed down. Everything had slowed down, really. For some years in the midst of it, when the children were growing up, Weezy had spent a fair amount of time talking with the other mothers on the block about everyone's business. It wasn't mean-spirited, or at least Weezy liked to think it wasn't. It was just something to get them through the day, at a time when their days were always so busy—school projects, money worries, shuttling Max to hockey, and grounding Claire. It was all so fast that sometimes it felt like you needed a reminder to breathe.

Weezy and Will used to talk about what they would do after the kids moved out, when they had their own lives and no children to take care of. "We'll be those crazy old people that buy an RV and drive cross-country," Will said once. Weezy had laughed. She would be happy with an apartment in the city and a cottage by the shore. They had looked forward to that time, when they could relax and just enjoy themselves. It was still coming, Weezy believed. It was just put on hold for a while.

Ten years ago, if Weezy could have predicted where her children would be at this point, she would have guessed that Claire would be married and maybe even have a baby or two. Martha was harder to guess, but Weezy thought she'd be living on her own, nursing, and enjoying every minute of it. Max was still in school, so for the moment, he was still on track. But who knew? These things could get derailed at any moment. She knew that much.

Sometimes Will got a surprised look on his face when Martha or Claire walked into the room, like he'd forgotten that they lived there now. It wasn't that he disliked having them there. Sometimes Claire would say something that would make him laugh loudly, a huge, surprising guffaw. And he and Martha enjoyed spending quiet time together, reading the paper in the mornings and drinking coffee. Sometimes he seemed confused by their presence, and sometimes he treated them just as he always had, as if they were still children.

Just the other day, Martha had walked into the kitchen to get some aspirin, and Will said, "You still have a headache? Poor baby." And something unsettled itself in Weezy, hearing him say that. Martha wasn't a baby. It didn't seem right to call her that, to say *poor baby* and pat her on the head.

It didn't help matters that when the kids were home they seemed to start acting like teenagers again. They left shoes and bags and jackets scattered all around. Glasses were missing from the kitchen, only to be found in bedrooms or the basement. Dishes rarely made it to the dishwasher. The best you could hope for was that they'd get rinsed off and left in the sink. Usually they were just abandoned in the kitchen, on the counter, presumably waiting for a fairy to come and clean them up.

This was not how Weezy had raised her kids. Not at all. She taught them to clean up after themselves, called them back to the kitchen to clean up the apple and peanut butter snack that was now smeared on a plate. But that was when she was younger and had more energy, when she was able to take the time to yell and insist and ignore the rolled eyes and sighs of injustice. Now, most of the time she couldn't quite face it, and so she ended up picking up after them, throwing armfuls of possessions back into their rooms, rinsing off dishes, wiping crumbs from the table.

After Weezy had stopped working last year, Will had suggested that they get rid of the cleaning lady. "Should we let Sandra go?" he'd asked, like it was the natural thing to do. He had just left his crumby toast plate, an egg pan, and a coffee cup right in the sink.

"Let Sandra go? Why would we do that? So I can fulfill my life goal of cleaning up after you? Believe me, I do enough of that. Who is it that you think is going to come along and clean up from your breakfast? The elves that live under the sink?"

Will had thrown up his arms and sighed like a martyr. "It was just a suggestion," he said. He went back to the sink and started cleaning up his dishes.

Sandra came in only once every two weeks now anyway.

Did he really think that Weezy would be happy to spend her days scrubbing toilets? Sometimes she didn't know where he got these ideas. She had remained angry for weeks, and whenever she started to get over it, she'd hear Will saying, *Should we let Sandra go?* and get annoyed all over again.

"Don't you think you're overreacting just a little bit?" Maureen had asked her.

"No," Weezy said. "I don't think I'm overreacting at all. My husband would like me to spend my days dusting and mopping. Maybe that's what he always really wanted."

"I think you're reading too much into this. Will says stuff all the time that doesn't mean anything. He just said it without thinking, that's all."

Somewhere, deep down, Weezy knew that Maureen was probably right. Will said stupid things all the time. She tried to let it go. But every time Sandra was due to come, and Weezy had to go around the house picking up stuff to make sure that the poor woman could actually get to the vacuum cleaner and dust without tripping over a pair of shoes, Weezy would say out loud, "It's a good thing Sandra's coming tomorrow. Look at this place. No one's picked up a thing in weeks." She couldn't help herself. She wanted Will to know that she had better things to do than to be his personal maid.

Once a month, Sandra was allowed to go into Will's office to clean it. It was disgusting in there. There were Kleenexes on the floor (near the garbage but not in it), dust all around the computer and desk, papers stacked everywhere. And as much as Weezy begged Will to bring dishes down as soon as he was done with them, there was always a glass or two that was left behind. The last time that Sandra was up there, she'd come down holding a coffee mug that had mold growing up the sides.

Weezy was embarrassed and also horrified for Sandra. Even if it was your job to clean someone else's house, it didn't mean that you expected to find a cup of mold while doing so. Will hadn't really understood. "That's her job," he'd said. "Sorry, I didn't know it was up there." But he wasn't sorry, and now Weezy was never going to be able to let Sandra back into the office without checking it out herself.

Will was still clunking around the kitchen, and Weezy wanted him to finish up so that she could go back to the blog post she was reading, the one that was all about the personal touches you could add to your wedding—old family wedding pictures, naming the tables after favorite books, designing your own guest book!

"So, what's on the agenda for today?" Will asked. He took out some lunch meat and sniffed it, as if he thought it had been left there to go bad.

"That's brand-new," Weezy told him. "I just bought it yesterday."

Will nodded and grabbed some cheese, bread, lettuce, and mayonnaise and started assembling a giant sandwich.

"Go easy on the mayo," Weezy said. Will nodded and then moved so that he blocked the sandwich from her view. "I'm going to meet Sharon, from work, in a little bit."

"Oh really?"

"Yeah, she said there's some things she wanted to talk to me about."

"I hope she's not trying to lure you back to work." Will took a large bite out of his sandwich and chewed while standing. This was a habit of his that got more annoying with time. "Sit down," she was always telling him. "Sit down and chew." But he insisted on eating standing up, like a teenager or a farmer.

"I'm not sure what she wants to talk about. I told her I'd meet her for a cup of coffee."

"Sounds good." Will's answer came so easily that Weezy almost felt guilty for lying. Almost.

THE FLORIST WAS LOCATED CLEAR on the other side of the city and it took almost an hour to get there. Sally Lemons had been the one to recommend him to Weezy. "I love working with Samuel," she'd said. "He's so creative. A true artist."

And so Weezy had called him to make an appointment. This was actually the first appointment she'd made since the wedding was called off. All of the others were ones that were already set up, and this felt in some ways like she was crossing a line. It was one thing to peruse websites, and to e-mail for information, but now she was actually meeting with someone. But she was so curious to see what he had to show her, and she loved flowers, and really, what was the big deal?

Samuel worked out of his own florist shop, which was small and damp. There was some temperature-controlled room to the left that housed plants, and a large refrigerated portion up front that held cut flowers. The smell of flowers was thick, but not overwhelming. Then again, Weezy loved the smell of flowers. She loved everything about them, watching them bloom and flourish in her backyard. It was so satisfying to plant something and know what would spring up from the ground—that is, as long as the squirrels and chipmunks minded their own business. You always knew what you were getting when you planted a flower, and Weezy liked that.

When she opened the door, the shop was empty. She walked to the desk and waited a moment, then rang the little bell that was there. A large, balding, sort of roundish man peeked out from the back. "Mrs. Coffey?" he asked, and Weezy nodded.

"I hope you don't mind," she said, pointing to the bell. "I didn't mean to be rude, I just wasn't sure . . ."

"Of course not! Come on, let's take a seat over at the table."

Samuel was not what she expected. He had the build of an old high school football player, his voice was deep and booming, and he was wearing a blue-checked button-down polo shirt, which was identical to one that Will owned.

"It's so nice to meet you," Weezy said. "Sally said the nicest things about you."

"She's great, isn't she?"

The two of them sat at a long table and Samuel spread several glossy books filled with pictures of floral arrangements in front of them. Weezy couldn't help but sneak looks at Samuel. She was surprised at how, well, manly he was. Then she was ashamed of herself for being surprised. What did she expect? That just because he owned a flower shop he was going to be a tiny, delicate, feminine man? Well, yes, that's exactly what she had expected.

"So, how long have you been doing this?" Weezy asked.

"Oh, forever," Samuel said with a laugh. "This was my parents' shop, and I worked here growing up, helping out as a little guy, then part-time during high school and college, and full-time after that. I really took to it, and I was lucky because when my parents got ready to retire, none of my eight siblings was even the least bit interested."

"Eight!"

"Yes, eight." Samuel laughed again. "You'd think there'd be a few more green thumbs in the bunch, but there was just me."

"I love to garden," Weezy said. "I think of myself as a green thumb too."

"Great," Samuel said. "Then this will be fun." He placed his hands, palm down, on top of the books. "So what I usually do is flip through these books, and just have you point out anything that grabs your attention—good or bad. Then we can look through some of my photos from weddings I've done. We can talk a little bit about what you imagine for the day, what flowers are favorites of yours, and so on. Then once we've worked through it all, I can draw up a proposal and we can go from there."

"That sounds perfect," Weezy said. "And of course, it's so unfortunate that my daughter couldn't come with me today."

Samuel nodded. "Not a problem. As long as the two of you have talked and are on the same page, it should be fine. And we can show her what we come up with and alter it if we need to. Nothing is set in stone—this is a work in progress."

Sally Lemons was right—Samuel was amazing. Weezy loved him right away, and the way he knew flowers, oh! He was a wonder. All she had to say was "those little round green ones," and he said, "Kermit flowers." They talked about bachelor's buttons and hydrangeas, lisianthus, and pincushion proteas. He knew the name of every flower, could describe the textures and colors so vividly. A couple of times, he went into the refrigerator and came out holding samples. He had flowers in every shape and size; he had green, and orange, and ivory. He talked about pairing textures and tones to complement each other. He agreed with her on the flowers she felt were a little tired (roses) and the ones that were timeless and elegant (lilies).

"Now, there's one more thing I'd like to show you," he said. "When the guests walk in, I like to give them a Wow!"

He gave her some jazz hands when he said this. "One of my favorite things to do is a tall vase with monochromatic gerbera daisies, maybe in a dark orange, surrounded by a spray of tall grass. Now, it's a little pricey, so don't feel pressured. I just wanted to throw it out there."

Samuel opened a photo album and pointed to a picture of the arrangement he just described. "It's fantastic," Weezy whispered.

On the ride home, Weezy's flower high wore off. She got more deflated as she drove. What was she doing? How could she not have anything better to do with her free time than to have a fake meeting with a florist to plan a fake wedding? What was the matter with her?

Weezy thought of her mother, Bets, and how committed she was to attending daily mass. Weezy was almost jealous of her. Not because she herself wanted to actually go to daily mass (she didn't, and anyway, if she did she could just go) but because it was an anchor in Bets's day. Every morning she woke up and met her friend at the church at seven thirty, sometimes getting there a little early to say the rosary together. Afterward, they walked down the block to a little bakery and got donuts and coffee. It was simple, but it seemed nice to have an activity like that every day.

There was nothing worse than feeling bored and restless at the same time. Maureen could always find something to fill her time, but Weezy always felt like there was something else she should be doing, even if everything was marked off her list. Maureen and Bets both loved those cheap Harlequin romance novels, and every so often they'd exchange grocery bags full of them, passing the overflowing bags to one another. Weezy tried to read them, but she just didn't get it. They were all the same. Why waste your time reading something that was just going to be thrown into a bag when it was done, and confused with the rest of the bunch? There was nothing special about any of them; you knew what the ending was before you even started.

She drove home slowly and pulled into the driveway feeling very low. When she opened the door, she smelled garlic and onions cooking. Claire's head popped out of the kitchen. "Hi, Mom. I'm making dinner. Hope you didn't have anything planned. I tried to call you, but your phone was off."

Weezy walked toward the kitchen. "That sounds great," she said. "I'm pooped."

"I'm making sausage and peppers and some pasta thing to go along with it."

"Mmm," Weezy said. She smiled and sat down in a kitchen chair. "Do you need help?"

"No, I'm good. Where were you? Your phone kept going right to your voice mail."

"I had some meetings. How was work?"

"Fine," Claire said. "The same. Pretty boring."

Claire had announced that she wanted something to do, a job, but she didn't care what it was. This disturbed Weezy. She suggested that Claire look at grad school programs or research some nonprofits here, but Claire wouldn't hear of it.

"I just want a job," she'd insisted. "Just a job. I don't care if it's boring or what it is."

Weezy wanted to tell her that this wasn't the attitude to take. She'd spent years working at places that were "just a job" and it didn't make it easier that you didn't care about it. If anything, it made it harder.

She'd always known that Claire would be able to thrive in a work situation. It was Martha that she had to constantly build up. "You're so smart and capable," she'd said to her last week. Martha needed reminding, needed to be shown how to showcase herself. Sometimes her skills didn't translate in the real world.

Claire didn't go into much detail on her temp job, which was nothing new. She was always private with her information, never offered up anything unless Weezy was there to pry it out of her. Even after she and Doug called off the wedding, Weezy had to push to get any sort of answer. "It's over, Mom," was all she said. "What else do you want me to say? It's done."

"Was he unfaithful?" Weezy had asked.

"No, God, Mom. No."

"I'm just trying to understand. Were you unfaithful?"

"Mom, stop. No." Claire had breathed loudly on the phone, as if she was trying to calm herself down. "No one cheated, Mom. Nothing happened. We just don't want to get married."

Weezy had started to say something else, but thought better of it and stayed silent. She didn't quite believe Claire, but there was no point in pushing further, she knew. Claire was the most stubborn of her children, and the more Weezy tried to put pressure on her, the more she dug in her heels and refused to move.

When the girls were little, Weezy sometimes resorted to trying to scare them into behaving. Once, in the grocery store, when they both refused to walk next to the cart, choosing instead to run in circles in the cereal aisle, she'd turned her back and left them. "Okay, then. I'll see you later. I'm going home."

Weezy walked down the aisle, turning once to look back at them for dramatic effect. Martha had screamed, "Wait! No! I'm coming," and raced after her, snotty and red-faced, already crying in a panic. Claire had remained where she was. She sat herself down on the floor of the grocery store and didn't budge. She just looked up at Weezy, daring her to go, her jaw clenched and her arms crossed, refusing to move.

And so Weezy went to the checkout, paid for her groceries, and then started walking to the car, sure that Claire would follow behind at any moment. Martha was still snuffling with fear because she'd almost been left behind. Weezy stood at the car, trying to remember what her childrearing books had said. Should she give in? Should she hold her ground? At what point did this become dangerous? Kids could be kidnapped anywhere at any time. Even if she was watching the front door, to make sure that Claire didn't come out, you never knew.

She probably stood there for only a total of two minutes at the most, although it felt like an hour, and finally, convinced that Claire was in some sort of danger, she'd grabbed Martha and run back inside, and found Claire sitting right where she'd left her, staring straight ahead, refusing to move.

DINNER THAT NIGHT WAS WONDERFUL, mostly because Weezy hadn't had to cook and Martha offered to clean up the kitchen. "Maybe having you two home isn't so awful," Will said, and the girls rolled their eyes at him.

Reading in bed that night, Weezy thought about the large flower arrangement of orange daisies, and how if she was really going to do this, she'd splurge for it. Even if it meant scrimping somewhere else in the budget, she'd do it. They were so beautiful and breathtaking. She could just imagine everyone's faces as they walked in and saw them.

Will leaned over to give her a kiss good night, and his lips stayed on her for just a moment longer than usual. "You smell nice," he said, smiling at her. "Like flowers." He kissed her one more time, and then rolled over and fell asleep.

CHAPTER 9

The people at Proof Perfect (or "PP," as they affectionately called themselves) took themselves very seriously. They wrote each other e-mails that said things like, "As we discussed," and "FYI," and "Per our earlier conversation," and "Loop me in." It was as if they'd all just read a book on office jargon and were in a competition to see who could use the most terms in one day.

People walked quickly, as if they couldn't waste a second (not one second!) by walking at a regular speed, and so they raced from their offices to the restroom, and back again, presumably to continue their proofreading. As they passed each other in the halls, they often called out to each other, "Shoot me an e-mail," because wasting time to stop and talk was clearly not an option.

Sometimes it was funny and sometimes it made Claire a little sad to watch them. They all seemed to have just discovered Microsoft Outlook meeting invitations and they sent them to each other for everything—weekly meetings, morning coffee breaks, birthday celebrations in the break room. It was the cause of many a scuffle when someone chose not to respond to an invite.

One of the women that Claire assisted, Leslie, called her anywhere from seven to ten times a day. She mostly called her Amanda, even though Claire was certain that she knew her name and remembered that Amanda was on maternity leave. Claire answered to it, figuring it was Leslie's way of trying to tell her that she was very important and couldn't be bothered to remember everyone's name.

The job was easier than Claire had imagined. It was also a lot more boring. She mostly just sat around and waited for someone to ask her to Xerox something or for the phone to ring. If Claire had had any desire to write a book or a screenplay, this would have been the perfect opportunity. She could have sat all day and typed, mostly uninterrupted. But she had no such desire, and so instead she played solitaire, and perused cooking sites for recipes. Sometimes, she added up how much she was earning each day, and how much closer she was to paying down her credit cards. That was usually the most exciting part of her day.

AT HOME, MARTHA KEPT SAYING, "It's good timing that you moved home now, since I'll probably be buying a place soon." Martha had been talking about buying a place for years now, so Claire didn't pay much attention to her.

Each morning, Claire got up and was in the shower by seven, in order to beat Martha, who took forever in the bathroom. The two of them still often ended up in there at the same time, brushing their teeth or putting on their makeup, which made it feel like they were in high school again. Claire left the house around eight thirty and then was home by six, where she immediately changed into pajamas, or headed over to Lainie's to drink wine. It was one or the other.

The first time that she came back late from Lainie's, Weezy started to say something about coming home at a regular hour, and wanting to know where Claire was. While she talked, Claire just stood and stared at her and finally said, "Mom, I'm almost thirty. This isn't going to work."

Weezy let out a little laugh then, and looked just a touch embarrassed, as if she'd actually forgotten how old Claire was. "I guess it's hard to get used to you living here as an adult," she said. But then she made Claire promise that she would still just leave a message so that they knew where she was. Claire was too tired to protest, so she agreed. "Just Twitter me," Weezy said, by which she meant send a text.

They ate dinner together every night, and Martha talked about her new job, Will talked about his students, Weezy asked Martha about nursing, and Claire tried to figure out how she'd ended up there. After a week of the same routine, Claire felt like she was right back in high school. Or jail.

The other thing about living at home (which Claire had forgotten) was that all of a sudden, she was expected to be so many places, to attend so many random things—Lainie's niece's baptism, lunch with Weezy's cousins, dinner with Will's professor friends. When she tried to back out of anything, they would all just shake their heads. "You're here," they'd say, as if that explained it. As if her presence back in the state of Pennsylvania required her to participate in everything.

She even got roped into going to a wake for the father of an old high school friend. "I haven't seen Kelly in, like, six years," she said, but Lainie wouldn't hear of it.

"You have to go," she said. "It's Kelly's dad."

And just like that, Claire was in the car with Lainie and Martha (who'd taken a math class with Kelly in high school) and they all stood in line at the wake, which was incredibly crowded, and then talked to Kelly's mom, who looked really drugged up, hugged Kelly, and then stood and looked at the dead body at the front of the room.

"Doesn't he look great?" Kelly's mom said.

No, he didn't look great. He looked dead. Kelly's mom grabbed Claire's hand, although Claire was pretty sure that she didn't know who she was. Lainie, meanwhile, was nodding and telling stories and saying gracious things, like she was an expert at wakes now.

Claire hated wakes. It was a bizarre tradition to stand around and look at a corpse. And so, as soon as she could, Claire excused herself and walked outside and around the corner of the building, where she almost ran right into Fran Angelo, leaning against the wall, his head tilted back and his eyes closed as he smoked a cigarette.

For a second, Claire wondered what he was doing there. Was everyone in town required to go to this thing? Then she remembered that he was related to Kelly somehow, a cousin or a second cousin or something like that.

"Hey," Claire said. He opened his eyes, but didn't look all that surprised to see her, like he'd been waiting for someone to come find him. He smiled at her and she looked at the ground.

"Hey," he said. "What's going on?"

"Not much. Just, you know." Claire motioned toward the wall of the funeral home, like that explained everything. She shifted from one leg to the other, hating that he made her feel like she was fifteen again.

"I haven't gone in yet," Fran said. "I hate wakes."

"Me too. I was just thinking the exact same thing."

"Do you want a cigarette?" He shook the pack and held it out to her.

"I don't really smoke anymore," she said. "But sure." She didn't bother to explain that she'd never really smoked in the first place, except when she was drunk and sometimes in college if she was bored. But now seemed like an appropriate time to smoke, and so she took one out of the pack and leaned forward to let Fran light it. She remembered parties in high school, clumps of teenagers standing around a backyard, smoking and looking bored. She inhaled and felt dizzy almost immediately. Fran smoked Reds, which seemed like a serious, old-man cigarette. He would probably smoke for the rest of his life.

"I was going to call you to hang out," Fran said, "but then I realized I never got your number the other day."

"Oh really?" Claire said. She sounded like an idiot. A teenage idiot.

"Yeah, we should get together." He reached into his pocket, pulled his phone out and handed it to Claire.

"So, should I put my number in?" she asked. He nodded and she typed herself into Fran Angelo's phone.

"I should probably go in, I guess." He closed his eyes and leaned his head back, aiming his face at the sky. Claire remembered him in high school, how he was always tilting his face up like that to drop Visine into his eyes, like he was stoned or wanted people to think he was.

"Okay," Claire said. "I'll see you."

Fran opened his eyes and looked at her. "I'll call you," he said. He walked back toward the front door of the funeral home, and left Claire standing there, holding her still-burning cigarette.

Lainie came out of the funeral home as Fran was going in. Claire walked around the corner of the building and called out to Lainie.

"Hey," Lainie said. "I wasn't sure where you went. Are you smoking?"

"Not really," Claire said. She dropped the cigarette on the ground. "Are you ready?"

"Yeah. We just have to wait for Martha."

"What's she doing in there? Making plans to go to the burial with the family?"

"She's just saying good-bye to a couple people. What were you doing out here anyway?"

"Nothing. I just didn't want to be in there anymore. I hate wakes."

"I don't think anyone really likes them," Lainie said.

"Martha," Claire said. "I think Martha likes them."

FRAN CALLED CLAIRE TWO DAYS LATER and invited her over. She'd lost her breath for a second when she heard his voice on the phone, and it was hard to recover and answer him when he said simply, "Want to hang out?"

"Sure," Claire said. And then, "Sorry, I'm out of breath. I just got back from a run."

"Cool," Fran said.

Fran was living in the basement of his parents' house. It looked just as she'd imagined it would. There were two old red-plaid couches that were scratchy when you sat on them, a banged-up coffee table, wall-to-wall brown carpeting, and a queen-sized bed in the corner. There was a small bathroom down there with a stand-up shower, a tiny refrigerator (the kind that kids keep in their dorm room), and a flimsy-looking desk with the oldest computer Claire had ever seen on it. In an adjoining room were the washer and dryer, and every so often, a whiff of dryer-sheet—smelling air would come drifting out, which was always surprising and pleasant.

"Here it is," Fran said when she walked down there. "My new place."

"It's nice," Claire said. She knew that since she was living in her parents' house at the moment, she didn't have a lot of room to judge, but it seemed worse that Fran was in the basement. Like it was more permanent or something.

Claire's friend Natalie had a brother who had lived in the basement for as long as she could remember. He was eight years older than they were, and by the time they were in high school, he was a permanent fixture in the basement of the Martin house. He smoked pot down there, and he and his parents seemed to have an agreement—as long as he sprayed air freshener and pretended that he wasn't smoking, his parents would pretend that they didn't notice the smell of weed drifting up to the kitchen.

When they were freshmen in high school, they were all in love with Dan Martin. They'd giggle when he came upstairs and talked to them, kept their makeup on when they slept over, just in case he was around. As they got older, they sometimes went down to the basement with him to hang out, and by the end of high school, they sometimes drank beers down there or even smoked a joint.

But by the time they graduated from college, Dan no longer seemed cute or even a little bit appealing. He was thirty then, and even though he was thin everywhere else, he had a gut that hung over his pants. They never went down to the basement to see him anymore, and when he came upstairs they didn't giggle. He transformed into Natalie's creepy older brother, who was sort of a perv, and everyone seemed to forget that they used to worship him. Even Natalie started rolling her eyes at him, calling him a loser, blaming her parents for letting him live there. "What a waste of life," she used to say. "What a complete waste of a person."

Claire sincerely hoped that Fran would not live in the

basement forever, but as she looked around she heard Weezy saying, "It's a trend, an epidemic."

Fran told Claire that he'd let Liz keep their apartment, which was a loft on the edge of a trendy new neighborhood. "I didn't want to stay there anyway," he said. "She picked out all the furniture and decorated it. I didn't want that place. It was full of fake posters and dream catchers."

He got them both beers and they sat on the couch with the TV on, but they didn't watch anything. Instead, he told her about Liz, who was a waitress and an artist who made jewelry that she sold at street fairs and some small boutiques.

"She thinks she's going to make it," Fran said. "She stays up half the night baking beads in a kiln that's in the middle of the fucking apartment, thinking that she's really going to make it." He took a sip of beer and sniffed. "I mean, her stuff's good, don't get me wrong. But how many people actually make it big designing jewelry, you know?"

"Probably not a lot," Claire said.

"Yeah, exactly. I used to tell her I wanted the kiln out of there, and she'd freak, like me saying that I didn't want a huge fire pit in the middle of our apartment was single-handedly killing her career. Like, because I didn't want to live in a fire death trap, I wasn't supporting her."

Claire laughed, and he smiled at her. He got them each another beer, and they set the empty ones right on the coffee table in front of them.

"Doug used to sleep with his BlackBerry. And I don't mean he had it by the side of the bed. He had it *in* the bed, right next to him, sometimes on the pillow like it was a little pet. No matter what time it went off, he'd read it and respond. Like he was so important that he couldn't even wait a second, like someone would die if he didn't answer them right away."

Fran nodded like he understood. He was just as confident as he'd been in high school, which surprised her. She thought maybe time or the breakup would have taken something off of him, but it hadn't. After their second beer, he got them each another, and when he sat back down, he put his hand on her upper thigh, just letting it rest there right next to the crotch of her jeans.

He didn't move his hand, just started moving his fingers, drumming them. Then he started moving his thumb in circles on the top part of her thigh, and rubbed his fingers on her inner thigh, his pinky just sometimes brushing against her, lightly, until she couldn't sit still.

He kept talking while he did this—about his job, his old apartment, what he missed about the neighborhood— just kept circling his fingers, as though he had no idea what he was doing, until she couldn't listen to him anymore, and when he leaned over to kiss her, she turned to face him, straddling one of his thighs, moving back and forth, grinding against him, both of them making appreciative noises as they moved.

Later, as they lay in bed and sniffed the dryer-sheet air, Fran laughed. "What?" Claire asked.

"I'm just surprised, that's all," he said.

"Surprised at what?" She rolled away from him and sat up, holding the sheets in front of her and feeling very, very naked.

"At this. You were always so quiet in high school."

"I wasn't quiet," Claire said.

"Well, you didn't talk to me." He stretched his arms above him.

"I talked to you. We hooked up, remember?" She felt like digging her nails into his arm until it hurt.

"I remember," he said. "Don't get so worked up."

"I'm not worked up."

"Okay," he said. He put his face next to her and started to kiss her, then pulled her on top of him. He still tasted like tobacco and cinnamon gum, but his face felt different now. He had stubble that seemed harder, more grown up. As they kissed, she was aware of all of this, and still had time to think, *This is a dumb move.*

LAINIE AND BRIAN HAD SEX freshman year of high school, and when Lainie told her about it, Claire tried to listen, but she was so far away from it, so far from that actually happening to her, that it didn't make much sense. It was like somebody telling you about a safari that they went on; you understood why they were excited, but you couldn't actually imagine a giraffe coming up and licking your hand, and so you just nodded and smiled.

After that happened, Lainie joined the Group of Girls Who Have Sex With Their Boyfriends. It was like a club. Claire never totally understood how they all identified one another, but somehow girls from all different groups of friends would smile knowingly at each other during the health portion of gym class, nod at each other in the hallways. Sometimes, Claire would walk into the bathroom at school and find Lainie whispering with Margie Schuller and Tracy King, two girls they weren't even friends with, and she knew without asking what the three of them were talking about.

When Claire finally had sex, her junior year in college, she didn't tell Lainie right away. She didn't want Lainie to welcome her into the club, like she was the president, like she owned sex because she'd done it first.

And even now, as she told Lainie about Fran, it was

strangely uncomfortable. Claire just blurted it out, knowing that Lainie would be hurt if she didn't tell her.

"You're sleeping with Fran?" Lainie asked her.

"Not sleeping," Claire explained. "Slept. Once."

"Why didn't you tell me?"

"I'm telling you right now. What did you want me to do? Call you from his bed?"

"I can't believe this."

"I sort of can't either."

"I do not see you guys together," Lainie said.

"Yeah, I know, right?" Claire was offended, but tried not to show it.

"So, do you think you'll see him again?"

"Who knows? Probably not," Claire said.

But Fran called her the next day, as she thought he would, and they saw each other that night. And then the next night and the one after that.

"It's fun," she said to Lainie, as if that explained it all.

The truth was that most of the time when they were together, they talked about Doug and Liz, telling stories and trading information with a sense of urgency, like the faster they could get it all out of their heads, the sooner they'd be back to normal. They talked about them when they were still in bed together, often when they were still naked. Claire wondered what Doug and Liz were doing at that moment, and she thought that it would have been nice if they could have been together, doing the same thing.

They were a good balance; Fran was angrier than she was, and Claire suspected he was a little more heartbroken too. Claire was mostly confused and embarrassed, and Fran was neither of these things, so it seemed to work out well. Claire never minded when Fran talked about Liz, even when she didn't have clothes on. She understood what was happening here, that they were trying to get rid of their memories, trying to figure out new bodies to forget the old ones.

Claire waited to come to her senses, waited for her grown-up self to show up and tell her to cut it out, to tell her that Fran Angelo was not who she should be spending time with. But every time he called, she happily went over there, ran down the steps to the basement as quickly as she could, to get to Fran Angelo and his dryer-sheet–scented room.

CLAIRE HAD BEEN DREADING THIS weekend for a long time. All of her high school friends were getting together, "for a reunion," they kept saying, like they didn't all see each other a few times a year at least.

Their friend Jackie was the one that demanded this reunion happen. "I miss you girls," she kept saying. "Come to my house and I'll send the kids to my mom's and we'll have a GNI."

"A GNI?" Claire asked.

"Girls' Night In," Lainie said.

"It sounds like an STD," Claire said.

They suspected Jackie just wanted to show off her new house, but for some reason they all still agreed to go to Red Bank, New Jersey, for the weekend. Claire, Lainie, and their friend Paula drove from Philly, and their friends Katherine, Clancy, and Erin came from New York.

Paula was recently engaged, and on the drive down there, every time she talked about the wedding, she turned to Claire and said, "Sorry."

"I'm fine," Claire said. "Really, you can talk about your wedding." She was already planning to drink as much wine as she could.

"I can't believe we're going to Jackie's," Claire said. "We could have at least gone somewhere fun. Why did we agree to go there again?"

Lainie just shrugged. They'd all been friends with Jackie in junior high, mostly because they were scared of her. Jackie was the queen of three-way calling, orchestrating one girl to stay silent, while she encouraged another unsuspecting girl to rip the listener to shreds, and then she'd announce the secret guest like she was a talk show host. She was like an evil preteen Oprah.

In seventh grade, Jackie left fake notes in Claire's locker, signed from Luke, the boy in the class that they all loved. It still made Claire's face burn to remember the excitement she felt when she found those notes, how she hoped they were real, as if any seventh-grade boy would ever declare his love for a girl on a piece of notebook paper and stuff it in her locker.

Jackie confronted Claire at a sleepover, announcing to everyone that the notes were fake. "You believed it, though," she said to Claire. "I saw your face and I know you believed it."

"I did not," Claire said. It still remained one of the worst nights of her life, as she found out that every one of her friends had known that Jackie was leaving the notes, including Lainie, who cried later and apologized.

"I wanted to tell you," she said. "But she told me that she'd get me if I did."

To distract Jackie from Luke and the fake notes, Claire suggested that they TP Molly Morrisey's house. "You know," she told Jackie, "she said you were the fifteenth-prettiest girl in our class. The only one lower than you was Lacey. And she said it was because she thought you were fat."

Claire was still ashamed that she'd thrown Molly under the bus like that. But looking back, she realized it was normal to crack under a regime of terror. She was just trying to survive.

In high school, Jackie had gone through a klepto phase. She had piles of bras and underwear in her room with the tags still on them that she'd stolen from Victoria's Secret. "It's so easy," she told them. "You just bring a bunch of stuff to try on in the dressing room, and then you wear it out underneath your clothes."

Sometimes if she grabbed the wrong size or was simply feeling generous, she'd dole the stuff out to the girls. Claire never wanted to take any of it, since it felt like stealing once removed, but Lainie didn't seem to have a problem with it. "What?" she'd always say. "It's not like *we* stole it."

The fact that they'd lived with Jackie as their evil ruler for all of junior high was hard to believe. Harder to believe was that they stayed friends with her throughout high school, where her power was diminished a little bit when it became clear (as Molly Morrisey so accurately pointed out) that she wasn't very pretty; but whatever power she lost, she made up for by always being the one to take beer to parties in her backpack, to be unafraid to talk to boys. She was not to be trusted.

Jackie had married a boy from high school, Mike Albert, who was a roundish guy with glasses and a fuzzy stare. He'd been friends with all the cool kids, even if he was a little on the periphery of the group, and Claire figured that this was very important to Jackie, that she had probably bullied him into dating and then marrying her.

As they pulled into the driveway at Jackie's house, Claire said, "I can't believe we agreed to this."

"Of course you can," Lainie said. She turned off the car

and the three of them sat there for a moment. "Come on, we'll get drunk and it won't be so bad."

"I CAN'T BELIEVE THAT I HAVE two under two," Jackie said. It was probably the twentieth time she'd said it, but who was keeping track? She sounded so pleased with herself that she almost couldn't stay seated.

"I'm so glad we're doing this," Jackie said. "And I'm so glad you guys get to see my house. Don't you love it?"

The girls just nodded and looked around. Clancy was eight months pregnant and was sitting so far back on the couch that it looked like she'd never be able to sit up again. Claire didn't envy her, having to stay sober this weekend. Clancy and her husband had just moved to Long Island. "It's really boring," she answered, when they asked her how it was. "I mean, I know we had to do it. We were running out of space and we would have had to put the baby in a drawer or something, but still. You can't order any takeout past like eight thirty, and it's just really boring."

Erin and her boyfriend, James, had just bought a new place in Brooklyn. She showed them all pictures of the huge new loft, and when she left the room, Jackie leaned forward. "What does James do?" she asked. "I mean, I know it's just an apartment, but still it's really nice." Jackie was easily threatened. "I mean, I'd sooner die than live in Brooklyn. There's a lot of immigrants there, you know. And gangs. It's really dangerous." Claire was almost positive that Jackie had never been to Brooklyn.

Jackie poured them all some more of the deep yellow Chardonnay from the huge bottle, unaware that they were all looking at each other. They'd begun to notice in the past few years that Jackie was definitely racist. At first, they'd thought she was just a little clueless, maybe had some bad timing or judgment with her jokes. But her comments kept getting harsher and way more embarrassing. "Don't be a Jew," she'd say, when someone tried to itemize a restaurant bill.

"Even my grandmother wouldn't say that," Claire whispered.

"Bets would totally say that," Lainie whispered back.

"Okay, fine, but she's like a hundred years old."

They all took large gulps of the wine, which was tangy and bordered on unpleasant, but thankfully seemed to go down easier the more you drank. When Jackie went into the kitchen to get another bottle, Katherine picked up the empty one and said, "I think my great-aunt Janice drinks this. And she's, like, the world's cheapest person."

The weekend went slowly. The next day, as they walked around the neighborhood and down a bike path, Jackie made an announcement. "We've decided to teach Emma to sign," she said, like they'd all been waiting for this news about her daughter. "We've all read the reports about its possibly delaying language. But Mike and I just really believe that it's positive, you know. We really think it will help her."

No one said anything, but Jackie didn't seem to notice. She was so sure that everyone was dying to know the details of her life that it probably never occurred to her that she could possibly be boring them.

Later that night, they ordered pizza and drank more wine. Erin suggested going out for dinner, but that idea was quickly shot down by Jackie. "It's so cozy in the house," she'd said. "Let's just stay here."

They drank more wine that night than they had the night before. Katherine told them all how she had broken up with her latest boyfriend, Jed, a computer programmer of some sort that looked like he really wanted to be a hipster, but was just a little off.

"What happened?" Claire asked.

Katherine shrugged. "I read his e-mails and found out that he'd been posting online ads for meeting men," she said. Lainie choked on her wine and started coughing. Erin leaned over and patted her on the back. "It happens sometimes, you know?"

Jackie nodded knowingly. "That's why you should always read your boyfriend's e-mails," she said.

"Seriously?" Clancy asked. "That's seriously what you just took from that story?"

Katherine sighed and drank her wine. She'd cut her hair short and dyed it blond. She looked tired, like she'd given up fighting. Even when she'd climbed out of Clancy's car the day before, it had seemed like she didn't want to be there but didn't have the energy to resist.

"So," Jackie said, turning to Claire. "I heard you and Fran Angelo have a little thing going on."

Claire turned to Lainie, who shook her head just a little, meaning that she hadn't said anything. "Who told you that?" Claire asked.

"I have my sources," Jackie said.

"It's nothing," Claire said. "Really."

Jackie let it drop, and Claire was relieved. But on the ride home, she was angry. "What are we doing still hanging out with her?" she'd yelled at Lainie and Paula in the car. "She's disgusting. I'm done. I'm serious, I'm ashamed of myself that I even spent this much time with her. What does that say about us? What is wrong with us?"

Paula and Lainie had muttered in agreement, which made Claire even angrier. She was silent the rest of the way home, arms crossed, hating herself for not cutting off all contact with Jackie when they were twelve. What was wrong with her? Why was she still putting herself in situations where she was around this person? Jackie was nothing but bad energy. She was pure evil. And how on earth had she ended up married and living in a house with two kids? How had she tricked people into not seeing that she was horrible?

It seemed to Claire that Jackie was a symbol for everything that had ever gone wrong in her life since junior high. She couldn't stand up for herself then and it had probably just spiraled from there.

FRAN WAS SITTING ON THE COUCH in the basement playing video games when Claire walked in. "How was your weekend?" he asked. He didn't look away from the TV, or pause the game.

"It was fine," she said. "Sort of boring. We just stayed at Jackie's house mostly."

"Oh yeah? Did you see Mike?"

"No. Jackie made him leave for the weekend."

"Jackie was always sort of a beast," he said. "I don't know what he was thinking." Claire felt better.

At least sitting in the basement with Fran, she didn't feel like the messed-up one. Even around Katherine and her boyfriend that dabbled in men, Claire felt like she was the one that was a disaster. It was only here, on the red-plaid couch, that she felt like things weren't totally falling apart. She sat and watched Fran play his game.

"Remember what video games looked like when we were little?" Claire asked. "The people were basically just little geometric shapes. You could barely see them. These look like real people."

"I know," Fran said. "It's awesome." He stood up and put his arms straight up in the air when the game was over, and Claire assumed that meant he'd won. "Want to watch a movie?" he asked her.

"Sure." Claire sat with her arm resting against the back of the couch, her feet right at Fran's thigh. She let him pick the movie. It was some story about gangsters or a fighter or something. It was mindless. She watched it without talking, just nodding whenever Fran said something.

"You okay?" he asked.

"Yeah, I'm fine."

Fran picked up her foot in his hand and held it on his lap. He started running his fingers over her toes, pausing to hold each one for a second, before moving on to the next one.

"What are you doing?" Claire asked.

"I'm looking for the one that ate roast beef," he said. He held on to her middle toe and squeezed it. "He's my favorite."

Claire leaned her head back and laughed, a big loud laugh that surprised her. She held her stomach and laughed until it hurt. Her whole body shook, and she laughed harder than she had in as long as she could remember.

"There we go," Fran said. He patted her leg. "There we go."

CHAPTER 10

Cleo never even went to the bathroom when Max was in the apartment. That was her first thought when the nurse told her. Of course, if she just had to pee that was one thing. But to really "do her business," as her mother would say, she waited until he left and then she'd run in there. A couple of times, when she really couldn't hold it, she'd pretend to take a shower, letting the hot water run (which she knew was wasteful), and just pray that he couldn't hear or smell anything on the other side of the door.

She wanted to say this to the nurse, but she couldn't quite get the words together. Instead, she said, "I'm sorry, that can't be right."

The nurse nodded and said, "I'm afraid it is."

"I don't understand," Cleo kept saying. "I don't understand."

The nurse was sympathetic, but firm and removed, which was annoying as all hell. Cleo wanted her to be just as shocked as she was. She wanted her to say, "I can't believe it either!" But she just stood there calmly. She probably thought Cleo didn't understand how the body worked, that it was possible she was one of those girls who would give birth in a bathroom, leave her baby in a garbage can, and then head back to the prom. This could not be happening.

"This is a mistake," Cleo said.

"There is no mistake," the nurse said. "You're pregnant."

"But I'm on the pill." It sounded like she was making excuses, even to herself, but it was the truth. She was on the pill. This wasn't right.

"It can happen." The nurse shrugged her shoulders, like, *What can you do about it? Isn't life a bitch sometimes?* Cleo wanted to punch her in the jaw, give her a side hook, like a boxer.

"Yes, it can happen. But it doesn't happen often, does it? There is a very minimal margin of error in these things." Cleo thought to herself that she sounded just like Elizabeth. And then she thought, *Elizabeth. Oh, fuck.*

The nurse was giving her pamphlets, asking her when the date of her last period was, looking unsurprised when Cleo said, "Ummm, let's see."

"It looks like you're about five weeks," the nurse finally said.

"Five weeks?"

She wanted to ask the nurse how many pregnant students she'd seen in her time here. Cleo would feel better if there were lots of them. She always felt better when she was part of a group.

Cleo could have stayed there all day, going round and round with the nurse about how this really wasn't possible, but the nurse told her she had another patient and told Cleo she should make an appointment with an ob-gyn to get more information. Then she'd herded Cleo out the door, nudging and guiding her like she was some sort of sheepdog.

When she went to health services, she really hadn't thought she was pregnant. Maybe it crossed her mind, the same way that cancer does—it's a possibility, sure, but really, not very likely. Cleo had been feeling nauseous and tired, but she thought it was the flu or maybe a parasite or something.

It had never occurred to her to take a pregnancy test at home. She'd never ever taken one. Cleo had slept with her high school boyfriend senior year, mostly because she thought she should before she went to college. He was a lacrosse player with nice hair. She'd never really had any sort of pregnancy scare—she was careful!—but there were a few times she was a day late, and she'd panic.

Her friend Violet took pregnancy tests like they were going out of style, sometimes just to reassure herself, sometimes because she was bored, sometimes because she thought it seemed adult. Cleo thought maybe she bought them in bulk.

If Cleo ever breathed a word that maybe she was worried, Violet would offer her a test and encourage her to take it. "Don't you just want to know?" she'd always ask. Cleo always refused. To take a test would be too final—you might get the answer you were dreading. If you didn't take it, there was always the hope that things were still okay. And so Cleo preferred to lie in her bed at night and pray and imagine that she would get her period the next day. It had always worked.

AFTER SHE LEFT HEALTH SERVICES, Cleo walked for a while. She left the campus, because she couldn't look at all of the students, just walking around with their stupid backpacks, thinking that they had real problems because they had a paper due or a test to take, when really none of it mattered at all.

She walked into town, and then around the neighborhoods, winding in and around streets, hoping to get lost. Just then, she missed Monica so much that it was a little bit like a stabbing pain in her stomach. She wanted so badly to find her, to be able to tell her what had happened, to cry hysterically on her bed, while Monica rubbed her back and said, "What are we going to do?"

And the strangest thing about it was that she missed Monica so much in that moment that it seemed to override everything else. Cleo didn't want to tell Max. It was embarrassing or shameful or something. What if he got mad or broke up with her or thought she'd done it on purpose? Even if he wasn't that kind of person, you had no idea how someone was going to act when he was in a situation like this.

Cleo ached to be able to tell Monica, but she knew she couldn't. The day she packed up her stuff, she knocked on Monica's bedroom door. "I'm sorry about this," she said. "I don't want things to be weird between us." This of course didn't mean much, since things had been weird between them for a while now.

Monica had shrugged. "It's pretty shitty, but I guess I understand."

She'd felt awful then, leaving her best friend who wasn't well. What kind of a person was she? To give up on a friend when she hit a rough patch. Well, she was paying for it now. She had no one. No friend to talk to, no safe place to go. And so she walked up and down the streets, hoping that maybe she'd wake up and it would be one of those dreams that you talked about for days, saying, "It was so real, you wouldn't believe it."

CLEO WENT BACK TO THE APARTMENT, and took a cigarette out of the pack that Max had left on the table. Max was a drunk-smoker, as he put it, buying packs when he was out at night, and then letting them sit untouched until the next time he was out drinking. Cleo had never really liked smoking all that much. Usually, if she got drunk enough to smoke a couple of cigarettes, she threw up the next morning.

She opened the window and leaned over the back of the

couch. The lighter was running out of fluid and she had to click it a few times before she finally got it to light the cigarette. She inhaled and coughed, then inhaled again.

Of course, she wasn't supposed to smoke. But she wasn't supposed to drink either and she reasoned that drinking was worse. Maybe the cigarette would jostle the pregnancy, cause a miscarriage. She could smoke this baby out. But that was stupid. If that was the case, anyone would just smoke a cigarette when they were pregnant and no one would ever have to get an abortion.

Was that what she was going to do? She couldn't imagine it. But imagining a baby, a creature that was going to grow inside of her and then come out of her, was even harder. She was so screwed.

When Cleo got nervous, she balled up her hands into fists and played piano exercises from memory. It probably made her look strange, if anyone noticed the way her fingers pulsed, how her mouth sometimes counted. She explained it to Max once, and he'd said it was something you'd think an autistic kid would do.

She wanted him to come home and didn't want him to come home at the same time. Once it was over with, it would be done. She could tell him and she wouldn't have to worry about that part anymore. It would just be all the shit that came after it.

When he finally came in the door, she'd stopped crying but her face was still red, and she knew she looked strange sitting there, her legs underneath her, a blanket wrapped around her.

"What?" Max said. "What happened?"

It occurred to her later that he probably thought someone had died. And then after she told him, just blurted it right out, he probably wished that it had been that—because if someone had died, it would be sad, sure, but not unthinkable. They would know what to do and how to deal with it. There would be things they had to do, actions they had to take. But with this, they were left on their own.

Sometimes when Cleo was in a moment that she knew was an important one, she could step back from it like she was watching it, like she wasn't part of it, like she was just an observer. And she knew she was going to remember for the rest of her life how Max responded when she said, "I'm pregnant," simply and without any lead-in. Because he'd remained standing and put both hands on either side of his head so that he looked the way people on TV look when they're witnessing a tragedy or an accident, like someone jumping from a building. And then he looked straight at her, waiting for her to take it back or say she was kidding, but she remained silent.

"Oh fuck," he said. And then again. "Oh fuck."

THEY DIDN'T SLEEP THAT NIGHT. They tried; when they were exhausted with talking and Cleo was drained from crying, they lay on the bed facing each other with their eyes closed. But neither of them slept, and soon they'd just start talking again.

"What are we going to do?" Max said. It was just what she'd wanted to hear Monica say. But it didn't sound comforting coming out of his mouth.

"I don't know," Cleo said. "I really don't know."

"Do you think you want to keep it? Or do you think you don't?"

He couldn't even say the word, which was driving her crazy. All night, he'd talked around it. It wasn't his fault, she tried to tell herself. It was a hard word to say, but if they were going to talk about it, they were going to have to say it.

"I don't know if I can have an abortion," she said.

"Okay."

"But I don't know if I can have the baby."

"Okay."

Cleo started crying again, quietly. Tears just rolled out of her eyes and she had no idea how she still had any left inside of her. She was surely dehydrating herself. She hadn't cried this much in her whole life. Never.

"I'll do whatever you want," Max said. He put his hand on the side of her head. "Whatever we do will be okay."

Cleo moved away from him and sat up to blow her nose. He sat up too, put his hand on her back. She knew that he was trying to make her feel better, trying to touch her so that she would know he was there, but it was suffocating. She blew her nose and added the Kleenex to the pile that was on the nightstand.

"I can't imagine doing either," she said. "But if I had to pick one that I really couldn't do, it would be having an abortion. I can't. I know I just can't."

"I know," Max said.

"And I don't want to even think about giving the baby away. I don't want to do that. I mean, we're young but we're not, like, thirteen. People our age have babies all the time."

"So that's the decision, then," Max said. He reached over and put his arms around her shoulders, pulling her down until she was lying in his lap. She was so uncomfortable, she wanted to scream. It felt like Max was trying to act like a straitjacket. But she knew if she moved then, he'd be hurt, and so she willed herself to stay still.

"We shouldn't tell anyone," Cleo said. "Not now. Not for a

while. Anything could happen. I could have a miscarriage. It happens all the time." She tried not to hope for this, but she couldn't help it. It was one thing to decide to have the baby, but if nature intervened, well, then, who was she to stop it?

"How long should we wait?" Max said.

"I don't know," Cleo said. *Forever,* she thought.

They decided they would wait until Thanksgiving to tell their families. It was three weeks away. If she was still pregnant by then, they'd suck it up and tell them.

"They're going to kill us," Max said. He sounded so young then, like a seven-year-old in trouble, and even though it was the exact same thing Cleo had been thinking, she found she was annoyed.

THEY WENT THROUGH THEIR DAYS, going to class and watching TV. Cleo studied for midterms harder than ever, trying anything she could to keep from thinking about being pregnant. She stayed in the library for hours, eating only bananas and drinking water. There was one cubicle she liked, on the fourth floor near the back. It was right by a window, and she could watch people below as they scurried around the campus, sometimes laughing with a friend, sometimes staring down at the ground with a serious look.

Cleo got more done at this cubicle than anywhere else. She began to think of it as only hers, and a couple of times when she arrived at the library to find it taken, she sat nearby, keeping her eye on it until the person there decided to leave. Once, when someone left an empty Coke can there, like it was his own personal garbage can, she'd followed him out.

"You forgot this," she said, and handed it to the boy.

"Oh, I'm done with that," he said.

"You're not supposed to have food or drink in here," she

told him. He'd just shrugged. She felt like someone had come into her home and littered.

TWO WEEKS LATER, CLEO FELT LIKE she was losing her mind. She was still pregnant, there was no doubt about it. And even though almost every night she or Max would say, "Let's not talk about it tonight," they couldn't help it. They always came back to it. Even if they were just watching TV or a movie, there was always a baby somewhere on the screen, and one of them would look at the other, or Max would lean over and rub her leg, and just like that they were in the middle of it again. There was no escaping it.

Cleo managed to avoid talking to Elizabeth much on the phone. She was afraid if they talked too long, Elizabeth would hear it in her voice. It was a lot like after she had sex for the first time and was afraid to look Elizabeth in the eye, like she'd be able to tell right away. Cleo kept her phone calls short, told her that she was really busy with schoolwork, that she was spending every minute studying.

"I'm glad you're focused," Elizabeth said. "Senior year is important."

Max stayed in the apartment with her every night. She wondered what his friends must think. Maybe that they were fighting, that they'd break up soon. Or maybe that she was making him stay home, controlling every part of him. If she thought about it too long, her head hurt.

One afternoon, Max was at class and Cleo was walking around the apartment. She felt jittery, like she'd been drinking Red Bull. And before she could think about it, she pulled out her phone and called Monica.

Monica answered on the first ring. She probably thought something was wrong, since even when she and Cleo were a pair, they mostly just texted. They preferred talking in person.

"Hey," Cleo said. She suddenly felt nervous. "I was just thinking about you and thought I'd call."

"Oh, hi," Monica said.

"I was—do you want to get lunch? I haven't seen you in forever."

"Sure," Monica said.

They met in the cafeteria. Monica looked thin, but she got a salad and she seemed a little less angry. The frown line between her eyes was gone.

A new girl that had transferred, Trish, had moved into Cleo's old room and Monica said she was nice. "She's clean—like almost OCD—so, you know, Mary and Laura like her."

"That's great," Cleo said. She felt weirdly jealous, like she was being cheated on.

"So, how's Max?"

"He's good. He's really good."

Monica poked at her salad. "I can't believe you guys are living together. It's so grown-up."

"Yeah, I guess so." Cleo knew she'd never tell Monica now.

Monica told her that she was almost definitely going back to Boston at the end of the year. "My parents want me close by."

"That seems like a good idea."

"Yeah, I guess. They want me to live at home for at least a year, which seems unnecessary, but whatever."

Then Monica went on to tell her about a party they'd had at the house. "We got all these boxes of wine, and had people dress up like it was fancy, and Laura made Jell-O shots, which I've never had."

"Really?" Cleo asked.

"Yeah, it was so funny." Monica stopped poking at her lettuce and put her fork down. "Oh shit, we should have told you about it. I don't know why we spaced on it."

"That's okay," Cleo said. She wouldn't have gone anyway. She couldn't have stood to be sober at a party where Laura and Mary were fun and took Jell-O shots.

"I feel so bad," Monica said.

"Really, it's fine. Laura and Mary probably wouldn't have let me in anyway, unless I spun the chore wheel and cleaned the bathroom or something."

"Oh, them." Monica waved her fork. "I think they're over it."

"Really?"

"Yeah, you know how they are. They get all bent out of shape, but then they get over it. You should have seen them with this party. They really went all out."

Cleo picked up her drink and took a long sip of her Diet Coke through the straw, even though it was hard to swallow. Monica and her old roommates were getting along just fine without her. Better, really. They were having parties and Jell-O shots. How did she get here? How did she end up pregnant and friendless, about to graduate from college with nothing to show for it?

Monica was watching her, like she knew she was upset but didn't know what to say. Cleo pulled the straw out of her mouth and set her drink down.

"That's crazy," she finally said. "I can't imagine it."

IT STARTED TO MAKE SENSE to her now, how people that undergo terrible loss or tragedy manage to keep living. She'd never really understood it before, but the thing was that the body will shock you, so that maybe you don't believe it all at once. And then, if you keep moving, a day goes by, and then another. And since the worst thing you ever imagined actually came true, that becomes your reality, something else takes the place in your mind, and you continue on.

Once. One day she had forgotten to take her pill. And she'd taken it the very next day, just like she was supposed to. Just like they said to. In what world did that make a baby? In what world? Cleo never really did much wrong. She'd always been a rule follower. She always went to class, always did her assignments, did her reading, handed in her papers on time. The worst thing she'd ever done was get drunk in high school. And who didn't do that? She'd forgotten to do the right thing for one day and that was it. Life was shit sometimes, it really was.

THANKSGIVING WAS GETTING CLOSER. Every time Cleo saw a paper turkey anywhere, she felt like she might throw up. She thought often about the presidential pardon of the turkey. It was a weird tradition and when she was younger it upset her. It still did, if she was being honest. Why on earth would everyone gather to watch one bird be spared when there were millions of others being eaten for dinner? Were you supposed to feel really happy for that one turkey that made it when the rest of his family was getting their heads chopped off? It didn't make any sense. It was cruel, really, and it made her stomach turn. It was enough to make anyone a vegetarian, and she found that she couldn't stomach the thought of it. During those weeks before Thanksgiving, she stopped eating meat altogether.

WALKING AROUND CAMPUS, Cleo just watched everyone and thought, *I fucked up more than you, and more than you, and more than you.* It was like nothing she'd done up to this point mattered anymore. Everyone else was free and she had a human growing inside of her.

Every day, Cleo thought about what it would be like after they told everyone. Max's family would hate her for sure. And Elizabeth was going to be so mad, she couldn't even imagine. She'd always talked about birth control, always made sure that Cleo knew what she needed to know. It was like she was telling her, *You were a mistake and believe me, you want to make sure you don't do what I did.*

Maybe they were some sort of hyper-fertile family. It was possible. She could tell Elizabeth that it wasn't her fault, it was biology. That would go over well.

Cleo hated when people were mad at her. She couldn't stand to disappoint anyone. The thought of Elizabeth and Max's family being so thoroughly disappointed in her made it hard to breathe.

Elizabeth used to always tell her she needed a thicker skin. "Not everyone is going to like what you do all the time," she'd say. "Sometimes you have to say, screw you, and do it anyway."

Senior year in high school, Cleo had decided not to play soccer. It had gotten to be too much, and she liked her other activities better, so it only made sense. She was sleepless for weeks, knowing that she'd have to tell the team, knowing that the girls and the coach were going to be disappointed in her. She hated disappointing people.

"Oh, for Christ's sake, Cleo," Elizabeth had said. "This is your life. You're the one that has to live with the decision you make, not anyone else. Just remember that. What you do in life is yours and it doesn't matter what other people want from you."

It was sort of funny, actually, that for the first time in her life, Cleo was going to take Elizabeth's advice, that for once she was going to do something that was going to make everyone around her angry as all hell. She repeated Elizabeth's words to herself every night. *What you do in life is yours.*

Cleo thought that maybe when she told Elizabeth, she could point out how ironic it all was, how she was finally doing just what Elizabeth suggested. "That's the thing about giving advice," she could say. "It might come back to haunt you."

CHAPTER 11

Martha's new job smelled like death. Or actually, it smelled like dying, which was worse. Death was at least clinical and final. Dying lingered. It was urine-stained couch cushions and shirts with drool on them. It was labored breathing and fake cheery voices that tried to distract the patient from the fact that this was it—his life was coming to a close.

Her first day, Martha showed up to find Jaz scrubbing the wood floor in the den with Pine-Sol. "Just a little accident," she said. Her voice was pleasant and no-nonsense, the kind of voice you would use when dealing with a child, to let them know that accidents happen, but they're nobody's fault, and it's nothing to be embarrassed about.

Mr. Cranston sat in his chair and stared straight ahead, not acknowledging Martha or Jaz's comment. Martha, unsure of what to do, stood in the corner and folded her arms across her stomach. "Accidents happen every day," she'd said. Then she wanted to die, because Mr. Cranston gave her an accusing look that meant he thought that either she was a moron or she was against him.

"Mr. Cranston loves to read his papers first thing," Jaz said. She wrung out her rag into the bucket. "Why don't you go grab those for him—they're by the front door—and go ahead and put them in the sitting room? When we're done here, I'll show you how to get breakfast ready."

Martha nodded and almost ran from the room to the front of the house, where she picked up the *Wall Street Journal*, the *New York Times*, and the *Philadelphia Inquirer*. She was so grateful to get out of that room, that she almost hit her head when she opened the door.

When they met in the kitchen, Jaz told her not to get overwhelmed. "I'm going to be here with you for a couple of weeks until you get it down. Any questions you have, you just ask. I'm not going anywhere, so there's no reason to get nervous, okay?"

Martha nodded and swallowed. Ever since her stupid comment about accidents happening every day, she felt like she might start crying. But Jaz was kind. And for that, she was very grateful.

"Okay, now. First thing you'll do when you get here in the morning is make breakfast. It's the only meal you'll have to make, but he's pretty particular about it. He has the same thing every day—two soft-boiled eggs and a piece of whole wheat toast. He used to have bacon too, but that ended about five years ago, when his cholesterol went through the roof. Every once in a while he can still have it, but don't let him fool you into thinking that he gets it every day, okay?"

Martha nodded again. She was trying to remember everything that Jaz told her, and then, without a word, Jaz handed her a black leather-bound notebook and pen. The breakfast was just the beginning of the instructions. Lunch and dinner were prepared by a cook who came in a few times a week, and stored the meals.

Jaz opened the big shiny refrigerator to reveal shelves full of delicious-looking meals, stored in clean, labeled Tupperware containers. It was the kind of refrigerator that Martha would love to have, full of meals that made her hungry just to read the labels—cold salmon and homemade mayonnaise, mini beef tenderloin sliders with horseradish sauce, fresh arugula with shaves of Parmesan, and little lamb chops, tiny and perfect.

"Don't worry about getting the food ready," Jaz said. "The cook writes everything down on this pad over here, and you just follow her instructions. It's easy. Also, there's always plenty, so help yourself to whatever you want."

Martha wanted to stand and stare at the shelves all day. They were so neat and orderly. Imagine having this be your refrigerator! You'd never find an old peach or a soft sweet potato in there, never find a block of moldy cheese and have to wonder when you bought it. Martha was still staring as Jaz shut the door.

The instructions continued. Mr. Cranston could go to the bathroom by himself, but he sometimes needed help walking there, or getting up from his chair. He did not want or need help once he got there. "For now," Jaz said.

He read all three papers every morning. He did not like to watch TV, except for the seven o'clock news, and sometimes *Jeopardy* if he was in the mood. If he was extremely tired, you could sometimes persuade him to watch a show; just suggest it like it was something you'd heard about and thought he would like. Nothing popular. No sitcoms. He did not like to watch shows where groups of adults lived together in the city and whined and acted like children. Stick to things like BBC miniseries, as long as there wasn't too much melodrama.

He was an avid reader and would (at least twice a month) make a list of new books that he wanted. The local bookstore could be called—they had his account information—

and they would drop off the books the next day. He had a computer, although he didn't use it all that often. He did not e-mail. He did sometimes ask to dictate a letter, to an old friend or work acquaintance, which he would want typed up so that he could sign it. "He had a secretary for years," Jaz explained. "It's just something he's used to."

Mr. Cranston enjoyed crosswords sometimes, and did not like to be interrupted while he worked on them. He did not like to go outside, but Jaz insisted that he get out at least once a day, to go for a walk in his wheelchair. It made him feel like a baby, to be pushed around the block, but Jaz was firm. He needed fresh air and he knew it. If you were firm with him, he would be okay. Just a quick walk, maybe fifteen or twenty minutes, down the street and maybe over by the park, but not *in* the park, because there were almost always children there, and they were so noisy, and he didn't like to see the way that children were raised these days, like wild animals let loose. Why did they always have snacks with them, their grubby hands full of yogurts and drinks and crackers, like they were going to starve before they got home? "Just trust me," Jaz said. "Stay out of the park."

Ruby came over a couple of times a week, whenever she felt like it, really. She usually brought some sort of gift, a book, or a pint of frozen soup that she picked up. "She tries to help, bless her," Jaz said. But Ruby was often in the way. She insisted that he go on an outing with her, to the store, or maybe to a restaurant for an early dinner.

"Even when he was healthy as a horse, Mr. Cranston never shopped. Never. And he never liked eating out," Jaz said. "That man would rather eat a peanut butter sandwich than sit in a restaurant."

His son, Billy, usually came only on the weekends, so Martha would probably never see him, but when he did come he just liked to sit with his father and wasn't a bother.

Martha wrote everything down. It was a lot of information, but she felt like she could get a handle on it if she could just write it down. The nurses came at night, and as soon as she let them in at six o'clock, she was free to go.

"Don't take it personal if he gets crabby," Jaz told her. "He's an old man and he's used to having things his way. And now his body's failing him and that's hard for him to handle."

"Okay," Martha said. "That's so sad."

"It's sad, sure. But it's just life. We're here, we live, and we die. Not much you can do about it, so we might as well enjoy it while we can. No use worrying about that."

Martha couldn't believe that Jaz really thought this. Who in their right mind wasn't afraid of dying? She was probably just putting on a brave face so that Martha would feel better about the whole thing. She must be.

Jaz moved around the house with so much purpose. Martha watched as she informed Mr. Cranston that it was time for lunch, suggested that he'd like to take a rest, announced that it was time for a walk. Martha walked behind her, afraid of what Mr. Cranston was going to say, her feet following Jaz's, stepping right where she had stepped, hoping that this would give her some sort of strength.

When she got home at night, she was so tired she could barely move. The first week, she was in bed by nine each night. She resolved every night as she went to bed that the next day she would act just like Jaz. She would be firm and purposeful. But each morning she woke up and she was still herself—nervous and unsure, following behind Jaz, afraid of upsetting Mr. Cranston.

. . .

"IT'S SAD," MARTHA TOLD HER FAMILY at dinner. "It's like everyone is just waiting for him to die, including him! Like they're just killing time. Literally."

"Well, what did you expect?" Claire asked. "You knew you were going to be a caretaker for an elderly person. It's not like there's a lot of different endings to that story."

"I know, I was just saying that it's hard. That's all."

If Martha was being honest, she missed J.Crew. She missed bossing people around the ribboned shirts and sparkly scarves. She missed her work smelling like new clothes. It had been so clean at the store. There'd been an order to the polos, a calmness to the khakis.

Every night, Weezy asked her how her day had gone as soon as she walked in the door. She asked it nervously, like she was waiting for bad news.

"I think people are waiting for me to fail," Martha told Dr. Baer.

"Are you waiting for yourself to fail?" Dr. Baer asked. "Do you think you want to fail?"

"No, I don't want to fail," Martha said. "Of course I don't want to fail." Sometimes Dr. Baer was an idiot.

Martha found herself losing patience during her sessions. *I'm a patient losing patience,* she often thought when this happened. Dr. Baer didn't seem all that impressed that she had a new job, that she was practically back to nursing.

"Well, I don't think that people are waiting for you to fail," Dr. Baer said. "I think you have a good support system around you, and when people ask you how things are going, they're really asking just that and nothing more."

"I guess so."

"So, how do you feel at the end of the day with Mr. Cranston?"

"Good, I guess." The truth was that sometimes it was very, very boring. Martha sat still and watched the clock during the days, just waiting for the next activity.

"That's great," Dr. Baer said. "It sounds like this job was the right move for you then, something to challenge you a little more."

"Retail is very challenging," Martha said. She tried not to sound too offended. "People don't understand that, but it's not easy. You don't just show up and sell things. Plus, I was a manager, which entailed a lot of responsibility. So actually, I don't think that this job is more challenging in that sense. Not at all."

"That's a good point," Dr. Baer said. "I guess what I meant was that it's different and new. And new things are always challenging, especially when you've gotten comfortable somewhere."

"Right, I guess that's true. New jobs are hard," Martha said. "Actually my sister just got a new job too."

"Really?"

"Yeah, she's temping for an agency, and they already placed her somewhere for a few months."

"You sound impressed."

"With Claire? No. I mean, not that I'm not impressed, but I'm not surprised, I guess."

"No?"

"No. She wanted a job and so she got one."

"That's all there was to it?"

"Pretty much. Things come pretty easily for her."

"Really?"

"Yeah, I've told you that before."

"You have," Dr. Baer said. "I just find it interesting that you're still so sure of that. She's had a tough year, hasn't she?"

"Yeah, but still. It's not like things have happened to her . . . She's made the decisions. She ended her engagement, she quit her job, she moved back home. I mean, it's a lot of changes, but it's all stuff she wanted to do."

"But haven't you made your decisions too?"

"Well, yeah, but it's different."

"Different how?"

"Claire has more choices?"

"How so?"

"She just does, she always has."

"Okay."

"It's true."

"I didn't say it wasn't true. I just think you can't be so quick to be so sure of other people's situations. Examine your own situation. You also have a lot of choices. It's not always easier for other people. It doesn't work like that."

"Sure it does. A lot of times it does work like that."

"Well, sometimes, I'll admit it might seem that way. But things aren't always what they seem."

After that session, Martha thought about her choices. She thought that maybe she should have been a therapist, so that she could say things like, "Your life isn't so hard," and "I see," over and over again. Now that seemed like an easy life.

NOW THAT CLAIRE WAS TEMPING and she was at the Cranstons', they were getting up and getting ready at the same time each morning, which they hadn't done since high school. Sometimes Martha knocked on the bathroom door, pretending to be in a hurry, so that Claire would let her in and they could brush their teeth together, put on makeup side by side.

· · ·

MARTHA LOVED WHEN RUBY CAME to the Cranston house. She was the prettiest person Martha had ever seen in real life— she always looked a little bit tan, her hair was always shiny. Once, when Martha commented on how glamorous Ruby was, Jaz said, "She should be. She works at it like it's a job."

Sometimes, Ruby would sit in the kitchen with Martha and have some tea. Martha always made it, but she didn't mind. Ruby sort of seemed like a little kid that needed things done for her. The first day that she came, she kept staring at the teapot and saying, "I'd love some tea," like it was a puzzle she couldn't figure out. Finally, Martha got up to make the tea, and Ruby smiled at her like she was relieved.

Now Martha offered as soon as Ruby walked into the kitchen, setting out cookies and starting the water boiling. Then, Martha would sit and wait for Ruby to start talking— Ruby loved to talk—hoping that she was going to spill some family secrets.

"We're not speaking," Ruby said one day. "My brother and me, I mean. We're on upsetting terms." Ruby had a strange way of talking, of putting words together, almost like English wasn't her first language, or like she wanted people to think that. She dotted her sentences with random phrases, arranged verbs and nouns in odd places, throwing them wherever she pleased.

"Oh really?" Martha asked. She didn't want to sound too eager, but she was dying to know about Billy.

Ruby sighed. "He's impossible, if you must know, my brother. He thinks of himself as the most important person in the world. Or rather, he thinks he's more important than he is, in truth." Ruby paused to think this over. "I don't know which one it is, or if there's even a difference. I'm just telling this to you, so that you understand why we won't be in the house at the same time. This is why the schedule exists."

"Of course," Martha said. "I mean, I understand. Has this been going on for a long time?"

"Forever, it seems like. But in actual time, only a few years. Since my mom died, really. Billy thinks he's in charge of everything."

"Families are tricky," Martha said.

"Isn't that the truest thing," Ruby said, and Martha felt like the cleverest person in the world.

MARTHA LOVED SENDING HER COUSIN CATHY long e-mails about her job and the Cranstons. She told her about Jaz and Ruby, and talked about how degrading it must be for Mr. Cranston to basically need a babysitter at this point in his life. Cathy loved hearing about her work, always responded by telling her how funny and insightful she was, sometimes suggesting that Martha should be a writer, which always thrilled Martha.

Martha and Cathy had always gotten along well, mostly because they found each other entertaining. Martha always said how lucky she was that her best friend was her cousin too. And the fact that she was a lesbian was just an added bonus. Martha thought it made her sound very cool and accepting when she said things like, "I'm going to visit my cousin Cathy and her partner, Ruth. She's great, Ruth is. They've been together for a while now, my cousin and her partner."

She used to talk about Cathy all the time at J.Crew, partly because she wanted Wally to know that she was not only accepting of his lifestyle, but that she too had gay friends and family. She made references to Cathy a lot, until one day

Wally said, "You don't have to call her *Cathy my cousin who's a lesbian* every time you talk about her. We get it, sweetie. You're related to a dyke."

Martha wanted to tell him that she didn't like that term, that she found it offensive, but she wasn't sure she was allowed to, since Wally was gay himself. She just cut back on her talk about Cathy at work.

Cathy had come out via e-mail to the family during her freshman year in college. Martha had read the note, and then called home immediately, knowing that Weezy wouldn't have checked her e-mail yet. She was excited to be the one to break the news, basically yelled it out as soon as Weezy answered the phone.

"Oh," Weezy had said. "Well, honey, you aren't surprised, are you?"

Martha actually was surprised, but not because she couldn't imagine that Cathy was a lesbian—she actually could, now that she thought about it. But she just hadn't thought about it one way or the other before. Cathy was just her cousin, who was sometimes bossy and always knew the most scandalous information growing up, like what French kissing really entailed, and what the definition of third base was.

"No," Martha had said. "I guess I'm not surprised." She was, however, sad that she wasn't able to shock Weezy with this information. Martha loved a good piece of gossip and this one was a doozy.

Cathy was very excited about Martha's new job, and even more excited at the idea that Martha might get a place of her own. Martha had mentioned this idea briefly one time, and now Cathy wouldn't let it drop.

"Things are cheaper in Ohio," she reminded Cathy one night on the phone. "I can't afford a place just yet."

"Martha, you're thirty. You can't afford not to afford your own place."

AFTER TWO WEEKS, JAZ STARTED leaving Martha alone with Mr. Cranston. First, she just ran little errands, but with each day she left for longer stretches of time. "I need to run to the store," she'd say. Martha knew that she was being tested during this time, to see if she could handle it and also to see if Mr. Cranston was okay with her being there.

"I get the feeling that if he doesn't like me, they'll just fire me," Martha told her family one night.

"Of course he'll like you," Weezy said. And Will had nodded in agreement, and that was that.

Most of her time with Mr. Cranston was quiet, sometimes just sitting together and reading. Martha learned to bring a book with her, so that if Mr. Cranston wanted to read all afternoon, she could do the same. At first, she would walk around the house, trying to find something to do, refolding blankets and hanging them over the edge of the couch, or getting Mr. Cranston a fresh glass of water.

Eventually, Jaz told her to settle down. "There are people that come to this house to do all of these jobs. All your job is, all you have to worry about, is keeping him company and making sure he gets what he needs. Most of the time it's not too hard, right? So just settle down and enjoy the quiet time."

Martha had nodded, although her feelings had been a little hurt. She was a doer. She couldn't help it. That's why she'd been so great at J.Crew. She loved moving around and keeping busy, making things look pretty.

But after a few days, Martha realized that Jaz had been trying to help her. She could see that it annoyed Mr. Cranston when she moved around too much, that it disturbed his reading when she walked in and out of the room. He didn't like to call for help, would never shout to the next room that he needed something. He liked someone to be right there, so that he could just turn his head and Martha could say, "Did you need to go to the restroom?" or "Are you thirsty?"

Jaz was agitated lately, on the phone with her family often, and she confided in Martha that she didn't like the "no-good" man that her daughter was dating.

"If she marries him, so help me God, I will kidnap her and leave the country."

"Is he abusive?" Martha asked. She was imagining Jaz and her daughter running for their lives.

"Is he what? No, child. He's just a lazy shit."

"Oh."

"Mark my words, if they end up getting married, my Marly will work herself to the bone, while he lays around the house smoking dope in his skivvies and watching talk shows."

"Did you tell her that you don't like him?"

"Did I tell her? I tell her every day that he's worthless. I tell him, too, when I see him. It doesn't seem to help. He don't scare easy, I'll give him that."

Martha tried to imagine what it would be like to have Jaz as a mother, or to be in a family where people just said exactly what they were thinking, shouting their opinion no matter what it was. She didn't see how much good could come from that.

ONE AFTERNOON, MARTHA WAS IN Mr. Cranston's office, looking for a new credit card to give to the bookstore. "The old one expired," Jaz told Martha on her way out the door. "The new one is on his desk, I think. Just call them with the new number. He's getting cranky and needs his books."

The desk was covered with folders and file cards that had notes and lists written on them. Martha felt like she was snooping, even though Jaz had told her to go through the papers. She carefully lifted one set of folders and placed them to the side, then picked up a couple of loose pieces of paper and that was when she saw the manila folder, labeled FUNERAL.

She couldn't believe it. She glanced at the door and then opened the folder before she could even stop herself. It was full of old funeral mass booklets, some of which were marked with Mr. Cranston's handwriting. There were readings that were circled, and some that were crossed over with a big X, sometimes a NO written next to it for good measure.

Martha heard a noise in the hall and she shut the folder quickly. She spotted the new credit card, grabbed it, and ran out into the hall holding it in the air, like it was a badge proving that she wasn't snooping. But no one was there.

All afternoon, Martha kept thinking about what it must be like for Mr. Cranston to plan his own funeral. How scary it must be to know that death was coming. Of course, she knew that death was coming for everyone, but it must be strange to know without a doubt that it was coming soon. He was so organized, so efficient. It looked like just another business file on his desk, just one more thing to cross off his list.

Sometimes, imagining her own funeral, Martha could make herself cry. She didn't sob, but if she pictured her parents and siblings sitting in a pew, pictured Cathy bent over with grief, she could get a tear or two out. After all, it would be such a tragedy, such a shame if she were to die now.

There were times when Martha imagined that she'd died of a long and drawn-out disease, which would give her time to prepare, as Mr. Cranston was doing. She would write letters to all the people that were important to her, and leave instructions for them to be opened on the day of her funeral. And of course, she'd write an open letter to be read at the actual service. She'd probably have Claire read it—her parents would be too distraught, and Max wasn't great at public speaking. She could have Cathy do it, but she was a little rough sometimes, and Martha would want the letter to be read with quiet emotion. Claire would be devastated too, of course, but Martha would explain that it was her last sisterly duty, and Claire would come through.

Martha wondered if she was the only one who thought about these kinds of things. She could daydream about her funeral for hours, imagining the people from her past that would show up, the ones that would be shocked to hear the news. She worried sometimes that this wasn't normal, but then she told herself that people talked about death all the time. At least once a month, usually after she'd had to go retrieve something from the attic or the basement, Weezy would say, "I pity you children, if your father and I die unexpectedly. It will take you a decade to clean out this house."

Once, her grandma Bets had announced at a family dinner that she'd like to be cremated and have her ashes split between her two daughters. Later that night, Martha overheard Weezy and Maureen talking about it.

"That gives me the heebie-jeebies," Weezy said. "What do you think possessed her to say that?"

"I think she wants to make sure that she'll always be with us," Maureen answered. "Judging and disapproving our every move from her urn."

The two of them had laughed, but Martha was disturbed. Maybe she'd like to be cremated too. Then she could be with her family, instead of underground, and they could take her with them wherever they went. But then what would happen after all of them were gone too? Her ashes would be passed around, and then, eventually, generations later, someone would say, "What is this thing?" and they'd get sick of taking care of the urn, probably find it creepy, and put it in the garbage. So maybe cremation wasn't the best choice.

When she was younger, she'd seen a mausoleum in a graveyard and asked Weezy what it was. "Can we get one of those?" she asked. To her, it seemed like the perfect solution, to be with your family, aboveground, so that no critters could get to you. It was just like a little house. But Weezy had told her no.

"You'll grow up and have your own family," she'd said. "And you'll want to be buried near them too." But that seemed impossible to Martha at the time, to grow up and have a family of her own. She'd always secretly thought that she could buy a mausoleum after her parents died, but then for their fiftieth birthdays, Bets had given each of her parents a plot in Saint Ambrose's graveyard.

RUBY KEPT BRINGING PRESENTS for her father—a blanket, a CD, a new movie for him to watch. Mr. Cranston never seemed to like any of the things that she gave to him, but she seemed determined to keep trying. Once she brought him an iPad, and insisted that he try to play Angry Birds.

"Here, Dad, put your finger here and then shoot the bird like this."

"What? Why am I doing this?" he asked.

"To try to kill the pigs," Ruby explained. "I know it seems strange, but I think you'll really like it. It's totally addicting." Ruby had a tendency to sound like a teenager when she talked to her dad.

Mr. Cranston humored her, putting his finger to the screen, and then looking surprised when there was the sound of a bird screaming and pigs snorting. "What the hell is this thing?" he asked.

Ruby had just laughed. "We can put it away for now," she said. "But you should try it later. I really think you'll like it." Martha was pretty sure that Mr. Cranston never touched the iPad again, and sometimes it made her sad, how badly Ruby wanted to find something that would make her father happy.

MARTHA HAD STARTED TO DREAM about the Cranstons. She figured it was just from spending so much time there. After all, she'd had more J.Crew stress dreams than she could even count. The number of times she'd woken up in a panic, sweating, because no matter how hard she tried she couldn't get the sweaters to stay folded and in a pile. Oh, those were the worst! As soon as she managed to wrangle one sweater, another one fell out, and another. Around the holidays, when the store was at its craziest, Martha barely slept.

But the dreams about the Cranstons were a little different. In them, Martha was part of the family. They weren't stressful at all, except for one where Ruby's hair fell out and she screamed at Martha. But usually, the dreams were just Martha sitting around with the family, watching TV or eating dinner. They sort of reminded her of the dreams she used to have when she was younger, where she was a part of the Huxtables or the *Full House* family.

Dr. Baer told her she might be getting a little too involved. "I understand it's hard when you spend so much time with a family, and you get wrapped up in their business. But just remember to keep a little distance. You're there as the caretaker."

People were always telling Martha not to get too involved. She didn't understand it. How could anyone be too involved? Didn't that just show people that you cared? What did people want? Did they want everyone to just walk around, pretending that they didn't see anyone else, didn't notice a thing? That was ridiculous.

In college, Martha was always the first one to step up and tell one of the girls if she needed to break up with her boyfriend. "He's not treating you right," she'd say. She'd demand that the girl end it. How could she not step in when she saw something bad happening?

The girls that she was trying to help almost always got annoyed with her. "Mind your own business, Martha," they'd say. But she wouldn't let it drop. After all, they were the ones who offered up the information in the first place, who told her about the things their boyfriends said, the suspicions they had about cheating. What else was she supposed to do?

"People don't want to hear that they're with the wrong person," Claire told her once. "And unless they're being abused in some way, the most you can really say is that you think they can do better. Or that they should be treated better. But that's it."

Martha disagreed. She'd just ended a friendship with a girl in her nursing program, Ann, who had refused to break up with her boyfriend.

"Look," Claire said. "I get what you're saying. But at the end of the day, it's not really your business. People don't always want the truth, and you don't always know what the real truth is. It's not worth losing a friend over."

But Martha had lost a friend. Ann never forgave her for the things that she'd said, and she ended up marrying the guy. Martha didn't get it. Weren't friends there to tell you the truth? Weren't you supposed to get involved?

WHEN MR. CRANSTON HAD A doctor's appointment, either Jaz or Ruby took him. He preferred Jaz, because Ruby usually got herself all worked up, thinking the doctor was going to find something fatal during these visits.

"Don't worry about it," Mr. Cranston told her once. "I'm already dying. What else could they tell me?"

"Oh, Dad," Ruby said. She went to the upstairs bathroom and shut herself in for almost fifteen minutes.

"Well, now we'll never get out of here," he said. He crossed his arms and waited for her to come downstairs.

"Why does he have so many appointments?" Martha asked Jaz. "Is there something wrong with him?"

"He's old, child. Things have started failing. He's having trouble breathing, his heart's giving out, you name it, it's happening to him." She didn't know how Jaz could be so matter-of-fact about it.

It seemed to Martha that Mr. Cranston got a little smaller each day, just a tiny bit weaker than he was the day before. Could she be imagining it? When they sat together and read, sometimes he fell asleep in the middle of a page, the book open on his lap, his mouth open with a little bit of drool at the corner. His skin looked so thin while he slept, the veins so close to the surface. Martha knew he should rest if he was tired, but what she really wanted to do was make noise until he woke up and moved around, until he looked alive again.

MARTHA COULDN'T HELP BUT TALK about the Cranstons when she was at home. She was always dying to share new information about them, or tell her family what she thought was behind the rift between Ruby and Billy.

"You sound a little obsessed with them," Claire said one night. Claire had started cooking dinner for the family, claiming that she was so bored at her temp job, all she could do was look up recipes on the computer. She'd made some truly amazing things, like tonight's dinner of tarragon chicken in cream sauce, scalloped cherry tomatoes, and twice-baked potatoes.

"You're going to send us all to the fat farm," Weezy said when she sat down that night.

"I'm not obsessed with them," Martha told Claire. "I'm just interested. They're interesting."

"It's a fine line between interested and obsessed," Claire said, but Martha wasn't offended. Claire had never met them, so she didn't understand. The Cranstons were the kind of people who had an interesting story, who had many interesting stories. They were the kind of people that once you met them, you just wanted to learn everything you could about their lives.

CHAPTER 12

Thanksgiving started weeks before it actually happened. It was the way it always had been. There was shopping to get done, the house needed to be cleaned, silver needed to be polished. There were logistics that had to be figured out—who was coming, who was staying where, who was a vegetarian this year, who was lactose intolerant. There were phone calls to be had with Maureen, to complain about their mother and her absolute refusal to cooperate with anyone on anything. "She doesn't want to come?" Maureen said every year. "Great, let's leave her in Michigan. I'm good with that, are you?"

Years ago, when they were both first married and had little babies in the house, they used to switch off hosting Thanksgiving. This didn't last long. Weezy ended up doing all of the cooking anyway, and most of the cleaning, and honestly it was just easier to have it at her own house in her own kitchen.

The past few years had gotten more complicated, since they started to think that Bets shouldn't travel by herself. Cathy and Ruth had taken on the responsibility of driving almost three hours from Ohio to Auburn Hills to pick up Bets and fly with her from Detroit. It wasn't convenient, but none of them could think of a better alternative. Bets, of course, still thought she was fine to travel alone, so Cathy and Ruth had to think of excuses for why they were going to be up that way anyway. "We're visiting friends," they always told Bets. She acted like she was doing them a favor, letting them stay at her house for a night before they all flew to Philadelphia.

"Cathy's coming again this year," she told Weezy. "I guess some of her lesbian friends live up this way."

"Great, well, that works out for everyone." Weezy didn't know how many more years they could realistically keep asking Cathy and Ruth to escort a crabby old lady on a plane.

Weezy and Maureen still alternated who Bets would stay with, and unfortunately this was Weezy's year. "Tough break," Maureen said. She didn't mean it. Bets was a horrendous houseguest. If Will emptied the dishwasher, she commented on Weezy's lack of housekeeping skills. Once, Weezy put out cocktail napkins and Bets had called her hoity-toity. There was no winning.

They used to invite their cousins the Nugents from Pittsburgh, but thankfully that had stopped after Bets's sister, Linda, died and all of the children's children had reproduced so many times that it was impossible to fit everyone in the same house. They were an odd bunch. Linda had once brought a basket of stuffed reindeer to the house, and Weezy assumed (as one might) that she'd brought them for the kids. "How nice of you," she said. "I'm sure Martha and Claire will be thrilled." She tried to take the basket away from Linda, who held on tight.

"These are my pets," she'd said. "Our last dog died and we're too old to get another one, so now these are my pets." She'd walked into the house with her basket and proceeded to tell anyone who would listen about each of the reindeer. "This is Misty, she's shy. Bernie is bossy." Martha and Claire were six and seven that year, and they'd petted the stuffed animals with wide eyes, as if even at that age, they knew that their great-aunt Linda had really gone bat shit crazy.

Linda was the only person who Bets refused to say a bad word about. She once admitted that she thought her sister had "married down," but that was all. Bets still went to stay with her sister's children between Thanksgiving and Christmas, taking the train from Philadelphia to Pittsburgh and spending a week or so with each of them. She bought their children gifts and raved about the cooking. "Your cousin Patty really knows how to fry a chicken," she'd say, while watching Weezy prepare chicken cutlets.

Weezy didn't really keep in touch with any of her cousins anymore, except for a Christmas card each year, and a call to talk about Bets's stay. But she was eternally grateful to them for taking Bets for the stretch between the two holidays. Getting her back and forth from Michigan twice a year would have been a nightmare, and while Weezy suspected that Bets was much kinder and more charming to her nieces and nephews than she was to her daughters, she still couldn't have been an easy guest.

Maureen was coming over today to talk about menus. Ruth was a vegan, which was a choice that Weezy respected, but it made cooking for her almost impossible. The girl was so nice about it, always brought over a side dish of her own, and assured Weezy that she was getting enough to eat, but Weezy didn't see how that was possible, considering that pretty much all she could eat was plain vegetables and nothing else. Last year, they'd made a special pecan pie for her, and out of curiosity, Weezy took a bite. She'd made herself swallow, but it wasn't easy. *Poor, thin Ruth,* she'd thought. *No butter or meat, what a sad life.*

She was happy that none of her children had entered

into the world of vegetarianism. Unless you counted the two years in high school when Claire refused to eat red meat, but even then she'd eat chicken occasionally. She was just doing it to be difficult, really. Even Cleo ate meat, thank God. Not that she considered Cleo one of her children—it was way too early for that. So at least she had that much to be thankful for, that her children were getting enough protein. Ruth should probably be taking iron pills, and Weezy made a note to ask her about that.

Maureen was late, which was not unusual. In fact, it was almost expected. It surprised Weezy how Maureen could be so organized and efficient in her work, and have none of that spill over to her personal life. Maureen was an executive assistant for John McLaughlin, one of the VPs at Price Waterhouse. She had been there for over twenty-five years and as he got promoted, she went with him. He called Maureen his "right-hand man" and he meant it. She kept his schedule, was loyal to him, and always had her ear out for talk among the assistants of any rumblings in the company. She kept his office running tightly and smoothly, and you would never know that she often ran out of dishwasher detergent at home and forgot to replace it for weeks.

Maureen had gone back to college after her husband left, and it had taken her almost three years, during which Cathy and Drew spent a lot of nights eating dinner with the Coffeys, and sometimes spent whole weekends there so that Maureen could make it to class and study. But she'd done it, and landed the job with John right after she graduated.

"You went back to college to be a secretary?" Bets asked when she got the news. "I was a secretary for years, and I didn't need to go to college."

"An executive assistant," Maureen corrected her. Bets

had rolled her eyes, but her job was one thing that Maureen never doubted. She loved working for John. She was friendly with his wife, attended his children's first communions and graduations, and accepted his investment advice. Maureen loved everything about her job, feeling in control and having lunch with her friends in the office. Hearing her talk about it always made Weezy a little jealous.

Now, John was over sixty and his role in the company was getting smaller. He wanted to retire. He and his wife wanted to move to Maine full-time. For the time being, he still had an office at the company, but he'd been moved to a small office, and while Maureen went in every day, she was done by one o'clock at the latest. There just wasn't much to do. She set up his golf games and answered e-mails and phone calls about when he would be in the office. Sometimes he came in and they organized files or went over things. But by next year, he would be gone, and Maureen would be retired as well. She wouldn't need to work, thanks to the investments she'd so wisely listened to him about, but she wasn't looking forward to it.

"All those days, stretching on, spending them all by myself," she'd said. "It seems so definite."

"You're not by yourself," Weezy told her. But she knew what Maureen meant.

Maureen kept suggesting that they start a business venture together, but she was just talking, just trying to grasp at something so that she wouldn't feel lost. She'd mentioned a dog-walking business and a paint-your-own pottery store in the same sentence, and Weezy knew that she was just going a little bonkers over the change.

The feeling of loss was understandable. It was like Max and his hockey. He'd played since he was four years old. He took to skates right away, a natural, which surprised Will and Weezy, since neither of the girls liked it at all. The few times the girls had gone skating when they were little, Weezy and Will had to drag them around on the ice, their little mittened hands gripping their parents' tightly.

But Max stood up on his own right away. It was really something to see. For a while there, Weezy was convinced that he was going to be an Olympian or a professional athlete. It was amazing, to watch this little boy glide on the ice, forward and backward, like it was nothing. And then, when the Pee Wee coach handed him a stick, he just smiled. It was like he'd always been holding it.

They threw him into the sport wholeheartedly. Will loved hockey, and Max's being the star of the team was just a bonus. What Will and Weezy learned about the sport very quickly was that they were required to be just as involved. There were club teams and tournaments. There were day camps and sleepaway camps. Soon, their weekends were filled with driving Max to different locations (often different states) to play hockey.

Weezy loved watching Max play. Her sweet, even-tempered baby turned into something else on the ice. He was fluid and graceful and also could be ruthless and sneaky, coming up beside someone, checking them with his shoulder, and then skating on, like nothing had happened.

Hockey took up almost all of their time, and they often grumbled to each other about it, but it was too late to back out. It was exhausting and it seemed that they were always trying to schedule around a hockey game of some sort. Holidays were cut short, and long weekends were spent in Canada and Michigan.

And then, just like that, it was over. Max went to college

and decided that he didn't want to try out for the team. He didn't think he'd start, he told them, and it seemed like a lot of time and work to sit on the bench. He decided to play on the club team, which was really just a bunch of boys getting together at eleven o'clock at night to play around on the ice and drink.

After that, Weezy felt like part of her life was missing. Did she really miss the hours in the car? The nights spent in questionable hotels in random Canadian towns? No, she told herself, she couldn't miss that. But there was a loss when it was gone. And so Weezy understood it when Maureen talked about missing work. Even if the whole point of a job was to be done with it someday, to be able to relax, it could become a part of you, it could become how you saw yourself. And when it was gone, it left a hole.

MAUREEN LET HERSELF IN THE back door, apologizing before she was even inside. "I know, I know," she said. "I'm sorry, I got stuck talking to someone at work."

"That's okay," Weezy said. And it was. They didn't have all that much to go over, actually. She'd spread the cookbooks out on the table, and had the lists of what they'd made for the past five Thanksgivings.

"So, Cathy and Ruth are all set with Bets?" Weezy asked.

"Yep. They're leaving Ohio on Tuesday, and they'll stay over with Bets that night, and they all fly out bright and early on Wednesday."

"God bless them."

"No kidding. But you know, I'm paying for their tickets, so it's not like they're getting nothing out of the deal."

"Still."

The two of them talked about the pies that they wanted

to make. Pumpkin, of course. Pecan was Max's favorite. Bets always wanted something with chocolate in it, and then there was an apple-cranberry crisp that looked good.

"Four desserts?" Weezy said. "That seems like a lot, doesn't it?"

"Yeah," Maureen agreed. "I guess we'll lose the crisp?"

Weezy nodded. The crisp was actually her favorite, but there was nothing else that could be cut from the list without a lot of whining and complaining from the group. And none of them needed four desserts. Especially not Weezy or Maureen, who were starting to both look just a little barrel-shaped in the past five years, no matter how much they exercised.

"So this is the trade-off?" Maureen had asked, when she'd started to go through menopause, just a year and a half after Weezy. "No more cramps, but now I'll just be hot as hell and fat?"

Weezy couldn't even find it in herself to tell her it would get better. Her hot flashes had persisted, well past the time when she thought they should have stopped. "How long will this go on? How many years is normal?"

"I don't like the term *normal*," her doctor had said. Weezy told him that was too bad, because she did like the term *normal*, loved it even, and so she would be getting a new doctor.

Will and the kids had learned not to say anything when in the middle of winter she'd open the back door and stand there, while the rest of them shivered and moved to the front of the house. She was glad when Maureen started, just so she could have someone to complain with. Weezy's new doctor had told her that there was a slight chance that she'd have hot flashes for the rest of her life. Maureen never had hot flashes like Weezy. She did, however, have raging mood swings that once caused her to tell Bets to go fuck herself on Christmas Eve.

WEEZY FILLED IN HER CALENDAR. She entered in when Max and Cleo would arrive, when Bets would get in, who needed to be picked up at the airport when. She woke up every morning and went for a walk, then came back and a few times a week went to that weight-lifting place with Maureen, the one that was made just for menopausal women and had popped up in every suburb across the country.

She was trying to keep herself busy, to keep away from the computer and the wedding blogs and websites. Thanksgiving was a good excuse, she figured. During the day, she did pretty well. But it was at night, when she couldn't sleep, that she crumbled.

Her favorite wedding blog was called WeddingBellesand-Whistles.com and featured a different DIY project every day. It was also filled with tips, and once a week a guest bride wrote an article about an aspect of her wedding. That night, Weezy read about a bride who'd been left behind at the venue, after all of the buses that they hired to take the guests back to the hotel (forty-five minutes away!) had driven off. "Oh no," Weezy whispered out loud. "What a nightmare."

Weezy told herself that staying away from weddings during the day was a good start. It was like the patch for smoking, and she felt virtuous when, at the end of the day, she hadn't checked in even once.

She went to the store and stocked up on all of Max's favorite foods. She got his room ready for Cleo, washing sheets, vacuuming and dusting, airing everything out. She set Max up in the basement, which was a shame really, that he wouldn't be able to stay in his own room when he came home, but they couldn't very well put Cleo down there. She got everything that was on Bets's list: creamer for her coffee, bran cereal, pistachios, and hard caramel candies. Bets had called several times to go over the list, and Weezy assured her that it was all taken care of.

Maureen had offered to have everyone over for dinner on Wednesday night, which was a nice thought, but just made extra work for Weezy since she'd have to make everything at her house, then pack it all up to take over. Maureen didn't cook, and she'd suggested ordering pizzas—"Why make it complicated?" she'd asked—but Weezy had shot her down and told her she'd whip up some meatballs.

By the time Max and Cleo arrived on Wednesday morning, everything was ready. Claire was at work for just a half day, and Martha was working all day, so Weezy was the only one there to greet them. She was so happy to see her son, her Max, who walked right in and gave her a huge hug.

Cleo, if it was possible, looked even more gorgeous than she had before. "Hi, Mrs. Coffey," she said. They gave each other a tentative hug.

"I brought these for you," Cleo said, and held out a box of chocolates, which was a nice gesture, but Weezy's first thought was that more food in the house was the last thing that they needed, and when was she going to put these out for people when there were already so many desserts?

But of course she just smiled and said, "Thank you."

The two of them stood there and smiled at each other, as though they both thought it would convey how thrilled they were to share Thanksgiving. Max was on the ground with Ruby, letting the dog lick his face, bending his head down so she could smell his hair and press her head against his. Ruby wagged her tail more for Max than for anyone, and she was always a little depressed when he left.

"Do you two want something to eat?" Weezy asked. "Max, I got some cold cuts for you. I could make you a sandwich or maybe you want something else? We're having spaghetti and meatballs at Maureen's tonight, so you probably don't want pasta."

"We're okay for now," Max said. "Actually, we're going to throw our stuff down and head over to John's to see him and meet up with some people. I think we'll stop at Gino's for a cheese steak."

"Not Pat's?"

"We went there last time. Cleo has to try both so she knows which one she likes better." Max gave the back of her neck a squeeze, and she scrunched up her shoulders and laughed.

And then they were gone. They dropped their bags in the rooms and were out the door a few minutes later. "Be sure to be back by four, because Bets will be here and then we'll head over to Maureen's." Max gave her a kiss and they left. She noticed that Cleo looked relieved to be leaving, even though she'd just gotten there.

MAUREEN BURNED THE BREAD. She basically had just one thing to do for the dinner, which was to cook the garlic bread, and it was black when they got there. Smoke filled the kitchen. "I didn't want to forget it, so I just popped it in," Maureen said, as if that explained it.

Will was sent out to get more. "Just get some frozen stuff," Weezy instructed. There was no telling what he'd come back with, but it was a risk they'd have to take. Bets was already sniffing and coughing in the kitchen over the smoke, and Maureen was in the corner sipping a glass of wine.

Weezy turned the fan on and cracked the window in the kitchen, then set to work warming up the meatballs, and instructed Maureen to empty the bags of prewashed salad that she'd gotten that day and to toss them with Italian dressing. She sat Bets down and got her a glass of wine. All of the kids were already in the next room, laughing about something.

"Maureen was never much of a cook," Bets said.

"Thanks so much, Mom," Maureen said.

Parents would probably be arrested these days if they talked the way their parents had. Sometimes she still heard her dad's voice: "Louise is the brains," he'd say to strangers, "and Maureen's the looker."

Will came back with the bread and asked Bets how things were going in the retirement village. "I call it Death Valley," she told him, "because every other day, there's a body taken out of there on a stretcher."

"Bets, you're a funny one," he said. He laughed and put his hand on his stomach, and Weezy was amazed, as she always was, that her husband was good-natured enough not just to put up with Bets but to actually seem to enjoy her company.

They finished getting the dinner ready—after sending Will out one more time to get meatless sauce for Ruth, which they'd forgotten—and everyone sat down to eat. The kids were chattering, all happy to see each other, and that made Weezy so happy. When she had Claire, everyone had told her, "Those girls are sure to be best friends," but they weren't. And then, when she'd had Max, she was worried that he'd be raised as an only child, not close to his sisters at all, but right from the get-go, he and Claire had been thick as thieves and still were.

She was always happy that Martha and Cathy were so close. It wasn't the same as a sibling, but at least it was a family member that was a friend. It was Cathy's poor brother, Drew, really, that was always the odd man out when he was around. Although most of the time, he didn't even seem to mind.

Will poured them all more red wine and made a toast, and the whole family ate, spilling sauce all over the tablecloth, which would have driven Weezy nuts if it had been her house, but Maureen didn't seem to notice or care, and so she relaxed and let herself enjoy the dinner.

IT OCCURRED TO WEEZY, after Max was born, that she now had the exact same family that she'd grown up in—two girls, a year apart, and then a boy. Of course, their baby brother, Jimmy, died when he was just a few weeks old and—this was awful, but true—sometimes she forgot that he'd been there at all.

After he'd died, her father delivered the news, very matter-of-factly. "He went to heaven," he said one morning. He'd already been to the hospital with Bets and Jimmy in the middle of the night. The girls had never even been woken up. A neighbor was called to come and sit in the house with them.

They'd had a funeral for him, a small and quick ceremony. ("Thank God he was already baptized," their grandmother kept saying. "That's why you do it right away. Right away. You don't waste a second.") There was a baby picture of him placed alongside pictures of Weezy and Maureen on the side table in the front hall. But he was rarely mentioned.

If that had happened these days, if a baby died, people

would talk to the kids. They'd probably be in therapy before the funeral was even planned. But Weezy and Maureen never really talked about Jimmy. They knew it was sad—unthinkable—to lose a baby, and after they'd both had kids they maybe understood that a little bit more. But they didn't feel the sadness, really. Not the way Bets did. She never talked about it, but something changed in her after that. The pictures before were of her smiling widely with lots of lipstick, and after she looked sharper, and always smiled with her mouth closed.

Bets had always hated Philadelphia, still referred to Michigan as home even after she'd been gone for years. She had met James when he was working in Detroit, and she'd been impressed with his "East Coast ways," as she always put it. They dated for a few months, and when his company transferred him back to Philadelphia, he'd proposed and she'd accepted.

But she'd never liked the people in Philadelphia; she missed her friends and family back home. She seemed to blame James in some way for taking her there, although Weezy always thought, she'd agreed to go, so she couldn't really complain. After Jimmy died, it was just one more thing that Bets hated about the place.

When James had a heart attack and died Weezy's freshman year in college, Bets wasted no time. She packed up the house, sold it, and right after Maureen graduated from high school, she moved back to Michigan. Both Weezy and Maureen thought this was a mistake, and they were devastated at losing their childhood home so soon after losing their father. "She's not going to be happy there," they told each other. "She has a memory of it, but it won't be the same when she gets there."

But they were wrong. Bets thrived back in Michigan. She reconnected with all of "the gals" she'd known growing up, and it was like she'd never been gone for those twenty years. She had no problem leaving Philadelphia, even if that meant moving away from her children. "That was never my home," she always said about it, as if all of her time there, raising her children, was just one little pause in her real life.

THEY ALL GOT HOME, STUFFED AND TIRED, and Weezy figured everyone would just go to bed, but Claire announced that she was going over to Lainie's with Max and Cleo.

"You're going over now?" Weezy asked. "It's so late already."

"Mom, it's fine. It's not even that late."

"What about Martha?"

"What about Martha?" Claire repeated.

"Did you invite her?"

"Yep. I told her we were all going but she wasn't interested."

"Well, why don't you invite her again?"

"Why? She already said no."

"You know sometimes she needs to be convinced to go somewhere," Weezy said.

"You want me to go beg Martha to come with me, to a party that she doesn't want to go to?"

"Claire." Weezy gave her a look, and Claire let out a sigh, but she went upstairs, and returned with Martha in tow. The four of them headed out the door and Weezy called, "Have a good time!"

Weezy settled herself on the couch and turned on the TV. There was so much to be done for tomorrow, but she could rest for just a minute. *It's a Wonderful Life* was on, which made it seem like Thanksgiving was already over, like time had just raced by and it was already Christmas.

She watched a little bit of the movie, but her heart wasn't in it, so she snuck over to the computer and pulled up Wedding Belles and Whistles. She read an article by a bride who was to be married that weekend, and how she'd already arranged to have a plate of Thanksgiving food set aside for her, since she wouldn't be able to indulge that day. She was making place card holders in the shape of turkeys, which sounded a little silly to Weezy, but they were actually sort of whimsical looking. *Just a few minutes,* she told herself as she settled into her chair and read all about Thanksgiving Bride's big day.

CHAPTER 13

Claire knew before she opened her eyes that it wasn't good. Her head was throbbing, and it felt like she was on a boat, or something that was moving very slowly, back and forth. She opened her eyes to find that it was just a couch—Lainie's couch—and not a boat. Her right hip ached, probably because she'd been lying on it for hours without moving. She looked in front of her and saw a full glass of wine on the coffee table, and Jack standing and staring at her. He was still in his pajamas, which were dark blue with light green monsters printed on them, and he was holding some sort of Transformer-looking toy, although Claire realized with a horrible throb of her head that it couldn't be a Transformer because kids didn't even play with those anymore—or did they? Were they back? She couldn't remember, and thinking about it was making her want to vomit.

"Hi," Jack said. He rubbed his nose with the heel of his hand. "Hey, you're still dressed for the party."

Claire closed her eyes. She was still wearing the same clothes she'd worn over last night. Sleeping on Lainie's couch wasn't a first—she'd done that plenty—but being so drunk that she couldn't bother to borrow a T-shirt and sweatpants was a new low. In the kitchen, someone was banging drawers open and closed, like they were in a hurry. Lainie walked out into the room holding a cup of coffee.

"Hey, bud," she said, touching Jack's head. Then turning to Claire, she said, "I feel awful."

Claire sat up slowly, and held on to the arm of the couch in an attempt to stop the spinning in her head. "Really? I feel great."

Lainie laughed. "You kept me up way too late last night. And made me drink way too much wine. I'm so screwed. I have to bring a pie to Brian's mom's house."

"Really, well, I have to actually stand up at some point today. And right now I'm not sure that's possible."

"Do you want some coffee?" Lainie asked. She was now moving quickly around the room, picking up the last of the party remnants, taking the empty glasses into the kitchen, and throwing out the napkins. Ever since Lainie had had kids, she didn't really get hungover. She claimed she did, but she never sat still and moaned about it. "I can't," she said once. "I don't have a choice, so it's like my body figured out how to get through the hangover while letting me move around." It made Claire feel worse to watch her up and cleaning.

"No coffee for me, thanks," Claire said. "I just need to lay here for a minute."

"Sure. Your phone has been ringing, by the way."

"Oh God." Claire knew it was Weezy. "I should go home soon."

Jack was folding and unfolding his little toy into a truck and then a robot. He was making those noises that little boys make to mimic an explosion, or a rocket, or a bomb.

"Hey, bud, you want to help me make a pie?" Lainie asked. Jack looked up and nodded. "All right, then, go get dressed."

Jack ran out of the room, and Claire sat up. She told

Lainie what Jack had said to her about still being dressed for the party, and the two of them snorted with laughter.

"Okay," Claire said, finally standing up. "I think I might make it."

"OH, CLAIRE," WEEZY SAID when she walked in.

"What?"

Weezy sighed. "Look at you. You're going to be exhausted. I need your help today."

"I'm right here, ready to help," Claire said. She smelled like liquor and cigarettes, and she stood on the other side of the kitchen so that Weezy wouldn't notice.

Weezy went back to stirring the stuffing, sighing as though Claire had just caused a huge inconvenience. The stuffing was in three different pots, each one overflowing, little stale bread pieces jumping onto the counter at random. "I just wish you hadn't stayed out all night. We've got a big day."

"I'm fine," Claire said. She was reminded of the recurring fight that she and Weezy had had after every grade school sleepover. Claire would get angry, Weezy would accuse her of being tired, and then Claire would scream that she wasn't tired, and then Weezy would threaten that she'd never go to another sleepover again.

All Claire wanted was to go to her room and lie down just for a minute, but Bets was in her room, probably going through her drawers, and snooping through her things. There had been some issues with the sleeping arrangements. Normally, Max stayed in the basement and Bets stayed in his room, but with Cleo here, they needed an extra place for her, so Claire was sent packing to Martha's room, which had twin beds, Cleo took Max's room, and Bets got Claire's room. No one was happy.

Claire grabbed a bagel from the counter, spread it with cream cheese, and ate it in huge, quick bites. She hoped that it would make her feel better. She headed upstairs to take a shower, but Martha was in the bathroom, so she lay down on one of the twin beds and waited.

Martha came out of the bathroom in a cloud of steam. She closed the door and then listened to make sure that no one was outside the room. "It smells like an ashtray in there," she whispered. "Last night, I woke up and there was smoke coming out from underneath the door."

Claire laughed. Bets was a secret smoker, but it was a secret that wasn't very well kept at all. When they were little, they used to ask Weezy, "Why does Bets smoke in the bathroom?" and Weezy would shush them.

"It's her secret," she told them. "She doesn't want anyone to know, so we can't say anything. She'd be embarrassed."

And so, for years now, Bets would disappear into a bathroom and emerge with smoke billowing behind her. Sometimes she'd cough. "I'm getting a cold," she'd say. And none of them would say a word.

Once, Claire and Doug had been sitting on the back deck, and Doug touched Claire's arm and silently pointed up to the bathroom window, where a hand holding a cigarette was going in and out of the window. Claire had shrugged. "It's her thing," she said. "She doesn't want anyone to know. We just let her be and pretend we don't see anything."

"Your family," Doug had said, "is just so Catholic, it kills me." Claire never exactly knew what he meant, since secret smoking didn't really seem like a Catholic trait to her.

Claire had also warned Doug that Bets was just a little bit racist. She wanted to give him fair warning. "You know," she told him, "not like *really* racist but like old-people racist."

Doug had tilted his head like he didn't quite understand, and she said, "You'll see."

"The president looks blacker on my TV," Bets told Doug that night. Doug coughed on his water. "I don't know what it is, but it's true. He looks so much darker on my TV at home. He looks practically white here."

"Mom," Weezy said, "that's enough."

"What? I'm just making an observation. Come over and watch him on my TV and you'll see what I mean. He looks blacker there."

"Mom, drop it."

Bets turned to Doug and shook her head. "No one can say anything these days. You can't say a single thing without someone being offended, without the polite police coming to tie you up."

That was Bets, always full of inappropriate comments. They spent every holiday whispering about her while she was in the next room. At least she made things interesting, and gave them something to talk about.

In her room, Martha was now drying her hair with the towel, then stopped and sprayed a can of air freshener in the direction of the bathroom and Bets. "One day," she said to Claire, "she's going to burn down the house."

"I know," Claire said. "And then we're all going to have to lie to the firemen about what started it."

CLAIRE STOOD IN THE SHOWER for a long time. She let the hot stream run over her, and then she had to sit down because she started to feel a little nauseous. Even from inside the shower, Claire could hear Weezy yelling up the stairs at people, giving orders.

"I can do this," she said to herself as she shampooed her

hair. It was fine. She could make it for an hour, then have a drink and some appetizers and she'd be fine. Thank God their cousin Drew wasn't coming this year. Not that Claire didn't love him, but when he came to family gatherings, they all abstained from drinking out of support. It was miserable. Well, all of them abstained except for Bets, who once told him that she thought alcoholics were people that couldn't handle their liquor. "Maybe you'll get the hang of it as you get older," she'd said to him. Maureen was out smoking on the deck, but Weezy had stepped in to defend him.

"Mom, Drew has a disease and he's been very brave in dealing with it," she said, in a speech that would have made any Lifetime Movie writer proud. It was embarrassing to watch Weezy standing there, knowing that she thought she was doing something very important.

Weezy put her hand on Drew's shoulder and the three of them stood in an awkward triangle, until Bets said, "Cancer is a disease. Not being able to drink is just a goddamn shame."

Claire was all for abstaining when Drew was there, although sometimes she wondered if he really was an alcoholic or if maybe that was just where his problems showed themselves. He was only twenty-two when he went into rehab—a baby, practically. Which one of them wasn't an irresponsible drinker at that age? But Claire kept this thought to herself, since Drew seemed to be doing well in the program and had gotten his life back on track.

The last time he'd come, two Thanksgivings ago, the dinner seemed to drag on forever as they'd sipped at Diet Cokes and some stupid raspberry spritzer that Weezy had made in an attempt to have a fun non-alcoholic cocktail. Bets had gotten drunk by herself, not needing any of them to join her.

She was happy as a clam to down glass after glass, and all of them realized that she was much harder to deal with when they were all sober. As Drew had pulled out of the driveway that night, Weezy was already opening a bottle of red.

"Good God," Claire said to Max. "It looks like Mom's going to rip the cork out with her teeth."

So, yes, it was better that Drew wasn't coming. After all, Cathy was enough to deal with. The first year after she came out, she'd made a point to mention her sexuality at every turn. When she first brought Ruth to meet the family, she'd made a point to introduce her to Bets in a way that left no room for misinterpretation.

"Bets, this is my girlfriend, Ruth," she said. "And by *girl-friend*, I mean *sexual partner*."

"Oh, sweet Jesus," Max had said under his breath, and he and Claire had laughed. Martha shot them a look, like they were being rude, but really. She didn't know why Cathy had to talk about her sex life all the time. No one else did. Claire was all for it, thought it was great and that Cathy should be who she was and they could all live life together. Cathy was the one that talked about it all the time, and that got tiring. It wasn't like she'd invented being a lesbian.

"IT'S INTERESTING," CATHY SAID ONCE at a family dinner. "Some people would think that my father being a misogynist had something to do with me being a lesbian. I don't believe that sexuality is something we choose, but others disagree. Some think it's something we learn." Then she'd turned to Claire. "What do you think?"

Claire had just shrugged. How was one supposed to even answer that question? She didn't remember Uncle Harold all that well. He'd been around when they were younger, and then he and Maureen had separated and he'd moved to Oregon. Claire hadn't seen him since.

She remembered the time (the only time, she was pretty sure) that Cathy and Drew went to visit him there, how Cathy had called Maureen from some strange person's house to tell her that she and Drew had been left there, that their dad had gone out and told them to "stay put." Maureen had come over to the Coffeys' that night, screaming and crying, was on the phone with the police in Portland, trying to get them over to her children. She'd flown out there the next morning and had come back with Cathy and Drew.

Maybe Harold visited once or twice after that, maybe he'd come to a birthday party that Cathy had, but Claire was fuzzy on that. And soon, as the years went by, they stopped talking about him at all. It was like he'd never even existed. Claire had no idea if he was a misogynist or not. Mostly she just thought he was a really shitty dad.

DOWNSTAIRS, WEEZY HAD A NEW APRON on that was already covered in stuffing and potatoes. The kitchen table had casserole dishes spread all over it, with different Post-it notes stuck to each one that said things like, *Bake at 350 for 20 minutes, uncover for last 10,* and *Vegan Stuffing!* And *Put in the same time as sweet potatoes.* And then there was one note that said, inexplicably, *Will and Green Beans.*

Weezy kept reaching up to push her hair out of her face. She looked hot and annoyed. Cathy, Ruth, and Maureen had arrived and all crowded themselves into the kitchen. They were chatting away, believing themselves to be kind in keeping Weezy company, but Claire knew that all Weezy wanted was for them to get the hell out of her kitchen so that she could spill and curse and cook in peace.

Will and Bets were in the living room, watching the TV in silence. They both seemed happy. Will just wanted to watch the football game, and Bets was probably just gauging the blackness of the NFL players on this screen as opposed to her own.

Max and Cleo were in the basement. They'd been kind of quiet all weekend, and she thought they might have had a fight of some kind. Poor Max. It wasn't easy to deal with a significant other in this household.

Martha was at the stove, stirring apples and cranberries and looking worried. She'd made this dish every year for the past ten years, and still every time she fretted about it and tasted it, apologizing to everyone that it wasn't quite right, until people praised it so much that she smiled down at her plate and said, "It's not that hard."

When Claire walked into the kitchen, Weezy was arranging appetizers on a platter and Cathy was eating crackers and talking about her job, which had something to do with computer programming. Ruth saw Claire and gave her a hug. "Hi!" she said, like they hadn't just seen each other the night before. Claire always liked Ruth, and sometimes wanted to pull her aside and say, "You know you can do better than Cathy, right? You're way nicer."

"Okay then," Weezy said. She clapped her hands and then held them together like she was praying, which maybe she was, for strength to make it through the day. "Ruth? Would you take these out to the family room and then why doesn't everyone head out that way to spend some time with Bets."

Ruth nodded and picked up the tray of cheese and crackers. Cathy followed behind her, still talking about her job—something about a man named Brett, and why he was responsible for spreading a virus throughout the company.

"What can I do to help?" Maureen asked.

"Nothing. Really, we're all set. You can go relax."

"I think I forgot to add cinnamon," Martha said. "Oh shoot!" The mixture boiled and spit a little bit, and Martha jumped back to avoid it.

"I can stay in here," Maureen said. But Weezy just shook her head, and Maureen got up and headed out, looking like she was being punished. During Thanksgiving, Maureen ended up sulking and smoking in corners of the backyard, looking like a teenage version of herself.

"I'll go see if people need drinks," Claire said. She took orders in the family room—white wine spritzer for Bets, beer for Cathy, white wine for Ruth, and for Maureen "anything with vodka."

"Do you want some help?" Will asked, but his eyes were still on the game.

"I'm good."

Claire went to the bar and first made herself a large Bloody Mary with olives. After a few sips of that, she took the drinks to the family room and delivered them to each person with a napkin. She took her drink and walked down to the basement, knocking on the doorframe.

"You guys? Are you in there?"

"Hey," Max said. He sounded tired. Claire peered around the side of the door and saw both of them sitting on the bed. Cleo's eyes looked a little red. They were definitely fighting.

"You should come up soon," Claire said. "Cathy's talking about her job, which is fascinating, and Bets is getting ready to tell us all why we're a disappointment. You don't want to miss it."

"We'll be up in a minute," Max said. He didn't smile.

Claire felt bad for them. Once, during a trip with Doug's

family, she and Doug had gotten into a fight about the cable bill. It was so stupid, but at the time she was so mad she thought she was going to scream at him, right in front of his parents. She'd found the bill and saw that he'd added this crazy football package that basically doubled the price.

"We split this bill," she'd hissed at him in their room. "And you didn't even have the courtesy to tell me about it? To ask me?"

"It's not a big deal," Doug said. "I'll pay for it." Then he tried to shush her, which she hated.

"Don't you shush me," she'd said. "Don't you dare shush me."

The Winkleplecks were a quiet family. They never yelled. At dinner, if someone accidentally interrupted another person, they'd say, "Oh, I'm sorry. Go on." There was no talking over anyone else. When someone started telling a story, the whole family turned and gave that one person their total attention. It made Claire feel very nervous to ever talk around them.

She knew Doug was scared that his parents were going to hear them fighting. "Shhh," he kept saying. "It's fine. I'll pay for it, okay?"

"That's not the point," Claire had said. But she couldn't quite say what the point was, exactly. Just that she was so mad at him that she wanted to scream, and she wanted him to scream back. But they couldn't, and that made it worse. And Mr. and Mrs. Winklepleck were always there, quietly reading or watching TV at a very low volume. There was nowhere to go, and Claire stayed mad at him the whole trip.

And now it looked like poor Max was in the same situation. "Okay, guys," Claire said. "See you up there. You want me to bring some drinks down here for you?"

"No, thanks," Max said. "We'll be up soon." Claire left them down there, wondering what it was that they could be fighting about.

CLAIRE FRESHENED HER BLOODY MARY, and sat down next to Cathy on the couch. She reached forward and grabbed some slices of cheese. *The worst part is almost over,* she told herself.

Cathy turned to her and lowered her voice. "I didn't get a chance to tell you, but I'm really sorry. About Doug and everything."

"Thanks," Claire said.

"I really mean it," she went on. "I know how sometimes news can be worse when everyone else gets ahold of it. You forget how you even feel about it. But just remember that however you feel about it is fine."

"Thanks," Claire said again. But this time her eyes watered a little bit and Cathy squeezed her arm. Maybe being with Ruth had made Cathy a nicer person. And maybe Claire should ease up on the Bloody Marys a little bit.

LAST NIGHT, FRAN HAD TOLD HER that she was "D-runk." That's how he'd said it, pronouncing the *D* and the *runk,* as if they were two different words. She'd protested, telling him she was just tipsy. And then, as they walked into the kitchen to look for snacks, she'd tripped on her heel and ended up facedown on the kitchen floor.

"I've fallen," she said, "and I can't get up."

"Come on," Fran said. He lifted her up and brushed the front of her, like she was a little kid that had fallen in dirt. "Time to go home."

"No, I was just kidding," she said. "Don't you remember that commercial? I was just pretending."

Fran had walked her across the street and down the block to her front door. "I should get home anyway," he said. "People are coming over early tomorrow. Why do people eat so early on Thanksgiving anyway? Who wants to eat mashed potatoes at noon?"

"We don't eat until late," Claire said. "Like six o'clock, usually." She sat on the front cement steps and rested her head on her knees.

"Okay, then," Fran said. He knelt down. "Do you want to go inside?"

"I think I'm just going to sit here for a while."

"What?"

Claire lifted her head. "I said, I'm just going to sit here for a while."

"Do you want me to wait with you?"

Claire shook her head. "No, you can go home." She put her head back on her knees and waved her arm. "Go, I'm serious."

"I'd feel better if you were inside," he said.

Claire stood up and walked down the steps. "Okay, I'll go in the back door, then."

She waved good-bye to him as he walked down the driveway and the sidewalk, and then when he turned the corner, she walked across the street and back to Lainie's.

Almost everyone had gone home, but Lainie's two younger sisters were still there, and they cheered when she walked in. "You're back," Lainie said. "Yay!"

They sat on the back patio and smoked cigarettes, until Claire started feeling like it was going to make her puke. Lainie smoked only when she was drunk, but she didn't like to smoke in the front of the house, in case any of her clients walked by. "Pilates people do not smoke," she always said.

They talked about Fran, and Claire re-created her "I've fallen and I can't get up" scene for Lainie, who loved it.

"What do you want with Fran?" Lainie asked. Claire shrugged. She really didn't know.

"I don't think I want anything," she said. "Or maybe just a little something. I don't know."

She barely remembered their moving back inside the house, and vaguely remembered sitting on the couch and then just laying her body down sideways to sleep. Then the next thing she remembered was waking up to Jack calling her out on sleeping in her clothes.

"RUTH, AREN'T YOU GOING TO HAVE any turkey?" Bets asked.

"Bets, Ruth is a vegan," Cathy said.

Bets sniffed. "Right, I forgot." She asked the same question every year, and Claire was pretty sure that she put "Vegan" right along with "Alcoholic" on her list of things she didn't believe in.

"Martha, how's the job going?" Maureen asked.

"Fine. I mean, good. It's going well."

"You must be the only white caretaker out there," Bets said. "All of ours are foreign, probably illegals. You'll be in high demand." She smiled at Martha.

"Mom," Weezy said. Bets just shrugged and held up her hands, like, *What do you want me to do?*

"Should we say grace?" Will asked. They all bowed their heads, and afterward Will raised his glass and said, "Let's eat!"

Claire noticed that Cleo was just poking her food around on her plate. "Are you okay?" she asked her quietly, but everyone heard her anyway.

"What's the matter, Cleo? Are you not feeling well?" Weezy asked.

"There was a bug going around the retirement community last week," Bets offered. "Four people died."

Claire and Ruth caught each other's eye and smiled, then looked down at their plates. It wasn't funny, of course, that four people had died. It was just that the first time Ruth met Bets, she'd been going on and on about all of her friends that had died. Ruth had very nicely asked Claire later, "Does your grandmother talk about death a lot?" and Claire had laughed so hard she'd peed a little bit. Ever since then, the two of them were in serious danger of getting the giggles when Bets announced that another bridge partner had dropped dead.

"The sweet potatoes are wonderful," Will said. "And so are the apples and cranberries. Martha, you've outdone yourself."

Martha smiled as everyone chimed in, "Yes, they're amazing, they really are. So tasty."

Claire had moved on to white wine and she finished her glass and refilled it from the bottle at the table. Thankfully, it was making her headache go away. There would be another one tomorrow, she knew, but for the moment it was worth it to get through this dinner.

"We'll call Drew after dinner," Weezy said.

"Where is Drew?" Bets asked. They'd told her maybe ten times already.

"Drew stayed in California. He's having Thanksgiving with some coworkers," Maureen said.

"Well, that sounds downright depressing," Bets said.

"I think it sounds nice," Max offered. "To be someplace where it's warm, I mean." He got up and returned with another beer. On his way back to his seat, he patted Cleo's shoulder. The table got quiet and all Claire could hear was chewing and forks hitting the plates.

"Do you like train travel?" Bets directed this question at Ruth, who looked as surprised as the rest of them.

"Um, yes, I do. I haven't done much of it, but I do like it."

Claire saw Weezy and Maureen give each other a meaningful look across the table. They were always on the lookout for signs that Bets was losing it, and bringing up train travel out of the blue was a bit strange.

"Should we go around and say what we're thankful for?" Weezy suggested. It was something they'd done when they were little, and every so often, when conversation was lacking, they did it again. One year, Drew said he was thankful for the dirt bike that he'd gotten for his birthday, and Bets tried to make him choose something else. He'd refused, telling her that really was what he was most thankful for. Bets got mad and told Maureen that she'd raised materialistic children. Weezy had come to her defense, and all the kids went upstairs to play and listen to their mothers fight with their grandmother. Will had gone into the kitchen to clean, which was more desirable than staying at the table and fighting over a dirt bike.

Now, when they went around the table to say what they were thankful for, everyone gave up and just said "Family" and "Health" as their answers. Weezy was about to start, when Cathy interrupted her.

"Well, actually, I have an announcement to make," she said. She looked around the table and smiled, looking a little nervous. "Last night I asked Ruth to marry me, and she said yes!"

Claire thought she felt time stop. Bets had her fork in her hand and she held it right above her plate, a strange little smile on her face. Everyone else stared at Cathy, as though it would take a minute to understand what she had said.

Finally, Martha squealed and jumped up to run around the table and hug Cathy and Ruth. Once she moved, everyone seemed to get unfrozen.

"This is so exciting," Martha said over and over.

"Will you be my maid of honor?" Cathy asked. Martha started to cry and Claire rolled her eyes before she could stop herself.

"Of course," Martha said.

"Well," Maureen said. "What a surprise. Well. What a happy Thanksgiving."

"To the engaged couple," Will said, holding up his glass. Claire knew he would repeat the story later, to friends and coworkers, saying, "You can't pick who you love, you know. As long as they're happy, we're happy."

They all raised their glasses and clinked them to the right, to the left, and the center. Now Claire knew why Cathy had mentioned Doug. She really did feel bad that she was going to announce her engagement so soon after Claire's ended. That's why it was sincere.

Cathy turned to Claire. "Will you be my bridesmaid?" she asked.

"Of course," Claire said. "I'd be honored." She took a sip of wine.

LATER, AFTER THE TABLE WAS CLEARED and the dishes were stacked, and the dishwasher was started, they all rested in the family room. It would probably be two days before the kitchen was really clean again. It never seemed worth it to Claire, to make all that mess for one meal. But then again, Thanksgiving was not her favorite holiday.

Someone suggested playing a game, but no one really wanted to, so they just sat around for a while. Will fell asleep in his chair and started snoring loudly. Claire leaned her head back on the couch and closed her eyes, and when she opened them, Maureen, Cathy, and Ruth were getting ready to leave.

Everyone hugged, and Bets went up to bed. Will stood up and stretched, pretended that he hadn't been sleeping and said that he was heading to bed as well. The house smelled like turkey grease, which made Claire feel a little sick.

Claire and Martha unloaded the dishwasher and got another group of dishes in, and then they started washing the china and crystal by hand. "Oh, thanks, girls," Weezy said. She was on the couch with her feet up. "You don't have to do all that. I'll be there in just a minute." But her eyes were closed, and she looked like she couldn't have moved if she wanted to.

Martha kept talking about Cathy's wedding. "I'll have to give a speech," she said. She almost dropped the wineglass she was drying. "What will I say? Oh, I'm already nervous. What do you think she'll want us to wear?"

"Burlap sacks," Claire said.

"Very funny. Ruth has a great sense of style."

"Yes, but we're Cathy's bridesmaids. I think she'll be the one picking out the dresses."

"Oh, well, we can suggest some things. Don't worry."

"I'm not."

They finished the second round of cleaning, and Claire went upstairs to get ready for bed. Martha came up a little while later, when she was already under the covers.

"I tried to get Mom to go to bed, but she's still on the couch. She kept saying, 'I'll get up in a minute.'"

"Mmm-hmm," Claire said. She was half-asleep.

"Happy Thanksgiving," Martha whispered.

• • •

CLAIRE WOKE UP WITH A START, in the middle of a nightmare where she was falling off of a balcony. She sat up to steady herself, and saw Martha squatting by the door, which was cracked open.

"What are you doing?" she asked.

"Shhhh," Martha said. She motioned for Claire to come next to her.

"What?" Claire said. But she got up and went to the door. She could hear her mom's voice, but couldn't quite hear what she was saying. Then she heard Max, who sounded like he was crying.

"What's going on?" she asked Martha.

Martha turned, her eyes wide. "I think Cleo's pregnant," she said.

"No—did you really hear that?"

"I think so. It's kind of hard to hear."

"No way. Max is probably just failing a class or something." But even as she said it, Claire knew that she was wrong. She couldn't hear what Max was saying, but she knew he was upset. And not much upset Max. In fact, almost nothing upset him. Claire tried to ignore the excited look in Martha's eyes.

Claire never understood the way that Martha got almost giddy when there was tragedy or drama. She fed off of it. She could find a problem in any situation, even the most pleasant. But when there was a real problem, like this, that's where she really thrived. She got involved, she talked about it constantly. It was like being a part of the drama made her feel included and important.

They sat crouched together, listening to the rise and fall of Weezy's and Max's voices. They heard Cleo's name and something about her mom. They heard Weezy say, "Decisions to make," and "young" and "difficult." And once, they heard an "Oh, Max," from Weezy, and then they heard Max really start to cry.

They looked at each other, and Claire knew that it was true. Cleo must be pregnant, because what else could it be? Unless Max had killed someone, but even then, Weezy would be on the phone with a lawyer or the police. And she wasn't. She was just talking to Max, her voice filled with disappointment. And that was never a good sign.

Poor Max, she thought. *Poor, poor Max.*

CHAPTER 14

Weezy didn't handle it as well as Max had thought she would. He'd said, "It won't be that bad" so many times that Cleo almost believed him. She agreed that he should tell Weezy by himself, and not just because she didn't want any part of that conversation. Weezy wouldn't be able to react truthfully if Cleo was there, and that didn't seem fair.

Max went upstairs late, after everyone had gone to bed. Weezy was asleep on the couch, but he'd woken her up. Cleo had stayed in the basement, sitting on the top step and listening.

Weezy had started crying almost immediately. At first Cleo felt bad, but after a while as she listened to Weezy heave and gasp, with what seemed like unnecessary drama, she started to get annoyed. She thought about storming up the stairs, looking her in the face, and saying, "What are you crying about? You don't have to have this baby." She didn't, of course. She stayed put and listened to Weezy repeat that she was so disappointed. Not *in* them, but *for* them. Whatever that meant.

Somehow, during the conversation where Max told Weezy that Cleo was pregnant, it had come out that they were living together. "You're what?" Weezy had said, like that was the real problem, like living together was the reason she got pregnant in the first place.

MAX STAYED CALM UNTIL THE VERY END when he started to cry. She couldn't blame him. She was about to cry herself, just listening to Weezy repeat herself, letting him know that she really was just so disappointed.

Cleo heard the word "options" and she sat up straight. She didn't want Weezy up there talking about her like she wasn't there. She was right here. They weren't Weezy's options, they were hers, and she had decided.

When Max finally came back down, she had moved one step down and had her head resting on her arms on the landing. She was exhausted. Max was walking quickly, and he still had tears running down his face, which embarrassed her so much she had to look away. She was embarrassed because she knew he wouldn't want her to see him cry. She never had before, and if this hadn't happened, she wondered how long, if ever, it would have been before she'd seen it.

"I think we should go," Max said. He was already grabbing his bag and putting stuff in it.

"Now?" It was five in the morning.

"Yeah, let's get out of here. I want to leave before anyone wakes up."

"Can you even drive? You had kind of a lot to drink."

"Yeah, I'm fine. It's morning now."

"What did she say?" Cleo already knew, but she wanted to hear it from him.

"I'll tell you about it later. Let's just go."

"But my stuff is upstairs," Cleo said. The last thing she wanted to do was to walk up there by herself, and run into Weezy in the hall, or see crazy Bets on her way to the bathroom. Her heart started to beat quickly just thinking about it.

"I'll run and grab it," Max said. "Can you finish packing my stuff?"

Cleo nodded and he ran up the stairs, taking them two at a time. They looked like a couple that was late for the airport.

IT WAS STILL DARK OUT when they got in the car, and they drove in silence for almost an hour. Cleo was afraid to say anything to him. Every once in a while she reached over and put her hand on his leg, or rubbed the back of his neck, but he didn't react much. Cleo forced herself to keep her eyes open, even though all she wanted to do was sleep. It used to be that she couldn't sleep if she was worried, but now she felt like she could sleep anywhere and anytime. Finally they passed a sign for a rest stop that was coming up, and Max turned to look at her. "Are you hungry?" She nodded, and he turned on his blinker and got off the expressway.

Max said he'd run in and get the food, and Cleo asked for an egg sandwich and a cup of coffee. Max shook his head. "I don't think you're supposed to have coffee."

"Oh," Cleo said. "Not even a cup?"

"I'm not sure."

"Forget it. Just get me a bottle of water."

Max nodded and got out of the car to go get their food. She was so sad just then, for both of them, as she watched him open the door and go in. It was so sad, just fucking depressing, really. Neither of them had any idea what they were doing. They didn't even know if she could have coffee or not.

Cleo started to cry a little bit, her nose running, and she dug around until she found an old napkin in the car to blow her nose. She was trying to stop the tears before Max came back, but when she saw him walk out with a drink tray and a bag of fast-food breakfast, she started crying all over again.

"I got you orange juice, too," he said. He put his hand on the back of her head and ran it down to her neck.

"What're we doing?" she asked.

"We'll be okay," Max said. This sounded like such a complete lie that Cleo let out a little laugh. "Here, you should eat." He handed the sandwich to Cleo and she unwrapped it in her lap.

"We're really in a lot of shit, aren't we?" she said. Max was pulling out of the parking lot and onto the ramp to get back on the highway, and he didn't answer her.

WHEN CLEO TOLD HER MOM, there was a pause and for a second she thought her mom hadn't heard her and she was going to have to repeat herself. And then she heard her mom say, "Oh god*damn* it, Cleo."

Cleo had breathed in quickly, like someone had surprised her, and then she'd started to cry. On the other end of the phone, her mom sighed. She hated when Cleo cried, she always had.

"Well, have you thought about it?" Elizabeth asked.

"Mom, of course I've thought about it."

"And?"

"And what? I'm keeping it. I wouldn't be telling you about it otherwise, would I?"

"Cleo, you really need to think about this."

"What do you mean, I really need to think about it? You think I haven't thought about it?"

"I'm just saying, it's a big decision."

"Yeah, no kidding. And I've thought about it. I have. You're talking to me like I don't think things through, like I'm some idiot who got knocked up and just decided to go with it."

"Well, right about now, that sounds pretty accurate, don't you think?"

Cleo hung up the phone and threw it at the couch. Then she started to really let herself cry, with big, indulgent, dramatic sobs. She waited for her mom to call her back, but all she got was an e-mail an hour later.

Cleo,

I'm upset at the way things were handled today. I understand that you are upset as well, so when you're ready to talk in a calm manner, I'll be available.

Mom

"Do you believe this?" she screamed. She ran into the bedroom to show it to Max, holding her phone right in front of his face until he took it from her and read it. Her first instinct had been to hide it, to hide the fact that she had a mom who was such a monster. But then her rage had taken over and she didn't care about that.

It sounded like a fucking business e-mail: *The way things were handled. I'll be available.* Good God, her mom was a crazy person. She didn't even know how to talk to people normally, didn't even know how to act when her daughter told her she was pregnant.

"I'm never talking to her again," Cleo said. "She can die alone."

"Okay," Max said. "You're upset."

"Of course I'm upset. My mom is a horrible person. And can I just point out that she also got pregnant by accident? With me. You'd think she'd be a little more understanding."

"She's just surprised."

"I'm surprised too," Cleo said. "Didn't she think about that?"

CLEO WAS STILL THROWING UP almost every day. They kept waiting for it to stop, but it never did. Max read the pregnancy books they bought and reported back to her. "It says it's normal for some women to be sick through the whole pregnancy. Mostly it's just the first trimester, but some people have it the whole time." He looked up at her with wide eyes.

"What a relief," she said.

In class, her lips were red and raw from all the retching. She could feel her professors looking at her, probably thinking that she was on a bender, that she was perpetually hungover, that her life was spiraling out of control. The last part was true, of course, just not for the reasons they thought.

As soon as she got home in the afternoons, she'd lie on the couch and watch TV. Sometimes she'd try to eat saltines, but the only thing that ever had any chance of staying down was Fig Newtons, which she'd never liked before.

"Our baby is going to grow up to be a fig," Cleo said. She was kidding, but Max looked worried.

"Maybe I'll call my mom to see if she has any ideas," he said.

Weezy had called them before they'd even gotten back to school. She apologized for the way she acted, Max relayed to Cleo. She was sorry that they'd already left. And she wanted them to know that the whole family would be there to help them through all of this.

Max was relieved, and Cleo was too. She was. For the most part, anyway. She still wished that her own mom would have come around, and if not, it would have almost been nicer if she and Max could have commiserated on how awful their parents were being. Instead, he talked to his mom every single day, filling her in on doctor's appointments and asking her advice on every little thing.

Cleo was tired. More tired than she'd ever been in her whole life. Sometimes when she'd be walking to class, she'd think that she was going to fall asleep standing up, because she couldn't keep her eyes open, and they would close and her head would bob. One night, after dinner, Max came in the room to tell her that Weezy had said that her nausea would be worse if she lay down after meals. "She said to stay upright, just walk around or sit up until you've digested."

Cleo was lying on the couch when he told her this, and she opened one eye to look at him standing there, so eager. "I'd rather throw up all over myself, than sit up right now," she said. She closed her eyes again and heard Max walk out of the room.

Sometimes Max would be talking to Weezy and he'd just hand the phone to Cleo, without giving her a chance to say no, or even just prepare. She wanted to tell Max that it hurt her feelings, that it made her feel sad when she heard Weezy's voice over the phone, telling Cleo what it was like when she was pregnant, asking her how tired she was, promising that it would get better. But she couldn't tell him that, because even she knew it sounded ridiculous, that talking to his mom hurt her feelings, and so she kept it to herself.

There was one night, though, when Max was on the phone with his mom, again, and Cleo was lying on the couch, trying to watch TV, which was hard since Max was talking kind of loud. She turned up the volume, but all she could concentrate on was Max's voice.

"Yeah, she's been having trouble with that for a while now," he said. "It's making her feel sicker, I think." Then

Max turned to her, lowered the phone from his mouth, and said, "My mom says to drink hot water with lemon. She said it really helps constipation."

Cleo opened her mouth to say something, but nothing came out. Then, when Max got off the phone, she finally found her words. "Could you please not talk to your mom about my constipation?"

CLEO MADE MAX PROMISE THAT he wouldn't tell any of his friends. "Please. Please don't say anything. I don't want to be the pregnant girl at college."

"Okay," Max said. "But people are going to find out eventually."

"I know, but let's just wait, okay? No one needs to know right now."

"People are going to think something's wrong when we just hole up in the apartment."

"Well, you can go out. Just because I can't drink doesn't mean you have to stay home."

"Really?" Max asked.

"Definitely. You can just tell everyone I'm studying or sick or out with other people."

And she had meant it. Or at least she had meant it until Max came home drunk one night with a bag of McDonald's and crept into their bedroom to say hello.

"Hey, baby," he said, and put his face next to hers. He smelled like rubbing alcohol.

"Hey," she said. She'd been asleep. She rolled away from him and heard him rustling in the bag of food. She looked back to see him unwrapping a Filet-O-Fish.

"Have you ever had one of these?" he asked her. "They're pretty good. I don't always feel like them, but tonight I wanted an appetizer to my Big Mac." Cleo now smelled tar-tar sauce in addition to the rubbing alcohol.

"Ugh, Max," Cleo said. She sat up and put her hand over her nose.

"What's the matter?" he asked. He was slurring just a little bit. "Do you want a bite?" He held the sandwich out to her.

"No! Just get out," she said.

Max looked hurt. "Do you want some french fries?"

"No, Max. Really, please just leave me alone."

"Fine," Max said. "I was just trying to be nice." He stood up and walked to the door, leaving a few french fries in his trail. He slammed the bedroom door shut behind him and turned on the TV in the other room.

Cleo found him there the next morning, fast asleep, mouth open, with the McDonald's bag resting next to him. They didn't talk for almost the whole day, just huffed around each other. Then, just when it was starting to get dark, Max apologized.

"I'm sorry," he said. "I didn't mean to make you mad."

"I know."

"But I did."

"Yeah."

"You're the one that yelled at me to get out."

"Yeah, but that was because you woke me up with a Filet-O-Fish on my pillow. Can you blame me?"

"I just wanted to say hi." Max smiled the tiniest bit.

"Max."

"I know, I'm really sorry. I am."

"I'm sorry too, for yelling," Cleo said. She went over and sat next to him on the couch.

"What a fucking mess," Max said. Cleo wasn't sure if he was talking about the apartment or their life.

"I know," she said.

MAX KEPT ASSURING HER THAT she wasn't showing, but she didn't believe him. "Look at this," she'd say, pulling her shirt tight across her stomach. "This is not what I normally look like."

"Well, I know that," Max said. "I just mean that no one else can tell."

"But I can tell," she said.

Max insisted she didn't look any different, like he thought that was the nice thing to say, but it wasn't. And so, she finally said, "If I'm normally this fat, then kill me."

AT THE FIRST DOCTOR'S APPOINTMENT, she'd been poked and prodded and had blood drawn and everything else. She kept waiting for him to say, "It's a mistake, you aren't pregnant," but he didn't.

"Your due date is July fifteenth," he told them.

It was already cold outside, the start of winter, so July seemed far away, which comforted Cleo. They bought a calendar on the way home, the kind that you hang on the wall, because it seemed like they should have one, and they hung it up on a nail in the kitchen, and circled July 15 with a red marker. In the circle, Cleo wrote, DUE DATE.

"Well, there it is," Max said. They stood and stared at it.

"Yep. There it is."

WHEN SHE WAS FOUR MONTHS ALONG, Max started telling people. "We can't just wait until your stomach starts to get huge," he said. He told his friend Mickey first, and then his friend Ben, and then more and more people. And those people told other people and Cleo figured that a few days after Max first told Mickey, the whole school knew. She didn't tell anyone. Who would she tell? Her old roommates that seemed to be thriving without her? Could she really call up Monica and tell her that she was pregnant, that she'd fucked up? She could just imagine Laura and Mary when they found out, sitting on the futon and saying to each other, "I knew it was a mistake for her to move in with him. I knew it. She's getting what she deserves. It's only fair."

Cleo felt like people stared at her wherever she went on campus. She felt like as soon as she passed, people whispered to each other, or pointed her out to the friend they were walking with. *There she is, that's the pregnant girl, can't you tell, her butt looks huge.*

"You sound paranoid," Max said.

"Well, I'm not," she told him.

CLEO AND HER MOTHER WERE ON e-mail terms. That's how she put it to Max. They had tried to talk on the phone once more, and Cleo had ended up screaming while her mom said, "This is not the kind of conversation I want to have," over and over. E-mail was better for both of them, they agreed. Maybe they'd just stay on these terms forever. Maybe Cleo could just e-mail pictures of the baby to her when it was born and then when the baby was old enough, it could start e-mailing with Elizabeth, have its own online relationship with its grandmother. It would be like they were all virtual people, like they were bodyless and floating in cyberspace.

MAX WENT WITH HER FOR the first ultrasound, even though she kept telling him that he didn't have to. It was so weird, that before she was pregnant, the thought of having Max in the room while she went to the gynecologist would have been disgusting, silly really, and so strange that no one would ever allow it. But now that she was pregnant, it wasn't just common but it was expected? Max was supposed to be there while she put her feet in the stirrups.

"Well, we can see the baby here," the doctor said. "And it is just one baby." The thought of its being more than one baby had never even occurred to Cleo.

"That's it right there?" Max asked. He pointed to the screen.

"It looks like a little doll," Cleo said. "Or a peanut."

The ultrasound technician froze the screen and told them that she'd print out some pictures for them.

"Can we get an extra copy?" Max asked the technician. "I want to send one to my mom."

"Really?" Cleo asked.

"Yeah, I think she'd like to see it. She'll probably hang it on the refrigerator or something." The thought of a picture of the inside of her uterus hanging in the Coffeys' kitchen made Cleo feel strange. But Max seemed excited, so she let it go.

They hung the ultrasound on their own refrigerator, and whenever Cleo went into the kitchen, her eyes went first to the picture, and then to the calendar that hung on the wall. And each time she glanced back and forth, between the calendar and the grainy ultrasound picture, she thought about how they were that much closer to that little baby's actually being a baby and coming into the world. As if she needed reminding.

15

Weezy had a high horse. And she could get on it whenever she wanted. Maureen used to always tease her, when she'd go off on other people's behavior. "Uh-oh," she'd say. "Giddyup! Here comes the horse."

Even when she was younger, her parents used to act like Weezy thought she was too good for people. "Don't get too big for your britches," her father would say.

It was silly, really. It's not like Weezy believed herself to be so morally superior to everyone. It was just that sometimes she simply couldn't believe the way that people acted. (Like Cleo's mother, for instance.)

Because what kind of mother would abandon her child at this moment? No matter how disappointed or upset a person was, to sever contact while your only daughter was pregnant? Well, it was disgusting. That's what it was. There was no other word for it, really. Except maybe *despicable*. And *selfish*.

"You know," she told Maureen, "I'm not thrilled with this either. I'm not jumping up and down that my son that's still in college is going to be a father. But I'm helping. I'm still talking to him."

"I know," Maureen said. "But you never know the details of other people's lives."

"I know enough. I know enough to know it's wrong. I

have half a mind to call her up myself and talk to her." She'd said as much to Max, but he'd begged her not to.

"Don't, Mom. Please don't. They're figuring it out, and Cleo would kill me if you did that."

"Fine," she'd said with a sniff. "I'll give it a few more months. But then she's going to have to be involved."

Right after Max told her the news, she'd been floored. This wasn't what she expected. Not that anyone expects this news, but still. She had to admit that this hadn't even crossed her mind. She'd thought about what would happen if one of the girls got pregnant, but not this.

"It's easier, probably, that it's your son and not your daughter," Maureen said.

"What's that supposed to mean?" Weezy asked.

"It just is. I don't know."

Weezy did know what Maureen meant, but she wasn't going to give her the satisfaction of admitting it. At least not without faking some sort of innocence. She had always made a point of being more open-minded than Maureen. When Cathy came out, Maureen admitted (when she was about three bottles of Chardonnay deep) that she was sad about the whole thing.

"I don't love her differently, I don't. I just wish . . . I just wish it wasn't the case," she'd said.

"Well, there's no use thinking that now," Weezy had said. She'd secretly been thrilled that Maureen had admitted such a thing to her.

"I know that," Maureen had said. She sounded annoyed. "I just mean, I had a picture in my head of how it was going to be. And now it's not. It could have been so much simpler."

They'd never spoken about it again, or at least not really. Weezy had found an article about how parents need to mourn for their straight children when they find out that they're gay. She'd been excited to give it to her, since it made so much sense. It said that you needed to mourn and fully understand that your child was going to lead a different life than you had imagined. And once you did that, you could fully accept who they were.

"Thanks," Maureen had said. She took it and folded the paper, and put it right in her purse.

Weezy knew why she didn't want to talk about it anymore. There was nothing worse than wishing that your children were something other than what they were. She'd had those moments, where she wondered what it would be like if Martha could function on her own, what it would be like if she were able to have normal relationships with people.

And of course, she wished that things had gone differently for Claire. It's not that she thought marriage and children were the answer to everything. Certainly not. She just wished that things had worked out between them, that Claire was settled now instead of lost.

When Max first told her about Cleo, she'd thought his life was ruined. So there it was, all three of her children in a mess, and yes, she wished things were different. She was ashamed at these thoughts, and she would never admit it to anyone. Maureen probably regretted even speaking the words out loud, and so Weezy swore she would never do the same.

WEEZY HAD BEEN PARALYZED FOR the weeks between Thanksgiving and Christmas. She'd managed to call Max, to tell him that they would be there for him, of course. But then she'd felt like she couldn't move. Christmas was a struggle. She'd do one thing, like get a box of decorations out of the attic, and then she'd have to lie down. Little by little, everything got done, but not before Weezy was convinced that she was anemic or possibly had some kind of cancer, because it just wasn't normal to have so little energy.

Max called her at least three times a day. He called to report on doctor's appointments and to ask her questions and to tell her what was happening. She knew that he was looking for reassurance. He'd been the same way as a little boy, needing to talk about things, needing to hear someone say that things were going to work out.

She talked to him whenever he called. She was happy to. At least this wouldn't tear their family apart, right? She felt righteous and good when they talked. She suggested that he and Cleo start taking walks for exercise, because it was never too early to start thinking about keeping in shape for the baby. Yes, she was happy to talk to him. But she did wonder if possibly that was what was taking all of her energy.

When she woke up in the mornings, her limbs felt heavy. She tried to explain this to Will, who suggested that it was just a reaction to Max's news. (That's what he was calling the whole thing. He hadn't said the words *pregnant* and *baby* at all.)

"I think I should see a doctor," she told him. She was still lying in bed when she said this.

Will turned to look at her. "Maybe," he said. "Or you could just give yourself some time to get used to this."

"Maybe there's a gas leak in the house," she said. There had to be something, some reason why her body felt like this.

"If there was a leak, wouldn't we all feel sick?" Will asked. Weezy had sighed and rolled over on her side. It was the kind of comment that could make you really hate Will.

Maureen brought soup over after Weezy told her on the

phone that she was coming down with something. "I don't know what it is, but it's bad. A virus of some kind."

When Maureen arrived, she found Weezy sitting on the couch in her pajamas and robe. She arranged the soup without saying a word, and then the two of them sat and watched some talk shows.

One morning a couple of weeks after Thanksgiving, Weezy walked down the stairs and surveyed the house. She decided that she'd do one thing every day to get ready for Christmas. How hard could it be to do one thing? She stood at the bottom of the stairs and looked all around. Dozens of little turkeys smiled at her from all around the house, sending her right back upstairs to bed. They all had such creepy gobbles, and she couldn't face that today. She could start tomorrow.

One day, she managed to arrange all the Santas that she'd collected over the years on the mantel, and then she'd gone over to the couch and lay there, staring at them. She'd cried a little bit, because her heart was breaking for her Max and she really didn't know what would happen.

Will brought the tree up from the basement and put on the lights, and the girls hung the ornaments. (They'd gone to a fake tree a few years ago, when getting a real tree seemed like too much of a hassle. Claire and Max had both protested, saying that it was pointless to put up a piece of plastic. Weezy tried to tell them that the pine-scented candles would make it seem like the real thing without all the needles on the floor that couldn't be vacuumed up no matter what. Even in April, she'd still be finding them hidden behind furniture and under rugs. This year she was even more grateful that the tree was in their basement, or they might not have had one at all.)

She didn't know how she was going to manage to buy presents and she put it off, until it was the week before Christmas and she had no more time to waste. She got in the car and drove to the mall. It was cold, but there was no snow on the ground, so she could be grateful for that.

For the first time in her life that she could remember, Weezy had no Christmas list with her when she shopped. She walked into department stores and bought generic gifts, scarves and mittens. She shopped in groups. When she found something she liked for one of the girls, she bought three of them. Will and Max got the same sweater in different colors, the same gloves, the same socks.

She was surprised at how quickly it went, buying piles of books at the bookstore, not caring who got what, just knowing that there'd be something to wrap. She had to buy for Cleo this year, who was coming for Christmas, but that just meant buying more duplicates. All of the shopping was done in one day, with Weezy making a few trips to the car in between.

When she pulled into the driveway after her shopping trip, she left all the bags in the car, poured herself a glass of wine, and got into her bed in her pajamas. It was five thirty. When Will found her, she was watching TV and had the comforter pulled up to her chin.

"I'm not feeling well," she said. Will looked at the glass of wine and nodded, then let her rest for the night.

Weezy spent her time in bed on the laptop, looking up information on weddings where the bride was pregnant. There were many tips. Ruching seemed to be a popular way to hide the stomach, although it didn't really look like it worked that well. There were some brides that decided to wait until after the baby was born, some that waited years and then had the child as a ring bearer or flower girl. (Which just seemed downright trashy.) She wondered what it would take to convince Max and Cleo that they should get married. She scoured the sites for tips and tricks, and thought at least they weren't the first couple to get themselves into this mess.

SHE HAD NO IDEA HOW she was going to manage to have everyone home for three days. That was all it was going to be, but it seemed impossible. She could fake sick, she thought, if things got really bad. It would be like the year that she had gotten the stomach flu and could barely make it downstairs for twenty minutes to watch the kids open their presents. They'd all eaten breakfast without her, gone to mass without her, and she'd stayed upstairs in bed, watching old movies.

Weezy felt safer that she had a backup plan. No one could argue with a sick person, and it wouldn't even be like she was lying. She was sick. She just didn't know what she had.

Somehow she managed to make it through. Will and the girls had helped with the cooking and while she had imagined that this year, the days would go on forever, it was like any other year and Christmas seemed to be over in a flash.

Now she could rest. She imagined sleeping all day, not having to shop or decorate. This is what her life would be like from now on. It was like she'd aged twenty years in the past month.

But then, after Christmas, things changed. She woke up one morning with her heart pounding, thinking of all the things that had to be done. And instead of feeling tired, she felt full of energy. She drank a pot of coffee each morning, and darted around the house, cleaning and organizing.

Claire told her that she had to slow down. Actually what she said was, "Mom, you're going to give yourself a heart attack." But Weezy couldn't stop. She sent out an e-mail to all

of her friends, telling them that Max's girlfriend was pregnant and that she hoped they could all be happy for the family, even if things were happening a little out of order.

Weezy knew that they were all giving each other looks
behind her back, but she didn't have time to deal with them.
There was too much to do, too much to figure out.

"I'm glad you're feeling better," Maureen said. She raised
her eyebrows and waited for Weezy to say something.

"Thanks. Me too," she said.

Will continued on through his days like nothing had happened. "What do you want me to do?" he asked Weezy. "It's
happened and we're dealing with it."

But *they* weren't dealing with anything—*Weezy* was
dealing with all of it. She made the plans and ran them by
Max, who ran them by Cleo, and then she told Will what was
going to happen.

"They'll be moving back here at the end of the school
year," she told Will. It had taken weeks to convince Max that
this was the right thing to do, but she'd done it.

"That's a good idea," Will said. And that was all.

Will spent almost all of his time in his office, typing away.
He took all his meals straight up there, probably to avoid
Weezy and talking about Max. Whenever she brought it up,
when she talked about how worried she was about Max, Will
just nodded.

"Don't you care?" Weezy asked.

"Of course I care," Will said. "I just don't think we need
to pretend like Max isn't responsible, like this is something
that happened to him and not something that he did."

But Will's inaction just made Weezy move faster. She
began to redo the basement, since she figured that Max and
Cleo would be staying down there when they returned. It

would be more comfortable for them, and easier on the whole family, if they had their own space.

The challenge of course was to make a basement look like a place where you wanted to spend time. There was something damp and chilly about the room down there, and Weezy had never liked it. But now, she would get it done. She felt like she was on one of those home-decorating challenge shows, where they find an unused space and make it into something amazing.

She got the floors redone, and bought new throw rugs to cover the tile. (They couldn't put wall-to-wall carpeting down there, because there was always a chance it would flood. But she made it look cozy.) She bought new furniture, a new dresser and two bedside tables with matching blue ceramic lamps. She had the walls repainted a soft yellow, which seemed welcoming and calming, and she bought new bedding that looked inviting and soft.

The bathroom in the basement was old and rusty and the floor was always freezing, no matter what time of year it was. She had some people come in to look at it and two days later it was all ripped up. "We've been meaning to do this for years," Weezy said when Will acted surprised. "Now this just gives us a reason to get it done."

She bought a bassinet for the baby and put it right next to the bed. That would do for the time being. They'd have to figure out a crib at some point, but for now this would be enough. Although she did go out and buy a couple of extra soft baby blankets, and just a few little stuffed animals to put in the bassinet so it didn't look so empty.

When she showed Claire and Martha the finished room, she was extremely proud of herself. They were shocked, she could tell. "Well?" she asked them. "What do you think?"

"Whoa," Martha said. She kept turning in circles looking at the walls.

"It looks great," Claire said. "It doesn't even look like the same place."

"Oh, it was just a few things here and there," Weezy said.

"I don't know how you did this all so quickly," Claire said. "Now you're all set."

But she wasn't all set. The room was just the beginning. There was so much more to do. Maureen told her to slow down. "You're running yourself ragged," she said. But no one understood. No one understood that Weezy had to keep moving, had to keep doing things, or everyone around her would fall apart.

The rest of her family seemed to go on just as usual. Claire was spending a lot of time with that boy Fran, which worried Weezy, although in the grand scheme of things she couldn't worry too much about it now. Unless Claire got pregnant as well, there just wasn't time. And of course once she had that thought, it was stuck in her brain. Imagine if that happened—if Claire and Cleo were both pregnant and living under her roof. *See?* Weezy thought. *Things could be worse.*

WEEZY GOT THE FEELING THAT her family was talking about her behind her back. Whenever she came into a room, it seemed that Will and Martha and Claire had just been whispering about her, just been sharing some information. "Just humor her," Will probably told them. "Just be helpful."

It reminded her of when the kids were young, when every once in a while she'd lose her temper and stomp off to her room, and when she'd come back down, she'd find Will playing with them or making them lunch and they'd all look up at her and say hello, cheerfully, as though nothing had happened. Will would be spinning the wheel for Candyland or making bologna sandwiches, and she just knew that they'd talked about her while she was upstairs. "Mom's upset," Will would have said, "so we need to be on our best behavior."

It should have made her feel better during those moments, that Will would step in and run interference, that her kids were so willing to put on a smile to appease her. But whenever she came downstairs, it just made her feel left out, like she was the moody member of the team, that needed special treatment, and they had all kept going without her. Will always looked so satisfied, like he thought that he could take over with the kids. He was so pleased that he could handle them for all of thirty minutes, and it didn't make her feel better—it made her angry, made her feel like she wasn't even a part of this family that she was running.

ONE WEDNESDAY, WILL HAD CALLED from his office to suggest they go to dinner. "Somewhere nice," he said. "Just the adults."

It occurred to Weezy that their children were now adults too, that there were really four adults living full-time in this house, soon to be six. But she didn't say that.

"I don't know," she said. "There's so much to do." Really, the thought of washing her hair and finding something to wear out seemed overwhelming. But Will had insisted.

They'd gone to Pesce, a seafood restaurant that was a favorite of theirs. Usually it was saved for anniversaries or birthdays.

"Well, this is fancy," Weezy said, when they pulled into the parking lot.

"I thought you deserved a nice night out," Will said.

They walked in and were seated at a corner table. The restaurant was dark and the table had a small votive in the center, as if that would be enough to help people see. Will ordered a Scotch and Weezy ordered red wine. It came in an oversized glass, the kind that almost looks like a bucket, which pleased her. She took a few sips and felt the warmth in her chest and stomach.

"I've been worried about you," Will said. "Because you've been so worried about everything. You're going to collapse if you keep this up."

Weezy sighed. "I have to worry. Just for a little while. Just until things settle down."

Will nodded and tilted his glass to the left and right, causing the ice cubes to clink against one another. "You're a fantastic mother," he said. He raised his glass. "To you."

He and Weezy clinked glasses and then took a sip. Weezy wanted to tell him how strange it was that she felt so energized lately. How for the past few years, she'd felt like there was nothing surprising to look forward to—that is, until Claire had gotten engaged, but then that had all gone to hell. Her children were mostly grown, they'd gone off to college, and she had just been waiting, stalled really, for the next stage of her life to start. And she thought that it was far away, many years down the line.

But then this had happened. And, of course, she was not pleased at first. Disappointed, really. Embarrassed, for sure. But once that went away, once she dealt with that, she was excited. She couldn't admit that to herself for a long time, but it was the truth. She was needed again. Max needed her and Cleo needed her. She was useful. And there was going to be a baby.

She thought of how to explain this to Will, who was looking at her with a mix of concern and pity. He felt bad for her! He still thought she was the martyr who was putting everything aside to help their child. So she didn't say anything except, "It's what any mother would do."

Will reached out and patted her hand, leaving his to rest on top for a few moments. "That's not true," he said. "It's what you do. And so you deserve a night out."

With that, he took his hand back and opened the menu. "Good God, can you see any of this?" He squinted and brought the menu close to his face, then picked up the votive and held it next to it. "I can't see a thing!"

Weezy pulled the magnifying card that Will had given her a few years earlier out of her purse. It had lights on the side to help as well. He'd put it in her stocking as a surprise one Christmas, as a joke about their old age. But lately she'd really had to use it. It had become their custom for Weezy to look through her menu with it, reading aloud the things that she knew he'd like.

"Seared scallops with asparagus risotto," she read. "Pecan-crusted tilapia, maple-glazed salmon."

Will got the scallops, which she'd known he would. Weezy got the tilapia, which Will had guessed. They both ordered white wine with their dinners, and ate slowly. Will cut one of his scallops in half and deposited it on her plate with a scoop of the risotto. She did the same with her fish.

They even split a dessert, at Will's insistence. "My diet is already shot," he said. "So we might as well go all the way." Will's "diet" consisted of his complaining about his weight and spending a few days each month doing sit-ups in his office and trying to give up butter.

"This was a perfect night," Weezy said as they left. Will had ordered a glass of port for each of them and they were both a little wobbly as they left the restaurant. Will had started slurring just the tiniest bit, and Weezy knew it probably wasn't smart for them to drive home, but it was only a couple of miles.

She woke up in the middle of the night with a headache and stomach cramps and spent the next hour in the bathroom. Will came in at one point to get the antacids. The rich food and all that alcohol. Oh, what was she thinking? There was a time when that wouldn't have bothered her one bit, when she would have slept peacefully through the night. But now? Well, now she was old. Practically a grandmother.

She thought of Will then, the way he'd said "just the adults" as if Claire and Martha were still little children they needed to escape from. She thought of the way that she'd passed Claire's room the other night, seen Claire asleep on the bed, her mouth wide open, her arms around an ancient stuffed moose. How Will had said "Poor baby" to Martha. Her head pounded and her stomach threatened to revolt again. What was going on? She took two aspirin and drank a glass of water and tried to go back to bed.

THE NEXT WEEK, WEEZY TOLD MAX that she needed Cleo's mother's number. Enough was enough. She understood that families work things out in their own way, but Max and Cleo were not in any position to deal with things on their own. "Just have her tell her mother that I want to talk to her," Weezy said.

She found she was nervous when dialing the number, and even more so when she heard someone else answer the phone. "Elizabeth Wolfe's office." Weezy identified herself and was put on hold. She wondered what Elizabeth would say, if she would even take the call. And just when she was beginning to think that she'd never get through, the line clicked.

"Am I ever glad to talk to you," Elizabeth said.

"Oh! Well, I'm glad to hear that."

On the other end of the phone, Elizabeth let out a breath, blowing straight into the receiver. "Can you believe this?" she asked. "Cleo is driving me absolutely insane."

"I've said the same thing about Max every day since I found out."

The two women laughed a little, and Weezy felt relieved. Elizabeth was just a mom after all. Weezy felt guilty for all the things she'd been saying about her, and even though there was no way Elizabeth could have known about them, she almost apologized. "I didn't want to intrude," she said. "I just thought we should talk."

They made plans to meet that weekend for lunch. "I can take the train there," Weezy said. "It'll give me an excuse to do some shopping."

The two women met at a restaurant on the Upper West Side, not far from Elizabeth's apartment. "I can't imagine raising a child here," Weezy said. "I admire you for it. If I hadn't been able to run mine like dogs outside, I think I might have gone crazy."

Elizabeth just nodded, and Weezy was afraid she'd insulted her. "It really is admirable," she said again. "Cleo's a lovely girl."

"A lovely pregnant girl," Elizabeth said. Weezy looked up, embarrassed that the waiter was standing right there and had heard, but Elizabeth didn't seem to care. She ordered a glass of wine and raised her eyebrows at Weezy, who nodded in agreement.

"I'm just so furious," Elizabeth said.

"I know, I know." Weezy found that Elizabeth's anger made her want to be even more understanding.

The two women talked about what was to come, agreed that their children had no idea what to expect, but promised to help in any way they could.

"I've told Max they can move in with us after graduation."

"That's a very generous offer," Elizabeth said.

"Of course, if you'd rather have Cleo here, I understand."

"It's really up to her. I doubt she'll want to come back here."

Weezy felt very sad for Cleo just then. If Martha or Claire were pregnant and abandoned, she'd drag them back home whether they wanted it or not. She'd make sure they knew they had their mother for support; she'd be in their faces every day.

"You're handling this all quite well," Elizabeth said.

"I'm just handling it," Weezy said. She tried to sound humble, but it actually came out sounding like she was bragging.

After lunch, Weezy wandered up Amsterdam, popping into some of the little boutiques. She was a little light-headed from the wine, but found it refreshing not to care who saw her. She ended up buying a ridiculously expensive pair of booties with giraffes on them. They were so tiny and perfect. She tucked them into her purse and went out to get a taxi back to the train station.

CHAPTER 16

This was what a psychotic break looked like. Claire was pretty sure of that. Sometimes, she wanted to stand up in the middle of the office, at dinner with her family, or while she was in Fran's basement watching ESPN with him, and scream, "I am having a psychotic break, people. I am having a breakdown and no one is noticing."

But that only happened if she let herself think about it, which she tried not to do most of the time. She found it was easier to ignore everything that was going on and just get through the day. She stayed busy. If she wasn't at Fran's watching a movie or drinking a beer, she was running around the neighborhood with her iPod on, sprinting down the dark streets in the cold until her chest was too tight to breathe and her legs hurt. Anything to make sure that when she got into bed that night, she'd fall asleep quickly.

AT HOME, THE AIR WAS FILLED with Max and Cleo. Weezy was acting like someone with a brain injury, sometimes slow and spacey, sometimes sharp and wild. The day after Thanksgiving, she'd told them the news in the kitchen, and although they'd already guessed, it was still a shock to hear.

"Don't tell anyone," Weezy said. She looked nervous, like they might have already spread the news around town.

"Of course not," Martha said. "Oh my God, we won't tell anyone."

"People are going to find out eventually," Claire said.

"I know that," Weezy said. "But let's just hold off. It's no one else's business."

"People are so gossipy in this town," Martha said. Her eyes filled with tears.

"Why are you crying?" Claire asked.

"They're so young. How can they handle this?" Martha's nose was running.

"Martha," Claire said, "stop acting like you're the one that's knocked up."

"Claire, that's enough," Weezy said. "This isn't easy on your sister. This isn't easy on any of us."

"Why isn't this easy for her?" Claire said. "What's so hard about it? Just because you're embarrassed doesn't mean you can act like this is all about you."

"This has nothing to do with being embarrassed," Weezy said.

Martha looked up at the ceiling then, just as the tears poured down her cheeks. She let out a strange squeak and left the room quickly. Weezy turned to Claire with a look that said, *Are you happy now?*

"Jesus," Claire said.

"It wouldn't kill you to be a little nicer to your sister."

"It actually might."

None of them spoke to one another for the rest of the day. Will looked like he wanted to get out of the house. He'd been angry in the morning, but by the afternoon, he looked exhausted. He and Weezy had been holed up in their bedroom having whispered conversations. Around dinnertime,

Will tried to act normal, asking if anyone else was interested in warming up some leftovers, then going ahead and taking out the Tupperware containers and warming up the turkey, stuffing, and gravy until the whole house smelled like Thanksgiving again. He was the only one who ate.

They didn't apologize to one another. That isn't how they worked. The three of them were just short and chilly to one another for a few days, and then eventually it went away. Even Martha and Weezy spoke to each other with pursed lips and stilted conversation, although Claire was pretty sure they hadn't been fighting with each other. It was like no one could keep track of who was mad at whom.

Even Ruby the dog was upset by the situation. She knew that everyone was out of sorts, and she spent her time walking up to each member of the family and licking them on the hand, as if to say, *Don't worry, it will all be fine.* At the end of each day, she looked exhausted, lying on her green bed in the corner of the TV room, her head on her paws. Ruby had taken to eating her food quickly, like she was afraid someone was going to take it away from her if she paused or looked up.

"She's not even chewing," Claire pointed out. And it was true. The dog was just scarfing down her food, swallowing the pieces whole.

"Maybe she's an emotional eater," Martha said.

"A what?" Claire asked.

"An emotional eater," Martha repeated. "You know, like she's eating her feelings because she's upset about Max."

Both Weezy and Claire stood and stared at Martha without saying a word.

AFTER THANKSGIVING, MAX HAD TAKEN to calling Claire's cell phone every day. "Just checking in," he'd say.

"Things will get better," Claire told him. She could think of nothing else to say.

"I can't even imagine that right now," Max said.

"Trust me. I know it seems bad, but in a few months it will be fine."

"Months?"

"Just give it time."

Claire convinced Max to come home for Christmas, telling him it would be worse if he didn't. So he'd arrived with Cleo in tow, who still wasn't talking to her mother and was so quiet that she didn't even seem like the same person. All of Christmas was quiet, actually. They sat around reading books most of the time, which seemed to be the perfect activity since they could ignore each other and still pretend to be spending time together. Everyone took a lot of naps. And even Bets, who didn't know that Cleo was pregnant yet, seemed to sense that something was off and was on unusually good behavior.

"Won't your mother miss you?" she asked Cleo.

"Oh, no. She'll be fine."

One night, Claire got up and had a cigarette in the bathroom. She never would have dared if Bets hadn't been there, but who was going to know the difference? She sat on the tile floor, her back against the wall, and smoked slowly, letting the cigarette burn down to her fingers. She sort of understood what it was that Bets liked about this. It was secret and solo. It was just one little thing that she had for herself. When she was done, she flushed the butt down the toilet and went back into Martha's room and climbed into the twin bed.

"Did you just smoke in there?" Martha asked.

"No," Claire said. "I didn't."

They all went to midnight mass on Christmas Eve, and came back home to have eggnog by the fire. Bets excused herself, telling everyone that it was well past her bedtime.

"I'm an old woman," she said. "Practically on death's door. I'm not cut out for this anymore." She'd worn her best red suit, which seemed too big for her. Bets had always been tiny. "I barely eat," she sometimes said. But now she was practically miniature. She seemed to be proof that old people really did shrink. It was a frightening thought.

The rest of them settled in the living room and Will started a fire. Claire was certain that they all wished they could go to bed like Bets had, but this was their tradition and they didn't really have a choice.

Weezy poured everyone eggnog with a shot of whiskey, except for Cleo, of course. "This one's a virgin," she said, handing the glass to Cleo. Cleo blushed and took it. "Well, that's an awful term, isn't it?" Weezy asked. It was like everyone was trying to be as awkward as possible.

Claire even wished that Cathy was there with them. It would have been lovely to have someone to talk loudly and hog the conversation. But Maureen, Cathy, and Ruth had decided to visit Drew in California for Christmas. "We're just in need of some sunshine," Maureen had said. But that was a lie. Maureen just didn't want to be anywhere near the Coffey house that Christmas. And really, who could blame her? She'd offered to come back and fly home with Bets on the twenty-seventh, which was her way of apologizing, and Weezy had seemed to accept it gladly.

Christmas morning, they opened their presents politely, thanking each other like they'd met not long ago; like they were acquaintances or office mates who were fond of each other. They balled up wrapping paper and threw it into a big black garbage bag that Will held open. Anytime someone made it in, Will would shout, "Two points for you!"

By the time they all sat down to eat ham at the table, their patience was thin and their small talk was bordering on nasty.

"Don't take so many potatoes," Martha told Max.

"Calm down, there's plenty left for you, porky," he said.

"I can't believe any of you are hungry," Bets said. "You all ate like pigs going to slaughter this morning. I can barely even imagine eating a meal right now."

"I could use some help in the kitchen," Weezy said.

"I'm right here, trying to help," Will said.

"This ham looks really fatty," Claire said.

Only Cleo remained almost completely silent. She was probably trying to will herself to be anywhere but there, thinking that no matter how much she was fighting with her own mom, this was worse. You could almost see her thoughts: *There's no place like home. There's no place like home.*

Fran spent the holiday in Florida with his parents, and when he returned, he brought her a little tchotchke, a tiny stage with a group of stones with googly eyes and little guitars. Underneath the label said ROCK BAND. Claire took it and laughed.

"It made me think of you," Fran said. She wasn't sure what to make of that.

He also gave her a beautiful light tan leather journal. She realized that he probably found both presents in some little gift shop that was nearby, but she didn't hold that against him.

She gave him a plaid scarf that she'd bought at the last minute, during a moment of doubt when she couldn't justify sleeping with someone for three months and not giving him a Christmas present. He seemed to like it.

IT WAS A RELIEF TO GO BACK TO WORK after Christmas, which was the first time Claire had ever thought such a thing. Even though the heat in the office was on full blast and the place was always too warm, and everyone always seemed to have wet shoes that smelled like dogs, Claire was glad to be back. It meant that time was moving forward, that winter was continuing on. The people of PP loved talking about the weather, and even when it was barely snowing outside, they'd come in sniffling and saying things like, "We're due for another whopper," or "It took me twenty minutes to clear off my car this morning!"

Right before Christmas, Leslie had called Claire into her office to tell her that Amanda had decided to take another three months off unpaid. "It's company policy that allows you to do that," Leslie said. "So legally we have to let her. I won't get into the details, but let's just say I'm not surprised we're in this situation."

"Uh-huh," Claire said. She couldn't blame Amanda for not wanting to come back to PP right away.

"We're hoping that you'll be able to stay on for the next three months."

"Sure," Claire said.

"That's great. That really gets us out of a bind."

It didn't seem like a bind at all to Claire, but she didn't say anything. If she couldn't do it, wouldn't they have just called the temp agency and gotten someone else? But she could tell that Leslie was the kind of person who enjoyed being annoyed at work, who liked to sigh deeply and tell her friends, "You just have no idea what I'm dealing with at the office. No idea."

"So you'll stay until the end of March?" Lainie asked when she told her. "That's good."

"I guess."

"Well, it's a job. And that's what you need."

"I know. It's just sometimes I feel like I'm going to be there forever. Like I'm just going to keep working at PP and keep living at home for the rest of my life."

"Claire, it's three more months. Don't be so dramatic."

"It's just when I look at the past year, I feel like I messed up so much that there's no telling what I could do."

"That's ridiculous. You're not going to live at home forever. You'll move out, and probably soon. You're just taking time to figure out what you want to do. It's just a time-out."

"Yeah, I guess."

Claire thought about Lainie's words when she was at Proof Perfect, making copies or opening the mail. "TV Time-out," she'd whisper sometimes at her desk. It was something they used to scream when they were little, when they were in the middle of a game and someone needed a break. They'd be running around, playing tag or kickball, and someone would yell, "TV Time-out!" and just like that, they'd all stop right where they were, put their hands on their knees, and catch their breath.

EVERY WEEK, MAX FORWARDED AN e-mail from a baby website to Claire that had been forwarded to him by Cleo. Claire was familiar with the website. Lainie had been obsessed with the same one when she was pregnant with Jack. "Do you believe this stuff?" Max would sometimes write at the top. The e-mail gave weekly information about skin and organs and fingernails. It gave comparisons to objects, so that you could imagine how big the baby was: The baby was a peanut, a grape, a kumquat, a cucumber. Okay, maybe they didn't use that last one, but Claire couldn't bring herself to read the e-mails. She knew that Max was overwhelmed, knew that he needed her to talk to, so that she could tell him that it was all going to be fine. So she did try.

Your baby is an orange, your baby is a peach, your baby is a plum, a watermelon, a fig. This is what Claire thought each night before she went to sleep. She listed them out of order, then went backward, making the baby smaller and smaller. Sometimes she'd keep going, creating her own list of objects: Your baby is a basketball, a watermelon, a dachshund, a couch. The list of items ran in her head fast, until it felt like she wasn't in control of them anymore. How could you tell the difference, she wondered, between hearing voices in your head and your own thoughts?

And then one day, when the IT guy was working on her computer, she saw his eyes get wide and he turned to her with a smile. "Well, I guess congratulations are in order."

"What?" Claire said.

"Your baby is a lemon," he said. "You can barely tell."

"Oh no, that's not me. That's my brother's baby."

"Oh, sorry about that."

After he left, Claire tried to figure out what he meant when he said, *You can barely tell.* Barely tell? "I can barely tell that you're a huge loser," she muttered. And then she felt mean. And she deleted the e-mail.

FRAN'S PARENTS WERE STILL IN Florida and Claire started sleeping there a few nights a week. Whenever she left the house with a bag and said she wasn't coming home that night, Weezy raised her eyebrows.

"What?" Claire would ask. Weezy would just shake her head.

It wasn't much different with Fran's parents gone all the time, since they'd seemed oblivious to Claire's presence anyway. She'd met them a few times and they'd seemed uninterested and bored. His mom was a thin woman with short gray hair who wore sweat suits and looked tired. His dad was the same.

Claire knew without having to ask that these were not the kind of parents who asked after her, or asked Fran much about his life, for that matter. They were the parents who were truly surprised when Fran was caught smoking pot in his car at the high school, who were annoyed about it mostly because it meant they'd have to go in and meet with the dean.

One Saturday, Claire went over to help Fran watch his niece. Fran's sister lived a few towns over, in an apartment building. She was divorced. Claire vaguely remembered her from high school. Bonnie was a couple of years older, and used to stand with the group of kids that huddled at the edge of the parking lot to smoke cigarettes in the morning and the afternoon.

Fran's niece was about three years old, and was not an attractive child. It seemed horrible to think that, but it was the truth. She had stringy blond hair and her nose was way too big for her face. She always had food on her clothes and cried often and loudly. Also, she was a hitter.

When Claire got to the house, Fran was smoking a cigarette in the basement and Jude was sitting on the floor playing with a doll. Two lines of snot were running out of her nose.

Claire tried, but she couldn't take an interest in the little girl. She pretended to, kneeling down to talk to her, but Jude just snatched up her doll to her chest and reached out to smack Claire. After that, she just watched. Fran seemed fond of his niece, or at least not opposed to her. He made her macaroni and cheese and got her milk in a sippy cup, which she immediately poured down her shirt. For the rest of the day, the little girl was slightly damp and smelled sour. When Claire got up to leave, she leaned down and touched the top of Jude's head.

" 'Bye, Jude," she said.

" 'Bye, stupid," Jude replied.

She and Fran never went out, which suited her just fine. Sometimes they picked up food or got takeout, but mostly they just sat in the basement. "Don't you two ever want to go out to dinner?" Lainie asked. Claire knew she thought it was weird, but to her it would have been weirder if they ever left the basement.

"Not really. We're fine just hanging out," she said.

It wasn't just that she never wanted to spend money (which she didn't), but it was like they both knew that their relationship, or whatever it was, worked best in the basement. If they took it out into the light of day, it would be different.

All through high school, Claire had imagined what it would be like to date Fran. Fran now seemed like a different person than the one she used to spend hours thinking about. In high school, Fran had worn a gas station shirt to school almost every day. It was navy and had the name BUD stitched above the left breast pocket. She would wonder what it would be like to lie next to him, rest her head right on top of the BUD.

She remembered the way Fran would sometimes take huge sandwiches to parties, how he would sit, stoned, in the middle of a room and shove a sub in his mouth, letting lettuce and onions drop all around him, like he was the only person in the room, or really, like he could give two shits about what these people thought of him anyway. In her whole life, Claire was pretty sure she had never felt that comfortable.

Sometimes when she was with him now, she would have a moment where she'd think, *I am lying in bed with Fran*

Angelo. It was a strange, out-of-body experience, like when she used to get stoned in college, stare in the bathroom mirror and think, *That is me. That is me looking back at me,* until she got dizzy and had to leave the room.

WINTER SEEMED LONELIER, although Claire couldn't say exactly why. She was barely home, but when she was, the idea of going somewhere else seemed so hard. It was like the idea of putting on boots and a coat exhausted her.

She didn't spend as much time at Lainie's, mostly because with the three boys stuck in the house, it seemed smaller and much more crowded. The last time she'd been over there, Jack spent most of the time leaping from the couch to the table to the chair. "I can't touch the ground," he screamed. "It's lava and if I touch it, I'll die." Then he'd leapt back over to the couch and hit his arm on Claire's nose. "Ow!" he yelled. He cradled his arm against his chest with his other hand and glared at Claire like she'd hit him. "That hurt," he told her.

Martha had gotten in the habit of coming into Claire's room every night. She'd sit on the edge of Claire's bed and rattle off a list of things she'd done that day. She talked about her job and Max and Cleo. It didn't matter if Claire answered her or even really listened. It was like Martha just needed to hear herself talk.

Claire tried to be patient with her, but it wasn't easy. Most of the time she just wanted to be left alone. She found herself shutting her bedroom door early, turning off the lights and getting into bed so Martha would leave her alone.

One night, Claire woke up outside the house in her pajamas. She stood there, heart pounding, and realized that she must have sleepwalked out of her room, down the stairs, through the garage, and outside.

There she was, barefoot, staring right into the living room and trying to figure out what had happened. It felt a little like waking up in a hotel room on vacation and not knowing where you were for a few minutes—only so much worse. Claire hadn't sleepwalked in years. As a child, she'd occasionally wander out of her room and down to the kitchen or into her parents' room. Once, she'd walked out the front door, but Will had been following her and managed to guide her back to her room.

At camp, she'd once woken up a few feet from the cabin, and her counselor, a snarly teenage girl with horrible acne, was behind her, looking like she'd just seen a ghost. "What the hell?" the counselor had said. "You're, like, possessed or something." From then on, Claire had a note in her camp file that said PRONE TO SLEEPWALKING. PLEASE MONITOR.

But she'd thought she'd outgrown this little habit. All those years that she lived in apartments in New York, she never even worried that she'd do such a thing. And here she was, standing outside in winter in the middle of the night.

A few nights later, it happened again and Claire woke up standing on the front porch. Ruby was right behind her, her head tilted as if she was getting ready to bark. Claire hurried back into the house, locked the door, scooped Ruby up, and headed to her room, where she scrunched underneath the covers and tried to get warm again.

Telling her family was out of the question. Weezy would freak out, Martha would insist that she needed to go see a therapist, and Will would start trying to figure out how to lock the doors so that she couldn't get outside. The whole family would talk about it at dinner for weeks. Martha would pretend that she knew the medical reasons for sleepwalking, as if being a nurse qualified her to diagnose Claire. No, it was out of the question.

The next night, Claire put a stack of books in front of

her door, so that she couldn't open it without knocking them down, which she hoped would be enough to wake her up. She was pleased with the plan, pretty sure that this would keep her safely inside. Although she did go to bed every night a little afraid that she was going to wake up somewhere strange.

AT THE END OF FEBRUARY, the whole family came down with the flu. It was a flu that sent each of them running to the bathroom again and again. Just when one would flop down on the couch, dehydrated and exhausted, the next one would hear a rumble in their stomach and get up, clutching their middle and running out of the room.

Martha and Claire lay on the couch, trying to watch a movie, but they couldn't get through much before one of them had to leave. They were starting to get delirious. The flu had been going on for almost three days now and there was no sign of its slowing down. They had all said out loud that they might be dying.

"We look like a diarrhea commercial," Claire said. Martha started to laugh. "What?" Claire asked.

"A diarrhea commercial? I know what you mean, but it sounds like you're talking about an ad that's selling diarrhea."

"Oh yeah," Claire said. She started to laugh too. "I meant like Pepto-Bismol or whatever."

The family shuffled around in their pajamas, getting ginger ale and toast from the kitchen and then heading back to the couch or their beds. For the first time, when Max called, Claire told him truthfully that they hadn't talked about him and Cleo in days. "We're too busy talking about each other's shit," Claire told him. "You're off the hook."

"I think I might be coming down with something too," Lainie said to Claire on the phone.

"Well," Claire said, "you would know if you had this."

"Yeah, I just feel so pukey all the time. Great. I'm sure the worst is coming."

But then a couple of weeks later, Lainie called and asked Claire if she could go out for a little bit. "Brian's watching the boys," she said. They met in Lainie's driveway, and Lainie drove to the Post Office Bar, a place that they used to frequent during the summers when they were home from college.

"This okay with you?" she asked.

"Sure," Claire said. "I haven't been here in forever."

They ordered two drafts of some sort of amber beer, and a basket of Parmesan-garlic fries, which looked like frozen french fries that had been warmed and covered with grated cheese, but were actually not bad. The bar was empty, except for one older man at the end of the bar, who was doing a crossword puzzle and drinking. Claire wondered where he went in the summer, when this place was overrun with underage kids and a DJ came in on Friday nights. She wondered if he was mad when that happened, if he felt like his house had been taken over, or if he had a different place that he found, another quiet place for the summer.

"I'm pregnant," Lainie said. She was addressing a thin, limp fry that she was holding. It seemed to bend further with the news.

"What?" Claire said. "When?"

"I just found out last week. It wasn't the flu."

"Oh my God. Well, congratulations."

Lainie's eyes had started to fill with tears. "I can't be pregnant," she said. "What am I, that reality TV woman that has like a hundred kids? I'm barely recovered from Matthew. I can't be starting this all over again." She took a sip of beer and the tears fell on her cheeks.

"Should you be having that?" Claire asked.

"It's just one beer," Lainie said. "It won't do anything."

"Okay," Claire said. She was unsure how to continue.

"It's just so fucked up. I can't believe I let this happen. We have, like, just barely enough money now, but not even really. And that's with me teaching, which I can't do much longer." Lainie's nose had started to run, and Claire handed her a napkin.

"You'll be okay," Claire said. "I know you will. It seems crazy now, I'm sure, but you'll be okay."

Lainie lifted the glass of beer to her lips and then put it down again without drinking. "I don't even want it," she said, pushing it away. "Not really. I just ordered it because I'm annoyed I can't have it."

"What did Brian say?"

"Same as me. He just doesn't know how we're going to afford it, or even fit in our house anymore, not that that matters, because we're not going anywhere. We can't."

They sat together for a while, Claire reassuring Lainie that it would be fine, and Lainie listing all the things that would be different. They picked at the fries, and Claire drank both of the beers, even though by the time she got to Lainie's, it was a little warm.

"Well, maybe it will be a girl," Claire finally offered, as they paid their tab. "You did always want a girl, too."

Lainie laughed and put the last group of french fries in her mouth, dragging them through the cold grease that was dotted with garlic before eating them. It was a bitter sort of laugh that sounded like she was a wise old person who'd seen it all. "It will be a boy," she said. "I know it. We're just going to have all boys."

WHEN CLAIRE GOT BACK HOME, she didn't even bother going inside before she called Fran. He was sleeping, but he answered the phone. "Come over," he said. And so she ran there, all six blocks to his house, like she was in a race. She stopped when she got to his driveway, and rested for a minute, putting her hands on her knees.

She walked down the stairs on the side of the house, and turned the doorknob carefully. Fran never locked the door, which usually bugged her, but tonight she was grateful. The room was dark, and she stood in the doorway for a minute, letting her eyes adjust, so that she could see enough not to crash into anything.

She walked to the side of the bed and looked down at Fran, who had fallen back asleep. He was so handsome, but when she looked at him, she thought what her high school self would have thought: *He's so hot.* She touched his head and he opened his eyes and gave her a sleepy smile.

"Hey," he said. "You're a nice surprise."

She bent down over him, putting her face in his neck and smelling him, all cinnamon and smoke, and for one scary second, she thought she was going to start crying. Fran pulled sleepily at her shirt and then her pants.

"Off," he said. "Take these off."

And so she unbuttoned her jeans, fumbling with the zipper, like she couldn't make her fingers move fast enough. She slid out of them quickly, tripping a little as she pulled them off her feet. Then she took off her shirt with one movement and finished the rest before getting into bed, sliding in between the sheets and moving over next to him so that her skin was touching his. "Come here," he said, and so she did. She would have done anything he told her to at that moment, would have listened to anything he said.

CHAPTER 17

Her mom had said not to tell anyone, but Martha knew that she'd meant not to tell people who knew them, like family friends and neighbors and that kind of thing. It didn't hurt anyone that Martha told Jaz. She had to. This was the kind of thing you had to talk about, so that you were able to process it.

"Can you believe it?" she'd asked. "Can you believe that in this day and age, someone could be so careless?"

"It happens," Jaz said. "I believe it."

"I mean, at colleges these days, people are practically forcing condoms on kids. Well, not at my school they didn't, but that's different. It was a Catholic school. Still, you can get them anywhere." Martha had heard Will say this exact thing the night before, wondering aloud how on earth his son hadn't been able to find a simple condom.

"It happens every day," Jaz said. Martha thought Jaz was probably trying to calm her down, but what she was really doing was making it seem like this wasn't a big deal. When it was. Her brother had gotten someone pregnant. There was going to be a baby. She was going to be an aunt. This was a very big deal.

Martha had been spending more and more time with Jaz in the kitchen. Mr. Cranston was sleeping a lot more and they'd all decided it was a good idea to have the nurses look in on him more often. Now they came in the afternoon as well as at night. Martha was sure that meant her job was gone, but Jaz assured her it wasn't.

"There's still no one here in the mornings. Plus, we need you for all the things that nurses don't do," she said. She was trying to reassure Martha, but it just made her feel worse. She was a nurse. She should be doing more than buying books and retrieving the TV clicker.

When she asked what was wrong with Mr. Cranston, she always got the same answer: everything. It was the winter, the recovery from the surgery, just general exhaustion. Martha had imagined that she'd come in as the caretaker and nurse Mr. Cranston back to health, then leave when he was better. She never told anyone this, of course. They'd all told her from the beginning it wasn't going to go like that. It was just harder to see in person.

Jaz asked Martha what Cleo was going to do. She said it very carefully, like she wanted to remove all judgment from her words.

"She's going to keep it," Martha said. She tried not to sound like that was a stupid question, but really. If Cleo was going to have an abortion, would Martha even be talking about this? "We're really happy about it," she added. Just in case Jaz misunderstood.

MARTHA HAD A LOT ON HER PLATE. In addition to her new job and the Max-and-Cleo family crisis, she was officially house hunting again. She'd called up the Realtor she'd been working with last year and told her she was ready to resume the search. When she'd told Cathy this, she hadn't gotten the response she was looking for.

"Martha, what are you waiting for? Just do it already," Cathy said.

Martha was too surprised to talk at first. She was used to Cathy's blunt way of speaking; it was one of the things that she admired about her actually. But this sounded mean, impatient almost.

"I am," she said. "I'm going out with the Realtor tomorrow. I'm just waiting for the right place for me. Last year just wasn't the time to buy."

Martha hadn't actually told anyone what had happened last year. The truth was that she'd been sort of fired by her Realtor. And even though she knew that's not how it worked, it still felt that way. She'd been working with Sarah for almost a year, meeting on Saturdays and driving around to different apartments. Sarah was a few years younger than Martha, and was funny in a predictable and not terribly clever way. She wore her hair in a high ponytail, and always talked in an upbeat manner when describing the places they were going to see, using Realtor short-speak that Martha liked—*washer and dryer in unit, en suite bathroom, outdoor area.*

She was peppy, which you had to be in realty. There were lots of awful places out there, and you had to be persistent to find the right one. Martha figured that Sarah identified with her, wanted to find her the perfect place in the right neighborhood. It had been fun to meet with her every weekend, sometimes stopping for lunch in the middle of their day, eating pizza and taking a break to go over what they'd seen so far. And then one day, when Sarah dropped her off, she turned off the engine and said, "Martha, can I ask you something?"

"Sure," Martha said. She thought maybe Sarah wanted her to rank the places they'd seen that day. But that was not what she wanted.

"Do you really think you're looking to buy an apartment?" Sarah asked.

"Of course I am," Martha said. She sniffed.

"Okay, well, I'm happy to help you find a place. And I want you to find a place that you love. But at this point I'm getting worried that you're not going to be happy with anything we see."

"I don't want to compromise," Martha said. "You're the one that said I could find my perfect home."

"I did," Sarah said. She put her hands on the steering wheel and breathed in and out like she was trying to figure out what to say. "But at some point, there's going to be something you're not thrilled with. I'm not saying you have to settle for a place, but there's trade-offs. A place with a balcony might not have a washer and dryer and you just need to decide which one you want more. Does that make sense?"

"I need a washer and dryer."

"Right, I know. That's why we put it on the top of your list." Sarah tapped the pad of paper and bit her lip. "Martha, I just need you to really think about this. We've spent seven of the last ten Saturdays together. And again, I'm happy to take the time if it's going to end in a sale. But I'm starting to think that this isn't going to. That you aren't going to find anything that you feel comfortable buying."

Martha didn't know why people said that they were happy to do something and then followed it up by saying they weren't happy about it. It didn't make any sense.

"Look," Sarah was saying, "maybe we just need to take a break for a month or so. Take all the flyers for the places we've seen and look them over and think about what you want. Maybe you're just oversaturated with looking."

Oversaturated? Martha was pretty sure that didn't make any sense at all. Sarah was kind of stupid sometimes. She used words wrong all the time, but Martha let it go because she felt bad for her. She just wasn't book smart, not at all. She'd told Martha where she went to college, but it was nowhere that Martha had ever heard of before. It was probably some online university, the kind that accepted anyone.

"Fine," Martha said. She started gathering up her papers.

"Martha, please don't be angry." Sarah put her hand on Martha's arm. "I'm not trying to upset you. I just have to be practical here. I hope that you'll call me in a few weeks and want to look at more places and that we'll find one. I'll keep e-mailing you with anything I think you'll like, okay?"

"Okay," Martha said.

When Martha got out of the car, she was embarrassed, although she couldn't say why exactly. She'd told Weezy that night that she was taking a break from looking. "I just think I need to take a step back," she'd said. Weezy tried to ask more about it, but Martha shut it down. "I'm just not finding what I want."

When she told Dr. Baer, she said that it was hard to commit to buying something. "It's a big step. There's a lot to consider."

"Maybe you should start smaller then," Dr. Baer said. "You could rent."

Rent? Martha had to take a deep breath before she said something rude. Why would she throw her money away, month after month? Money she worked hard for and spent so long saving. It was a buyer's market. But maybe Dr. Baer didn't know a lot about real estate. It seemed a little ridiculous to have her try to give Martha financial advice, especially when it was so bad.

"I'll think about it," she'd said.

But she hadn't. She hadn't thought about it at all. Once she stopped looking, it was easy to forget. And even if she did want to try again, the thought of calling Sarah was too humiliating. But now it had been a year, and she was ready to look again. She thought about finding a new Realtor, but that seemed silly. Sarah knew what she was looking for.

Sarah answered her phone, perky as ever, and for a second Martha considered hanging up. But then she thought better of it.

"Hi, it's Martha Coffey."

"Martha! How are you? I'm so glad to hear from you."

Martha smiled before she could help it. She told Sarah that she was ready to start looking again.

"I'm so glad to hear that," she said.

"Things are really busy now," Martha said. "I have a new job, and I'm the maid of honor in my cousin's wedding. And there's just a lot of stuff going on with my family at the moment."

Sarah didn't ask about specifics, and Martha figured she didn't want to pry. They made a date for the next weekend.

"I'm really looking forward to it," Sarah said.

"Me too."

MARTHA WAS BEYOND EXCITED FOR Cathy's wedding. Every day, she called or e-mailed Cathy with an idea for the bridesmaid dresses or the ceremony. Cathy told her that she was thinking simple—an outdoor ceremony somewhere.

"Just because it's simple doesn't mean it can't be lovely," Martha said. She didn't want her cousin to get married in a campground somewhere with Porta-Potties and hot dogs.

Martha talked about the wedding often at home. She figured the more that she talked about it, the better. She didn't want Claire to feel awkward about it, to feel strange discussing someone else's wedding when hers was canceled. Martha thought the more they discussed it, the easier it would be.

Cathy wanted to do it soon. "We're thinking April," she said.

"April? That's not enough time," Martha said. She was already panicked.

"I think you're imagining the wedding a little differently than we are," Cathy said. She said it gently, as though she knew she'd be letting Martha down if she admitted this.

"Different how?"

"We just want it a little more casual than your typical wedding. You know, just a fun party but nothing crazy."

"Well, okay. Have you thought about what you want the bridesmaids to wear?"

"You can wear whatever you want."

"You mean, like all wear a black dress or something?" Martha hated this new trend where brides let the bridesmaids pick their own black dresses. If it was your one day to tell people what to wear, wouldn't you take advantage of that?

"No, it doesn't even have to be black. Just wear a dress that makes you happy."

"Makes me happy?" Ever since the engagement, Cathy had talked a lot about letting yourself be happy. Martha figured it was a good sign, but it was still a little annoying.

"Yeah. Just wear something you feel good in. It's just going to be you, Claire, and my friend Carol anyway. You'll all look great."

"Um, okay. Hey, how about this? Why don't I look into getting the dresses from J.Crew? They have cute bridesmaid dresses, I promise. And I can probably still get my discount, because I'm really good friends with the manager there now. I'll just get Carol's measurements and we'll be all set."

"I guess that would be okay," Cathy said. "Whatever you guys want."

Martha was relieved. She could at least do this for her cousin, who was apparently under the impression that weddings were the same as potluck picnics.

"I'll pick out something really pretty," she promised.

"Whatever you want," Cathy said.

ON WEDNESDAY, MARTHA GOT HOME from the Cranstons' and found a package waiting for her. "Bets sent something for you," Weezy said. "I'm not sure what it is."

Martha tore into the package. It wasn't even her birthday. What could Bets have sent? Maybe some sort of congratulations present for the new job? Inside was a little statue of a saint and a note. Martha read Bets's letter a few times, trying to understand.

"What is it?" Weezy asked.

"It's a statue of Saint Jude. She says to bury him in my closet and that it will help a husband find me. She said that a few of her friends have seen it work for their grandchildren."

"Oh lord." Weezy closed her eyes. "Your grandmother is a real piece of work."

"I thought Saint Jude was the cancer saint. No?" Claire asked.

"There's no such thing as a cancer saint," Martha said. "The note said he was the saint of lost causes."

"Is she kidding?" Claire said. "How rude is that?"

"She's probably just trying to be helpful," Martha said. Bets was old, and Martha figured she no longer knew what was insulting and what wasn't.

"Honestly, girls. Your grandmother doesn't know what she's doing or saying half the time."

"She probably thought it was a nice thing to send," Claire said. She laughed a little bit.

"I think I'll put him in my closet anyway," Martha said. "It can't hurt, right?"

"Look at it this way," Claire said. "At least she thinks you're worth sending it to. She probably thinks I'm past the point of a lost cause."

Martha took the statue upstairs and wrapped it in an old shirt that she never wore anymore, then stuffed the bundle in the back of her closet. It seemed a little sacrilegious, and she knew this wasn't how things were supposed to work, but why not? She was surprised that Bets thought such a thing was possible. How did such a religious woman end up thinking that her beliefs basically boiled down to voodoo?

MARTHA DRAGGED CLAIRE TO J.CREW to get fitted for the bridesmaid dress. "I know what my size is," she kept saying, but Martha insisted.

"It's better to get measured. I've seen it happen a million times that girls think they know their size and then the dress doesn't fit them properly. Plus, I want your opinion on what style we should get. We can all do the same or do it a little different. Cathy said it was up to me."

"Okay, fine. Whatever."

It was strange to walk back into J.Crew. It felt sort of like going back to visit your grade school after you'd been gone for a couple of years. Things looked the same, but also Martha was overwhelmed with the brightness of everything, the sheer amount of stuff that was in the store. She felt dizzy at first.

"Did things move around?" she asked Wally.

"Nope. Same as it's always been, Squirrel."

Wally took Claire back to put her in some of the dresses and to measure her. The two of them were fast friends, which irritated Martha just a little bit. She could hear them giggling behind the curtain.

"Everything okay in there?" she called. It was not only a waste of time, but also pretty unprofessional of Wally to be giggling away instead of helping customers.

"We're fine," Claire said. She came out in a strapless light gray dress.

"Oh, I love it," Martha said. "That's the one I was thinking. Driftwood, right?"

"Yep," Wally said. "She looks amazing in it."

Again, Martha felt just a little irritated because first of all, he didn't say that Martha would also look amazing in it, and that was just rude. He should know that if you were dealing with bridesmaids, you shouldn't single one of them out. That was Retail 101. And granted, she wasn't a regular customer, but still . . .

"Do you like it?" she asked Claire.

"Yeah, it's cute actually. It's fine." She shrugged as if she couldn't care less.

"Just fine? Do you want to look at some of the others?"

"No, this one's good."

"Claire, a little help here would be nice. A little more enthusiasm and effort, please."

"It's fine. I'm going to wear this dress once, to a wedding at a yoga retreat that's probably going to be filled with lesbians, so it's fine."

Martha was horrified and turned to Wally to apologize, but he was laughing. "Probably not going to meet a man at this wedding, are you?" he asked, and the two of them laughed and laughed.

On the way home, Martha told Claire, "You know, maybe you're having trouble with this wedding because of your situation, but I don't think it's fair to not put any effort forth as a bridesmaid for Cathy."

"Excuse me?"

"I'm just saying, this is Cathy's day. We need to be there for her, no matter what our feelings are."

"Are you serious right now?" Claire asked.

Martha hated that people (especially Claire) always asked her that. Did it seem like she was joking? "Yes, I'm serious."

"Martha, didn't I just go with you to pick out the bridesmaid dresses? And that wasn't even something that Cathy wanted—that was something that you wanted. Plus, the only reason I'm a bridesmaid is because you are and Cathy was just being polite."

"That's not true," Martha said. "Don't think that."

"Um, I don't care, so you don't have to use your voice like you feel bad for me, but of course that's true. And it's fine. Cathy and I have never been close. She used to basically torture me when I was little, remember?"

"She had a lot of issues," Martha said.

"Yes, she did."

"I'm just saying, maybe you should be a little more enthusiastic about the wedding."

"And I'm just saying, if you don't shut up now, I'm going to jump out of the car."

By that time they were just about home anyway, and they drove up the street in silence. Claire slammed her door shut and was inside the house before Martha even got out of the car. She sat for a moment, then pulled herself together and went up to Claire's room, where she knocked, but then opened the door right away.

"You know, Dr. Baer said that she once knew two adult sisters that moved back home and had so much trouble, that they went to couples counseling."

"Jesus."

"It's just something to consider."

"We are not going to couples counseling."

"You shouldn't judge therapy so much. You know, you might benefit from it."

"Martha, seriously. If you don't get out of here, I'm going to push you out. I mean it." Claire stood up from her bed, like she was going to come after Martha, like they were going to have a physical fight, which they hadn't done in about twenty years. Even then, it rarely happened, where they actually pulled each other's hair or pinched one another. But Claire was moving toward the door, and Martha turned and ran, hearing the door slam behind her.

MR. CRANSTON SLEPT MORE AND MORE. At first Martha thought maybe he was just coming down with something, but he never really seemed to bounce back. Everything exhausted him. He never even read the papers anymore. He would start to, and then get tired or frustrated, and they remained folded up on the table until the next morning, when Martha would throw them in the recycling bin and replace them with the new ones.

Jaz seemed to be around more, like she was nervous to leave. Martha didn't mind, since it gave them a chance to talk. She told Jaz about the Saint Jude statue, which made her laugh, but then she said, "It can't hurt, can it?"

"No," Martha agreed. "It can't."

Most mornings, Jaz was there to fix breakfast for Mr. Cranston. Martha noticed that she started giving him bacon every once in a while. "He needs a pick-me-up today," she said, whenever she fried the bacon slices up in the pan.

All of a sudden, it felt like everyone was waiting. There was no more talk of new doctors, and even Ruby and Billy decided to get over their fight and began spending time at the house together.

"I decided to start looking for a place to buy," Martha told Jaz one day.

"That's good," Jaz said. "You should keep moving forward for as long as you can, until you can't move forward anymore."

Martha started to write that one down, but found it was too depressing. She ended up tearing the page out of her notebook and throwing it away.

SHE WAS HAPPY TO BE SPENDING her weekends with Sarah again. She'd been a little nervous, but they fell back into a routine pretty quickly. Sarah would come and pick her up, they'd stop at Starbucks and go over the listings for the day, and then they'd head out.

On the second time they were out, they looked at an old converted loft. It had two bedrooms, two bathrooms, an open kitchen, and a balcony.

"I know you said you didn't want a loft space," Sarah said. "But I think you should look at this one. It's all brand-new, which I think you'll like. Brand-new appliances, a washer and dryer, the works. It's really beautiful."

Martha was sure she wouldn't like it, especially when she saw there was still sawdust in the lobby. "They're still working on most of the units," Sarah explained.

It wasn't at all what Martha had pictured as her new home. It had high ceilings and exposed brick and pipes. But there was something about it.

"Do you think it will be loud?" Martha asked.

"There might be some echo," Sarah said. "That can happen in spaces like these. But I don't think it will be too bad."

"Okay," Martha said. She walked into the smaller bedroom.

"So what do you think?" Sarah asked. "Should we say it's a maybe?"

"Yeah," Martha said. "Let's put it at the top of the list."

IN MAY, THEY THREW CLEO a baby shower. Weezy kept saying, "It's the right thing to do. This baby is coming, so let's get on board." She pretty much just kept repeating this to herself as the days went on, but Martha figured whatever helped her was okay.

Martha and Claire put together the invitations, rolled-up pieces of paper in actual baby bottles that they mailed out. Martha had seen this on a crafts show once and she'd been dying to try it. Claire had sort of grumbled about the idea, but finally agreed, and the two of them went to Target to buy all the supplies, stocking the cart with baby bottles, ribbon, and confetti shaped like little rattles.

"We should get some streamers," Martha said.

"Really? Streamers?"

"You don't think so?"

"That seems more junior high dance than baby shower."

"Yeah, I guess you're right." They continued walking up and down the aisles. "I still can't believe this is happening. I feel so bad for Mom and Dad."

"Don't you feel bad for Max?"

"No. I mean, look what this is doing to Mom and Dad. He's the one that put himself in this position."

"Martha, it was an accident. You think he meant to do this?"

"I'm just saying it was irresponsible. And he's always been that way. I'm just worried about Mom being able to handle this."

"She's fine."

"She's not fine. Haven't you noticed? And it's really affecting the whole family."

"Have I noticed that she's being dramatic because that's how she is? Yeah, I've noticed."

"You're being really insensitive."

"I'm being insensitive? You're the one that doesn't even feel bad for our twenty-one-year-old brother who's about to be a dad and is scared out of his mind. Stop making this about anyone else. It's Max that has to deal with this, and he's the one you should be worried about."

The two of them pushed the cart down the aisles, sighing and shaking their heads. "Have you thought any more about coming to therapy with me?" Martha finally asked.

"Oh my God, Martha, I'm not going to couples therapy with you. Seriously, what is your problem?"

"It's not my problem. We're having trouble communicating."

"No, we're not. You're just looking for something to be wrong. You're looking for a problem to have. It's like you like it when you have issues to deal with."

"That's not true."

"Well, it seems like it is. It seems like Max is taking a lot of the attention lately, and you want some disaster of your own to focus on, and so you want to go to couples therapy with your sister, which isn't just ridiculous—it's totally weird."

"People have done it," Martha said. She sniffed.

"I'm sure they have. But we're not going to. Look at us—we're communicating right now. So let's finish shopping for this baby shower and go home."

"Fine," Martha said. Later that afternoon, she sat on her bed and evaluated her behavior. This was something that Dr. Baer had suggested she do. She wasn't being insensitive to Max, like Claire suggested. That was absurd She just didn't think that everyone needed to be falling all over themselves feeling bad for Max and Cleo, when really, they were the ones who got themselves into this mess in the first place.

MR. CRANSTON CAME DOWN WITH A COLD, that turned into bronchitis, that turned into pneumonia. When he coughed, his whole body shook, and sometimes it sounded like his chest was going to rip right out of him.

Ruby and Billy agreed that it was probably smart to have nurses there round the clock, at least for a little while. "He's having so much trouble breathing," Jaz told Martha. "They just want to make sure that there's someone here to help."

Martha wished that she could be the nurse that was there, but she couldn't. She hadn't done one thing—not one thing!—to start getting recertified. What had she been doing this whole time? She was ashamed of herself for wasting these months. Sure, there had been family drama that had taken her attention away, but still. That was no excuse. She promised herself that she would start looking into it.

THE BABY SHOWER WAS A SUCCESS, despite the arguments that had taken place. She and Claire strung a clothesline across the living room, and hung little onesies on it. Claire had wanted to make strawberry cupcakes, but Martha thought that made it look like the baby was going to be a girl.

"I think it's fine," Claire said. "It's a girlie cupcake, the kind you would have at a shower." But Martha was really against it, and eventually Claire gave up and made chocolate chip cupcakes instead, which were delicious.

Martha was dying to meet Cleo's mom at the shower. Cleo had described her once as "driven," and Martha wanted to know what that meant exactly. Elizabeth arrived a few minutes after the shower started, as though she were just another guest and not the mother of the mother-to-be. She wore a suit, and stood out among all the other women. Martha wasn't surprised to see that Elizabeth was a very attractive woman, although she noticed that her beauty was a little different from Cleo's, more focused and angular. Elizabeth had a firm handshake and she was direct and in command, which Martha admired. When Cleo opened the presents, Elizabeth stood in the very back of the room, like a Secret Service agent watching the crowd.

Cleo got so much gear that Martha couldn't even imagine where she was going to put it all. People had so much stuff for babies these days. There was a bouncy chair, a vibrating chair, and a swing. There were mats and mobiles and play sets. It was craziness.

But at the end of the day, when Cleo was done unwrapping her presents, sitting among the piles of her loot, she thanked Weezy, Martha, and Claire for the shower, and even started to cry a little bit. Martha felt satisfied, like she'd done a good deed. She wanted to point out to Claire that an insensitive person wouldn't have felt that way, but she kept it to herself.

CHAPTER 18

Winter finally started to melt, and after a quick and wet spring, it became hot. The weather people kept calling it "a burst of summer," like it was something fun, when really it was just miserable. No one was ready for the weather. People still walked outside with jackets, confused. They hit eighty degrees at the end of March and it just kept going up from there. And Cleo, who was already hot all the time anyway, became more annoyed with each day.

"Tell me there isn't global warming," she said to Max one morning. He was eating cereal at the little table they had in the kitchen, and he just raised his eyebrows.

"I mean, are people kidding when they try to pretend it's not happening? Eighty-seven degrees in April? What the hell is going on here? It's like those people that try to say the Holocaust didn't happen."

"I know," Max said. He ignored her comment about Holocaust deniers. "The air conditioner isn't doing much, is it?"

"It sounds like it's dying," Cleo said. They had only one air conditioner in the apartment and they kept it in the bedroom. It was an old one that Max had taken from the Coffeys' attic, and it growled and whined as it tried to spit out cold air. If you stood directly in front of it, you could sort of feel a breeze.

"Even I'm going to the library today," Max said. "It's too hot to stay here."

"Actually, I think I'm going to stay here today."

"Really?"

"Yeah, I just need to work without distraction."

"Okay," Max said. "But I'll save you a seat just in case you change your mind."

The weather was a problem for lots of reasons, the main one being that all the kids on campus stripped down like it was spring break, and Cleo, who was not ready to show her stomach to all, still wore sweaters, as if the extra layering could hide what was happening underneath. She ended up sitting in her classes, sweating and uncomfortable, trying to cool down by pulling the fabric away from her skin and fanning papers at her face. When she was alone in the apartment, she usually wore nothing more than a tank top and boxers, and she'd sit on the couch with her feet on the coffee table in front of her, hands stretched across her stomach. She sat like that for hours, not moving, just holding her stomach like that was going to stop it from getting bigger.

They opened the windows wide, in an attempt to cool the apartment down. All it did was invite every fly to come in through the screenless openings. Once they were inside, they buzzed around, too dumb to figure out how to get back out. Cleo watched them frantically fly around, hitting the blinds and the walls. Sometimes she tried to sweep them out with papers, but it didn't help much. Always, right before they died they got especially crazy and aggressive, looping around and dive-bombing Cleo and buzzing out of control as if that last burst of energy could save them. A few hours after that happened, Cleo usually found a little black corpse on the ground, and she'd scoop it up and throw it out the window. One morning, she woke up to find a bunch of dead flies on the table. "A massacre," she whispered, and then cleaned them up.

After Monica heard that she was pregnant, she came by the apartment. "You could have told me," she said.

"I couldn't," Cleo said. "I couldn't even say it out loud."

She finally had what she wanted: Monica was here with her to talk to her about being pregnant. She could have cried or screamed or told her that she was so scared all the time, that she felt like they were making every single decision wrong. They weren't living in a movie. Things weren't going to work themselves out offscreen and result in a cute baby. There was going to be blood and fighting and a lot of crying. She knew that much. But she couldn't say any of that to Monica. What she'd really wanted was her old friend before they'd fallen apart. Now she had someone who looked familiar but felt sort of strange. It was almost better when she was gone altogether.

"It's pretty messed up," is all she said.

Monica started to come by the apartment more often. Sometimes she brought an orange or a bag of licorice or a gossip magazine, like little offerings. Most days they ended up sitting side by side on the couch, watching bad reality TV.

"You know," Monica said one day, looking at Cleo's stomach, "you'll get used to people staring. Or not used to it, but it won't bother you as much after a while. Like when you get a haircut and it feels so different, you feel the missing ends, and then one day you wake up and it's just your hair again. It's like that."

"It doesn't feel like that," she said. She knew that Monica was trying to help, but what she wanted to say was that being pregnant was way worse than being anorexic. She wouldn't say that, of course, because it sounded horrendous. But still, she thought it.

And it was true. There were things that college professors were used to. They were used to kids getting drunk, or getting overwhelmed, or failing a test and then crying. They were used to girls like Monica getting pulled out of school and returning a semester later. But they weren't used to seeing pregnant seniors wander around the campus. They could barely look at Cleo. When it finally became clear to her economics professor that she was pregnant, he started avoiding her eyes when he taught. The staring was bad, but it was worse when people pointedly didn't look at her, when they just avoided her altogether, fixing their eyes on the air around her.

CLEO WAS READY FOR THE SCHOOL YEAR to end, ready to be away from everyone her age that was celebrating and talking about where they were going to move. They talked about Manhattan and Boston and Chicago and San Francisco. Sometimes they changed their minds just because they felt like it. They were going to live on the East Coast and then decided to try the West Coast. Why not? They had choices. They could do whatever they felt like. She was moving into the basement of her boyfriend's parents' house in a suburb of Philadelphia. Was a sadder sentence ever said?

She and Max had both agreed to move to the Coffeys'. She didn't want to, but what other option was there? Where else were they supposed to go? Even if Elizabeth had wanted them, her apartment was way too small, and it was still too hard for her to really talk about the baby without causing a fight of some kind. The last time they'd spoken on the phone, she'd said, "You have to understand, I just feel like I failed as a mother, Cleo. To have you pregnant in college is a nightmare and I can't help but think it was my lack of parenting." Cleo wasn't sure if this was supposed to make her feel better, but it certainly didn't. Then Elizabeth said, "I should have never let you go to that school," like that was the cause of all this.

She and Max also decided to get married, although that still seemed not quite real. Max had brought up marriage the day after he'd woken her up with McDonald's on her pillow. The fight was over, but they were still talking carefully to each other, stepping out of the way when the other walked by, saying *sorry* and *please* more often than normal.

They were both in bed, but not sleeping. Max was on his computer and Cleo had her eyes closed, a book resting on her stomach. Max cleared his throat once and then again and again, until Cleo opened her eyes.

"I was thinking," he said, "that we should probably get married."

"Married?"

"Yeah. I mean, we're going to be together anyway, and with the baby, I just feel like it's right."

"I just . . . I don't know. It's a lot."

"But don't you want to marry me? I want to marry you," Max said. He shut his laptop and turned to face her. "Will you marry me?"

She said yes, although she felt unsure. It seemed mean to say no. It was a horrible story, really. That was her engagement, Max saying, "We're going to be together anyway," and her saying yes, because that seemed the polite thing to do.

Later in the week, Max came home and threw his bag on the floor. "I got something for you," he said. He pulled a small box out of his backpack and opened it for her. In it was a ring with a large round diamond on it. Cleo looked up at him and tilted her head.

"It's fake," he said. "Sorry, I should have said that right

away." He took it out of the box and held it out to her. "I just thought you should have something now, until I can get you something real."

"Oh," Cleo said. "Thanks."

"Should I kneel?" Max didn't wait for her to answer, before getting down on one knee. It felt like they were play-acting and Cleo wanted it to be over soon. She took the ring and put it on her finger.

Cleo felt funny wearing the ring, like she was pretending to be something she wasn't. She turned the ring around often, so that the fake diamond faced the other way. She was embarrassed whenever one of her professors noticed it.

When Cleo told her mom that they were getting married, Elizabeth was silent.

"What?" Cleo asked.

"Oh, Cleo," her mother said. "What do you think is going to happen? That you'll get married and live together, all happy playing house? Come on, Cleo. You're smarter than this."

Cleo wanted to tell her mom that clearly she wasn't smarter than this. If she *was* smarter, wouldn't she be in a different situation? It reminded her of the time she got a B in calculus senior year, and Elizabeth had been angry, had shaken her head. "No B's," she'd said. "You're smart enough to get an A."

That never made sense to Cleo. If she was smart enough to get an A, wouldn't she have gotten one in the first place? She often wondered if she was even smart at all, or if Elizabeth just expected her to be, so she had to live up to it. Of course, the next semester she had brought home an A in calculus. Elizabeth had just nodded. "I told you," she said.

She wore the ring for Max, since it seemed to make him

happy. After a while, her fingers got bloated and she had to take it off. She was scared it was going to get stuck on there, that her fat little sausage finger would lose circulation and have to be amputated.

A little while later, Max came home with an identical ring—except this one was bigger. She wore it until that, too, got too tight, and she placed it on her dresser. She was ring-less until Max replaced it again. Sometimes she took all three rings and lined them up next to each other. She never asked Max where he got them. They were probably from Walmart but she didn't want to know.

WHEN SENIOR WEEK CAME, Cleo was relieved. At least when it was over, people would stop talking about it all the time. Max kept insisting that he should skip it. "I don't even want to go to Hilton Head," he said. "I hate it there." Because he was nice enough to lie, she told him he had to go. It didn't go unnoticed that he was acting in a way that very few college boys would. She saw the way his friends looked at her, like she'd ruined his life, like he didn't have as much to do with this situation as she did. And so, because of this, she kept saying, "You have to go."

Max finally agreed, but tried to get her to come with. Cleo was firm on this. There was no way in hell she was going to Senior Week with a huge pregnant stomach to be the only sober person in a sea of Bucknell students. She'd rather be trapped in a cave with Mary and Laura for seven days straight than go through that.

"Then I'm not going the whole time," Max said. "Just for a few days."

Cleo figured that was better than nothing.

With Max gone, the apartment was so quiet. Even when

she walked outside, the town felt empty, since all the seniors were gone. Before he left, Max went to the grocery store and bought Cleo enough food that she would have survived a war. She stood in the doorway of the kitchen and watched him unload frozen pizzas, boxes of cereal, macaroni and cheese, and soup. It made her start to cry, watching him pile up all this junk food for her, and she had to turn and go into the bathroom so she wouldn't bawl in front of him. These hormones really were a bitch.

Secretly, Cleo had been sort of looking forward to her time alone in the apartment. She realized that it would be the last time ever that she'd really be all by herself. After graduation, they'd be at the Coffeys' and then there'd be a baby. And while that was hard to imagine, hard to think that it was really going to happen, she knew enough to be grateful for this time.

She watched marathons of old TV shows, and stayed up well into the night, then slept past noon and ate huge bowls of cereal. She read stupid books and ate ramen. And after two days, she felt like she was going out of her mind. She'd started to have nightmares about the baby, where she forgot it someplace and left it behind. In one, she was buying shoes and Weezy came up to her and screamed at her for leaving her baby in her purse. Cleo was confused as to how the baby had gotten there in the first place, and tried to say so, but couldn't get the words right. She woke up sweating.

She had wanted time alone, but now she wanted Max. She felt desperate for him. She wanted someone else to be there when she woke up to tell her that the baby wasn't even there yet and to assure her that she didn't (and wouldn't) leave it in a purse. She couldn't help but imagine Max at the beach, drinking and talking to girls. Every night, she thought, *Please, God, don't let him make out with anyone. Please, God, don't let him decide to leave me.*

When Max came home, Cleo almost knocked him over. She sat with her legs on his lap while he told her about the week and who got really drunk, who hooked up, who threw up all over the floor. Cleo laughed at these stories, so happy to have him home. They talked into the night, and Cleo kept her leg linked around his in bed. She wanted to make sure that he was really there. What had she been thinking, taking him for granted? Was she out of her mind? This might not be what she had imagined, and this certainly wasn't perfect, and maybe she was wearing a ten-dollar ring from Walmart, but Max was still the best thing she had in her whole life at the moment, and she couldn't forget that.

GRADUATION WAS LONG AND HOT, but the upside was that in her robe, Cleo looked like she was just chunky and not necessarily pregnant. The downside was that both of their families were there, and they were all together for the first time ever.

Weezy and Elizabeth had been in touch and even met up for lunch a few months back. It was a strange thing to imagine, these two women getting together. Cleo waited for her mom to call and ridicule Weezy, to make fun of her coddling ways, how she talked about her children like they were all still toddlers. But she never did. She actually seemed to enjoy her. It was amazing how much an accidental pregnancy could bind you together against your children.

Weezy made the two of them pose in front of trees and buildings, with their caps on, then with their caps off, holding their diplomas, and just standing. She tried to make the two of them throw their caps in the air, which was when Max put his foot down. Then she made Cleo pose with Elizabeth, and then they took pictures of the whole Coffey family. "I'll get you copies," Weezy told Elizabeth. Elizabeth just nodded. Cleo was pretty sure she didn't even have a camera with her.

After the ceremony, Cleo and Elizabeth ran into Monica and her family. Cleo and Monica hugged, and then Monica's mom and dad each hugged her. Elizabeth looked at Monica with a fond but distant smile, like she was sure she'd seen her somewhere before, but couldn't say where. When they went to say good-bye, Monica's mom hugged Cleo again, and whispered in her ear, "We're all thinking of you," which made Cleo feel strange, and weirdly like Monica had told on her. She pulled away and said the only thing she could think of, which was, "Thanks."

They all went out to an Italian dinner at a restaurant where Weezy had made reservations months earlier. Every restaurant was booked, of course, and unless you remembered way ahead of time, you were out of luck. Cleo wondered what they would have done if they weren't with the Coffeys. Elizabeth probably would have just driven back to New York.

They all said good-bye outside the restaurant. Cleo and Max had to go pack up their apartment, and everyone else was driving back that night. It felt weird packing up the apartment with Max. "I don't feel like we graduated," she said. "I don't feel like anything's over."

WEEZY MADE THEM UNPACK THEIR BAGS on the driveway. "Who knows what you're bringing back from that place?" she kept saying. Cleo wasn't sure if she thought they had bedbugs or that mice were hiding in their clothes, but she was offended. She managed to convince Weezy to let them bring the stuffed chair from their apartment down to the basement, after Weezy inspected it and sprayed it with some sort of foam that she then vacuumed off of it.

Cleo wondered what the neighbors must have thought, looking out to see Weezy in cropped workout pants and an old hockey T-shirt of Max's, sweating as she pulled the vacuum around, the orange extension cord trailing out of the house, while Cleo just stood there and watched, her hands resting on her stomach, which was as big as a beach ball.

After they moved everything in, Max sat on the edge of the bed and Cleo stood by the dresser. They were exhausted and sweaty. The room felt tiny, like it could barely hold the two of them.

"Well, here we are," Max said.

"Here we are," Cleo said.

MAX STARTED LOOKING FOR A JOB the very next day, which was annoying. There was no point in her even applying anywhere, since no one was going to hire a girl that was almost eight months pregnant. Cleo looked at his résumé and wanted to tell him that she should be the one getting a job, that she'd be able to get a better one than he could. It was always understood between them that she was the smarter one, and now she wanted it acknowledged. She had to bite her lip to keep from saying something out loud. Instead, she sat and watched Max send out his résumé, feeling like a big blob of nothing.

THEN MAX GOT A JOB DOING AD SALES for a small business magazine, and Cleo spent her days sleeping late, wandering around the house, reading, sleeping, and waiting for Max to come home. Then when he did, she listened to him talk about his job. She wanted to hear everything about his coworkers. Who brought tuna for lunch every day and who napped in their cubicle? She herself had nothing to share, except for the day that she took Ruby for a walk and the poor thing got diarrhea. Max was so tired every night. "I can't believe this is what a job feels like," he said. Most nights, he fell asleep while they were still watching TV in bed.

The days got even more boring. Weezy tried to help, which some days Cleo appreciated and some days it made her want to scrape her teeth with her fingernails. "Shall we go look at some strollers?" Weezy would say. Or, "Why don't we go get you some new tops?" That last comment made Cleo cry a little, since she was sure that Weezy was telling her that her shirts were too tight.

One day, even Weezy seemed at a loss, and the two of them sat upstairs on the couch, reading. Weezy had given Cleo an old copy of *The Thorn Birds* that she'd found on a bookshelf in the basement. The book was wrinkled, like it had gotten wet and the pages had dried all wavy, but Weezy promised she'd enjoy it. "It's so dramatic, full of love affairs with a priest, and—oh, I don't want to ruin it. You'll love it, I promise."

And so, even if love affairs with a priest didn't really sound like a huge selling point for Cleo, she was reading the book, which actually seemed a little bit trashy to be on Weezy's bookshelf but did hold her attention, which wasn't easy these days.

"You know what we should do?" Weezy asked her. "We should go get some yarn and start knitting blankets for the baby."

"I don't know how to knit," Cleo told her.

"You don't know how to knit?" Weezy sounded appalled, as though Cleo had just told her she didn't know how to tie her shoes. Really, what did Weezy think, that girls still took

Home Ec classes? In what world was it that strange not to know how to knit? Cleo thought all of this, but just shook her head in response to Weezy's question.

"Well, then, I can teach you. It will be wonderful."

Cleo was so bored that she agreed. She even hoped it really would be wonderful. Here she was, getting excited over yarn and books with philandering priests. She didn't even recognize herself.

She and Weezy went to the yarn store, to stock up on needles for Cleo and get some easy patterns and fun yarn. The place was called At Knit's End and was tucked in an old house off of a busy road. A few of the women greeted Weezy when she walked in.

"Hello," Weezy said. "Ladies, we have a first-timer! This is my daughter-in-law, Cleo." The women didn't seem all that excited, and Cleo stood frozen, shocked to hear herself be called Weezy's daughter-in-law. She wasn't yet, but she didn't correct her. She guessed that's what she would be soon.

"Since we don't know what the baby will be," Weezy was saying, "we'll have to get some neutral colors. Yellows, greens, and I guess even light blue would work. We'll get you some yarn to practice on. And let's see . . ." She thumbed through a stack of books. "Here. This looks like an easy pattern. Just knitting with increasing and a yarn over. Or you could do this one, it's a basket weave. Just knitting and purling. What do you think?"

Cleo hadn't understood one word that Weezy had just said, but she pointed to the simpler pattern, and Weezy nodded. She chose a light yellow yarn, which was super-soft and pretty. Weezy had found a complicated pattern, with sheep dancing across it, and she was picking up ball after ball of yarn and throwing it into the basket.

When the ladies rang them up, Cleo was surprised by the total. How did yarn cost this much? Cleo tried to offer to pay, but Weezy patted her hand away. "This was my idea and it's my treat. It will be fun for me to get knitting again, and now I have a good excuse."

The cashier, who was a large sour-looking woman, put their purchases into a bag and handed it to them without smiling.

" 'Bye, ladies," Weezy called. Some of them grunted in response. When they got out to the parking lot, Weezy lowered her voice. "Knitters are not friendly. I don't know what it is, you'd think they would be, but I've learned over the years that most of them act like they have a needle up their behind." Cleo laughed and then Weezy laughed a little bit too.

It turned out that Cleo loved knitting. Well, that wasn't exactly true. She loved the feeling of concentrating, the magic of turning the yarn over the needles and coming out with a perfect little stitch. When Weezy taught her to do a yarn over for the first time, she gasped. "Oh, look at that!" and Weezy looked pleased. It was magical, sort of.

She could knit for hours, sit with the TV on or music in the background and let her fingers go. She didn't enjoy the actual process; it sort of made her fingers ache, and sometimes it was so boring that she felt like her skin was going to split. But she liked the goal, and she loved checking off the boxes as she was done with each row, marking her stitches with the little stitch counters. She was determined.

At night, she'd sit up in bed and knit. Max thought she was becoming obsessed. "Maybe I'm nesting," she told him.

"Maybe that's it," he said. He pulled her down for a kiss and then put his face on her stomach and kissed that. "Good night, baby."

She and Weezy took to knitting every night after dinner.

They had different programs that they liked to watch, and Weezy could always help her if she knotted a stitch or did something wrong. She sometimes hoped that Claire or Martha would join them, but they seemed to have their own thing going on. Will always went up to his office to work, and Max was so tired with his new schedule that he went to bed early.

Weezy's blanket was really complicated. Sometimes she would explain it to Cleo, the stitches she was doing, and Cleo would watch, fascinated. It took Weezy more than an hour to do a row, and almost every row required something different. When she was done, she would knit the sheep over the blanket. "It's not as hard as it seems," she said. But Cleo could tell she was pleased at the attention.

Cleo finished her first blanket, and as Weezy taught her how to do the final stitch and tie it off, they both cheered. Cleo felt exhilarated. She couldn't believe that she'd made this thing. "I love it," she said over and over. She put it next to her and rubbed it on her face.

"We'll wash it in Dreft and it will be all clean and ready for the baby. It's really beautiful. You are a natural."

They got Cleo more yarn and she started on the basket-weave blanket. This one she did in a light blue that was almost aqua. It was really more of a girl color, but you could use it for both. Plus, Cleo felt like she was having a girl, but she hadn't told anyone in case she was wrong. She didn't want to sound like an idiot.

"A baby can never have too many blankets," Weezy said. "And you can always give them as gifts. It's such a wonderful thing to receive."

Sometimes Weezy had a glass of wine while she knitted, although one night, after she'd had a few, she ended up messing up the blanket so much that she had to take out two entire rows. "This is why you don't drink and knit," she told Cleo. They laughed, and Cleo wished that she could knit and drink, but it wasn't an option.

It was funny, those nights, how peaceful it was to sit together, the TV chattering in the background showing some silly sitcom or fashion reality show. She and Weezy could talk about the people on the TV, who their favorites were, or they could talk about their knitting. But most of the time they were silent, both pairs of hands working away, fingers moving in rhythm, and Cleo felt a certain sense of happiness, to be making something for the baby, to be sitting quietly with Weezy and creating something for this little person.

Ruby liked to sit on the couch next to Cleo while she knitted, sometimes resting her body on the completed part of the blanket, like she was testing it out. At first Cleo hadn't really liked Ruby all that much. The dog had goopy eyes and some strange-feeling lumps on her back. But after seeing how much Max adored her, and after being at the house long enough to get used to her, and the sort of foul smell that she carried with her, Cleo grew fond of her.

Ruby seemed to know that Cleo was pregnant, and she would come sit next to her and rest her head on Cleo's stomach, as if she were talking to the baby or protecting her somehow. "Are you talking to the baby?" Cleo would sometimes whisper, and Ruby would press her snout into her stomach, as if to say yes.

Max was always worried about Ruby. "She's walking weird," he'd say. "She's limping, on her right side."

"She's just getting older," Weezy would tell him. But she didn't sound so sure herself.

Ruby moved slowly around the house, and sometimes when they got ready to take her out, by the time she walked to the back door, she seemed to have forgotten where she was going.

. . .

SOME DAYS, IF CLEO DIDN'T think too much about anything, she was okay. But she was never much good at putting things out of her mind, and so most days she spent worrying. She thought about getting married to Max, and how silly it probably was. Then she thought about how, if they didn't get married, Weezy would probably sneak down to the basement one night with a judge and marry them in their sleep. She did not want her grandchild to be born to unmarried parents. She'd made that much clear.

Cleo loved statistics. But she knew that what they would tell her now was that she and Max wouldn't make it. Not for the long term anyway. Who knew what would happen ten years from now? She'd be only thirty-two. Not old at all. She tried not to dwell on these thoughts, but she couldn't help it. Look at what happened with Monica. She couldn't even keep a best friend. What hope did she have that she and Max would stay together?

There were nights that she lay in bed and stared at the back of Max's head, just thinking, *Well, this won't last long.* Or worse, sometimes when she woke up in the middle of the night, she'd stare at the lump of him in the bed and think, *Who is that?*

Sometimes if she couldn't stop thinking about their doomed fate, she'd remind herself that the odds of her getting pregnant while on the pill were small too. Almost impossible, really. If she was feeling good, she'd think that these slim statistics would revisit them again, that she and Max were some sort of magnet for the improbable, and that they'd have a long and happy life together. If she was feeling bad, she'd think that they'd used up all of their impossible odds, and that she and Max were bound to split up soon.

CHAPTER 19

Claire had broken even. Which was a miracle of sorts, really. She had barely any money in the bank, but her credit cards were paid off. And she felt rich. Now, when she signed on to her bank accounts, she felt like she could breathe, like her chest was open again. It hadn't even taken as long as she'd thought it would. Apparently having someone else give you a place to live and pay your bills was a great way to get rid of credit card debt. Moving home had been the right thing to do.

It was good to remind herself of that, to remember that living at home had saved her. Because at the moment, the house was so crowded it felt like hell.

How had they all lived there at the same time? Sure, there wasn't a pregnant Cleo living with them when they were growing up, but still. Claire didn't remember it being like this. It seemed like every time she went down the stairs, she ran into someone. She'd go to the kitchen to get a glass of water and find that there were no clean glasses. Bowls of cereal were left out, balled-up napkins were all over the counter, and there were always crumbs—on the floor, on the counter, in the sink. Everywhere. It made Lainie's house seem tidy and calm.

The bathrooms were a whole other story. The Coffey house was old, and some of the plumbing issues had never quite been resolved. If the dishwasher or washing machine was running while someone took a shower, there were bound to be shocks of cold water that spurted out. And if someone flushed a toilet while someone else was in the shower, the water turned scalding for about five to seven seconds. They'd all lived with this before, coming out of the bathroom looking to accuse whoever was rude enough to flush the toilet while they were in there, but they hadn't had to deal with it in a while, and now it just seemed absurd and impossible.

"I'm sorry," Claire heard Weezy saying to Will one morning, "but there is too much laundry to do, and if I wait until everyone is showered, it will never get done. Maybe if the people in this house learned how to use a washing machine instead of throwing their laundry down the chute for me to handle, we wouldn't have this problem." Will grumbled something and walked away.

Trying to explain the water rules to Cleo proved harder than they thought. Over dinner one night—after Cleo had started the dishwasher while Weezy was in the shower and was faced with a screaming Weezy running down the stairs a few minutes later—Max tried to explain the situation.

"So if I flush the toilet, it will make the shower cold?" Cleo asked.

"No, it makes a spray of hot water come out," Max said. "So you can do it, but you have to warn the person."

"So what you're saying is that you want me to knock on the bathroom door and tell whoever is in the shower that I have to use the bathroom somewhere else in the house?"

"Exactly," Max said. He sat back and looked pleased.

"Maybe I just won't use anything if anyone's in the shower. Does that work?"

"You could do that too," Claire said. She smiled at her and

reached across the table to pat Cleo on the arm. She couldn't believe that her brother was asking his girlfriend to interrupt showers at his family's house. How stupid could boys be?

AT THE END OF MARCH, Amanda decided not to come back to Proof Perfect. Claire wasn't surprised one bit. As soon as Amanda had taken the extra three months, Claire could have guessed that she'd never be back. Who could blame her? The thought of returning from maternity leave to face crazy Leslie and all of the strange people here was pretty horrible. Leslie called Claire into her office to tell her the situation.

"What's unfortunate is that we've paid for her health care for the past three months. We believed her when she said she was coming back," Leslie said.

"I'm sure a lot of people change their minds once they're home with the baby," Claire said. But Leslie shook her head.

"The good news is that we've discussed it and we've decided to offer you the job full time."

"Oh, Leslie, that's so nice, but I can't take it."

Leslie wrinkled her eyebrows and tilted her head, like she couldn't possibly understand what Claire was saying.

"It's just . . . I don't plan to stay here long term."

"Well, we all know that the best-laid plans always blow up in your face."

Was that a saying? Claire really didn't think so.

"I think I'm pretty set on moving back to New York," Claire said. "But thank you for the offer and for the opportunity."

"Why don't you sit with it for a while? We're not in any rush to find someone new. You can keep the job as a temporary situation and think about it for a month or two."

Claire agreed, but her heart was pounding when she left

her office. She felt like there was a chance she'd just end up trapped there. She tried to talk herself down, tell herself that it was a ridiculous thing to think. But she still felt a slight panic and she knew that sooner rather than later, she'd have to get out of there. June, she decided, was her limit.

LAINIE AND CLEO HAD TAKEN TO going for long walks together after dinner. "You should come," Lainie said, but Claire declined. She watched from her window as the two pregnant ladies walked down the sidewalk, their heads turned toward each other, Cleo laughing at something that Lainie said, while she gestured and shook her head. Lainie had invited Cleo over for lunch one day, and ever since then the two of them had been spending a lot of time together.

"She just needs someone to talk to," Lainie said. "She's scared out of her mind, and there's no one she can really ask about this stuff."

"That's nice of you," Claire said. She didn't really mean it.

The first time Cleo and Lainie had met, a couple of years ago now, they seemed to like each other immediately. They'd smiled at each other right away, and spent the night talking, bonding over (Claire could only assume) both being really, really pretty. And now, here they were, waddling off into the sunset together, talking about pregnancy and hormones and placentas. It reminded Claire of seeing Lainie talk to Margie Schuller in the bathroom that day, knowing that she was on the other side of something and that there was nothing she could do to join them. It felt a little lonely.

Her friend Katherine was calling her more often, asking her when she was coming back to New York. "I don't think you should stay there any longer," she said. "You really need to come back."

When Claire thought about going back to New York, she felt calm. Was it wrong that part of it was because she knew that there were so many other women there her age who had jobs and were unattached and weren't even close to having babies? Was it such a bad thing to want to be surrounded by your own kind? People had been doing it for years, really. Look at the ethnic neighborhoods that popped up all over. There were Little Italys and Chinatowns in every city. And weren't there even midget colonies somewhere? She'd heard that once and it made so much sense to her, to want to be somewhere where everyone and everything was your size, where things were within your reach and you weren't struggling all the time to fit in a world that wasn't built for you.

That was all she wanted. To be back somewhere where no one looked at her strangely, where she fit in. And she knew that place was New York. Sometimes the thought of going back there overwhelmed her—she'd have to find a job, look for an apartment, and be shocked and disgusted at how much she was going to pay for a tiny place. But she could figure it out. She knew where she was supposed to be.

ON THE DAY THAT WAS SUPPOSED TO BE her wedding day, no one said anything to her. She wouldn't have forgotten anyway, but all of the places that she and Doug had registered sent her congratulatory e-mails. She had never bothered to take the registries down, or take her e-mail address off the list.

She wondered if Doug had gotten the same e-mails. It was so strange to think that Doug knew nothing about what was happening in her life, and she knew nothing about his. She'd e-mailed him when she left New York, because it had seemed like the right thing to do, to let your former fiancé know that you were going to be living in a different city. He'd written back and wished her luck, but they hadn't been in contact since.

She wondered what he'd think if he knew that she was living at home still, what he'd say about Max and Cleo having a baby, and about Martha's trying to get her to go to therapy. She couldn't imagine what he'd say if he knew that she was acting like a whole different person, smoking cigarettes pretty often, hanging out with Fran, sometimes smoking pot on weeknights just for fun. She would bet he wouldn't believe it.

When they'd split up their stuff in the apartment, they had both wanted the expensive ceramic Dutch oven that they'd gotten as an engagement gift. It was bright orange and cheerful, and Claire loved it. When they registered, Doug had wanted a blue one, but she fought for the orange. She pointed out that he would eventually be with someone else, and that girl wasn't going to want something that his ex-fiancée had chosen. He'd looked hurt when she said it, but nodded and let her have it. And she wondered now if he was with someone else, if he also was acting totally different than he had with her. Maybe he was engaged again. He could be married already with a baby on the way. (Okay, sure, it wasn't likely, but Max and Cleo were proof that things sometimes happened much faster than intended.) She thought about e-mailing him, just to see. But in the end she left it alone. He wasn't hers to know anymore.

AT THE END OF MAY, they'd all trekked out to a yoga retreat in Ohio for Cathy and Ruth's wedding. The place was called Bear Den Cottages and they spent the weekend sleeping in cabins, doing Downward Facing Dog, and drinking green tea. She'd told Fran that it was family only, which wasn't true, but she didn't want to invite him and anyway, she didn't think he'd even want to go.

Claire had been dreading this weekend, but surprisingly it wasn't awful. Even pregnant Cleo seemed to enjoy her sun salutations. And while they all agreed that a lot of it was "hippie nonsense," as Maureen whispered to them, it was all in all a pretty pleasant trip. And when Claire stood up front with Martha and Cathy, wearing her Driftwood bridesmaid dress that Martha had freaked out over, all she thought was that Cathy and Ruth seemed really happy. And when she realized that this made her feel happy, she was relieved, because she figured that meant she wasn't a horrible, jealous person after all. And that made her even happier.

HER THIRTIETH BIRTHDAY WAS AT THE BEGINNING of June, and she really meant it when she said she wanted to ignore it. But that wasn't an option. Lainie insisted on throwing her a party. "We'll have a barbecue," she said. "It will be fun."

"I really don't feel like having a party," Claire said.

"Don't tell me you're freaking out about turning thirty. Come on. It's not that big of a deal."

"Fine," Claire agreed. It seemed easier than trying to fight it. "Fine."

For three days out of the year, Claire and Martha were the same age. When she was younger, Claire loved this. She used to torture Martha with it, telling her that she was just as old as she was. Now it didn't seem that fun.

Martha was concerned that turning thirty would send Claire into a tailspin, and she talked to her often about it. "It seems worse than it is," she said. "The idea of thirty can be scary but once it happens, you're totally fine."

"I'm fine," Claire repeated over and over again.

Martha thought Claire's birthday was even more reason to go to therapy with her. Sometimes Claire thought she should just agree to go to shut her up about it.

"You're probably stressed about things you don't even know that you're stressed about. That's the best part of therapy," Martha said.

"Martha, I'm going to tell you for the last time. I am not going to therapy with you." Claire couldn't help but yell it. That was another reason she had to get out of this house. Each day made her act more and more like a teenager.

"You are being really closed-minded," Martha said. She yelled a little too.

"Good," Claire said. She didn't care if she wasn't making sense. The two of them left the room and slammed their respective doors. Anytime Weezy looked at them, she just shook her head.

LAINIE TIED BALLOONS TO THE CHAIRS in the backyard and hung an old silver banner that read HAPPY BIRTHDAY. Claire hugged her when she arrived. "This is a big birthday," Lainie told her. "You should enjoy it."

Lainie's boys were all dressed alike, in khaki shorts and light blue polo shirts. When she got there, Jack ran right up to her. "Remember when I was five and you babysat me?" he said. She nodded and he smiled. "That was fun." He had made her a birthday card and helped her blow out her candles. He seemed to have changed his mind about her. Apparently, they were now the best of friends.

Lainie invited a couple of her sisters, Claire's whole family, a couple of friends from high school, and Fran, of course. When she brought Claire's cake out, which was a yellow sheet cake with chocolate frosting she'd made from a box, she said, "I just want to wish my best friend a happy thirtieth birthday. I don't know where I'd be without you."

It was a funny speech, considering Claire had always thought that Lainie would be just fine without her. She was the one that needed Lainie more. But maybe that was how all friendships were—one person was the littlest bit needier than the other one. And maybe sometimes it switched. Not often, but sometimes.

Fran had shown up at the barbecue wearing a collared shirt and no hat. It looked like he'd made an effort to look nice, and seeing him stand there and talk to her family dressed like that hurt Claire's heart a little for reasons she couldn't totally identify.

After Claire blew out her candles, Lainie brought out a cupcake with another candle in it and lit it for Martha. "It's a few days early," she said, "but we can't forget the other birthday girl."

Martha was pleased, Claire could tell. And Weezy was too. Even Claire felt good about it, and she realized that in every relationship, Martha was the needier one. And she knew that would never change.

MARTHA WAS CLOSING ON A CONDO, which took up a lot of the discussion at the dinner table. Cleo always looked happy to talk about it, since it took the attention away from her and the baby, and actually everyone else also seemed relieved to have another topic to discuss.

"It would make sense to rent out the other bedroom, but it would also be great to have it as a guest room. Cathy was saying that she and Ruth would love to come stay for a few days soon, and I'd love that too. I just have to decide what to do." Martha sighed, like she'd just been faced with deciding whether or not she should euthanize a puppy.

"I'm starting to apply for jobs in New York," Claire said. It seemed as good a time as any to let everyone know.

"Already?" Weezy asked.

"I've been here for almost a year," Claire said.

"What sorts of things are you looking for?" Will asked. He took a bite of peas.

"I think the same sort of thing I was doing before . . . nonprofit stuff."

"But we'll miss you," Cleo said. Claire smiled at her. She really did feel bad leaving her and Max, but at least they'd all be happier for the space.

"It might be a good idea to wait," Weezy said. "Until your money situation is more stable."

"I'm fine," Claire said.

"Well, it couldn't hurt to give yourself a cushion is all I'm saying. Just have a good amount socked away. You could stay for a few more months, get yourself in a better position," Weezy said.

"I don't think so," Claire said.

"Well now, don't dismiss the idea before you even think about it. You don't want to find yourself right back in the same situation." Weezy shook her head just a little.

"Thanks for the vote of confidence. But I'm ready to go and I'm fine. You can't have all your children living with you for the rest of your life, you know."

"Claire." Will gave her a look.

"Who will be our babysitter?" Max asked. He tried to laugh.

Weezy sniffed. "I'm just saying you should think about it, that's all."

"It's not a bad idea," Martha said. "When you look at how much I've saved, how easy this buying process has been. It's worked out great."

"So, we should have all lived at home for all of our twenties? Sounds like a great plan," Claire said.

"Don't be nasty," Weezy said.

"This is ridiculous." Claire got up from the table. Cleo was looking down at her plate, like she wanted to disappear, like she'd been dropped in the middle of a loony bin and had no way to escape. Which, really, wasn't too far from the truth.

Claire grabbed her bag and walked outside, although she didn't really know where she was going. She hated the way she acted here. As soon as she stepped on the sidewalk, she felt guilty. What a brat she was. They'd let her come back and stay with them, and she couldn't even stand to listen to their suggestions. Why was she like this? The worst part was she couldn't help it. The anger seemed to come out of her before she even knew what was happening.

She wandered around for a while, pretending that she didn't know where she was going to go, before she finally called Fran. "Come over," he said. That's what he always said. She loved that.

He had a beer waiting for her on the coffee table. He was just in his boxers, even though the basement stayed pretty cool. "Here," he said, handing her the beer. "You sounded like you could use one."

Claire tried to tell him about the fight, about why she felt so bad. He listened, but she knew he didn't really understand. Fran wasn't one to feel guilty for being mean to his parents. It made sense, really, since they didn't seem to think about him so much.

"I just can't stand being there anymore," Claire said. "I

feel like this horrible person, because I'm annoyed at them all the time. And they're just trying to help, I know that. But it's so smothering." Fran made a noise like he agreed with what she was saying, but she knew he didn't. She put her feet in his lap and they fell silent, watching TV.

They were lying on the couch a few hours later, when she told him. She was wearing just her bra and underwear, and all she could think about was how scratchy the couch material was on her hip. Fran was lying on his back, and she was on her side, her head on his chest. He was holding a chunk of her hair in his hand, twisting it and then letting it unravel on his fingers. She knew he would fall asleep soon if she didn't say anything.

"I think I'm moving back to New York," she said.

"You think?" He held his hand still, and she could imagine her gob of hair in his hand, raised above her head, like it was waiting for something.

"I mean, I know," she said. She lifted her head to look at him. "I'm moving. Soon, I think. I just need to figure it all out."

Fran didn't say anything for a few seconds. He dropped her hair and put his hands behind his head. "I'm not surprised," he finally said.

"Really?"

"Yeah. I mean, last week you said you were going to kill someone if you had to live in your house much longer."

"No, I didn't," Claire said.

"Yes, you did," Fran said. "So, before it comes to murder, it's probably best if you get out of there."

"I just think it's time," Claire said. "It just feels like everything is going on without me. Like I took a break, but no one else did and now if I stay here I'll just fall further behind. Does that make sense?"

"Not really," Fran said.

"Oh."

"But I mean, I get it. You're not happy here."

"I'm not unhappy."

"There's not that much room in between, you know."

"I guess that's true."

"It's probably a good idea." Fran picked up her hair again and started twirling it.

"I just wanted to tell you. Because I don't know what we're doing, exactly, but I've liked it. I really have. You were one of the only good things here."

"That's nice," Fran said.

"I mean it." Claire sat all the way up and moved her hair away from his hands. "I might have been unhappy, that's true. But I wasn't unhappy when I was with you." She got a feeling that she was going to start crying, so she looked at the far wall until it started to go away.

Fran pulled her back down and kissed the top of her head. "Look," he said. "We had fun, right? It's okay, I swear. We're good, I promise."

"Okay."

"Claire, really. We're good. Both of us. We needed time to get over those fuckers, and we did. And you can't feel bad about that."

"I don't."

"You're such a liar. I mean it. Stop feeling bad. You feel guilty all the time, about everything. And you shouldn't."

Claire didn't say anything. She was impressed that he had been so observant. It didn't seem like he noticed. "You should move out too," she said.

Fran laughed. "You mean to tell me a thirty-year-old living in his parents' basement isn't that attractive? Point taken."

"I didn't mean that."

"Nah, you're right. It's time. Soon."

"I like this basement," Claire said. She felt even worse now for saying that to him.

"It's all right," he said. "I bet you'll be happy to get back to New York. I have to say, I never really got it. I could never live there."

"You could visit," Claire said.

"Yeah, maybe I'll come see the elephants when they come to town," Fran said. Claire didn't even remember telling him that story, but she must have. Had she left Doug out of the story when she told him or not? She couldn't remember.

"You should," she said. "It really is something to see."

"Okay," Fran said. "Maybe we'll do that. Maybe I'll come and we'll see the elephants."

They were both lying. They knew he'd never come to visit her in New York, that he would never see the elephants. But just then, she really wished he would, so he could see how weird, how unreal, the whole thing looked; how magical it was to watch these huge animals marching down the streets of Manhattan. Just thinking about it now made her homesick and a little sad. The way it felt like a dream, how even after you saw it with your own eyes, you never really believed it had happened.

CHAPTER 20

The wedding was ridiculous. All of it. Max had insisted that it take place in the backyard, and at first Weezy tried to get him to change his mind. But now she was glad that they were at home, and not out in public for the world to see. The bride was walking down the "aisle" eight months pregnant, in a flowy white dress that showed off the bump underneath it, like she was a movie star, some starlet that was flaunting the fact that she was getting married in this condition. *Look at me,* the dress seemed to say. *I'm pregnant and I don't care who knows it.*

Weezy tried to be open-minded. After all, her children were living in a different world than the one she'd grown up in. But honestly. A white dress? Really? Why even bother?

She'd suggested to Max early on that he and Cleo should think about getting married. She waited for him to disagree, or to tell her that it was none of her business, but he surprised her.

"I think that's a good idea," he said. "I think it's something we both want."

Even though Weezy had just suggested the same thing, she immediately wanted to tell him that marriage was a mistake. He barely knew this girl. They were children. How did they think they could make a marriage work? But she kept her mouth shut.

She imagined the children would want a quick justice of the peace ceremony, that maybe they'd all go out for a nice lunch afterward. And then after the baby was here, they could have a small church ceremony, really do it right. But Max told her they had other plans.

"We want our friends to be there," he said. "And our families. If we're going to do it, we want to do it in front of everyone."

It sounded just like something Cleo would say, and Weezy knew that her son was repeating Cleo's words, and she resented that. It was enough to make her scream.

"You know, if you have it in the backyard, it won't be recognized in the church," she finally said.

"It'll be recognized everywhere else, though," Max said. "Plus, Cleo's not even Catholic."

And that was how Weezy found herself in early June, staging this spectacle, this crazy event for everyone to see. "One day, we'll look back on this and laugh," Will said to her that morning. She didn't have the heart to tell him that she didn't believe that for a second.

THE DAY OF THE WEDDING WAS WARM, but not too warm, and Weezy felt that she deserved at least that much. "Aren't you grateful for the weather?" Maureen asked her, and Weezy just shook her head a little bit. If your son got his college girlfriend pregnant, if her mother was still so angry she could barely speak to her, if they were going to live in your basement while they had the baby, then you deserved a beautiful day for the wedding. That was all there was to it.

Bets was over at Maureen's house, along with Cathy, Ruth, and Drew. And somehow Maureen knew enough not to breathe even a word of complaint. When Weezy finally picked up the phone to call Bets and tell her the news, Bets was surprisingly calm.

"Oh, Weezy," she'd said. "Don't worry about it so much. Once kids are out of your house, you can't control what they do. Not one bit. Believe me, I've learned that."

And even though it sounded like Bets was placing some sort of judgment on her and Maureen (what on earth could they have done that would have disappointed her, really?), she didn't care. She kept waiting for Bets to start being, well, Bets. But it didn't happen. She'd been quiet during her visit, sitting and smiling at the family, and not even muttering anything about "bastards" under her breath. It was a wedding miracle.

The girls had been fighting—were at each other's throats, actually—and it was driving her crazy. They were acting like they were back in high school, stomping up the stairs and knocking loudly on the bathroom door, screaming, "I need to get in there!"

"Girls, *enough*," she'd yelled that morning. They were in the kitchen, bickering about cereal, and she couldn't take it anymore. And the two of them, still in their pajamas with their hair messy, had turned to look at her like she was the crazy one. Cleo and Max had both just come up from the basement, and were standing at the kitchen door, staring at her as well. She felt like telling all of them to just shut up, to do exactly what she said. She had half a mind to just leave the house and let them all deal with the wedding on their own. But she knew she'd never do that. It wasn't her way.

"We all need to work together today," she finally said. And all of them had nodded, like quiet, obedient children.

Outside, workers were setting up white wooden folding chairs in two groups, to create an aisle in the middle. At the front, there were two large potted plants, which sort of made it look like an altar. Sort of. All of the flowers were white, which is what Cleo wanted. And even though Weezy would have gone a different way, she had to admit that it looked pretty.

When they'd started planning the wedding, Weezy considered finding a new florist. After all, how could she explain this wedding to Samuel? But in the end, she knew he would be the best, and she called him to set up an appointment.

"This is a delicate situation," she'd said. "I'm actually not calling about Claire's wedding. It's—well, it's my son's."

She'd gone on to tell Samuel the whole story—more than she'd told most of her friends, in fact. He'd listened kindly, told her gently that he'd done more of these sorts of weddings than she could even imagine. He told her that she was a lovely woman, a kind mother to be there for her son and his wife-to-be, promised her that once the baby was born, she wouldn't remember any of the mixed feelings she had about this.

When she'd gotten off the phone with him, she felt better than she had since the news had broken. (That was how she thought about it, like it was a news story that broke on television, of an awful event like a murder or the death of someone famous and beloved.) She met with Samuel alone, telling Cleo that the flowers needed to be picked immediately, promising that she would stick to her wishes for the white flowers. And she had. And now they were the loveliest part of the day—the hydrangea blooms that were tied to the chairs, the lovely textured bouquets, the potted plants.

Samuel had come to set up the backyard himself, which she knew he almost never did. He'd given her a hug and wished her luck, told Cleo that she looked beautiful (even though she was still in her robe). He arranged the pots up front, straightened the bows and blooms on the chairs, made sure that every detail was perfect.

She saw him talking to Claire outside, and for a moment Weezy hoped to God he wasn't talking about her wedding, but before she could head out there, the caterer had another question and she was drawn back into the kitchen.

Even though this wedding was almost nothing compared to what they had been planning for Claire, Weezy still found herself totally swept away with it. Maybe it was because they had so little time, or maybe that's how it always was with a wedding. They'd all been running around like chickens with no heads for weeks now, and the day of the wedding felt like a nightmare—the kind where you're trying to pack to go on a trip, and all your clothes keep falling out of the suitcase, no matter what you do.

They'd all gotten up early, but there still didn't seem to be enough time. Weezy had this fear that guests were going to start showing up and they were all going to be half-naked, running around the backyard barefoot. If anything was going to get done, Weezy was going to have to make it happen.

"Why don't you two go get dressed?" she said to Claire and Martha. They were both bridesmaids, although they had both just picked their own dresses (white, of course) and didn't really match. But when they came downstairs, they did both look very pretty. Even if Cleo did seem to be rubbing this white-themed wedding in everyone's face (*I'm pregnant, but I want everything to be virginal!*), it actually all came together beautifully.

She kept sending Will on errands, or out to check on the setup of the bars outside. He was driving her sort of crazy, just standing there all ready for the day, like he couldn't think of anything to do unless she told him. Weezy couldn't help but snap at him, more than once, for just standing there, or for not being in the same room when she needed something from him. Honestly, sometimes men were no help.

The caterers had taken over the kitchen, and set up strange little ovens on the countertops to cook the food. You could barely move in there without running into someone or something.

Cleo had been very opinionated during the meeting with the caterer. She wanted wine and appetizers served as soon as the guests arrived, before the ceremony, so that when the two of them said their vows, people would be eating and drinking, just snacking away, like they were watching a TV show. Weezy tried to talk her out of it. "It's just not how things are done," she said. But Cleo's mind was made up.

"I want it to feel like a party, like a celebration," she said.

Weezy tried to give the caterer a look, to raise her eyebrows as if to say, *I know this is a ridiculous request, do you believe this?* But the caterer had just nodded.

"I love that idea," she said. "Very fun and relaxed."

They'd gone on to decide on "stations" of meat and sushi instead of a sit-down meal.

"I don't want any seating arrangements," Cleo had said. "I just want it so that people can eat whenever they feel like it, wherever they want."

"I think that will confuse people," Weezy said.

"That's very in right now," the caterer said. "People will catch on." Weezy could only imagine what Sally Lemons would say about something like this. She was not one to throw seating arrangements away like they were nothing.

The kicker of the wedding planning was when Max announced that they wanted a friend of theirs to marry them. "Absolutely not," Weezy had said. "It's not even legal."

"Mom, it's legal," Max said. "Everyone does it now."

"Why don't you have Deacon Callaghan? Or even a judge?" But it was like Weezy wasn't even talking, and somehow it was decided that Max's friend Ben (a boy who was once almost kicked out of school for ripping the doors off all of the bathroom stalls in their dorm freshman year) would be the one to marry them. They might as well have had a Muppet do the honors.

THE CEREMONY WAS BRIEF. Cleo and Max had put it all together on their own. After Ben was chosen as the officiant (Weezy still couldn't say that without a sneer), she decided to just let them do what they were going to do.

Claire and Martha walked down the aisle, and then Cleo followed them, alone. Her mother was sitting in the front row, and she looked just like Weezy felt: *Let this day be over with, please God, soon.*

One of their friends read a love poem by George Eliot, which Weezy had to admit was nice. Then Max and Cleo filled a glass jar by pouring two different-colored sands into it, Max with blue and Cleo with yellow, which seemed a bit silly. Another friend played the guitar and sang, a lovely but very sad song called "Hallelujah." Weezy had been excited when she'd heard the name of it, but then quickly realized it wasn't the least bit religious, and wasn't even joyful. There were parts about tying people to kitchen chairs, cutting hair, and bathing on the roof. She hoped that no one was really listening to the words.

Before they exchanged vows, Ben talked about the couple, and said how after Max had met Cleo, he'd told everyone that he'd met "the hottest girl he'd ever seen." People laughed at this, but Weezy was just plain embarrassed. Then the two of them were facing each other, promising to be friends forever, to love each other, and then Ben was pronouncing them husband and wife, which seemed impossible, Weezy thought, because it was just some words spoken in the backyard. It didn't seem real at all.

The whole crowd cheered as they walked down the aisle, and then someone handed each of them a glass of champagne and everyone was clinking glasses and hugging. Weezy went up to both of them and kissed and hugged them. She figured if she pretended like this was a real wedding, eventually it would start to feel like it.

One of Max's friends was a DJ, and he and Cleo had insisted that he should do the music for the wedding. So Weezy hired a twenty-one-year-old kid to be in charge, and just as she predicted, it was a mistake. As soon as the vows were done, he decided it was time for the music. He started off playing a loud song, and the only words that Weezy could make out throughout the whole thing were "bad romance." So, not only did all of the adults look shocked at the noise, but it didn't seem to be a very wedding-appropriate choice.

As the night went on, the older people made their exit quickly. Weezy couldn't blame them. The music got louder with each song, and more vulgar. Her friends came up to say good-bye to her, hugging her and kissing her on the cheek, as though this was a normal wedding. Almost everyone had brought a card with money in it for Max and Cleo, and they'd deposited them into a birdcage that was set up for the purpose. (The birdcage was Samuel's idea, and it was a genius one. It gave the cards a safe place to go, but it wasn't so obvious that it looked like they were begging for money.) It seemed a little sad that all the new couple were getting was cash, but then again, what else would people give a young couple who were expecting their first child in the very near future? A place setting of china? A Cuisinart? No, cash was the only practical thing. Weezy would have done the same if she'd been a guest at the wedding.

Max and Cleo seemed to be having a good time, which was nice, although Weezy was a little shocked to see Cleo out there dancing, shaking her round stomach around the dance floor, rubbing it against Max and laughing.

She and Will danced just once, when the DJ found it in his heart to play a Frank Sinatra song, something for the old people, and Will found her right away and led her out to the dance floor. That was a nice part of the day, swaying and twirling with Will. Of course, right after that, the next song played repeated the words *sexy bitch* over and over, and everyone who had been dancing to Sinatra scattered like cockroaches.

Finally the day was over. It was funny, on all the sites that Weezy had looked at, the bride and the bride's family always commented that the reception went so fast, in the blink of an eye. But this one seemed to go on forever. At one point, Weezy thought they were going to have to kick the straggling college friends out of the backyard and tell them to go home. Thankfully, by the time it was getting to that point, they all seemed to get the hint and were on their way.

Maureen had hired a limo to take Max and Cleo to the Ritz-Carlton for two nights. "My present to you," she'd told them the week before. "I know you won't be going on a honeymoon, so think of this as a mini trip." She'd made them appointments in the hotel spa, and dinner reservations for the next night. "Enjoy yourselves," she said.

And so Max and Cleo had driven off in a limo, while the rest of the family finished saying good-bye to the last guests that were hanging on, and watched the caterers fold up the chairs and remove the leftover food. Weezy felt tired through her whole body, right down to the bones in her fingers, which ached just a little bit.

They'd all gathered on the back patio to have a glass of wine, although that was the last thing Maureen needed. She'd downed her glass quickly, then announced that she thought it would be a good idea if she went home, and Drew, who had been waiting quietly the whole day, piled Maureen, Bets, Ruth, and Cathy into the car and drove them off.

"And then there were four," Weezy said. She felt sad, the way you do after holidays or vacations, just a little let down that the whole thing is over. Isn't that what she'd wanted the whole day, for the thing to be over? But now, she felt let down. Her own head felt a little swimmy from the wine, but she somehow didn't want to go to bed just yet.

"I think it all went well," Will said.

"It did," Martha said. "Except when the caterers tried to set out the buffet before the ceremony even started. I went right in there and told them they'd have to cool it. I mean, can you imagine?"

Martha had repeated this story a few times already, and Weezy saw Claire close her eyes briefly.

"Well, thank goodness you were there," Weezy said. "It could have been a disaster."

"I mean, really," Martha went on. "How hard is it to follow simple directions? What if the food had been out there for all that time, getting cold and congealing as they said their vows?" She sat back and shook her head.

"Well, it wasn't," Claire said. "So there's no need to keep talking about it."

"I'm just saying it could have been a disaster," Martha said.

"We know. You've said it only about a million times already. We understand—the caterers were incompetent and you saved the day. We heard you."

"Girls, stop. Please stop." Weezy felt the beginning of a headache.

"Give your mother a break, would you?" Will said.

"I'm not doing anything," Martha said. "I don't know what Claire's problem is. All I tried to do today is help."

"You were a big help today," Weezy told her.

"Oh my God," Claire said. "Can we please stop praising Martha for acting like a normal person for once?"

"Claire, stop it." Weezy could tell that Martha was on the verge of tears.

"I'm serious. This is why she's like this, you know. This is why she thinks everything's about her. Because you make it about her. All she did was say thank you to people as they left today. And you're acting like she performed a miracle."

Martha got up and walked inside, and Claire rolled her eyes.

"You should apologize to your sister," Weezy said. Her whole body felt so tired. Had she ever been this tired in her whole life?

"I'm not apologizing to her. She needs to hear it. This isn't good for her, the way you treat her."

"You should try to be a little more understanding," Weezy said.

"Understanding is all I am. You make her worse, do you realize that? She thinks the world revolves around her because you make it seem like it does. You make it seem like every little thought she has is so important. It makes her crazy. She thinks the whole world is supposed to treat her like that. And God forbid we should hurt her feelings. How is she ever supposed to live like an adult if you never treat her like one?"

"When you're a parent, you'll understand this more."

"When I'm a parent," Claire said, "I won't focus only on one kid."

"You know what?" Weezy was mad now. "Sometimes the world isn't perfect, Claire. Sometimes you just need to be grateful for what you have. Sometimes you need to be a grown-up." She hadn't yelled at Claire like this since high school.

"A grown-up?" Claire looked up to the sky and laughed. "Right, a grown-up. Well, since you're such a great example, maybe you can explain to me why the florist somehow still thinks I'm getting married. Why he told me that the two of you have been planning things, and that my flowers would be beautiful."

Will turned to Weezy, but didn't say anything. Weezy felt her face get hot. She hadn't felt like this since she was in high school, when Bets had found out that she'd snuck over to Steven Sullivan's house. She swallowed a few times and finally answered.

"I have no idea what you're talking about. He does tons of weddings a year. He probably just mixed you up with someone else."

"Really?" Claire asked. "He seemed pretty sure it was me. He knew Doug's name, he told me how even though we'd changed the date and postponed the wedding, he was still so excited to work with us. How he'd loved going over the flowers with you, how you had great instincts."

"Claire, that's enough," Will said. "Your mother has had a long day—we all have—and we need to just step back."

"I can't wait to get out of this house. I can't wait to get

away from this crazy family. I hate it here." Claire stormed out, and Weezy had a strange feeling of déjà vu, of the girls' being teenagers, when their storming out of the room in tears was just another Tuesday. It used to hurt less when Claire said she hated them. Now it stung, like someone had whipped her.

Weezy felt tears come to her eyes, and she tried to blink them back. Oh, she was so tired. Her children all thought she had failed them, probably even Max. Had she? Because even though Claire was being horrendous, she was right—they did treat Martha differently. They'd had to. All those years, ignoring her outbursts, doing anything to make sure that she was happy, or at least stable. Was it true that they'd made things worse for her? Had she ruined her even more? Weezy's head throbbed and she closed her eyes.

"Don't let this upset you," Will said. "It's been a long day for all of us. Hell, it's been a long year."

"Yes, it has," she said. She waited for Will to ask her about the florist, but he never did.

"We should get some sleep," he said. "Come on."

"I'll be up in a minute," Weezy told him. He nodded and walked over to kiss her good night.

Weezy sat there for several hours. She was so tired, she thought she might just fall asleep right there on the porch, like a crazy old woman. But she stayed awake. She wondered why Will didn't ask her about the florist. She let herself admit that she was secretly thrilled that Samuel had said that she was a pleasure to work with, that she had great instincts. She thought about her children—Martha, Claire, and Max—and how none of them was where she wanted them to be. None of them was where *they* wanted to be. She wondered if it was all her fault, wondered whether if she'd done things differently, they'd all have turned out okay.

She thought about Bets, and how she'd just left Pennsylvania after her husband died, just left her two daughters without a home base and gone back to Michigan to live her own life. She'd just assumed that they'd be okay, that they'd be able to manage. And they had. Was that what she should have done with her own children? She couldn't imagine it. Couldn't imagine how Bets had just separated her life from theirs.

When the sky started to get light out, and the birds started to sing, Weezy got up from the porch and went in the house to go to bed. It was no use torturing herself anymore, she thought. She couldn't fix anything by wondering what if.

She finally got into bed, and Will, who was snoring, turned over in his sleep and put his arm on her stomach as if to say, *There you are.* For a second, she felt a little bit calmer, a little bit less lonely. She pulled the covers up to her shoulders and closed her eyes. She thought she might just sleep all day.

PART Three

CHAPTER 21

Mr. Cranston's funeral wasn't as dramatic as Martha had imagined it would be. They didn't have a separate wake and funeral, just had an open casket for an hour or so before the service started. Martha came early, and then sat in the back. When they finally closed the top of the casket, Ruby started crying, loudly. It echoed in the church, and actually was a little dramatic, which was probably what Ruby was going for. But her brother was the one to take her arm and lead her to the pew, so it looked like they were getting along now. Who could tell how long that would last?

There weren't too many people there, actually. Martha remembered Bets saying once that the older you got, the smaller the funerals were. Because everyone that you knew was dying and there weren't many people left, which was depressing when you got right down to it. Which was worse? To be one of the first to die and have a packed church or to outlive everyone and have almost no one at your funeral to show for it? Martha couldn't decide.

The funeral was at a Presbyterian church, and the service was just what Mr. Cranston had written down. Martha felt like she'd gotten a sneak peek, since she knew which hymns and readings she was going to hear. She was a little surprised to see Jaz get up to do a reading, but thought how nice it was that Mr. Cranston had chosen her. It was right.

Ruby and her brother both gave the eulogy, although Ruby didn't get too far. She talked about being a little girl and having her dad read the comics to her while she sat on his lap. Then she said something else that Martha couldn't understand, and her brother put his hand on her back and gently moved her out of the way. He spoke about Mr. Cranston like he was a businessman that he admired. But Martha tried not to judge, because maybe he had to keep his speech a little removed or he'd lose it like Ruby.

Martha went back to the house for the lunch, which was catered, but it was still Jaz that was in charge, taking over and giving orders. She seemed happy to have something to do, to be bustling around, arranging and rearranging cold cuts and tiny rolls. Switching out the serving spoons for the salads, inspecting the glasses. If anyone noticed that she was crying while doing all of this, they didn't say anything. Jaz just kept moving, and every once in a while reached up to wipe away a tear.

She didn't stay at the house too long. Since Jaz was so busy and Ruby and her brother were greeting guests and accepting condolences, Martha didn't really have anyone to talk to. She made herself a tiny ham sandwich and ate it standing in the corner of the living room, where she'd had her interview with Ruby. She wondered what they'd do with the house now, if they'd sell it, if they'd have to redecorate it before they put it on the market. To think of it cleared of all the personality (as stuffy as it was), to think of the pictures gone, the furniture taken away, made Martha sadder than she'd been all day.

After she ate, she put her plate in the kitchen and found Jaz to say good-bye. Jaz gave her a big hug, and cried a little in her hair, but Martha didn't mind.

"It was so great working with you," Martha said. She meant it.

"You too, baby. Take care now. You take care of yourself."

They squeezed arms and then Jaz kept moving, picking up plates and glasses that had been abandoned, picking up crumpled napkins. Martha looked around and saw Ruby, so she went up to say good-bye.

"It was really an honor to work for your father," Martha said. It seemed like the right thing to say.

"That's sweet," Ruby said. "Oh, I almost forgot. Come with me."

Ruby led her back to the office, and gave her an envelope with her name on it. "To thank you for all your work," she said, sounding strangely formal.

"Oh, no, I already got paid," Martha said.

"This is just a little extra."

"I couldn't." Martha held the envelope out to Ruby.

"Take it," Ruby said. She looked like she didn't really care if Martha was going to or not, but didn't want to deal with the back and forth.

"Well, thanks."

"Sure. I know he wasn't always that easy to deal with."

"Oh, no. He was great. Really. He loved your presents, I think."

Ruby laughed. "No, he didn't. I never knew what to get for him."

"He did, I think. Even if he didn't use them all the time, I think he really loved getting them."

"Thanks," Ruby said. She looked around the office.

"Thank you again." Martha felt like she'd done a good deed, like she'd made the day better for Ruby. She smiled as she let herself out the back door.

• • •

MARTHA HAD GOTTEN A CALL from the caretaking company, just a few days after Mr. Cranston passed, which seemed a little insensitive, but it was their job, she supposed. They asked if she'd be interested in a new placement, and because she hadn't thought too far ahead, she said yes.

This was a different sort of job. She'd be with a woman in her early sixties who had fallen and broken her hip. The woman lived alone and would need help getting to the store and moving around. Martha was happy to take a job with someone who wasn't going to die anytime soon. Although sixty was fairly young to break a hip. This woman probably hadn't gotten enough calcium or done any of the light weight lifting that could help prevent bone deterioration. Well, no matter. Martha could talk to her about all of those things.

They met once, briefly. Sharon Cooper lived alone in a much smaller house than the Cranstons'. Her husband was dead, she told Martha, but she didn't elaborate on it. Martha wondered if he was older or if he'd had an untimely death. From what she could tell from the pictures in the house, she had a few children and a couple of grandchildren. Martha stopped in front of one picture of a blond girl, about three years old, hugging a teddy bear.

"She's so cute," Martha said. Sharon just smiled. "I'm just about to become an aunt. My brother's going to have a baby."

"Congratulations," Sharon said. And that was that. Well, never mind. They had plenty of time to get to know each other.

It would be strange to be in a new house all of a sudden, surrounded by a new family and a new story. It seemed not right to just leave the Cranstons when she'd been such a part of it. But she knew she could always go and visit Jaz over the next few months. Jaz would be happy to have a friendly face, she supposed, while dealing with the house and the loss of Mr. Cranston. Yes, that's what she'd do. She'd make a plan to go there next week and have tea with Jaz.

AT HOME, CLEO SEEMED TOO PREGNANT to even breathe. Martha had never spent this much time up close with a pregnant person—other than when Weezy was pregnant with Max, and Martha didn't remember that much. It was fascinating. Sometimes Cleo leaned back on the couch, shifting around.

"The baby's feet are in my ribs," she'd say.

"Really?" Martha asked. What a strange thought to have feet kicking you in the ribs.

Cleo nodded and puffed a little. She was pretty irritable, but it seemed to be that Max was the only one she took it out on. Martha couldn't really blame her. She looked like she was about to pop.

"You're so close," Martha told her one day. The due date was just a week away. The two of them were lying on the couch watching TV, and Cleo's breathing was so loud it was almost distracting.

"I hope I make it until then," Cleo said.

"You will." Martha patted her big, swollen feet. It was the first time she'd seen any part of Cleo that wasn't pretty and perfect, and she couldn't help but feel just a tiny bit happy about it. "You will."

DR. BAER TOLD MARTHA THAT she was going to have to let Claire make her own decisions about therapy. "Not everyone is ready or willing to give it a try. And if they're not ready, then it won't do them any good."

"I know, but I just know it would help," Martha said. Dr.

Baer held up her hand, as if to say, *That's enough talking for now.* Martha sighed.

"It's not up to you. You made the offer, you told her why you wanted her to come with you, and she doesn't want to do it. Sometimes you just have to let it be."

"Fine," Martha said. She hated when people said to let things be. If everyone in the world just let things be, it would be a disaster.

Claire wasn't home much these days anyway. She took the train to New York for interviews and to look at apartments. Martha knew she'd be on her way soon. They had totally different schedules now, and even when Claire was home, they rarely ran into each other in the bathroom, which made Martha feel sort of sad. But then, the other morning, Claire had come in while she was brushing her teeth and gone over to put toothpaste on her own toothbrush.

They stood there and brushed their teeth, each at their own sink, looking in the mirror. Claire spit and then sang, "Brush, brush, brush, in a rush, rush, rush." She looked at Martha from the corner of her eyes, and Martha started laughing. It was a song they had made up when they were little, and they'd insisted on singing it every night while they brushed their teeth together.

"Spit and rinse, spit and rinse, brush in a rush," Martha sang. The song wasn't exactly genius, but they'd been little kids. The two of them smiled at each other in the mirror.

Claire cleared her throat and looked over at her. "I'm sorry if I've been hard to live with the past few months. I really am. I didn't mean to take it out on you."

"It's okay," Martha said. And it really was. She knew that even when Claire was saying stuff about her, it was really more about Claire.

"Good," Claire said. "It's just not been the best year for me, you know? But I'm sorry if I was being an asshole."

Martha opened her mouth and was about to say something about how maybe therapy would have helped her work through it, but thought better of it and just said, "Thanks."

"I'm glad you got your own place. Really. I think it's great."

"Me too," Martha said.

MARTHA WAS REALLY DIVING INTO being a homeowner. She got paint samples and wallpaper books from the store, and spent hours studying each one. Some people thought wallpaper was old-fashioned, but Martha liked it. She thought maybe she'd do the guest bathroom in a small floral pattern. And who cared if other people didn't like it? It was her house after all.

She was starting to get a little nervous about moving out. It was strange to think she wouldn't see her parents every day. But with the baby coming, it was probably for the best. Even though once she and Claire were gone, Weezy wouldn't have nearly as much help around the house as she did now.

The great part about Martha's situation was that she didn't have to move at any specific time. She now officially owned the condo, but she was taking her time getting it set up. She went over and measured and thought about how she wanted everything to be. It was a pretty big job, actually, since she had to buy all new furniture.

"Just take it piece by piece," Weezy said to her one night. "You don't have to have it all done in a day."

That was true, Martha thought. And that calmed her down a bit.

SHARON COOPER TURNED OUT TO BE a tougher patient than Martha had thought she'd be. She was much tougher than

Mr. Cranston, that was for sure. Martha was there every day from nine to five, and she helped her get into the shower and get dressed. She took her to the grocery store, which seemed like a big trip out, but Sharon insisted. She was using a walker and was not very steady, and it made Martha nervous to watch her shoot down the aisles of the store.

"Why don't you take it easy?" she said one day.

"I'm fine," Sharon said. "I'm not going to get better just sitting around."

"No, but if you make yourself fall again, it's going to take you a much longer time to get better."

Sharon didn't answer her, but she did slow down a little bit. She had a fight to her, which was good. But it also made it seem like she was annoyed all the time, and that got tiresome. Mr. Cranston had been frustrated, sure, but that was different. He was looking back at his life, mourning the fact that he was almost done. Sharon was fighting like hell to get back to the way she'd been. And you had to admire her for that. Still, it didn't make her an easy patient. Not at all.

Sharon's children took turns coming over at night, to bring her dinner and get her settled. They always looked frazzled and tired, and kind of put out to be there, which bothered Martha. If Weezy was in this situation, Martha would be happy to help out. Although maybe Sharon was a harder mother to take care of than Weezy would be. She could see that.

Her oldest daughter, Megan, was a nurse and often came by in her pink scrubs. "You should change," Sharon said to her one night. "There's probably germs all over those things."

Megan rolled her eyes, and Martha knew she was annoyed, but really, it was true. Her scrubs were probably festering with disease. The next day, she told Sharon that she used to be a nurse, that she was planning to go back to it.

"Really? What's stopping you?"

"I'm just figuring things out," Martha said.

"I could never have been a nurse," Sharon told her. "I don't like seeing people sick and lying around in beds. Blood is not for me. Vomit even less. When the kids had the stomach flu, it was their dad that dealt with them."

"It doesn't bother me so much."

"That's like Megan. She never had to turn away from those things."

"That's a sign of a good nurse."

"Well, I can't say I understand your choice, but I have to say it seems better than this gig. You should figure it out soon, you know. Or you'll be stuck wiping the asses of old people like me for the rest of your life."

Martha didn't say anything. She could see why Sharon's children weren't tripping over themselves to come here and help her. Yes, she could certainly see why.

THAT NIGHT, MARTHA HAD TROUBLE falling asleep. She was annoyed at Sharon, at how harsh she'd sounded when she told her she should go back to being a nurse. What did she know? She had no idea what Martha had been through the past year. Good lord. Some people were so quick to judge.

Although, if she had to be honest, she was a little bothered with herself for not doing anything about it the whole time she worked at the Cranstons'. Not one thing. She had so much more free time there! She could have figured out what needed to be done, could have gotten started on it. It was always so quiet and peaceful at the house. Even when Ruby was making a scene or Mr. Cranston was crabby, it was nothing like being with Sharon. Martha hoped her hip healed soon.

She told herself that she deserved a break. Time had gotten away from her, but that happened. And she'd just bought a new condo, for goodness' sake. That was a big change, a life change, and anyone would need to take a breath after that, to take some time and regroup. She was okay. *One step at a time,* she thought. That was also the motto for alcoholics, wasn't it? No, that was one day at a time. Well, that made sense too. She still had to adjust to her new place, decorate it, and get settled. She could only do so much at once or she'd drive herself crazy. *One thing at a time,* she told herself. There was always time for the rest of it later. Yes, there was always time.

CHAPTER 22

Cleo wanted a natural birth. And no one could talk her out of it.

"Take the drugs," her mother had said. "Oh, sweetie, believe me, you'll want the drugs."

Weezy told her to keep an open mind. "Sometimes you don't know what you want until you're there. Sometimes you don't have a choice. You might even need a C-section."

Even Lainie told her that she should be flexible. "It's good to have a plan," she said. "I didn't really know what I wanted, but then when it started with Jack, I was sure that I wanted an epidural."

"What about the rest of them?" Cleo asked.

"Well, with Tucker, he came so fast that we didn't even have a chance. I started labor and then it's like he slipped right out as soon as we got to the hospital. And with Matthew, it took a while and I got the epidural right away. Just be ready to do whatever you want in the moment, okay?"

Cleo agreed, but she knew deep down that she was going to stick to her plan. She'd found a doula to be with her when she went into labor. The plan was to labor at home for as long as possible before going to the hospital.

"Think of the hospital as a drive-thru birthing center," the doula said.

Cleo liked that idea. She didn't want to be in the hospital

for any longer than she had to be. "Hospitals make me nervous with all the germs and infections," she explained. Max pointed out that the doctors were there too, and that was a plus, but he said it was up to Cleo.

It was nice of Lainie to offer advice, but Cleo wished she'd never said, *He slipped right out.* It made it sound like the baby came down a greased slide, made her want to cross her legs, as if that would keep the baby inside her. Sometimes when she lay down at night, she would hear the phrase *He slipped right out*, and she knew she was going to be awake for a while.

It didn't matter what anyone said anyway. She wanted a natural birth and she wanted a doula and that was that. Cleo explained this to Weezy and her mother while they were sitting around having tea after the shower, and talking about her like she wasn't even there.

"I don't know where she got these ideas," Elizabeth said. "Certainly not from me. She wasn't raised in a hippie house." And Elizabeth and Weezy laughed together, like they were friends now, like they were ganging up against her.

"It's better for the baby," Cleo said.

"Next thing you know, she'll tell us about plans to bury the placenta or, worse, eat it!" The two women really got a kick out of that one, and Cleo pressed her lips together to keep from saying anything else. It was like when she told them that she wasn't going to find out the sex of the baby because she wanted to be surprised. Elizabeth had snorted and said, "Because getting pregnant in college wasn't a big enough surprise for you?"

She relayed the whole scene to Max later that night. She was propped up against the headboard, with two pillows behind her back, and she was somehow still uncomfortable.

"They think they know so much more than me," she said.

"Well, they did both have babies." Max took her hand and tried to hold it with both of his, but she pulled it away and got out of the bed. She grabbed her pillow and held it in one arm.

"That's not the point," she said. "Didn't you hear what I said? They were mocking me, like I'm so stupid. Like I don't matter at all." She stood there for a moment, thinking that she'd go sleep somewhere else, that she'd show Max. Then she realized there was nowhere to go. What was she going to do? Sleep on the couch in the TV room and be lying there with her giant stomach when the whole family came downstairs in the morning? She sat back down on the edge of the bed.

"I just want you to be on my side," she said.

"I'm on your side," Max said. He sat up and rubbed her shoulders too hard, so that it almost hurt, but Cleo didn't say anything because she knew he was trying to help. "I'm always on your side."

Cleo never told anyone where she got the idea for the doula. She let them think it was in some article she'd read in a baby magazine, or in one of the how-to books, when really she'd read about it on some celebrity's blog and it had convinced her.

When she couldn't sleep, she searched the Internet for any article or website that would make her feel better about what was going to happen. One night Max woke up and rolled over to find her looking at birthing pictures.

"What the hell?" he said. "That looks like murder."

"I know," she said. The computer glowed in the room and the two of them looked at the pictures in silence.

WHEN HER DUE DATE WAS one month away, Cleo honestly didn't know how she was supposed to make it any longer.

"I'm too big," she said. "I'm huge. I can barely walk and I think the baby is stuck in my ribs."

"You're not huge," Max said. But Cleo knew he was lying. He'd walked into the room the other day while she was changing, and when she turned, so that her bare stomach was facing him, he'd said, "Whoa," before he could stop himself.

"I just don't think there's anywhere else for this baby to go," Cleo said. She sat back so that she was on an angle. "It feels like it's in my chest. It's probably hitting my heart."

"I don't think that can happen," Max said. "Plus, the doctor said all of what you were feeling was normal, remember?"

"Yeah. But maybe he doesn't know what he's talking about. Maybe the baby is ready to come now. Maybe it will be early."

"Maybe," Max said.

But she wasn't early. She kept waiting, each morning, to wake up and be in labor. She knew that the baby was ready to come out, could feel it inside of her, and sometimes could see its elbow or foot pushing at her stomach, like it was trying to get out.

"I know," she'd whisper, when this happened. She'd touch the little bump that the baby's hand made, and rub it. "I know you're ready."

TWO DAYS BEFORE HER DUE DATE, Cleo went into labor. She walked upstairs to find all of the Coffeys sitting around the table having breakfast together, which was weird, because they never did that. "I'm in labor," she said. All of them looked at her and Will took another bite of his toast. "I said, I'm in labor."

"Are you sure?" Max asked. He got up and walked over

to her, touched her stomach like that was going to help him figure out if she was telling the truth.

"Yes, I'm sure. I feel cramping, like a contraction. I've had a few of them."

"Why don't you sit down and have some breakfast?" Weezy said. "It may be false labor or maybe you're just hungry. And if you are in labor, it will probably be a while."

"I'm not hungry," Cleo said. "I'm in labor, I know it." She turned to Max. "I want to go to the hospital."

"I thought you wanted to wait," Max said. He was shifting his weight from one leg to the other, like a little kid, and Cleo reached out and held him still.

"I did, but I don't want to anymore. I just want to get there." Cleo's heart was pounding and her breath was uneven.

Weezy stood up, took Cleo by the arm, and led her to the couch in the TV room. "Okay, let's do this. You sit for a few minutes and we'll start timing the contractions, okay? Max, go get the stopwatch." Max ran out of the room and up the stairs. He looked grateful to have an order.

"Okay," Cleo said. "But not too long. I want to be in the hospital. I don't want to have the baby here." Her eyes filled with tears and Weezy patted her shoulder, which was the last thing she wanted. She didn't want to be here with these people, didn't want to be in this place.

"We're not going to let that happen," Weezy said. "I promise. We'll just sit for a few minutes, let you rest, and we'll get all your stuff together and get ready to go. Okay?"

Max came running back into the room, breathing hard. "I got it," he said. He held up the watch and Weezy stood and pointed to her seat.

"Great. You sit here and start timing. Remember what the book said and what they told you in class, okay?" Weezy was talking to them like they were schoolchildren, like she was instructing them how to tie their shoes. If she'd been able to catch her breath, Cleo might have said something.

"Can I get you anything?" Weezy asked. "Water?"

"Maybe water," Cleo said. "Also, could you call my mom? Could you tell her to come here now? Or to go to the hospital?"

Weezy nodded. "I'll do it right now."

Cleo heard Weezy on the phone with Elizabeth. "She thinks she's in labor," she was saying. Cleo wanted to run over there, grab the phone, and yell, "I *am* in labor," just to set the record straight, but she stayed put.

Weezy called the doula too, informed her that Cleo wanted to head right to the hospital, and then she was quiet and then said, "Mmm-hmm, yes," over and over again. When she hung up the phone, Weezy told Cleo that the doula was coming to the house. "She's very opinionated, isn't she?" Weezy asked.

NO ONE AT THE HOSPITAL seemed to be alarmed that Cleo was in labor. After waiting at the house for a few hours, with everyone watching her and the doula trying to get her to lie in different positions, Cleo announced that she was really ready to go. She expected the hospital staff to at least react, but they seemed almost bored with her. A nurse told her that they'd have the doctor come in to see how far along she was. "He might send you home," she said. Cleo thought it sounded like a threat.

In the room, Cleo went into the bathroom. While she was on the toilet, her water broke. She couldn't wait to tell that nurse who wanted to send her home that it was too bad, because she was staying put. She sat there for a while, feeling too tired to get up. When she finally pulled up her leggings, she felt them get wet almost immediately.

Cleo waited on the examining table, feeling like she was leaking. When the nurse came back in, Cleo said, "My water broke."

"Are you sure?"

"Yes, I'm sure. Why is everyone asking me that? I'm sure that I'm in labor and I'm sure that my water just broke. I am inside this body. I am in my body and I know." Max was typing something on his phone, and he looked up at her with his eyebrows raised.

"When did it happen?" the nurse asked.

"Right after I went to the bathroom."

The nurse sighed. "Are you sure you didn't just wet yourself?"

"Yes, I'm sure."

"It's very common."

"I know I didn't wet myself, okay? I know for sure because I just wet myself yesterday and I know what it feels like." Max raised his eyebrows at her again, but stayed quiet.

"Well, then, get changed into the gown. You were supposed to do that already, and we can't check anything with you still dressed." Cleo snatched the gown from her. She'd show that nurse.

THE PLAN WAS FOR MAX to stay by her head. "There's no way he's going anywhere else," she said. She told Lainie this one night while they were over at her house. Brian was in the other room and he laughed.

"Good luck to you," he said. "That was our plan too. But once it starts, it's like a war zone in there. You just go where you're needed, and you can't help but look."

Lainie rolled her eyes at Cleo as if to say Brian was ridiculous, but now Cleo was more determined than ever to keep to the plan.

"By my head," she kept saying. "Stay right here. Up here."

"Got it," Max kept saying.

After being in labor for ten hours, Cleo was sure she was going to go crazy. "I want an epidural," she said. "I want it now."

The nurse nodded. "We'll get the doctor and we'll talk about it."

"I know my rights," Cleo told her. "You can't deny me what I want. I want the epidural."

The doula quietly reminded Cleo of her birth plan, suggested that maybe she was just having a low moment and should try to get through it. "We can do some breathing and meditation," she said.

"Get out," Cleo told her. "Get out of this room."

"I know you're uncomfortable," the doula said. "Let's try to switch positions."

"I said get out of the room."

The doula looked at Max and nodded. "I'll give you two a few minutes, but I'll be right out in the hall."

Max stood next to her and held her hand, and sometimes smoothed her hair back from her face and put a wet washcloth on her forehead. She knew that he was trying to be helpful, but it felt like water torture to her for some reason. The washcloth dripped down the side of her face and neck, pooling at her shoulder. Finally, she picked it up and whipped it across the room.

"Okay, Dad," the nurse said. "I think we can take it easy on the cool compresses."

Max gave Cleo a look like she'd hurt his feelings, and if

she'd had any room left in her body to feel anything, she might have felt bad. He was so easily hurt.

Weezy had been surprised that Cleo didn't want her mother in the room. Cleo didn't know how to explain that they weren't that kind of family. She and her mom didn't talk about bodily functions the way that the Coffeys did, like Will's constipation or heartburn was just another normal breakfast topic. They never walked out of a bathroom and warned people not to go in there for a while, like she'd seen Weezy do, or announce that their cramps were just unbearable this month, as Martha had done last week.

No, she and her mother didn't talk about those things. When Cleo had gotten her period, she'd never even mentioned it, just put her underwear in the laundry and the next day there was a pack of pads and another of tampons. "Any questions?" her mom had asked. And Cleo hadn't had one.

So she didn't want her mom in here while her water was breaking. She didn't want her here while the doctor explained that it was that color because the baby had just pooped inside of her. And she didn't want her mom to be here if she pooped on the table, or bled, or did all of the stuff that you do when you have a baby.

And she hoped to God that Weezy knew that she'd never consider having her in the room. That would be absurd. She wasn't even thrilled about having Max in the room, but she had to have someone and he was the dad so he was supposed to be there. He would probably never want to have sex with her again, she imagined. And who could blame him? This was why you were supposed to wait until you'd been together longer before you had a baby, because of all the gross and embarrassing stuff that happened along with it. They should advertise that when they tried to stop teen pregnancies.

The last thing that Lainie had said to her was this: "You're going to be in the room, and you're going to think, 'I can't do this, I take it back, what was I thinking, I changed my mind.' And here's the best part: You can't change your mind. So there's no use thinking about it. You'll just have to do it. If there was any turning back, there'd be no babies in the world. So just remember, the decision is done and you'll just have to get through it."

AFTER SHE GOT THE EPIDURAL, Cleo said to Max, "I know why people are drug addicts."

"Okay," he said. He tried to smile, but he looked concerned.

Her labor went on and Cleo even managed to rest a little, to close her eyes, and even though she didn't think she really slept, it made her feel better.

Afterward, it was hard to remember the pain. It wasn't that she didn't remember that it was awful—she knew that much. But if she tried to talk about it, tried to imagine it again, she couldn't. It was like there were no words for it. Even saying that it was the most awful thing ever didn't do it justice.

Someone took pictures, but she didn't know who. When she looked at them later, she didn't remember the actual moments that were captured, didn't remember smiling and posing for anyone.

Elizabeth and Weezy were the first ones in the room, telling her she did a great job and marveling over the baby. They asked Cleo the name, but she let Max answer.

"Nina Grace," he said.

"It's perfect," Elizabeth said, and Weezy agreed.

Will came in later, looking uncomfortable at being so

close to Cleo in her ragged state. But he did hold Nina in the corner, smiling at her as she slept. Claire and Martha came in together, hugged her, and then took turns passing the baby back and forth.

"She's perfect," Claire said. "She's so beautiful."

"She really is," Martha said. "Are you two going to send her to the nursery for the night? You should, just so you can get some rest."

After everyone had gone, she and Max stared at the little red face. Cleo had told him that he could go home, but he'd insisted on staying and sleeping on the window seat that turned into a bed. She was grateful that he was there—even though they did send the baby to the nursery like Martha suggested—so that when she woke up in the middle of the night, there was someone else with her.

"I CAN'T BELIEVE THEY'RE LETTING US just leave with her," Cleo said to Max. "Don't you feel like someone's going to come and stop us?"

"Yeah, kind of." Max had insisted to his family that they were going to take Nina home themselves.

"Why don't you just let us come to help?" Weezy asked. "We can even take a different car, if you want."

But Max wouldn't budge. And so, it was just the three of them in the car, Cleo riding in the backseat next to Nina, because she was just so small and they couldn't really see her, even with the mirror.

When they pulled in the driveway, there was a wooden stork in the ground and pink balloons tied to the front door. They walked in and found everyone waiting in the front hall, and they all gathered around the baby as if they'd never seen her before. Ruby came over to see them, and Max knelt down on the ground and held the little bundle out to her. She sniffed Nina's legs and then poked her snout on her arm.

Cleo almost told him not to let Ruby lick the baby, but she thought better of it and stayed silent. Ruby looked up at her, like she understood, like she was saying, "I know this baby, I poked her with my nose when she was still in your stomach."

"Here she is," Max said to Ruby. "Here's your new niece." Then he looked up at Cleo. "Right? Nina would be Ruby's niece, because Ruby's like my sister?"

"Yeah, that sounds right," she said. Cleo was crying now, thinking that Ruby understood everything about Nina, which was absurd. She needed to sit down and she needed that weird donut thing that Weezy had gotten for her. She'd been mortified when she received it, but now she thought it might have been the nicest present anyone had ever given her.

THE FIRST NIGHT HOME WITH THE BABY, they were both too scared to sleep, not that Nina gave them much of a chance. She screamed and cried and nothing they tried seemed to work.

"She was so quiet in the hospital," Cleo said. They were standing above the bassinet, looking down at Nina's red face.

"Maybe she was in shock from being born," Max said. "But she's adjusted now." They were grateful when the morning came, like they had survived something. It had been only one night.

The days blended together, all of them sleepless and filled with feedings and diaper changes. Their time was marked by the cycle of Nina's sleeping and waking. Cleo gave up trying to breast-feed almost immediately. "She doesn't like it," she explained to Max. "She seems to know what she wants and she doesn't want this."

The doula was supposed to stop by to check on them, to help with breast-feeding if needed, but Cleo refused to call her back. She couldn't face the woman after she'd yelled at her and thrown her out of the room. She was fine with giving Nina formula. After all, that meant that Max could feed her too, which meant she could stay in bed sometimes.

Max stayed home with them for a week, and the first morning he went back to work, Cleo watched him get dressed and was filled with terror.

"I'll be back so soon," he said. "And my mom will be here all day. It will be okay."

With Max gone, the days seemed longer and more tedious. Weezy was there almost all the time, making comments or offering to help. Whenever Weezy suggested anything, Cleo's first instinct was to do the opposite. She had to stop herself from yelling, "You're not my mom" several times a day. It was just the hormones, she told herself.

Weezy often mentioned how Nina was such a good baby, and Cleo got the feeling that she was lying to her. If Nina was a good baby, what were the bad ones like? How much fussier and needier could something be?

Sometimes, she and Nina would wake up from a nap and outside the door would be a laundry basket, filled with clean, folded clothes for Cleo—onesies, pajamas, baby socks, and burp cloths. Things like this usually happened just as Cleo was thinking particularly horrible thoughts about what a beast Weezy was. She'd grab the laundry basket, more thankful than she could ever express, and hope that she'd be a better person soon.

WHEN NINA CRIED FOR A LONG TIME, Ruby would lift her head and look at Cleo with sad eyes, like, *Really? This is really what our life is now?* Other times, she would come over and lick Cleo's hand softly, as if to say, *I know you didn't mean to bring this one home. It's okay. It was clearly an accident.*

One night, Cleo was up feeding Nina, and she noticed Ruby lying in the corner of the room. Cleo watched her for a while, and then became convinced that Ruby wasn't moving, wasn't breathing. She crept over to her, holding the baby in her arms, trying to figure out how she was going to tell the family that the dog had died. She wondered if Ruby had just given up, if she was so unhappy with her house being so noisy that she simply willed herself to stop living. Cleo didn't think she could handle being responsible for the death of the Coffeys' dog. But just as she bent down, she saw Ruby's pink tongue dart in and out of her mouth, licking her nose, and Cleo sighed with relief.

CLEO HAD NEVER KNOWN TIRED like this before. It was constant and violent, like someone had beaten her up when she wasn't paying attention. She was still sore, everywhere, and sometimes the edges of her vision were blurry, like she was going blind. She was heavy-limbed and clumsy. She found herself walking into doorframes, tripping over her feet, and knocking glasses over. She had no sense of space. Once, she sat on the toilet and started going to the bathroom before realizing that she hadn't pulled her underwear down.

Cleo ached for her mom in a way she never had before. Elizabeth felt so far away when she was living in the Coffeys' basement, even though they talked every day, something they'd never done before. Elizabeth listened to her talk about Nina's spit-up and diapers. She drove to see them often, sometimes twice a week.

Of course, no matter how much Cleo ached for her, as

soon as they got together, there was some sort of squabble. Often Cleo ended up snapping at her mom, then felt like crying when she left, like a guilt-filled toddler who had done something wrong.

Cleo prayed that this would be over soon, this feeling of wanting things and then not wanting them as soon as she got them. It was exhausting not to know your own heart.

CLEO AND MAX WERE AFRAID that Nina was going to die, always; or that they'd hurt her or break her in some way. Clipping her nails almost always resulted in drawing blood, and Cleo often wondered why anyone let them take this baby home. Surely they were not equipped.

Some days she and Max fought over nothing, over everything. They were so tired that it didn't take much to get them going. Once she yelled at him for putting Nina in a day outfit in the middle of the night.

"It was the closest thing I could find, and who cares? They all look the same anyway? Her pajamas were all wet."

"The yellow pajamas were there for her," Cleo said. She held them up as proof.

"You and your yellow pajamas," Max said. Neither of them was making any sense, but the anger was real.

Cleo often imagined packing herself and Nina up, heading to New York, never talking to Max again. There was power in this image, scary and absolute. Whenever she thought about it, she felt strong, then immediately sick and afraid.

They apologized all the time, and sometimes Cleo was grateful that they were in such a tiny space. There was nowhere else for them to go, so eventually one of them had to say something. After they fought, Cleo often felt a wave of panic rise up. But usually, she was too tired to let it overtake her, and she just let the fight go. She figured it was the only upside of exhaustion.

THEY PROBABLY WEREN'T SUPPOSED TO let Nina sleep in the bed with them, but almost every morning she got up to eat around four thirty, and they'd feed her and change her, and then take her back into the bed. They'd put her right in the middle, and the three of them would doze for a couple of hours before Max had to get up for work.

Right after she ate, Nina acted like she was drunk, eyelids fluttering, happily drooling. Max would always say, "You hit that bottle hard, didn't you?" and lean down to rub his nose against her hair.

Those were Cleo's favorite moments, when they were all in bed together, before the day started. She and Max would both open their eyes every so often to check on Nina, and sometimes they opened them at the same time, looked at each other across Nina's full round tummy, and smiled.

When that happened, Cleo let herself feel happy, let herself believe that there really was a chance—no matter how small—that things just might turn out okay for all of them.

Lying in between them in bed, Nina would often wake up with a start, jerking her arms and legs, looking around like she was surprised to find Max and Cleo there. Then she'd settle down, ready to fall back asleep almost immediately. And with her little chin shaking, her eyes would close and she'd sigh like she was saying, *Okay then, everyone's here. Let's get some rest.*

CHAPTER 23

When the baby cried in the middle of the night, Weezy's first instinct was to get up and go downstairs to help. She'd wake up groggy and think, "Oh no, the baby's up again," and it would take a minute for her mind to catch up, to remind her that it wasn't her baby, that there were two parents down there to take care of it. So she'd stay right where she was in her own bed, listening as they paced the floor with Nina, sometimes singing or talking quietly, and sometimes pleading for her to stop crying.

Well, Weezy stayed in bed most of the time. Sometimes, if Nina was crying for an especially long time, she'd go down and offer her help. Even if it was only to hold the baby for a minute or two, while Cleo or Max went to the bathroom or drank a glass of water, or just got themselves together for a moment. She remembered how it was, the way it could drive you crazy sometimes, the endless crying for what seemed like no reason.

Once, when Martha was a baby, she'd been screaming all night and Weezy, who was already pregnant again at the time, was pacing back and forth and finally held the baby up, looked in her face, and said loudly, "What? What do you want?" Martha had been so surprised, had started the way babies do at loud noises, and then after a few seconds of silence began screaming again. Weezy had felt like the worst mother in the world, had brought her into the bedroom and woken Will up, told him that he had to take her. Then she'd gotten back into bed and cried herself, feeling like the cruddiest person ever.

So yes, she remembered the exhaustion and she was there to help if they needed it.

It was a strange thing to have a baby in the house again. As much as Cleo and Max tried to pick up after Nina (which truthfully wasn't that much), there was stuff everywhere. Cloth diapers for burping, almost-empty bottles sitting on the coffee table, clean bottles drying in the kitchen, pacifiers on the floor, blankets and baby socks and onesies with spit-up strewn all over the couch and the floor.

Had it been like this with her own children? Weezy didn't remember it that way, but it must have been. Maybe you just got used to it, got used to the milk and dirty-diaper smells that seem to be on everything. But now, in her house that used to be orderly, every time she stepped on a pacifier, she got a little annoyed.

She worried about Cleo and Max. The two of them often sat on the couch in their pajamas, looking exhausted and sort of dirty, wordlessly passing the baby back and forth, staring straight ahead at the TV. Sometimes Weezy would take Nina, suggest a shower or a change of clothes, and they'd get up like zombies and go do what she said. Was this normal? Maybe. She couldn't remember. She tried not to judge. After all, she hadn't had an audience when her children were babies. And she did remember one day when Will came home from work and stepped on an open dirty diaper that was on the floor. So yes, she would try not to judge.

Cleo had tried to breast-feed, but the poor thing never really got the hang of it. Weezy tried to give her tips, told her to stick it out. Weezy had never had any trouble, of course, but she knew some women that had. But after a few weeks, Cleo gave up. Weezy was disappointed, but there wasn't too much more she could say. Max, in fact, got a little snippy with her one morning when she was just saying that she felt bad for them about it. So she kept her mouth shut after that.

And she did have to admit, that once Nina was only on bottles, things ran a little more smoothly. For one thing, Cleo wasn't crying most of the day because it wasn't working. Also, she got more sleep, was able to go for walks with the baby, seemed to get it together a little bit more. Nina started sleeping like a champ, since she was always full now. And the other good part was that once Cleo stopped nursing, her breasts went back to their normal size. Right after she came back from the hospital, Cleo had looked a little bit like a porn star with her huge chest, and it didn't help that she seemed not to notice, that she wore little tank tops without bras all around the house. So yes, she looked a little more decent now.

Of course, some nights Weezy would look down at Nina, snoozing away with her belly full, and hope that she wouldn't end up an obese child because of the formula. You never knew. You really never knew.

There were so many days when the only thing any of them ever talked about was Nina. Had she eaten? Was she fussy? How much had she spit up? Did she smile? It consumed their days and nights, and sometimes Weezy would be in bed before she realized that not only had she not called her other children, she had barely thought about them.

It was almost hard to notice that the girls were gone, since tiny little Nina took up so much of the space. But both of her girls were out on their own, and it was strange to remember that they had been there not too long ago.

She decided to make them both blankets, as housewarming presents. (She had shown the patterns to Cleo, who barely looked up at them. She hadn't had the time or energy to get back to her knitting.) Weezy's first instinct was to start with Martha's blanket, since Martha would surely see the one she was working on for Claire and wonder where hers was. But Weezy thought that maybe she would do it differently for once, and start Claire's first so that she could take it with her when she went to New York. She would try not to worry about Martha's reaction, try to treat her like an adult, which she was. It didn't mean anything to make Claire's blanket first. And also, she thought, as she cast on the stitches, she could just hide it whenever Martha came over.

Martha was still getting settled in her new place, and she stayed with Weezy and Will at least one night a week, but usually more like two or three nights. Weezy tried not to worry about this. After all, it just took Martha longer to adjust to new things. And it was a big step. She came over with paint samples or catalogs so that she could show Weezy things she thought she might want to buy for the new place. She was even thinking about renting out the second bedroom, and was working on an ad. Weezy hoped that maybe she'd find a nice roommate that would become a friend, that she'd find a group of people that could be hers.

When Martha held Nina, Weezy felt her heart tear a little bit. She worried that it would never happen for Martha. She was already thirty-one, with no prospect of any sort of relationship in sight. And while she knew Maureen would make fun of her for wanting her babies to have babies, she couldn't help it. She wanted Martha to experience that, and at this point she had to admit to herself that it didn't seem probable. Martha had never had a boyfriend or, to be truthful, even a best friend. It was hard to imagine that she would just go through life like that, but with each year that passed it became more likely. Still, Weezy could hope. So she did. She hoped.

She remembered the way that no matter what, Maureen always cheered for the sports team that was supposed to lose. "You have to go for the underdog," she always said. And Weezy supposed that was true.

Claire was doing well. She and Will both agreed that she seemed happier than she had in a long time. And Weezy tried not to let it hurt her feelings that part of that had to be due to being away from them. She tried to remind herself that it was the natural thing to be on your own. But sometimes she thought back to the time when Claire was at home, and wished they could all do it over again, do it differently.

"What does it matter as long as she's happy?" Will asked one day as she was thinking out loud. And she said that he was probably right.

ONE NIGHT SHE TIPTOED DOWN the stairs to find Cleo leaning back on the couch, watching an old movie. It was a little after three in the morning, and Nina was snuffling in her arms, sort of sleeping, but she was fighting it. Any time she started to drift off, she'd wave her arms, like she was waking herself up.

"How's she doing?" Weezy asked.

"She's okay." Cleo looked down at her face. "She won't go to sleep. She's refusing. She is so stubborn."

"Claire was the same way as a baby."

"Really?"

"Oh yes. She seemed to know what I wanted her to do and then she did the opposite."

Cleo laughed. "What about Max?"

"Max? Oh, he was so easy. He was the kind of baby that makes you want a few more. He was so sweet, no matter what. I could put him in his seat for the whole day, and he just sat, content."

"I can imagine that," Cleo said.

"Do you want me to take her?" Weezy was tired, but she loved holding Nina while she was sleeping.

"I'm okay," Cleo said. Weezy sat down anyway.

"I love this movie," she said. It was the original *Parent Trap*. "Martha and Claire loved it when they were little. They used to beg to watch it almost every day."

"Really? I've never seen it."

"What? Oh, it's a riot. Just a riot."

The two of them stayed up to watch the whole movie, well after Nina was asleep. It was the moments like these with Cleo that made Weezy feel especially protective of her. When she was just in pajamas with no makeup on, holding Nina, and looking very young herself, Weezy wanted to take her in her arms and tell her it would be okay.

Cleo and her mother had been on better terms since Nina was born. Elizabeth came down a few times, and Cleo had been up there with the baby to spend a week or so, which made Weezy feel empty and almost panicked, like she was just going to take Nina away and never come back. Weezy imagined never seeing Nina again, pictured going to court to try to get visiting rights. But then they returned.

Cleo and Elizabeth were maybe on better terms, but they didn't have an easy relationship. There was one time when Elizabeth was visiting and made a remark about all the jobs that Cleo had missed out on this year. "It will be a hard thing to explain this empty year on your résumé," she said to Cleo, who left the room in tears. Weezy thought she sounded a little harsh, but then again, who was she to say? Mothers and daughters had their own language.

Cleo and Max fought fairly often, which was to be expected. They were in a small space in someone else's house, with a new baby and no sleep. But still. Whenever Weezy heard them arguing, she wanted to hold her breath. What if they split up? What if Cleo took Nina and never let them see her? Sometimes she would interrupt to take the baby, just to try to help so that the two of them could calm down and talk in peace; this was sometimes welcome, and sometimes Cleo and Max looked at her like she was out of her ever-loving mind.

It was a hard thing, to try to stay out of it. All she wanted to do was to get in the middle of their fights, sit them down, mediate, point out who was in the wrong. But she didn't. She stayed above it, and afterward always felt very saintly.

She kept suggesting that they start thinking about getting Nina baptized, that they should do it soon. But every time she talked about it, they just looked at her like she had suggested they take Nina to get a tattoo on her back. She complained about this to Maureen, who listened and then said, "Well, in the end it's their decision, isn't it?" Weezy hadn't really seen it that way, and wasn't sure she really agreed. But she dropped the subject for the time being. She'd bring it up again later, when they were a little more settled.

WILL WAS UP IN HIS OFFICE more than ever. He was in love with that little bundle of a baby, but he preferred to hold her while she was sleeping, or to feed her every once in a while. Anything else, and he was ready to hand her off. He complained more about the crying in the middle of the night.

Even if they weren't the ones getting up with her, it woke them and it was hard to get back to sleep at their age. Many mornings, Will was grumpy, but what could you do? He knew what they had signed on for.

After the wedding, Weezy kept thinking she should tell Will about the wedding planning, but she couldn't quite find the words. She took all of her wedding stuff, her binders and folders, and went to throw it out. Then she thought better of it and put it all in a large Tupperware storage container in the back of her closet. It was a lot of information and it seemed a waste to throw it out. Who knew? She might need it one day.

One afternoon, Weezy decided she needed to come clean. They were both in the kitchen and Will was eating toast when she said, "Do you remember how Claire accused me of lying to the florist?" Will nodded. "Well, it was a little bit true. I just got so enamored with the wedding planning that after Claire called it off, I just kept doing research. It was silly, I know."

It sounded much better when she called it research. Why hadn't she thought of that before? She looked at Will to see how he'd react, and her stomach fell. He was looking for something to say, but his face told her that he'd already known.

"Well," he finally said, "I can see how that could happen."

She'd nodded and begun loading the dishwasher. In the other room, Nina began to cry and Weezy had never been so happy for that little baby's ability to distract them from everything else.

MAUREEN WAS OFFICIALLY RETIRED, which meant that she stopped by more often than ever. She loved seeing Nina, and spent many afternoons just holding her, walking around the house with her. Also, she used this time to pitch business ideas to Weezy. Maureen suggested starting a nanny company, buying a gym franchise, and once—in one of her strangest moments—starting a purse design company.

Weezy just listened to her talk, nodded when she'd say, "Okay, I know you're going to think this one is crazy." She was like a wind-up toy, and Weezy figured she just needed to wear herself out.

Then one day Maureen brought over a catalog with continuing education classes. "I'm signing up for something," she said. "And you're doing it with me."

A cooking class sounded a lot more pleasant than watching Maureen try to design purses, and so Weezy sat down and looked at the catalog with her. Paging through, she found a class on flower arrangement. "What about this one?" she said. "I bet it would be fun. I loved the florist we worked with for the wedding. He was amazing. If I could do what he could do . . ."

"We should open a flower shop," Maureen said.

"I don't think we're really qualified," Weezy said. "But I will take the class with you."

"Okay, great. Let's do it. And you never know. Maybe we'll be great at it. Maybe we'll start working for a florist, and then we'll decide that we should open our own shop." Maureen was off again, and Weezy let her go.

"I doubt that working for a florist would pay very much," Weezy pointed out. "And they would probably never even hire someone our age. Plus, who knows what this course will be like? We don't even know if it will be worth it."

"No one ever does," Maureen said.

FOR THE FIRST TIME IN A LONG TIME, Weezy began to wish for her house to be just hers and Will's again. No babies crying, no worrying about making dinner for more than just the two of them. And while it probably wouldn't happen for a while (they weren't going to throw Max and Cleo out on their ears!), it seemed like it was actually a possibility, that in a year or two they might be able to watch TV alone, just the two of them.

As much as she knew she'd miss the kids when they were gone, she also knew that she'd be happy to reclaim her house, to maybe just have a quiet dinner with Will one night on the back patio, with wine, no interruptions, no one handing the baby around to give everyone a chance to scarf down their food. Yes, she was looking forward to that.

WEEZY WAS CHANGING NINA'S DIAPER ONE DAY, and the little buster was crying so hard her face was bright red. Nothing Weezy said or did seemed to do anything to begin to quiet her. "Okay, sweetie pie," she said. "Let's just get through this. We're in it together. A dry diaper will make you feel better, I promise."

Nina continued to scream and then Max came back to the house. "Hey," he called out. "Who's that crying?"

Nina stopped and her eyes opened, looking around to find the voice that she recognized from all that time she was in the womb. Weezy stopped and stared at her, feeling tears start to form in her eyes. She blinked them back before Max came into the room, so he wouldn't accuse her of being just a sentimental old lady. She finished fastening the diaper and picked up Nina in time to hand her to Max, and he took her easily, put his face against hers.

"There you go," he said. "There you go."

Anytime Weezy felt she was losing her patience with Cleo and Max, anytime she wanted to scream at them for being so irresponsible, for letting themselves get to this place, she would take a breath and observe them with Nina—the way they watched her, the way they rushed to her bassinet to make sure she was still alive. More than once, she watched Cleo place a hand on the baby's back while she slept, waiting to feel the little body rising and falling so she could make sure she was still breathing.

She wanted to tell them that it would never go away, that feeling, that worry that your child was going to be okay, but she was pretty sure that they were figuring that out already. They'd have to watch Nina start walking, watch her walk up the stairs, sure that she was going to tumble down. They'd have to take her to school, pray that she made friends, hope that no other little kids were mean to her. They'd watch her get in fights, get left out, get cut from a sports team, not get into the college that she wanted. They had so much heartbreak ahead of them.

And so, after she had watched them for a minute or two, she found that she wasn't angry anymore. Not much, anyway. At least, she didn't feel like yelling at them. What else could she have said anyway? What could she have said to make them feel worse, to make this bigger? They had Nina to take care of and worry about for the rest of their lives.

They were in it now.

CHAPTER 24

Claire slept on Katherine's couch for a few weeks, while she started her new job and looked for an apartment. It wasn't the most ideal situation, but Katherine offered and Claire didn't want to be rushed into finding a place she didn't love. Plus, Katherine had a new boyfriend and as long as she had someone at the apartment to stay with Mitzy the dog, she could stay over at his place as often as she liked.

Most mornings, Claire woke up with Mitzy breathing on her, asking to be taken outside. She wasn't the best-trained dog by a long shot, and she often just squatted in the apartment, relieved herself right where she was, looking right at Katherine or Claire, like she was daring them to punish her. The whole place smelled a little bit like urine, no matter how quickly Katherine cleaned up after her.

Also, Katherine had become very eco-conscious, and while Claire admired this, it could be a little hard to live with. She'd stopped one day to buy paper towels and cleaning supplies, and had spent the afternoon dusting and cleaning, but when Katherine came home to find her Windexing the front windows, she'd screamed like she was watching the execution of a near-extinct animal. "What are you doing?" she'd said. "I have rags for that. And this"—she held up the blue solution with two fingers—"is basically poison."

Katherine also kept a compost bowl in the kitchen, which smelled and attracted flies. "She's just a little *too* green," Claire told Lainie over the phone. Claire was grateful for the place to stay, but she knew she couldn't stay too long.

Claire interviewed for almost a month before she contacted her old boss, Amy. She had just started to panic and think that she was never going to find another job, that she shouldn't have quit any job in this economy, and she felt desperate. Amy was happy to hear from her, probably because she was just happy to hear that Claire was still alive and functioning and hadn't had a complete breakdown. "I'll put the word out," Amy said. And true to her promise, Claire had three calls in a week, one from a nonprofit called Gallery 87 that was looking for a project manager to replace someone immediately. "We're in a bit of a bind," they kept telling Claire during the interview. She figured this worked in her favor.

The office that they gave Claire was a mess. All the drawers were still full, and there was a long sweater hanging on the back of the door, like the woman that had been there before had just not bothered to come back one day. The office assistant, Abigail, apologized when she showed Claire the office. "She moved to California with her new boyfriend," Abigail said. "They hadn't even been dating that long, like two months, and one day she just came in and said she was leaving." Abigail shook her head. "We think she was dying to get out of New York and just looking for an excuse."

Claire had no idea what she was doing at the job, but no one seemed to care. They were all just happy to have a body there again. The purpose of Gallery 87 was to pay high school kids to beautify the city—they painted murals on the sides of graffiti-covered buildings and in the subways, and spruced up parks, and playgrounds. Claire was thrown into the middle of projects that had been in the works for months, accompanied teenagers to parks and watched them paint benches with designs they'd created. They would descend on the park in the morning, and at the end of the day the benches were bright spots of color, some painted with checkerboards and swirls, one with tiny animals marching all over it. Claire was surprised at how much better the park looked when they left, how much it had changed. She wondered if she could get the kids to come paint her new apartment when she moved.

Every night when Claire left work she was so tired she was almost dizzy. Her head swam with information, and she felt like she'd never catch up. She slept better than she had in a year.

Whenever she had a few free moments, Claire would go through the drawers and files in her office. She threw out old receipts and packs of gum, and kept paper clips and pencils. In a cardboard box, she put all of the woman's personal stuff—her sweater, an old pair of heels, a stuffed duck, and pictures that were on the bulletin board. She was going to throw it all out, but it seemed nicer to put it all in a box together first.

In one of the drawers, Claire found a shopping list that read: *Tulips, Carrots, Q-tips,* and *Celery*. She taped the list up on the wall behind her computer. It made her smile. She liked reading it out loud, reciting it under her breath like a prayer or a poem, a crazy little list of the things someone needed.

A BROKER SHOWED HER TWO APARTMENTS in Manhattan before Claire decided she was going to live in Brooklyn. Most of her friends were there now anyway, and she didn't want to go back to the Upper West Side. She'd walked by her old building one day, expecting to feel drawn to it, but instead she found herself speeding up to get past it quickly. She waved at the doorman when she passed, but didn't think he remembered her. He waved back like she could be anyone.

Katherine tried to convince Claire to live in Windsor Terrace near her, but Claire was set on Brooklyn Heights. She'd fallen in love with everything about the neighborhood. Even the street names were adorable—Poplar, Orange, Cranberry, Pineapple, and Vine. She didn't care how small her place was, she just wanted to be there. It was too perfect for words.

"I think you should try to widen your search," Katherine told her. Sometimes she looked at Claire like she'd lost her mind, like she'd forgotten how hard it could be to find a decent apartment in New York and would end up living on Katherine's couch forever. But Claire remained hopeful.

THE DAY THAT CLAIRE MOVED OUT OF THE HOUSE, Max followed her around with Nina, making Nina's arm wave. "Say good-bye to your aunt," he said. "Tell her how much you're going to miss her." She remembered how, when she left for college, Max had cried in her dorm room. He was ten at the time, and tried to pretend it wasn't happening. He seemed sort of the same now, holding Nina up and talking behind her, saying, "Aunt Claire, how can you leave me? You're going to miss me so much."

And she did miss them, of course. As soon as she left, she missed them all, more than she had before she moved back. It was like she felt their absence more now. That was the worst part about leaving home—no matter what, it always felt a little sad. But not for one second did this mean that she doubted her decision. She was leaving and that was that.

When Claire told Lainie she was moving, she nodded like she'd been waiting for the news. "I hoped maybe you'd stay. That you'd like it here so much you wouldn't want to go back."

"Lainie," Claire said, "I can't stay here."

"I know, I know. I knew you'd go. I just thought maybe you'd change your mind."

"I'll come visit, I promise. Probably more than I ever did before."

"Good," Lainie said. "Because once I have this baby, I'll probably never be able to leave the house again. I'll be under house arrest, so you'll have to come to me."

"I will," Claire said. "I promise."

And she had been home three times already since she moved out. She loved seeing Nina, holding that sweet little baby. And then Lainie had her fourth baby, a boy that they named Tommy. Lainie and Cleo got the babies together pretty often, would put them next to each other on blankets and let them play side by side. They referred to Nina as Tommy's girlfriend and talked often about their future wedding. Claire knew they were kidding, but she swore those little babies smiled at each other.

Every time Claire came home, Weezy made a big deal of it. They all had dinner, and Martha came home to be there too, like it was a special occasion, like they all hadn't eaten together every single night just a few months ago.

WHEN THE BROKER TOLD CLAIRE that there was a studio on Pineapple Street that was for rent, she almost screamed. She tried to stay calm, but she knew that barring a major disaster (a serious mice infestation, for example), she was going to take it. Pineapple Street had been her favorite one from the start, the place where she hoped to find an apartment. She started to think that she was getting very lucky.

The apartment was one of the smallest that Claire had ever seen. But it was clean and solid and the girl that was moving out told her that she loved it there. (And she seemed honest, even if she did have Care Bear sheets on her bed.) There was a little half wall that hid the bed from the rest of the apartment, and enough room to put a tiny couch and TV comfortably. Claire didn't have any furniture anyway, since she'd sold it all, and she promised herself that she was going to get only the basics—a bed, a couch, and maybe a little table.

Katherine had come to see it with her, had looked around and then at Claire. "You could find a much bigger place by me," she said. But Claire took it and Katherine just shrugged. "It's your overpriced apartment," she said.

The night Claire moved in, she had a few friends over and they sat on the floor and drank wine out of plastic cups. They ordered Thai food and ate it out of the containers, passing around spring rolls and noodles. After dinner, they left to go to a bar, since they were all feeling a little cramped by then. Claire was almost hyper that night, was excited at every suggestion someone made, could barely keep from skipping to the bar.

"You look like you just moved to New York for the first time," Katherine told her. "You're acting like a tourist or something."

Claire knew it was true. She was so happy to be back in New York that sometimes she'd be walking down the street and she'd get a rise in her chest and a giddiness that bubbled out of her throat. It made her smile at strangers. She couldn't help it. These strange surges of happiness seemed to come out of nowhere. Even if she'd wanted to stop herself from bouncing up and down and smiling, she didn't think she'd have been able to.

It was strange. Claire was back in New York, working for a nonprofit, just like she had been a year ago. It was almost like she was right back where she'd started, but it didn't feel that way at all.

There were things that Claire didn't even know she'd missed until she moved back. At home, everything was done for her—grocery shopping, laundry, dusting, cleaning the bathroom. Now, she was responsible for all of it again. The first time she went to the grocery store after moving into the apartment, she had the best time. She bought a random assortment of things—sugar, cereal, Diet Coke, yogurt, cheese, crackers. There was nothing in all of it that could make a meal, but it didn't matter. She was only a little embarrassed at how free she felt, how grateful she was to throw whatever she wanted into her cart.

Weezy came to visit, carrying a potted plant and a new afghan that she'd made. "Oh," she said when she stepped into the apartment.

"I know, it's small," Claire said. "But I love it."

"It's adorable," Weezy said. She set the plant on the kitchen counter and arranged the afghan on the back of the new couch.

"It looks perfect," Claire said.

Claire and Weezy walked around the neighborhood, and then on the Promenade. Weezy kept looking over her shoulder, like she thought someone was following them. She'd never been a fan of any of the places that Claire lived in New York, and this one was no different. Claire tried to ignore it.

They talked mostly about Nina and Max and Cleo, but also about Martha's new condo. They'd never really addressed the fighting that took place during Claire's year at home, the accusations that she'd made. Weezy had tried to bring it up before she'd moved out, saying, "You have such a support system that we don't have to worry about you as much," and she had looked like she was going to cry and so Claire just said, "It's fine, Mom, it's fine." Claire had apologized for her behavior, and then really wanted to drop it. There was no use in talking about it, in making everyone uncomfortable. It was just the way it was.

Now Weezy was talking about the shore again, telling Claire that they'd pay for her train ticket, that the whole family was going to be there, that Martha really missed her and would love it if she came.

"Of course I'll come," Claire said. "I wouldn't miss it."

"Oh good," Weezy said.

It was so much easier to be gracious with distance.

THE END OF AUGUST WAS COOLER than normal, and everyone seemed to shift with the weather. Usually when they were at the shore, it felt like they were waiting for summer to end, dreading the return to fall. This year, it felt like summer was already over. There wasn't the same sense of longing in any of them.

They didn't spend much time at the beach. It was hard to take Nina down there and everyone seemed just as happy sitting out on the deck in the morning and going for walks in the afternoon. Their days revolved around Nina, and they could spend hours watching her, talking about how much she ate or what she was wearing or how funny and cute she was. Nina was a topic they all agreed on, and Claire couldn't remember what they'd talked about before her.

One afternoon, they had Nina set up in the middle of the

room, lying on her back on a blanket, a mobile set up above her. She was looking intently at a stuffed corn on the cob, frowning at it, like she didn't like the way it was smiling at her. She sized it up for a while, then wound up her arm and swatted it. She looked pleased when it went flying, and waited for it to settle down, then gave it another whack with her arm.

"I wonder what the corn said to piss her off," Max said.

"She's so focused," Claire said.

"Oh, she is so smart," Weezy said. Everyone laughed a little, but Weezy just shook her head. "She's one smart cookie, I'm telling you."

Claire woke up one morning before anyone else and went down to the kitchen to find Cleo and Nina. She started a pot of coffee and then took Nina from Cleo. Nina had a habit of curling up when anyone tried to put her over their shoulder.

"She's like a roly-poly bug," Claire said.

"That's what Max called her," Cleo said. "It took me a while to figure out what he was talking about. We used to call them pill bugs."

"Max loved poking them with sticks and watching them curl. It used to make him laugh so hard when he was little."

"That's what he told me. I can imagine it."

"So, how's it been going?" Claire asked.

"Okay," she said. "I mean, it's good. Just overwhelming, you know? I keep thinking that this baby's parents will be by soon to pick her up and take care of her, and then I remember that it's me. I'm the parent. Is that crazy?"

"I'm sure it's normal."

Cleo nodded. "It's not that I want someone to take her, I just sometimes forget that I'm the one in charge of her. That she's really mine. Don't tell anyone, okay?"

"I promise. But don't worry, I think it's normal. Once,

right after Lainie had Jack, we were out at the bar and she all of a sudden looked shocked and said, 'I just forgot I had a baby. Just for a second.' "

Cleo laughed. "Thanks," she said. "That makes me feel better."

It was strange watching Max with Nina. He picked her up with so much ease, changed her diaper and fed her with authority. He burped her with a great amount of confidence, patting her back hard, then smiling when he was successful, always laughing when she burped especially loud, saying, "That's my girl."

It was the first time ever that Max couldn't and wouldn't ask for Claire's advice. What did she know about babies that could help him? It was so bizarre and a little sad to watch Max going ahead of her, to picture herself having a baby someday and asking Max for tips. But most of the time, she was just impressed with him, how unafraid he was of Nina, how in control he seemed when he held her with one arm or buttoned her into a new outfit.

Martha kept saying, "Thank God for this vacation," and shaking her head. Her new patient was apparently diffi-cult and Martha loved to talk about her. "She's running me ragged," she said. "She's sort of a wretched old woman. Last week she told me that I should dress for my body type. Can you imagine?"

Claire found herself actually laughing at Martha's sto-ries. Now that they weren't living under the same roof, and Martha was no longer pushing for sisters couple therapy, Claire found her kind of amusing. She even managed not to get annoyed when Martha talked to her about the benefits of owning her own place. "You really should make that a goal," she told Claire. "What you're paying in rent, just throwing that money away month after month." She shuddered, like the thought was repulsive.

"I'll think about that," Claire said.

Maybe it was because of the weather, or maybe it was because she'd just had a baby, but Cleo didn't wear a bikini once. Whatever the reason, Claire was grateful.

THE LAST NIGHT THAT EVERYONE was at the house, they barbecued and ate outside. Claire and Weezy had marinated cubes of chicken and beef, and skewered them with red, green, and yellow peppers, mushrooms, and onions.

It was a nice night and everyone was laughing a lot. They were sharing Nina like a toy, passing her around nicely, even if they were all a little reluctant to let her go. Claire noticed the way that everyone leaned down to smell Nina's head before they had to hand her off to the next person, how they breathed in deeply, like teenagers sniffing glue to get high.

Nina fell asleep while Claire was holding her, and she didn't make a move to pass her to anyone else. She wasn't trying to be a baby hog, but Nina was her goddaughter and they were all leaving tomorrow, so it seemed only fair. Nina snuffled in her sleep, like a tiny little pig. She was a beautiful baby, which wasn't a surprise to anyone.

Everyone talked late into the night, like they didn't want to go to bed and admit that it was the end of vacation. Claire was a little sad to leave, but also excited to get back to her new apartment, to spend time there. The apartment was new enough that it didn't quite feel like hers yet. She still had the sense when she opened the door that she was walking into an unfamiliar place. It didn't bother her, though. She knew that would change soon enough. She knew that one day, she'd walk in and it would be like she belonged there. All of the dust and dirt would be what she created, the smell would be her own. And she would be able to walk barefoot everywhere without thinking that someone else's foot germs were there. It would be like no one else had ever lived there before, like no one else would be there after; it would feel like home.

Maureen went into the house and came out carrying a new bottle of wine. "Just one more splash for everyone," she said. "It's our last night here, we can't go to bed early."

They all obeyed, holding out their glasses like children, while Maureen stood in the middle of the circle, turning and pouring. Claire wrapped the blanket a little bit more up around Nina's face, even though it wasn't cold out. Will was talking about his new teaching schedule, listing all of the things he had to do to get ready as soon as they got back.

It was quiet for a few moments, and Claire could tell that everyone was getting sleepy. But then Martha started talking about her job again, explaining how her patient sometimes tried to sneak away from her in the store. And they all turned to her to listen, gave her full attention, and watched her as she said, "I have to chase her down, scream her name in the supermarket like a crazy person." Martha looked pleased as everyone laughed, then looked down at her lap for a moment and twisted her hands around, like a middle school girl, embarrassed by the attention. They were all silent for a few seconds, waiting. And then she recovered and went on.

ACKNOWLEDGMENTS

For my husband, Tim Hartz, who lets me take over the dining room table with piles of papers for weeks at a time and talk about my characters over dinner—when I come out of my writing haze, I'm so happy that you're the one there to greet me. Thanks for everything, friend. I think marrying you was a good decision.

My agent, Sam Hiyate, always, always believes in my writing and in me, which means more than I can ever say.

As far as editors go, Jenny Jackson is the very best. She is thoughtful and wise in her edits, so fun to gossip with, and always starts e-mails to me by saying, "this is a no-pressure e-mail." For all of these reasons (and because she makes my books better), I am delighted to know her.

I am a lucky writer to have such a great family. My parents, Pat and Jack Close, are the best cheerleaders ever. They are willing to attend multiple readings, assure me things will work out if I get nervous (Mom), and try to sell my book to strangers (that's you, Dad). Thanks, you guys.

Kevin Close, Chris and Susan Close, and Carol and Scott Hartz are a constant support and eager readers. I couldn't ask for more.

My adorable and brilliant niece, Ava Close, responded to the cover art for this book by saying, "Ooooh, Santa." Ava, I am always happy to have your honest feedback.

Wrigley Close-Hartz keeps me company while I write and also makes sure that I get outside at least once a day, by demanding his walk.

I AM ALSO GRATEFUL TO:

All of my students at George Washington University, who remind me of why I wanted to be a writer in the first place.

Tom Mallon, who was kind enough to give me a job teaching creative writing at GW.

My virtual coworkers—all of the people who make my days a little less lonely, by chatting over e-mail, answering writing questions, reading drafts, and always offering encouragement: Megan Angelo, Jessica Liebman, Martha Leonard, Lee Goldberg, Courtney Sullivan, and Molly Erman.

Moriah Cleveland is forever willing to talk to me about imaginary people as though they were real. There is no first reader/e-mail companion that I would rather have. You are invaluable.

My friends are constantly telling me funny things, and sometimes I have to steal bits of their dialogue and stories for my writing. Thank you, and I'm sorry, but if you guys weren't so funny I wouldn't have to do it—Becky Schillo, Margaret Hoerster, Mairead Garry, Erin Claydon, Erin Bradley, Mary Colleen Bragiel, and Hilary Murdock.

Being at Knopf has been a dream come true, and I am thankful every day for all the people there who support me, and my books. This team is superb at what they do and are also just genuinely nice people. I am indebted to: Sonny Mehta, Paul Bogaards, Ruth Liebman, Nicholas Latimer, Julie Kurland, Jennifer Kurdyla, Andrea Robinson, Elizabeth Lindsey, and Abby Weintraub.